CASIMIR PULASKI

A Hero of the American Revolution

Leszek Szymanski, Ph.D.

Foreword by
Brig. Gen. Thaddeus Maliszewski

HIPPOCRENE BOOKS
New York

For information, address:
HIPPOCRENE BOOKS, INC.
171 Madison Avenue
New York, NY 10016

Library of Congress Cataloging-in-Publication Data
Szymanski, Leszek, 1933–
Casimir Pulaski : a hero of the American Revolution /
Leszek Szymanski : foreword by Thaddeus Maliszewski.
     p.   cm.
  Includes bibliographical references and index.
  ISBN 0-7818-0157-5 :
1. Pulaski, Kazimierz, 1747-1779. 2. Generals—United States—
Biography. 3. Generals—Poland—Biography. 4. United States
Army—Biography. I. Title.
  E207.P8S97 1993
  973.3'46—dc20   93-37006
                                         CIP

Dedicated to the memory of Kazimierz Pulaski's
biographers, especially Wladyslaw Konopczynski,
Wladyslaw Kozlowski, Wladyslaw Wayda, Konstanty
Gaszynski, Leonard Chodzko, Paul Bentalou, Martin
Griffith, Jared Sparks, W.H. Richardson, to the memory
of Marian Kukiel, a great Polish emigre historian; but
primarily to the memory of my father, Kazimierz
Szymanski, who first told me about Kazimierz Pulaski.
—Leszek Wladyslaw Szymanski

ACKNOWLEDGMENTS

I wish to express my sincere gratitude to all the people who helped me either in my research or who assisted and helped me then and later on. Special thanks go to the following: Brig. Gen. Ret. Thaddeus Maliszewski who revised this edition; Edward Dusza; Father Cornelius Dende; J. C. Walls; Dr. Edward Rozanski; Professors Antoni Michalek and Tymon Terlecki of PUNO; Dr. Michal Zawadzki and his wife Danuta; Wladimir Kowal; Josef Glowacki; Alan F. Perry, Archivist, Center for the Documentary Study of the American Revolution, Washington, D.C.; Kathleen Halsey and her staff of the Interlibrary Loan, Learning Resources Center, University of Wisconsin, Stevens Point; Arthur Fish of the Documents section of that Center; Dr. Ira Cohen; Library of CSULB; Wanda Jazwinska of Polish Millennium Library, Los Angeles; Joseph A. Borkowski, Edward Pinkowski, Ed. Dybicz, Morton Deutsch, historians; Howard H. Peckham, Director of the W.L. Clements Library: Dr. Z. Jagodzinski and his staff of the Polish Library in London; Library of Hartford University, Hartford Public Library, and Librarian, Connecticut Historical Society; Joseph W. Zurawski and the Rev. Donald Bilinski of the Polish Museum, Chicago; Dr. Eugene Kusielewicz; Jerzy Kosinski; Dr. Alexandra Kaminska who translated for me some of Kazimierz Pulaski's letters written in French; the Polish press abroad, especially to Jan Krawiec, Dziennik Zwiazkowy, Chicago; Stanley Krajewski, Dziennik Polski, Detroit; Ewa Czarnecka and Boleslaw Wierzbianski, Nowy Dziennik, New York; Thedore L. Zawistowski, Straz, Scranton; Joseph Wiewiora, Narod Polski, Chicago; Czeslaw Maliszewski, Listy do Polakow, New Britain, CT.; Karol Zbyszewski, Waclaw Zagorski and Wojciech Plazak of *Polish Daily*, London; Stefania Kossowska, *Wiadomosci*, London; Eugeniusz Stuliglowa and Tygodnik Polski, Melbourne; Irene Prazmowska Coulter and Kirkley S. Coulter, *Polish Heritage*; Stanley F. Maxwell, Sovereign Grand Commander of the Supreme Council 33 AA Scottish Rite.

Leszek Szymanski

CONTENTS

MAPS

Battle of Brandywine
September 11ᵀᴴ, 1777

Map taken from *The Pictorial Field-Book of the Revolution* by Benson J. Lossing (1860).

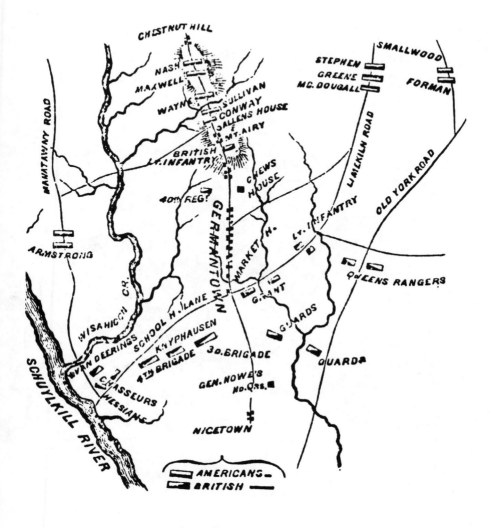

Battle of Germantown
October, 1777

Map taken from *The Pictorial Field-Book of the Revolution* by Benson J. Lossing (1860).

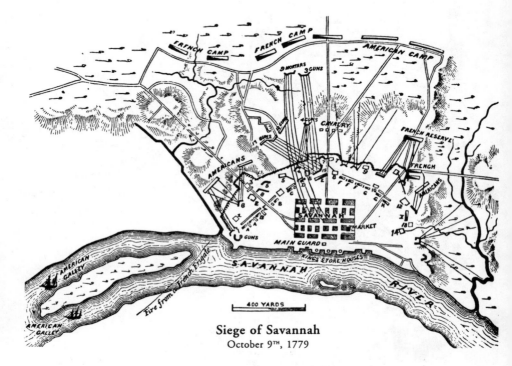

Siege of Savannah
October 9ᵀᴴ, 1779

Map taken from *The Pictorial Field-Book of the Revolution* by Benson J. Lossing (1860).

FOREWORD

"WHEN there is a need a person of purpose will come forth to fulfill that need." For too long, a void has existed about General Casimir Pulaski's life and service in the Revolutionary War. At last, Leszek Szymanski's *Casimir Pulaski: A Hero of the American Revolution* fills the gap of early American history with his scholarly, extensive, and exhaustive research. Not only has the author studied all available correspondence to and from Pulaski, but he has covered all areas and the periphery of global, historical reminiscences of the Revolutionary War participants, biographers, and narrators, leaving no stone untouched in his search for scholarly truism. This he has done with a zeal and persistency matching the standards and performance of Lancelot's quest.

As the first Commander of the Horse, Pulaski earned the title of "The Father of American Cavalry." Pulaski's father, an attorney, and his brothers were founding members of the Bar Confederacy, formed to fight the Russian occupiers of Poland. The loss of family and fortune did not deter him from this patriotic stuggle against almost hopeless odds, but his guerrilla-style cavalry tactics and defense strategies (like the successful defense of Czestochowa, the "Lourdes" of Poland) earned him an excellent European reputation. As a volunteer waiting at Washington's headquarters for Congress to act on his service application, he distinguished himself at Brandywine, which brought immediate Congressional appointment as a Brigadier General and Commander of the Cavalry Regiments. The American historian Jared Sparks notes: "That he gained and preserved the friendship of Washington, who more than once in a public manner commended his military talents, his disinterestedness and zeal, is a sufficient proof of his merits as an officer, and his conduct as a man."

Szymanski enthusiastically presents Pulaski's services to the American cause. Eventually, the Colonials mustered four regiments of cavalry. However, they would be detached from Pulaski's command for escort duty, guard duty, messenger service, bodyguards, etc., leaving Pulaski with 40 or 50 men for tactical fighting purposes. He

9

and Kovatch produced the first cavalry regulations, and vigorously trained his men in winter encampment, only to have the Commander-in Chief write him of his officers' complaints about overwork. There was intense jealousy and dislike for the foreign volunteers. Since he could not, under existing conditions, use the cavalry as they were used in Europe—as a tactical, strike and offensive force—he grew weary and impatient for more action. Thus, he resigned and was granted the command of an independent legion, popularly called the Pulaski Legion or the Polish Legion.

The reader will enjoy this treasure of Americana. It is a welcome and much needed addition to the lustrous lore on the library shelves of readable American history. America needs a resurgence of patriotism, as we recently experienced in the Persian Gulf crusade. In these dire days, we need so many more of our children to heed the Kennedy admonition: "Ask not what your country can do for your but rather: What can you do for your Country?" This book will certainly aid that laudable effort. One may even characterize the author with mimicking Pulaski's cavalry style in his literary labor of love, for Szymanski literally charges into the mass of known and unknown or undiscovered historical material to achieve a successful, scholarly work.

As a good chef decorates his gourmet offerings with tempting appetizers, so does Szymanski in like fashion garnish his creation with appropriate quotations from original sources to whet the appetite of the reader. These quotes provide us with eyewitness facts and observations or evaluative opinions about his subject, giving the work the stamp of objectivity, which is the essence of historical writings.

As for his treatment, he handles controversies in a fair and impartial manner, waiting for his concluding Epilogue to present personal opinions or conclusions. Proper attention to detail is illustrated by a meticulous itemization of the equipment of the Pulaski Legion. He carefully gathers and assiduously writes historical facts as a lawyer briefs a case. The colorful career of this dashing cavalryman lends itself well to novel form but Szymanski resists the temptation to novelize. Similarly, he does not dramatize because the simple narration of Pulaski's American experiences is inherent drama itself. As a newcomer to these shores, the author readily understands Pulaski's sensitivity and hurt feelings flowing from the provocative actions of jealous colonials, the prevailing antipathy towards the foreign volunteers, and Szymanski empathizes with Pulaski in this regard, for acceptance is the key to assimilation. This enhances and personalizes the author's literary style of historical reporting, for one can then spot the nuances and sense the ramifications of many an otherwise bald but boring fact or opinion. He does not flood us with his emotions, but he fills the plains and forests of history's landscapes with the bold, broad strokes of a stimulated artist who knows his subject all too well.

Szymanski comes to us with impressive credentials, a Ph.D. in History and an M.A. in Political Science. An honor graduate in the Polish language and literature from London University, he was able to examine the Polish and European writings on Pulaski and blend it in with the American material. He has penned a number of other books, both fiction and nonfiction, but this book belongs in every American library and should be used in every American History class as a supplementary textbook.

As Pulaski exasperatingly wrote in his last letter to a Continental Congress, which was still harassing him about the financial accounts of his Legion, "I came to hazard all for the freedom of America." Indeed he did hazard all, for he sacrificed his life on the altar of America freedom. As the 57th Congress Record intoned; "His invaluable services to America entitle him to be numbered among the heroes of America and to be perpetuated in the memory of the people for whom he sacrificed his life." So in these crucial times, when our progeny lack role models to follow, American students could well emulate Pulaski in serving a country which now, more than ever, needs dedicated and patriotic partisans.

Thaddeus W. Maliszewski

PROLOGUE

PULASKI is the best-known Polish name in the United States, but from the historical point of view, Kazimierz Pulaski, the father of the American Cavalry, the Commander of the American Legion, remains an unknown general of the Revolution, at least in his adopted country.

The best work on Pulaski in America, and the pioneer effort, was published by Professor Wladyslaw Kozlowski in *Biblioteka Warszawska*, Warsaw, 1903, under the title *Pulaski w Ameryce*. This is an extensive, laborious, well-researched and annotated paper, but its idealistic approach to the Revolution and insufficient background information without which a just appraisal or a clear understanding of Pulaski is impossible, makes it obsolete.

The same subject, i.e., Pulaski in America, and under the same title was covered by Dr. Wladyslaw Wayda, whose work was published in Warsaw in 1930, to honor the 150th anniversary of Pulaski's death. This is also a well researched work, and especially valuable for its appendix containing much documentary material, Though more realistic than Kozlowski's work, it too suffers from a deficiency of background material. Moreover, Dr. Wayda evidently influenced by Pulaski's literary talent, visible even through his awkward English, gratuitously and too often paraphrased instead of quoting the General's letters and reports.

The authority on the Polish career of Pulaski, Professor Wladyslaw Konopczynski, has an excellent chapter on Pulaski in America in his *Kazimierz Pulaski*, Krakow, 1931. This is, however, as the author states openly, simply a compilation.

The Polish-American historian Mieczyslaw Haiman wrote a number of articles and essays on Pulaski and his Legion, but they are mostly elaborations of English language works of a secondary nature, and dispersed in various books and publications.

The apocryphal memoirs *Reszta Pamietnikow Rogowskiego*, Paris 1847, written probably by their publisher, the poet Konstanty Gaszynski, introduced much confusion amongst Pulaski's biographers, lasting even to this day. The historical veracity of that work is on a level with

Louvet de Couvrai's fiction, *The Interesting Story of Baron Lovzinski*, Hartford 1800, and its various versions. Those memoirs, amongst others, misled Leonard Chodzko in his *Zywot Kazimierza na Pulaziu Pulaskiego*, Lwow 1869.

At this time all the books in Polish written on or including the American services of Kazimierz Pulaski utilized these works, adding nothing new to research. This may be stated even about the modern publications such as *Polacy w Wojnach Amerykanskich* by Bogdan Grzelonski and Isabela Rusinowa, Warsaw 1973, or Zdzislaw Sulek's *Polacy w Wojnie o Niepodleglosc Stanow Zjednoczonych*, Warsaw 1976.

Of the English language works of permanent value remain the Paul Bentalou-William Johnson polemic, which is referred to in the body of this monograph and will also be discussed in this introduction.

Charles Francis Adams's remarks on Pulaski in his *Studies Military and Diplomatic*, N.Y. 1911, albeit marginal and patronizing, make the most serious attempt to analyze Pulaski's role as the chief of the American cavalry, thus deserving discussion at this point rather than in the epilogue. C.F. Adams, continuing that irreverent attitude towards Washington which ran in his family, analyzes critically but justly Washington's talents as a general, and especially his approach to the cavalry. Correctly, Adams points to the obvious but obscured fact that Washington had no military experience nor education worth talking about. His ideas of the military campaigns were contrary to the spirit of cavalry action. Adams was right in stating that for Washington the cavalry's utility rested in its functions as convoy and mounted guard. But Adams was wrong in thinking that Washington did not realize the essential services which could be rendered by the horsemen in the field of military intelligence. Adams observes that the cavalry, in spite of the fact that war was already in its third year, was still an inchoate branch of service, and that it devolved on Pulaski to make the first serious attempt to give form to a systematic American cavalry organization for actual use in practical warfare. Cavalry colonels Bland, Moylan, Sheldon and Baylor are mentioned in various descriptions of the parade through Philadelphia on the eve of the Battle of Brandywine in September 1777, but we do not hear that their cavalry was used in that battle. Perhaps, Pulaski, Zielinski and Kotkowski (all Polanders) charged the enemy at the head of the Philadelphia Light Horse.

Suddenly Adams after giving a penetrating analysis of the whole cavalry situation proceeds to complain that Washington recommended and Congress confirmed a square peg in a round hole, i.e, Pulaski. According to Adams one had to be a native American to be a good cavalry officer in that war. That a foreigner (and a papist) became its commander was probably for him blasphemous, and the same with Pulaski's request to be beholden only to the Commander-in-Chief, though General Knox made the very same demand on the same grounds of European military practice.

Adams forgot that historically the cavalry of many nations operated deep in foreign territory. In 1241 it was the Polish knights who saved Europe from hordes of Tartar horsemen operating thousands of miles from their native lands, and, after all, the British cavalry operated in America on foreign terristory and successfully, to mention only Banastre Tarleton or John Simcoe.

Pulaski because of his background was well suited to be leader of the Revolutionary cavalry. The differences between Poland and America were nothing he could not get used to or comprehend.

Maps had been in existence in Pulaski's times. Moreover, each of the colonies was a separate state and its citizens were foreigners outside of their native state as much as Pulaski. Poland in the eighteenth century was not a plain connected by roads and admirably suited for cavalry action. Most of the country was covered by forests, and indeed, a squirrel could travel through Poland on its journey from Paris to Moscov without stepping down from the trees.

Professor Konopczynski pointed out certain similarities between the situation in Poland during the Bar Confederation Insurrection and the American War of Independence. Congress was an equivalent of the *Generalnosc*, as were the Rebels of the Confederates, the Tories of the Royalists, the British of the Russians and Indian allies of the British of the Ukrainian peasants who revolted on Catharina II's instigation (Koliszczyzna). There was even an epidemic of smallpox in both countries. (Konopczynski missed this last similarity) Also both revolts were republican and against "tyrannical despots."

C.E. Adams, mentioning Harry Lee's Light Horse Legion wrote that it was modeled on Pulaski's ill-conceived idea of an effective American cavalry service. But that such an effective cavalry leader as Lee chose to model his force on this could be only a compliment to the ex-Commander of Horse and a measure of Pulaski's effectiveness. In fact, Pulaski's corps were conceived as an independent self-sufficient military unit, not as a cavalry troop.

Charles Francis Adams, skillfully proving Washington's ignorance and neglect in cavalry matters and admitting that Pulaski's difficulties were both great and irritating, but not insurmountable if approached in the way Pulaski proposed, concludes that Pulaski was inadequate for his task because he was a foreigner.

But was Pulaski such an inadequate cavalry leader? Have we heard that after his resignation Bland, Moylan, Sheldon, Cadwalader or Hancock took command and proved their genius and worth of the Continental cavalry under proper leadership? And how came it that Congress authorized Washington to appoint an infantry brigadier to lead the cavalry?

In the south where Adams observes Washington's influence was negligible, the cavalry on both sides achieved importance. The names of such cavalry leaders as Banastre Tarleton, John Simcoe, Francis Marion, Thomas Sumter, Andrew Pickens, Harry Lee, William Washington, Daniel, Peter and Hugh Horrys became famed, but by that time the first commander of the Continental Cavalry was resting in his watery grave.

Judge William Johnson, the eminent pupil of Charles Cotesworth Pinckney, in his polemic with Paul Bentalou, offers the second most serious appraisal of Pulaski. The gross is contained in "Remarks Critical and Historical on an Article in the 47th Number of the North American Review relating to Count Pulaski, etc.," Charleston, 1825.

Judge Johnson does not limit his analysis to the American services of Kazimierz Pulaski but discusses his whole life. I have to dispute his assertions, however, as they throw a wrong light on Pulaski's character and actions, thus supplying a false key to his personality and actions. As the Johnson-Bentalou polemic is fully evaluated in the text, I shall limit myself to the Polish question and to the Legion.

Describing the Bar Confederation, Johnson condemns the entire insurrection out of hand: " the confederates amongst whom Pulaski figured were a band of intolerant persecutors, and their opposition to the grant of the most reasonable liberty of conscience to the Dessidents, caused the latter to place themselves under the protection of Catharine. To represent such men, with such purpose as combating for liberty, is a farce; nor indeed is it less so to laud the republican virtues of an individual whose life was devoted to the maintenance of despotism which chose to assume the title of *The Polish Republic.*"

To which the judge added, "...it is ridiculous to attribute to Pulaski hatred of kings since, had Stanislaus been the king of his own choice, he would have been a sound Royalist."

It is outside the scope of this monograph to discuss such complicated questions as Polands unique political system, and the partitions of that country, but as Johnson's ideas are shared by many contemporary historians who contribute to maintaining Pulaski's image as a young, feudal aristocrat, some words of explanation are called for.

Poland in 1768-that is, at the time of the Bar Confederacy-had a more representative and democratic system than England in 1832 or the United States in 1783, by which I mean that a larger percentage of Poland's population had the right to vote and to be elected to Parliament (Sejm), or even to the office of King, than in any other contemporary country.

Regarding religious tolerance, for hundreds of years Poland was famed because of that. Eventually the Catholic bigots reduced it but the Polish dissidents were manipulated by the neighboring absolute rulers for political reasons. And may I remind the followers of Johnson that the Quebec Act was considered to be one of the oppressive acts and slavery was ended only after the Civil war.

The basic reason for Poland's partition by her neighbors was that she maintained a democratic system, though imperfect from today's point of view, in the middle of absolute military states. Pacifist ideas were loudly and absurdly expressed and a good example set by reducing the Army. The love of freedom turned into anarchy. Furthermore Poland was in the forefront of federalism as the Polish Republic had been a Commonwealth with Lithuania since 1569. As to the part played by Pulaski in an attempt to kidnap King Stanislaus Poniatowski, the judge was correct, and probably this enterprise if successful would have finished that Civil War. The reverence for kings surfaced amongst the American revolutionaries only after the success of the War of Independence.

In regard to Pulaskis Legion Johnson states: "...But the truth is that the whole history of this corps is but a catalogue of misfortunes. It is known in Revolutionary history only by successive disasters. Scarcely had it acquired existence before it was surprised and cut up at Egg Harbor, and scarcely had its skeleton form reached Charleston before rout and destruction awaited it in the face of all the world. From Charleston it moves to Savannah to undertake the chivalrous exploit of storming a garrison and meets with the only fate that could await such an enterprise. And when it appears again upon the arena, it is only to sustain that decisive surprise at Monk's Corner from which nothing was saved but Captain Bentalou and the colors, a most shameful surprise in open day, as Moultrie calls it. From that time its existence is lost, its very form was annihilated, its name almost forgotten until its shade lately rose in Nile's Register. That corps never distinguished itself in battle."

For the surprise at Monk's Corner Pulaski was not responsible since he was dead. General Isaac Huger had an overall command, and the remains of Pulaski's dragoons comprised only a part of the force.

The history of the Legion is one of the bloodiest episodes of the Revolutionary War. The rolls of Pulaski's Legion read as an honor roll on a war monument. On December 29, 1779, Congress asked that the survivors of the Legion be disbanded. General Benjamin Lincoln incorporated the cavalry into the First Light Dragoon Regiment while the infantry was reassigned to the First South Carolina Regiment. I was not able to establish the date of disbandment The officers of the Legion, however, were incorporated into Armand's Legion in November 1780.

Up to this moment there is no adequate history of Pulaski's Legion after its Commander's death. The fullest account so far is given by Mieczyslaw Haiman in his *Polacy w Walce o Niepodleglosc Ameryki*, Chicago 1931, the work being, though praiseworthy, a compilation of English language works of fragmentary nature.

As much as the full history of Legion after its commander's death is needed, I could not, working without support of any grant, university or organization, afford the time and expense necessary for further research.

I cannot restrain myself, however, from quoting the following document showing the state of the Corps after they were orphaned:

> Camp at Shelden, November the 30, 1779.
>
> Dear General,
>
> It is my duty of informing you of the pityfull case of poor general pulasky's dragons; never has been a troop used in such a manner; being quite naked, they do duty in a cold contry and are continually exposed to the injury, and inconstancy of the weather. The have never received any blanket, they have neither clothes, nor shirts, nor...in short, they stand in need of things that you would not have denyed to neger or a beggar to cover his nakedness. The Muster Master general is an eye wittnes of their deplorable situation, and able to give credit to my assertion. I complain also of the unnatural behavior of the Pay Master you have been pleased to appoint for the Legion, some of my people have received no pay these nine months, and our wagonners have eight to claim. I complain too, and as a grievance, that the people draw no rum in this camp, while they are acquainted that the soldiers laying in good and warm casernes in town are drawing every day. I don't know if all these grievances conforms to the regulations of the Honorable Continental Congress; but a thing which I am very well acquainted with is that if the people under my command are not receiving in a forthight clothes monny, and every necessary supply due to them, no body shall be astonished at me leaving them and going where they will be pleased being extremly tyred to be the spectator of such a misery.
>
> You, general, and evry body will remember which a fine, and

brave troop I have bring along me from the North, well, where is not a single one man of them to be found among us. They have been so ill-used near Charleston, that some of them are deserted, and t'others, their time being out, preffered to work like negers in some contry farms as to inlist again; I call such a loss a real one to the United States, for it is not to be repaired in a short time, waiting great many days to form a soldier. Well, the same loss is very near at hand if nobody will prevent it. I am very sorry of being obliged by rank and duty to write to you in such a manner, for no body is more pleased in calling him self with respect. Dear General-your Mos obedient humble servant Petr Vernier, Mjr.

To His Excellency, General Lincoln, Esqu.
Commander in Chief the forces of the
United States in the South to Charlestown.

(Pulaski's Collection, Polish Museum of America, Chicago, Cf. Segond to Mifflin, PCC 247,102,78,307)

Martin Griffith's biographical sketch, "Count Casimir Pulaski, Father of the American Cavalry," in volume III of *Catholics and American Revolution*, Pa, 1911, is a valuable contribution in being a collection of important and eloquent documents, but the author's commentary is naive and uncritical. Naive also and obsolete is Jared Sparks's biography of Pulaski in the *Library of American Biography*, second series, vol. 4, Boston 1847, but written with an appreciation of Pulaski, and an occasional insight into his difficulties.

W.H. Richardson's pamphlet written to commemorate the 150th anniversary of Pulaski's death, "Brigadier-General Casimir Pulaski," Jersey City 1929, is surprisingly well researched for such a short work but too popular in character. Penetrating and skillful is a sketch about Pulaski in Joseph Borkowski's "Prominent Polish Pioneers," Pittsburgh 1975.

W.W. Gordon's "Count Casimir Pulaski," printed in the Georgia Historical Ouarterly, October 1929, is based mainly on secondary works.

Of the modern American works Clarence A. Mannings's "Soldier of Liberty," David Abodaher's "No Greater Love" (previously published as "Freedom Fighter'), Dorothy Adam's "Cavalry Hero", Pearle Schultz's "Generous Strangers," Red Reeder's "Bold Leaders" seem to be aimed at the adolescent readership. R.D. 'Jamro's Pulaski—A Portrait of Freedom" is well researched and annotated. But, unfortunately, not large in scope. It was not available to me during my research.

The newspaper and magazine articles on both sides of the Atlantic are mainly characterized by repetition, naivety, lack of historical criticism and partisanship. Amongst few exceptions I need to commend here two very valuable articles. They are: Richard Henry Spencer's "Pulaski Legion" in the Maryland Historical Magazine, vol. 13, Sept.1918, and Donald W. Holst's and Mark Zlatich's "Dress and Equipment of Pulaski's Independent Legion" in the "Military Collector and Historian," Winter 1964. Two eminent historians, Edward Pinkowski and Morton Deutsch, have been working on this subject, but their works were not available to me, neither was the "selective list" of J. Hoskins.

It is regrettable that there is no comprehensive work on the American Cavalry which discusses its beginnings at length. Consequently Pulaski is denied the pioneer place normal to the revolutionary generals in the military histories of the other branches of service.

The full bibliographic information and most of the footnotes are interwoven in the body of the text. The purpose of this reassessment is to show in a general manner the state of historical research on the American services of Pulaski up to the moment of this writing; thus only the more significant books were discussed here.

This work is a monographic study of the American services of Kazimierz Pulaski. Also, I compared most of the printed Pulaski letters with the available originals. No important discrepancies were found. I compared too, most of other printed documents with their earlier or full versions. All the facts were compared in as many contemporary sources as possible. It is the result of an extensive archival research and the perusal of contemporary sources such as journals, memoirs and works of the contemporary or close to contemporary historians. The stress was put on utilizing the primary sources. This monograph brought to light new facts, established some details and discussed aspects of Pulaski's American career previously not elaborated upon.

Additionally, this study is the most comprehensive collection of Pulaski's letters and documents bearing on him. Many documents were never published, or never published in connection with works on Pulaski. To facilate their perusal the orthography and punctuation was sometimes modernized.

An extensive study of the American Revolution from the military, political, social and economic points of view was necessary for this work. But only material helpful to understanding Pulaski was utilized

I was not able to explain satisfactorily Pulaski's role at the Brandywine battle nor an oversleeping incident at Germantown nor the nature of his connections with the men involved in the so-called

Conway Cabal, nor the reason for Charles Cotesworth Pinckney's animosity towards Pulaski and consequently William Johnson's, nor the pretext on which Judge Thomas McKean based his order to arrest Pulaski, nor how much Pulaski put of his own money into the Legion, nor do I understand the Legion's bookkeeping. Pulaski's connection with the Freemasonry remains a mystery to me as does the place of his burial.

I hope, however, that in spite of these omissions, this work establishes Kazimierz Pulaski's due place in the Pantheon of Revolutionary Generals.

Leszek Szymanski, Ph.D.

PART ONE

COMMANDER OF
THE HORSE

1777! It was the crucial year of the American Revolution. The brothers Howe had left New York, and were keeping Washington and Congress in suspense as to the direction of the coming blow. Congress had a multitude of business, from trifles to the all-important matter of Confederation.

But a certain famous general, sent to America by Dr. Franklin[1]to help the revolutionary cause, thought that the project of a speedy expedition against Madagascar required Congress's prompt decision.

Casimir Pulaski was in the United Colonies[2] barely a week before he wrote his Madagascar memorandum on 28 July 1777, in Boston, and it was on July 26 that General William Heath noted, "Count Pulaski, a Polish nobleman, came to Boston and dined at headquarters," but the newcomer had already forwarded to Congress some suggestions on how to conduct the war.[3]

If anyone bothered to read through the memorandum[4] he had to have some reservations about the whole project. There was not only the problem of logistics, but France was actively, though covertly, helping the revolting colonies and Madagascar was certainly not in the United Colonies'sphere of influence.

Wrote Pulaski, "The project of expedition to the isle of Madagascar, of which, I suppose, the commissioners have spoken already, demands a speedy decision, because the commander of the place waits for my answer.'[5]

The commissioners whom Pulaski mentioned were Franklin and Deane, then the colonial representatives in France. Most probably, they failed to forward the project to Philadelphia. The Madagascar commander of the place was Maurycy Beniowski, a famous adventurer and an old comrade-in-arms of Pulaski from the Bar Confederacy.

Beniowski succeeded in being elected by the natives a "ampan-sakab," Caesar of Madagascar, much to the chagrin of the local French authorities, and he arrived in France at the beginning of 1777 to seek an alliance with the Most Christian Majesty, very much like Dean and Franklin, but less successfully. Disappointed, he already thought about freeing that island of the French influence and evidently confided in Pulaski.

However, had John Adams or John Hancock had the patience to read Pulaski's memorandum thoroughly, they would have found some sound ideas expressed therein. Pulaski had given a great deal of thought to the military situation in North America, and Paris was well informed about these affairs. French public opinion was supporting the struggle of Americans for liberty. It was the age of enlightenment, and the poets, writers, political wits, philosophers and progressive aristocrats were very much concerned about the brave Americans who sought to establish their republic on French philosophical principles in their struggle with the tyranny of England's George III. In salons and coffee houses and, of course, in the papers, the military developments were freely discussed. To the French, Americans were representatives of political liberties and political reforms that were so necessary in France as well. Pulaski was not concerned with that kind of talk, however, but about the military situation which he knew so well. During the long journey, he had plenty of time to reconsider his ideas, and, as the second point of his memorandum he proposed that the American ship captains should recruit volunteers abroad. In so doing,he may not have appreciated the current situation in the colonies. There were already too many native candidates for officers and too few candidates for privates. Pulaski's next idea was very sound: "There are many officers who cannot obtain employment, and will return to Europe. It is of importance to the American States to maintain a good fame in Europe, but all those who shall return discontented will produce only a bad report. Some project of employing them should be hit upon by placing in service all those who arrive."[6] Pulaski's solution to the problem was the creation of an elite, a crack troop of officers, a kind of international brigade. Acceptance of this idea would save Congress a lot of trouble with the foreign volunteers as well as with the surplus of American officers.

The fourth idea was to interrupt the communication lines between Ticonderoga (lost to Burgoyne on July 6, 1777) and the British Army by building a chain of small, well-fortified posts operated by skillful partisans. This proposal was the result of a briefing by someone (perhaps Heath) on the current military situation. Thus, he discovered

26

the resemblance between the strategic situation here and the war in Poland when the French advisers, Dumouries and Viomenil, advocated a chain of such forts against the Russians. Pulaski himself was a successful commander of an important fort at Czestochowa, one of the main strongholds in this plan, which withstood a protracted Russian siege.

As to the fifth point, Pulaski proposed that a list of all prisoners should be made. The old and maimed should be exchanged, others should be incorporated into the American forces, and those not inclined to serve the American cause should be dispersed to rural areas to work upon farms to replace Americans serving in the Army.

I shall discuss the matter of deserters at some length as the question will emerge in the future career of Pulaski. The use of deserters in eighteenth-century warfare was not so obnoxious as in modern times. The loyalty of the professional was purchased by contract, e.g., the Hessians who served the British or the Swiss guard of Louis XVI. At the best the loyalty was to the contract, witness the Swiss Guard of Louis XVI. Professionals and volunteers were motivated by pay, rank, opportunities to distinguish themselves, and possibilities of advancement, e.g., witness the numerous instances of desertion on both sides during the Revolution. Pulaski himself had deserters in his Polish army, though it is doubtful if they were attracted by the pay, which was practically non-existent for the majority of Bar Confederates. Patriotism motivated Poles to desert the Polish King's service and join Pulaski and the Bar Confederates in their fight to expel foreign Russian troops from Poland. Thus, Pulaski's views on enlisting deserters, based on his Polish experience, was different than the Continentals, as we will see in the recruitment of the Pulaski Legion.

The Continental Army was always desperately short of men during the fight for American independence. They even thought of using slaves as soldiers but on the whole they did not use them. It was too risky to antagonize the influential slave owners who thought Lord Dunmore, the British Governor of Virginia, very unfair in promising liberty to Negroes who joined British troops. Their military uniforms displayed a slogan "Liberty to Slaves." John Page, writing to Jefferson, stated that numbers of Negroes and cowardly scoundrels were flocking to Dunmore's standards in such numbers that militia, under Patrick Henry of "give me (but not to the slaves) liberty or death" fame, would be helpless against Negro insurrection. Though the armed Negroes were never employed in large numbers by their rebellious owners, their services were not disparaged for military works.

As a professional military man and the ex-leader of a war similar to the American Revolution, Pulaski knew that patriotism and enthusiasm were not enough to ensure victory. That he was right in his belief was shown by the subsequent development of events. In 1779 the steady increase of taxes and departure of farm workers for military duty put the burden of production on women. Sometimes that burden was onerous and state and town officials had to support the warriors' families.

Already in September 1776 Mrs. John Adams described the effect of drafts and enlistments on a small town: "Forty men are now drafted from this town. More than one half from sixteen to fifty are now in the'service....I hardly think you can be sensible how much we are thinned in this Province....if it is necessary to make more drafts upon, the women must reap the harvest...." (American Archives V, vol. 2, p.599).

Poor and married men found that their military service meant starvation for their families at home. Inflation drove prices beyond the reach of soldiers' wives: "At this rate what will become of people who depended on their absent friends in the Army for subsistence?' (Am. Archives V. vol; 3, p.1176).

Such were the conditions that influenced Pulaski when he proposed enlistment of deserters and use of war prisoners for manual labor.

The memorandum was signed Count Ko Pulaski. It is an interesting question whether Pulaski had the right to use the title of a count and whether he really was using it. Professor Kozlowski, who stated in his "Pulaski w Ameryce" that he was very familiar with Pulaski manuscripts, claimed that Pulaski was mainly using a letter "C" which stood for Casimir.

In researching this matter, I have found that Pulaski used that title sometimes. Such is his signature on a letter written to Richard Bache in August 1777 (N.A. RG 360 PCC, 41,8,34) i.e., "Com. de Korwin Pulaski." (Com. for Comte or Count). The signature on his letter to Congress dated September 3, 1777, from Philadelphia is "Casimir Victor Count Korwin Pulaski"(PCC, 41,8,40–41). But on most letters it is simply "C. Pulaski," which, of course, was frequently taken for count, but could be Casimir.

In Poland the use of aristocratic titles was foreign to the principle of equality amongst nobles, whether low born or high born magnate. Consequently by a Bill of Parliament (Sejm) the use of titles was forbidden in 1638, and that bill was repeated a number of times and enforced.

Pulaski's family (coat of arms - Slepowron), though newly rich, was of high social standing, and in America being titled was useful. Lord

Stirling, though his title was a matter of discussion, was duly addressed as His Lordship. The Marquis La Fayette was, of course, a real marquis, and Baron Steuben was unerringly addressed as Baron, and numerous chevaliers remained chevaliers.

Pulaski realized the benefits of a title, feeling probably morally right[7], especially as in France he could observe numerous titled persons, inferior socially to him, but boasting of their titles. Pulaski appropriated the title of "comte" which was below "marquis" but above "baron," "seigneur" and "chevalier." Even democratic Tadeusz Kosciuszko, according to his biographer, Polish-American historian Mieczyslaw Haiman, once appropriated the title of count.

Pulaski was using his title with discretion (at least on paper) in the manner in which some people with scientific titles use theirs when they want to impress somebody with their standing. A request from Doctor Smith is generally dealt with more promptly by a librarian than such a request from plain Mr. Smith, and advantages of possessing the title of professor, even if no solid knowledge stands behind this title, are numerous.

★ ★ ★

New York was in British hands. Therefore, Pulaski could not proceed directly to Philadelphia. He arrived at Washington's head-quarters close to Neshaminy Creek, Warwick Township, Bucks County, about twenty miles north of Philadelphia, not south as Clarence A. Manning maintains in *Soldier of Liberty*, (p. 205), for this would make subsequent movements of Washington senseless. The main body of the army was encamped around a large two-storied house and on the opposite side of the road was a sight which Pulaski could not miss - a whipping post (W.J. Buck, *Pennsylvania Mag. of Hist.* p.275, vol. 1).

Some of Pulaski's biographers wondered why it took him such a long time to reach Neshaminy. The fastest travel by coach took 16 days. Paul Revere, traveling with a message for Congress from Boston to Philadelphia, averaged 63 miles a day. It took about four days for delegates to Congress to cover the distance from New York to Philadelphia. He was there on 20 August.

The answer is contained in Pulaski's letter to Claude de Rulhiere on 27 June to 3 August 1777 (Cor. du Gen. C. Pulaski avec Claude de Rulhiere, Paris, p.34). After hearing the news that the British were to attack Boston, Pulaski waited until 4 August and perhaps left on the 5th. Characteristically Pulaski noted "...that alarm (false) did not give a good opinion about the bravery of the country inhabitants, and up to this moment I have nothing to be satisfied with..." (The threat of British invasion is confirmed by the reports in the contemporary American journals.)

So if one assumes that Pulaski left shortly after his meeting with General Heath, it made for a long journey. Knowing it was about August 5, it then was a rather fast journey, if one takes into consideration the circuitous route which he had to take to avoid the British.

Besides appropriating the title of count, Pulaski was armed with some letters of recommendation. Among them was one to Franklin's son-in-law, Richard Bache, as we ascertain from the letter he wrote to Bache (PCC 41,8,34). This letter is presented mistakenly in "Ex. Doc. No 120 as written to Washington.

> SIR: Having just arrived, I hasten to express to you my very great desire to merit your friendship. Mr. Franklin recommends me by his letter, and for my own part, I shall do all in my power to gain your esteem. I shall leave here for the Army; thence I intend to go to Philadelphia, where I shall endeavour to convince you that I am, with respect,
>
> Sir, your most humble and obedient servant,
> COUNT DE KORVIN PULASKI
>
> By the inclosed letter you will become acquainted with my views, sir. I ask your assistance. I have written to his excellency, John Hancock, President. I herewith inclose my letter to him, begging you, after you have delivered it, to acknowledge its receipt. I shall await your [illegible] the Army.

On the same page of the "Executive Document No. 120" there is another letter of Pulaski's in translation, addressed to Washington. Wayda in "Pulaski w Ameryce" wrote that it was Pulaski's first letter written in America, and to Washington.

> SIR: I have the honor to inclose to your excellency the letters which show the hardships that I have undergone on account of having taken up arms in defense of my country. That country no longer exists for me; and here, by fighting for freedom, I wish to deserve it. Life or death for the welfare of the state is my motto; and thereby I hope to earn the esteem of the citizens of this country. I ask your assistance, sir; it will facilitate my first efforts to obtain the honor of serving you. I inclose a statement to your excellency; if it is worthy of your attention, I shall be glad to have it laid before Congress. I hope to be excused for my lack of skill in writing as handling the pen is not my forte. I leave

for the Army, where I shall await orders. Your excellency's most humble and obedient servant,

C. Pulaski

It seems to me that this letter was written to John Hancock or some member of Congress, because according to the French original he asks for some memorandum (or plan) to be put to Council (committee?), and most importantly he adds that he would be waiting for orders at the Army. Writing to Washington, Pulaski would be more likely to say something like "hoping to join your Army" or "I am on my way." Also, the letter ends in an identical manner as Pulaski's letter to Hancock of September 3. This gives credence to my theory that it was written to John Hancock, the man who once had ambitions to be commander-in-chief but eventually limited himself to the modest rank of Major General for which his millionaire revolutionary and merchant background, no doubt, was a great asset. It is significant that Casimir Pulaski did not come as a total humble petitioner, though he had no binding contract from Deane as, for instance, Dekalb had.[8]

At camp he handed a letter from Adrienne Lafayette to her husband. (Lafayette, *Memoirs*, N.Y. 1837, I, p.104).

As it was the first letter from his wife, who was expecting a baby, and since Pulaski was comparatively fresh from Paris, he was probably warmly welcomed by the Marquise. Perhaps it was Lafayette who took escorted and introduced the Polish general to the Commander-in-Chief of the Armed Forces of the United Colonies. What impression the generals made on each other is not known but we can at least reconstruct somewhat their physical appearance, and see how George Washington looked to two other distinguished Polish visitors.

Julian Ursyn Niemcewicz, a writer and politician, wrote on May 21, 1798: "His is a majestic figure in which dignity unites with sweetness. His portraits which we have seen in Europe did not resemble him at all. He is about six feet tall, with broad shoulders and very well built. He has an aquiline nose, blue eyes, a regressed lower jaw and plenty of hair, in one sentence, 'I am senior, *sed cruda, Deo virdisque senectus*' (The old man, but God's old age full of vigorous strength)" (B. Grzelonski, ed., *Ameryka w pamietnikach Polakow*, p.64 *Interpress* Warsaw).

Tomasz Kajetan Wegierski, a younger writer, wrote on October 8, 1783: "All the portraits of Washington which I have seen in Europe do not resemble him. He is one of the most beautiful people I ever met. His figure is noble, a martial face and graceful manners. The politeness which he has shown me from the first moment I saw him till the last moment pleased me very much!" (Ibidem, p.15).

George Washington Parke Custis wrote in *Life of Washington*-p.480:"All of the many portraits which have been given of Washington possess a resemblance from the drawing on a signboard to the galleries of taste. He was so unique, so unlike anyone else, his whole appearance so striking and impressive that it was almost impossible to form a total likeness of him, on whom every god appeared to have set his seal, to give the world the assurance of man."

A contemporary of Pulaski's arrival at camp said: "the firm, composed and majestic countenance of the General inspired confidence and assurance..." (John Howland, quoted in Douglas Southhall Freeman's *George Washington*, vol.4, p.343. (This book will henceforth be referred to as GW)

"I could not keep my eyes from that imposing countenance, grave not, yet severe; affable without familiarity. Its predominant expression was calm dignity, through which you could trace the strong feelings of the patriot, and discern the father, as well as the commander of his soldiers. I have never seen a picture that represents him to me as I saw him at Valley Forge." (Pontgibaud in Chinard, ibidem).

Pulaski had to look up at Washington. According to Dr. A. Waldo: "Count Pulaski, General of the Horse, was a man of hardly middling stature - sharp countenance (behavior) and lively air - and he has now joined the American Army where he is greatly respected. He is also acclaimed for his martial skill and courage." (*Pennsylvania Magazine of History and Biography* (further on referred to as PMH) vol.21, p.320).

This physical description is confirmed by a Polish memoirist, Jedrzej Kitowicz, but though of hardly middling stature, Pulaski could certainly impress Washington, himself a horseman but not a cavalryman, with his equestrian art.

In the annals of the Cincinnati Society of New Jersey we have the following description as quoted in Wm. H. Richardson's *Brigadier General Pulaski* (Sesqui Centennial, Jersey City, 1929, p.29): "...he was accounted the finest swordsman and one of the best horsemen in the Army...When his horse was at gallop, he would discharge his pistol, throw it in the air, catch it on its descent, again hurl it with all his power in front of him but with one foot in stirrup pick it from the ground and time his position in the saddle."

B.J. Lossing, in his *Pictorial Book of Revolution* (N.Y. 1851), describing Morristown, relates similar feats of Pulaski. The account is impressive but puzzling because of its dating. Washington had his headquarters in Morristown in the winter of 1777 (January - May) and again in the winter of 1779/80. Pulaski arrived in America in July 1777 and died of wounds in October 1779. The dating error is repeated by many other authors.

On the same day that Pulaski arrived at camp, a council of war was held, which concluded that Howe would proceed to Charleston The council then recommended concentrating on the Burgoynne problem, and perhaps on that day Washington's mind was preoccupied with plans of the great northern expedition and the problems of command there.

However, busy as Washington may have been, we may presume that he spared a little time to observe and converse with Pulaski, a Marshal and well-known commander of cavalry and infantry units in conventional and hit-and-run tactical warfare - a hero of the war of liberation in distant Poland. Their conversation must have been limited by a language barrier, however, as Washington spoke no French and Pulaski no English. We can fairly assume that Lafayette or one of Washington's officers was the French-English translator.

Dr. Benjamin Franklin's letter of recommendation which Pulaski handed to the Commander-in-Chief stated the following:

Count Pulaski of Poland, an officer famous throughout Europe for his bravery and conduct in defence of the liberties of his country against the three great invading powers of Russia, Austria and Prussia, will have the honor of delivering this into your Excellency's hands. The Court here have encouraged and promoted his voyage, from an opinion that he may be highly useful to our service. Mr. Deane has written so fully concerning him that I need not enlarge, and I add my wishes that he may find in our armies under your Excellency occasions of distinguishing himself. (*Writings of Washington*, Ford, VI, p. 57)

This letter is more than a polite introduction. Pulaski's qualifications are stated most strongly and effectively in Franklin's recommendation. The mention of the Court was the key. It was only because of his connections with that Court that the boyish La Fayette was taken seriously by Americans, given the rank of General, and placed in a command position. The statement about Pulaski's fame was also true and was repeated in Franklin's recommendation of Kotkouski (Kotkowski?). However, the mention of Deane, though given in good faith, was of doubtful value and, in the present circumstances, could have had the reverse of its intended effect. Franklin could not know in Paris how far the concentrated attack against Deane had progressed in Congress[9].

Washington, usually a very polite man, whatever his personal opinion about foreign adventurers, supplied Pulaski with this letter of August 21:

> To the President of Congress. Sir, I do myself the honour to inclose you a Copy of Doctor Franklin's letter in favour of Count Pulaski of Poland by whom this will be handed to you. I sometime ago had a letter from Mr. Deane, couched in terms equally favourable to the character and military abilities of this gentleman. How he can with propriety be provided for you will be best able to determine. He takes this from me, as an introductory letter at his own request... (*Writings of George Washington*, J.C. Fitzpatrick, 9, p. 112).

I was not able to trace the original recommendation of Pulaski, but in his letter to Washington of 14 June 1777 Deane writes, "the Count Pulaski whose character is established as one of the first officers in Europe..." (PCC 247,129, 103,79). To judge from his other recommendation, his endorsement of Pulaski had to be enthusiastic.

It would apprear that in the beginning of their acquaintance, Washington was perhaps lukewarm towards Pulaski, but he gave him a letter of introduction (written in an almost identical manner as the letter to Congress) to his friend George Clymer, a rich merchant from Philadelphia who was a member of the Board of War, member of commerce and financial committees and a delegate.

Also, the Marquis La Fayette graciously supplied Pulaski with a letter to one of the most influential and active members of Congress, James Lovell of Massachusetts, but Lovell, a member of a Committee on Foreign Applications, was hostile to foreigners.[10] (PCC M247)

It is strange that La Fayette entertained any illusion on that subject. When he and other French officers, eager to serve the cause, wanted to discuss their commissions with John Hancock, he had passed the buck to Robert Morris who, in turn, after keeping the applicants duly waiting, referred them to Lovell. Lovell delivered them a lecture on impudent and unwanted foreigners and disappeared into Independence Hall, leaving the eager volunteers in the street.

La Fayette eventually received a commission as Major General, which it seems was intended to be honorary. It was no secret in Philadelphia that this was a political appointment.

Similarly treated was Du Coudray who at the age of 39 was a Chef de Brigade (three battalions of about 1000 men) and a military author of reputation. He had a contract with Deane by which he was given the rank of Major General and command of artillery and engineers subject only to Congress and the Commander-in-Chief. This is a point worth remembering in viewing Pulaski's parallel request in this regard.

But Generals Greene, Sullivan and Knox rather than be subordinate to Du Coudray threatened to resign. To avoid this, Du Coudray was made, on 15 September 1777, an Inspector-General of ordnance and military manufacturers.[11]

On the same day on which Washington handed to Pulaski his letter of introduction to Hancock, he wrote to John Page: "The conduct of Genl. Howe is extremely embarrassing. He left the Capes of Delaware the 31st ulto. and has never been heard of since the 7th inst. off Sinapuxent. It was generally believed here that he had passed the Capes of Virginia, and that Charlestown in South Carolina was the object of his expedition." Washington on the same date also writes to Governor William Livingston "...I have just received advice from Virginia that the Fleet was seen on 15th instant standing in towards Cape Charles, but whether with a real design of enter Chesapeak could not be then determined..."

(W.W. 9. p.112-113).

Still on the same day, Washington received information that Howe was to land in Maryland. That was the possibility which was not considered by the council of war. Washington, to block Howe's progress and protect Philadelphia, the continental capital, moved southward. To improve citizen morale and influence the doubters, Loyalists, and disaffected amongst the Philadelphians, the commander decided to march his troops through Philadelphia. The army was to march in one column down Front Street to Chestnut Street and up this street to the Common. The Horse was to be divided upon the two wings, Blands and Baylor's regiments upon the right, Sheldon's and Moylan's upon the left. There were to be no strollers and the female camp followers were to be kept out of sight. Spectators lined the streets of Philadelphia, on August 24th, some wishing well, some evil, to the soldiers. Amongst the marchers, homespun shirts prevailed. Though uniforms were promised as a bounty for enlisting, a comparatively small number of soldiers actually received them. In general the American Army wore mostly the ordinary workcloth, and even that in rags and tatters. But says La Fayette: "Their heads covered with green branches and marching to the sound of drums and fifes, these soldiers, in spite of their state of nudity, offered an agreeable spectacle to the eyes of all the citizens." ("La Fayette - Memoirs," correspondence & MS, N.Y. 1831, p.120).

★ ★ ★

35

To understand Casimir Pulaski's situation and subsequent career in America it is necessary to consider the American military structure and also to look at the case of Charles Francois Comte de Broglie.

The American Army was structured according to the English tradition which included militia organization, similar in concept to Poland's *pospolite ruszenie*, a call to arms to all the Polish szlachta who comprised a considerable portion of the nation and were obliged to answer such a call armed and on horseback.

But to return to the Americans, their main regular military training was gained in the service of the British Army and the most recent experience had been in the French and Indian war of 1756-63, called the Seven Years' War in Europe. That war was fought in America practically without cavalry and artillery, in wild and forested areas, and was not typical of contemporary warfare. Braddock's defeat at the hands of an inferior force of Indians, Canadians and Frenchmen, using Indian tactics, caused an unhealthy contempt for the British regulars among the Colonists, and this contemptuous feeling was reciprocated.

The armies of those days were small and professional. Use of professionals and mercenaries was customary. Frederic, called the Great, had a habit of kidnapping Polish subjects and forcing them into his army. His soldiers were more afraid of their officers than of enemies; and cavalry, in addition to its normal tactical functions, had to serve as prison guards, otherwise the impressed soldiers disappeared at the first opportunity. Shanghaing was a popular way of recruitment internationally, the ideal objects being vagabonds, criminals and foreigners. The peasants and craftsmen were too precious to be wasted in a monarch's war plays.

Warfare itself had a highly formal character and was conducted according to set rules which gave ideas to many aspiring Ceasars, and also to Washington. O.L. Spaulding, author of *The US Army*, mentions that a captain of German jagers reported with surprise that he frequently found military books on tactics, treatises on military engineering and Frederic's "Instructions to Generals" in enemies' baggage. Washington, also, ordered his officers to read military books.

The wars fought in Western Europe at that time were not wars of national survival or of a religious or ideological nature. They were wars of kings and emperors for territorial gains and prestige. Soldiers were formally drilled and were taught to perform complicated maneuvres. Generally there was no mass conscription. Consequently, a soldier had his price and was not wantonly destroyed. Generals had not yet learned to treat men as gun fodder.

The American War of Independence, in spite of its civil war

character of cruelties and ruthlessness, was fought between the oppos-
ing regular armies, generally in the gentlemanly ways of the eighteenth
century, as exemplified by Washington returning Howe's lost dog
with kind regards.

But the war between the Loyalists and Revolutionists had the
character of a war of survival.

As I said previously, the American military system was basically an
English one, with modifications. However, there was one great
difference. There was a system of favoritism and commission purchases
in appointments in the British Army. Almost all the generals were men
of high social rank and connection. They were sons of peers, friends
of dukes or earls. Lord Howe was an Irish peer; Keppel, Barrington
and Byron were sons of peers; Digby a grandson of one, and Pye and
Rodney also were related to the nobility. There were, too, politicians
amongst the generals and in 1780 twenty-three generals in the House
included Howe, Clinton, Burgoyne, Cornwallis and Vaughan who
shared between them twenty-one colonelcies, nine governorships and
some staff appointments.

However, that system, to a certain degree, was checked by George
III who, as Captain General, tried to place the military abilities of the
applicants above other considerations.

Such counterbalancing power was lacking in the American military
system. Congress did not represent a unanimous body but thirteen
individual colonies, each with their vested interests. Washington, who
had only limited military experience but was appearing at sessions of
the Congress in a military uniform, was chosen to block New
Englanders. Generalships were divided among the states, and Benedict
Arnold, who was one of the ablest officers in the Army, had his
promotion blocked because the quota of generals from his state was
already full. Generals were appointed by Congress but the states were
appointing, for their respective lines, all officers below that rank. In
that way, military appointments were dependent on the state legisla-
tures, which were partial to the military requests of their local
politicians or their proteges.

Whatever the qualifications or aspirations of the officers, the basic
gun fodder (soldiers) in the American Army were not regulars but
militia with practically no military experience. The Continental Army
developed basically from Massachusetts and neighboring states' militia
gathered around Boston who on July 4, 1775, became troops of the
United Provinces of North America. They were to be reinforced by
six companies of riflemen to be raised in Pennsylvania, Maryland and
Virginia. Riflemen were considered at that time to be the secret

weapon of the American Revolution. These militiamen were volunteers. Whoever was able to gather men by bribery, persuasion, political influence, oratory or whatever appeals induced a man to enlist against his King, became their leader. A regiment consisted of ten companies of fifty-nine men each. Any man who could raise such a company became captain, and the senior captain, one who directed the larger recruiting, became the colonel of the regiment. A private from New Jersey left such a description of electing the officers: [the men were] "sworn to be true and faithful soldiers in the Continental Army under the directions of the Right Honourable Congress. After this we chose our officers....When on parade, our first lieut. came and told us he would be glad if we would excuse him from going, which we refused: but on consideration we concluded it was better to consent; after which he said he would go; but we said, 'You shall not command us, for he whose mind can change in an hour is not fit to command in the field where liberty is contended for. In the evening we chose a private in his place." (Charles K. Bolton, *Private Soldier Under Washington*, p.25, Scribner's 1902).

La Fayette described the American generals in the following manner: "...Lord Stirling, more courageous than judicious, was another general who was often intoxicated, and Greene, whose talents were only then known to his immediate friends, commanded as major-general. General Knox, who had changed the profession of bookseller to that of artillery officer, was there also..."

Albigence Waldo wrote: "...Major-General Stirling is a man of a very noble presence – and the most martial appearance of any General in the Service – he much resembles the Marquis of Granby – by his bald head – and the make of his face – and figure of his body. He is mild in his private conversation, and vociferous in the field; but he has always been unfortunate in action....Genl. Greene and Genl. Sullivan are greatly esteemed..."

Says John C. Miller in *Triumph of Freedom* (Little, Brown and Co, 1948): p.20: "Most of the soldiers on the American side in the War of Independence saw action for the first time in that struggle, and almost half of the number of generals received the training in the war itself. Of the generals with some previous military experience, over half were the Englishmen who had held commissions in the British Army and subsequently settled down in the American colonies."

So it was not surprising that the experienced French officers who arrived in America, some for idealistic reasons, expected to be appreciated and receive commissions according to their rank or higher. Nor was it strange that Deane was supplying them.

On the other hand, there was nothing strange in the reaction of the native officers, who with great effort raised their companies or who had political or military ambitions. They did not want to step aside for the foreigners, even if these were the better professionals. After all, it was the American Revolution, not the French. They were to have one of their own!

Today, from the perspective of two hundred years after triumphant revolution, for most of the Americans, the mere idea that there could be better leaders than Washington and his officers comes as a shock. Washington became by a process similar to aging in wine, a better and better general.[12] He became a father figure, almost sanctified in the popular imagination, (the same thing happened with Thaddeus Kosciuszko in Poland). However, to the French officers and Pulaski, Washington was an ex-colonel of militia with almost no military experience. Up to the date when Pulaski met Washington he had lost the battle of Long Island and had to retreat through Jersey. Trenton and Princeton, according to the chivalrous rules of warfare, were nothing particular to be proud of, being skirmishes rather than battles.

We do not know how many letters Pulaski brought and whom he met before meeting Washington. The mention of Deane in Washington's polite letter of introduction could have only an adverse effect, but Franklin's letter carried weight and it was impolitic to treat lightly the applicant so recommended by the old man of the revolution. Besides, Pulaski, though clandestinely, was recommended probably by the French Court and French help was essential to the success of the revolution.

Washington had no reason to be friendly to Deane as the American Agent on December 6, 1776, wrote to the Committee of Secret Correspondence recommending the Comte de Broglie to lead the Revolutionary Army. (Francis Wharton, Ed. *The Revolutionary Diplomatic Correspondence of the U.S.A.*, Washington, 1889, vol. 2, p.218-20).

However, the proposal to supercede Washington, today so blasphemous, was at that time was not so outrageous, except, of course, to the person involved and his friends.[13]

Charles Comte de Broglie was a scion of the distinguished family which supplied two marshals to the French Army. They filled distinguished positions and enjoyed close relations with the sovereign. Charles Francois, as a young man was sent to Poland, which to a suspicious mind could associate him with Pulaski. After that sojourn he returned to his profession of soldier and served in the Seven Years' War. He was associated with Louis XV's secret diplomacy which gave

Poland an important role in its sterile plans.[14] At the ascendence of Louis XVI the Count found himself out of favor with the new king who, however, had nothing against de Broglie assuming an important role in the American Revolution, alough at that time the Court was sending its best wishes to George III and was not openly supporting the insurgents.

In 1776, De Kalb submitted to Deane a paper entitled

'A project, the execution of which will perhaps decide the success of the cause of liberty in the United States.'

According to it,

'Congress should ask of the King of France someone who would become their civil and military chief, the temporary generalissimo of the Republic. The course which had been so beneficial to the Dutch provinces when suffering from the tyranny of Spain would be equally advantageous in the present case. It is necessary to furnish the infant states with foreign troops and especially with a chief of great reputation whose military capacity will fit him to command an army against the Prince of Brunswick or the King of Prussia himself, who will join to a name made illustrious by many great heroes great experience in war and all the qualities necessary to conduct such an enterprise with prudence, integrity and economy... Numerous armies and great courage are not sufficient to obtain success if they are not sustained by ability and experience...But my plan is to have a man whose name and reputation would discourage the enemy...Such a leader with the assistants he would choose would be worth twenty thousand men, and would double the value of the American troops. (*Kalb to Deane*, Dec. 1776, Deane Papers I, 427, N.Y. 1887)

Such a man was in short Broglie, and to promote personally the Comtes aspirations, De Kalb and most of his companions arrived in America shortly before Pulaski.

Deane was convinced of the logic of De Kalb's reasoning and wrote to the Committee of Secret Correspondence:

I submit one thought to you. Whether you could engage a great general of the highest character in Europe, such for instance as Prince Ferdinand Marshal Broglie, (Deane, it seems, confused the Comte de Broglie with his brother the marshal and duke), or another of equal rank, to take the lead of your armies whether such a step would not be politic, as it would give a character and credit to your military and strike perhaps a greater panic in our enemies. (*Deane Papers* I, 404).

Deane's recommendation and suggestions had, of course, a reverse effect, accelerating only his future fall. The mere thought of a civil and military chief, a generalissimo, was anathema to Congress. To suggest a foreigner and a Frenchman at that, was to add insult to injury. Congress on the whole was afraid of the possibility of the subjugation of the colonies by France. After all, it was only a very new and fresh role of France to be a friend of the colonial Americans.

In reaction to Deane's proposals, a Committee on Foreign Applications was formed to check strangers applying for service in the American Army, and an absolute refusal to accept any foreign generalissimo. It seems to me that to some members of Congress Pulaski could have been seen as a candidate for generalissimo. After all, Casimir Pulaski was the most famous of the leaders of the Bar Confederacy and there was a political group in Poland which would have liked to see him in the role of military dictator of that insurrection.

On August 24, 1777, Pulaski in Philadelphia forwarded his second memorandum to Congress:

To the honorable Congress:

The gentlemen, your commissioners, have written in my favor. I will strive to act up to their recommendations as far as my abilities and the trust which shall be reposed in me will permit. I desire to obtain a single company of volunteers of cavalry, with a title which will authorize me to command an entire division when I shall merit it.

My first military years were passed in very rough trials. I may be permitted to aspire to an employ in which I shall be subject only to the orders of the Commander-in-Chief of the Army. If that cannot be, yet joined to the Marquis de La Fayette, I would take pleasure in sharing his labors and executing the orders of the Commander-in-Chief as subaltern of the marquis. The principal thing which I ask is to be near the enemy, that I may more readily seize occasions of acquiring the name of a good officer. If an incursion is to be made into the country which the enemy possesses, I shall not probably be unskillful at that, or in defending an advanced post. I imagine one must be fortified near Ticonderoga. If I should be trusted with the choice of a spot, and with the defense of it, I would fulfill those orders with the greatest exactness.

I will not enlarge this memorial by different ideas which present themselves to me; but if what I ask shall be attended with any difficulties as to the grant, I beg the right of presenting others which may be better received. I commanded in Poland 18,000 in different battles. The sieges and attacks of places which I have managed give me a title to be counted among men of military experience. America cannot despise their talents. It was under this idea that I have passed hither from Europe, to do myself the honor of being admitted among worthy citizens in the defense of their country and their liberty.

COUNT PULASKI.[15]

(*Executive Document No. 120*, Senate, 49th Congress, 2d Session, Message from the President of the U.S., March 3, 1887. This document further on will be referred to as "Ex. Doc.")

He was obviously irate at the delay in his appointment and sternly lectured Congress that it should not despise men of talent. Pulaski clearly wanted to be subordinated only to the Commander-in-Chief. If he had agreed to accept orders from La Fayette, it was perhaps only because Pulaski (then a mature man of 30 with great military experience) thought that the youthful marquis would become for him a rubber stamp. La Fayette was obviously in search of adventure and of a father image, and his military experience was limited to two summers of practice maneuvers.

Pulaski requested the command of only a single company of cavalry volunteers, but he was certain that he would prove himself worthy of commanding a division. The statement that he had under his command eighteen thousand men was misleading. But the total he had ever commanded could be well above that figure. Generally he commanded a single unit of about four thousand men. The number and strength of Pulaski's command varied with the mission (i.e., whether offensive or defensive), the terrain and location (e.g., towns or fortresses under siege involving citizen soldiers) and the military-political fortunes of the Bar Confederacy, which was constantly changing.

★ ★ ★

On August 25, 1777, that one possibility, which was not considered by Washington's Council of War happened. Howe's fleet was sighted returning, and soon the British troops started embarking at the Head of Elk (now Elkton) on Chesapeake Bay, about 50 miles from Philadelphia. This news and the martial sight of Washington's army which paraded through the streets of Philadelphia prompted Pulaski to join the army without further waiting for the commission. He fired a parting shot in the form of a letter to Hancock. That letter is the first known English language autograph of Pulaski.

Philadelphia 25 Aust 1777 Ans.

I have Dought it not my Duty to stay here any longer, in as much as I have heard; that his Exy Genl Washinkton is gon to meet the Enemy; wherefore I will go to the Army, it is. I can not do much, but Hover I will shew my good will. I depent upon His Excelly and leef him my Memorials. I shal sent to France for every Articel Necessary, and Congress will to me advancing of money, of it I will waght for a Swift and decisive Answer. If On is possible before that I shall get or optain a Comission, by which I may not stand unter any other Comand as onter General Washinkton in such a case I shall think it my indispensible Duty, to Exert my self to the utmost in my Power, this is the supstange Conserning my Afars. But your Favour to uptain I Atest my greatest Desier and Respect by which I remain Your Excelencys Most opitient Humble Serv Cr Pulaski.

("Revolutionary Papers Miscellaneous" quoted in Martin I.J. Griffin, *Catholics and American Revolution*, General Count Casimir Pulaski, vol. 3, p.8, Pa, 1911)

He enclosed a ruled plan of "Establishment of Corps of Vallentears appertaiying to the General that is emploi During the War in various operations. Vageners 2, Horses for Vagens 8, vagens 2, spates 40, picks 40, trumpets 2, standart 1, swords 200, cardrich poxes 200, helmets 200, fusell 200, pistols 200, saddles 200, horses 200, establishment in every necessary respect. – Summed of Men with two coachmen – 208. Saddler 1, farrier 1, surzon major 1, Light Horse 180, trumpeter 2, caporal 12, quartermaster 2, Estandard bearer 1, Cornette 1, Lieutenant 2, Adjutant 1, Second Capt. 1, Commander First Capt. 1."

Pulaski's request to be subordinate only to Washington or La Fayette was considered by the Committee on Foreign Application which reported to Congress thus:

> The Committee to whom was referred the Memorial of Count Pulaski
> in which he solicits for such rank and command in the Army of these
> United States as will leave him subordinate to the Commander-in-
> Chief alone or to him and the Marquis de la Fayette – report as their
> opinion that a compliance with those expectations would be as contrary
> to the prevailing sentiments in the several states as to the Constitution
> of our Army and therefore highly impolitic. J. Lovell. (DCC 8 p. 6739
> and P.C.C. 41 vol. VIII, p. 25).

However, Pulaski, not willing to wait idly for Congress's decision, stayed with Washington at Wilmington. Somehow, he must have impressed Washington as the Commander-in-Chief sent a letter to the President of Congress:

Having endeavoured, at the solicitation of Count Pulaski, to think of
some mode of employing him in our service, there is none occurs to
me liable to so few inconveniences and exceptions, as the giving him
the command of the horse. This department is still without a head;
as I have not, in the present deficiencies of Brigadiers with the army,
thought it advisable to take one from the foot for that command.
The nature of the horse service with us being such, that they commonly act in detachment, a general officer with them is less necessary than at the head of the Brigades of infantry. In the absence of
General Smallwood who is ordered to put himself at the head of the
Maryland militia, we shall have two Brigades without general officers. But though the horse will suffer less from the want of a general
officer than the foot, a man of real capacity, experience, and knowledge in that service, might be extremely useful. The Count appears,
by his recommendations, to have sustained no inconsiderable military character in his own country; and as the principal attention in
Poland has been for some time past paid to its Cavalry, it is to be presumed this gentleman is not unacquainted with it. I submit it to Congress how far it may be eligible to confer the appointment I have
mentioned upon him; they will be sensible of all the objections attending the measure, without my particularizing them, and can determine accordingly.

This gentleman, we are told, has been, like us, engaged in defending the liberty and independence of his country, and has sacrificed
his fortune to his zeal for those objects. He deserves from hence a title to our respect, that ought to operate in his favour, as far as the
good of the service will permit; but it can never be expected we
should lose sight of this. (Aug. 27, 1777, W.W. p. 173)

However this letter strikes an extraordinary cautious tone, extreme
even for the usually reserved Washington.

It is interesting to restate the Commander-in-Chief's opinion of
cavalry as shown in this letter. The nature of cavalry is that they do
not act in unison but in detachments. They do not need, in fact, a
commanding officer as much as infantry. Putting a general of infantry
at the head of cavalry branch of the Army would be a simple matter
but for the shortage of brigadiers.

As far as Casimir Pulaski was concerned, should Congress decide
that that gentleman with some connections with the French Court
should be placated with the almost honorary title of Commander of
Horse, they could appoint him on their own responsibility. But

whoever recommended him should not be hasty and have the good of the service foremost.

★ ★ ★

When Howe landed his forces on August 25th the British had spent over seven weeks on board crowded ships, and in taking the Chesapeake Bay route Howe had inclined to the advice of Naval officers, but calms and thunderstorms made it a tedious voyage. According to Captain John Montresor, the chief engineer:

"The fleet and army were much distressed for the want of fresh water having been for some time put to an allowance, but not so much as horse vessels, having been obliged to throw numbers of their horses overboard." (Lynn Montross, *Rag, Tag and Bobtail*, N.Y. 1952, p.189)

More for political than strategic reasons Washington had to protect the continental capital of Philadelphia. For two weeks he kept a close watch on the advancing foe and was ready and willing to give him battle at the fords of Brandywine. Until that battle, only small skirmishes had occurred.

At the head of Military Intelligence was an amiable physician Dr. Theodoric Bland, Jr., who had also been a poet and journalist. He had no military experience, but was friendly with Washington.

By the convention at Williamsburg, on June 13, 1776, Bland was appointed captain of the first troop of Virginia cavalry, which he helped to form. His relative, Henry Lee, Jr., was commanding one of the six troops.

According to the Marquis of Chastelleux (who met him in Philadelphia in 1781) Bland was a tall, handsome man who acquired French in the West Indies. That Bland could speak French is confirmed by Thomas Anburey in his *Travels*. Whatever the quality of his French, it made it possible for him to establish contact with Pulaski who possibly shared in Bland's task which was: "... diligent and constant patrols both of horse and foot, on the flanks and in front of the enemy, as near them as prudence will permit, so that they cannot possibly move any way, without your having information." (*The Bland Papers*, ed. Charles Campbell, Petersburg, 1843, p.63)

Charles Campbell stated in this book that Bland was at the time of the Brandywine battle in Pulaski's detachment. As Pulaski had no commission this was not officially possible. However, while waiting for Congress to act, his impatience and restlessness would have led to contacts with Washington's cavalry. You can't keep a cavalry man away from horses and it would have been natural for him to ride with Bland on some missions.

The American Army, except for intelligence gathering, on the whole remained inactive. But Pulaski was well aware of the approaching conflict and his impatience prompted him on September 3, 1777, to send a sharp letter to Congress. As it is marked "Philadelphia," it is possible that Pulaski was personally pleading his case.

PHILADELPHIA, September 3, 1777.
The name under which I have served my country is sufficiently known to authorize me to pretend to something in military service. I have had the command of an army before, and here my pretension is to obey. If it does not please, I desire only to hear yes or no; the last word shall not surprise me. I have been unfortunate, and I have proved in my life most obstacles. The grace which I require of Congress is to obtain an answer to the letter from General Washington. Be it what it may, it will not abate my desire to serve the States of American. I recommend myself to your memory, and I have the honor to be,
Your excellency's most humble servant,
CASIMIR VICTOR COUNT KORVIN PULASKI. (PCC 41, 8, 40-41)

This is a letter of a man who knew his value and was certain of himself. At that time Congress was busy with many important matters. There was an investigation into the Ticonderoga defeat which led to the court-martial of some officers and there were ominous Quaker plots. There were also problems of taxation, this time of domestic origin, and various troublesome financial matters. After Pulaski's letter of September 3, Congress found time to deal with the exasperated foreigner for on the next day, the question of appointing him Commander of the Horse was negatived. (JCC, 8, p.711)

★ ★ ★

On September 9, the American Army occupied a position on the north bank of Brandywine River. Only a few fords were passable and Washington positioned the center of his forces opposite Chadd's Ford. Bland was patrolling across the river. Also, Infantry General Maxwell crossed at Chadd's Ford and was skirmishing with the vanguard of Knyphausen, while Porterfield and Waggoner attacked Ferguson's riflemen. "Lieutenant-General Knyphausen, as had been previously concerted, kept the enemy amused in the course of the day with cannon and appearance of forcing the ford..." (General Sir Wm. Howe dispatch to Lord Geo. Germain, quoted in H. Dawson's *Battles of the USA*, N.Y. 1858, p.282).

A large force under Lord Cornwallis crossed the Brandywine upstream and moved around, intending to attack the Americans from the rear or on the flank, hoping to repeat the successful British maneuver at the Battle of Long Island. Sullivan was caught in the act of changing flanks when the British struck and his men retreated in confusion. According to La Fayette, Sullivan fought with "such courage as...will deserve the praise of everyone." (*La Fayette Memoirs*, p.23). Conway, an Irishman once in the service of France, commanded eight hundred men in a most brilliant manner. La Fayette himself sustained a leg wound while rallying the troops and made good his escape only through his aide-de-camp, Gimat. Baron St. Ovary, who assisted La Fayette in his attempt to rally the fugitives, was taken prisoner. Altogether, the foreign adventurers and little Caesars acquitted themselves well.[16]

It was General Greene who saved Sullivan's forces from total destruction. In about fifty minutes, his Virginia Continentals covered four miles of broken country and upon arrival checked the enemy's progress.

The battle was lost! The Americans retreated towards Chester. However, the defeat, as described in Washington's report, did not look too serious: "..But though we fought under many disadvantages and were from the causes mentioned obliged to retire, yet our loss of men is not, I am persuaded, very considerable; I believe much less than the enemy's."

Richard Henry Lee in a letter to Patrick Henry stated: "But Gen. Howe may say with Pyrrhus, 'Such another victory will ruin me.' Every account of officers and country people, who have been in the field since the action, say the enemy's loss in killed and wounded must be between 2 and 3000. Nothing proves this more strongly than their remaining yet upon the field of battle when every interest calls upon them to push on. Our loss in killed and wounded scarcely comes to 500..." (The letters of R.H. Lee, J.C. Ballagh, editor, N.Y. 1970, p.322). Lee's statistics are in conflict with Peckham's.

According to the authoritive statistics in the *The Toll of Independence*, edited by Howard H. Peckham, Washington had 11,000 men against Howe's 13,000. The British had 90 killed, 448 wounded ad 6 missing. The American estimated losses were 200 killed, 500 wounded and 400 captured. Hardly a pyrrhic victory!

The unreliable and confused intelligence was chiefly blamed for the American defeat, and there were two scapegoats, Colonel Bland and Sergeant Tucker.

Says Henry (Light Horse) Lee:

Washington was quickly informed of the separation of the enemy's columns, as he was subsequently informed not only of its continuance, but that the left column was making a very circuitous sweep. Persuaded of the fact, he wisely determined to pass the Brandywine with his whole force and strike at Knyphausen. In the very act of giving his orders to this effect, Colonel Bland of the Virginia Horse, brought him intelligence which very much obscured, if it did not contradict, the previous information, and the original judicious decision was abandoned. Colonel Bland was noble, sensible, honorable and amiable, but never intended for the Department of Military Intelligence. (*Henry Lee, Memoirs of the War in the Southern Department of the USA*, Philadelphia 1812, [not 1827 as says M. Boatner] revised edition, 1869, N.Y. p.88)

In the *Bland Papers* (edited by Charles Campbell, 1843, p. XXVII), Colonel Bland's grandson writes: "In reference to General Lee's opinion of Colonel Bland's inaptitude for the Department of Military Intelligence, it may be sufficient to observe that in this department he was employed by Geo. Washington whose confidence Colonel Bland had the happiness to enjoy, without abatement or interruption during his whole life." Anyway it is obvious that the titular head of intelligence cannot be responsible for each one of his subordinates or for the actions and judgments of his superiors (as it was with Major Spear and Sergeant Tucker) and General Sullivan's decision to send two contradictory reports to Washington. However, Colonel Bland did his duty well as he crossed at Jones Ford, spotted Cornwallis, and immediately informed Sullivan. Besides, there were such factors as difficult terrain, full of shrubs and trees, and the morning fog, which spread over the creek.

What part, if any, did Pulaski play at the Battle of Brandywine? As he had no commission, his status was that of a volunteer. Probably he kept close to Washington and and his staff, possibly reconnoitering with them before the battle. There is an interesting and little-known account of the following incident, and if it is true then Pulaski's life perhaps hung on the magnanimity of his alter ego, Frederic Ferguson.

The following account is contained in *The New York Mirror*, April 1831, p.327:

General Washington-we present to our readers the following anecdote relating to General Washington, with a desire to preserve it in the pages of the Mirror. What corroborates Mr. Cooper's statement in the eyes of the remaining few acquainted with the times and events of the revolutionary war is that the hazardous situation of our army near Brandywine, and the incessant duties imposed on the commander in chief, could scarcely have permitted his absence from the encampment to reconnoitre the foe, and thereby expose a life on which the salvation of the country almost depended. The story is therefore improbable, and the conjecture of Captain De Lancey that the officer in question was Count Pulaski, who was present at the battle of Brandywine, on the eighth of September, 1777, is most probably correct. General Lafayette, who was wounded in that engagement, and is one of the very few surviving field officers of that disastrous day, might probably elucidate the circumstance.

Count Pulaski was a Polander of high birth, who, with a few men, had carried off King Stanislaus from his capital, Warsaw. The king afterwards effected his escape, and declared Pulaski an outlaw. Thus proscribed, he came to America, and offered his services to Congress, who conferred on him the rank of brigadier general. He was mortally wounded in the abortive assault, under Count d'Estaing and General Lincoln, on Savannah, on the morning of the fourth of October, 1779, while attempting to charge the enemy at the head of two hundred horsemen, in full gallop. Congress resolved that a monument should be erected to his memory.

Captain De Lancey, although in the opposite ranks, was a brave, resolute, intelligent officer, and allied to one of the most respectable and wealthy families of the then province of New-York.

The letter, from which the following is an extract, was addressed from Paris, under date of twenty-eight of January, to Mr. Skinner, editor of the American Turf Register and Sporting Magazine.

While troubling you with this letter, I will take an opportunity of correcting an error, which has been very generally circulated, and is even to be found in several historical works, as well as in numberless magazines. Among others who have fallen into the mistake to which I allude, Bigland, in his 'View of the World,' related an anecdote by which it would appear that at Brandywine the life of Washington was at the mercy of the celebrated British rifleman, Major Ferguson, who was too generous to profit by his advantage.

Mr. J.P. De Lancey, (father of Mrs. Cooper) though of a well-known American family, was regularly educated for the British army, in which he received a commission at eighteen. In 1774 he was quartered at Philadelphia with a part of his corps, the eighteenth of the royal Irish. Washington was then a delegate in congress; and, in consequence of his having dined with the mess of the eighteenth, and of the intercourse which naturally existed between gentlemen of the different provinces, through their family connections and acquaintances, Mr. De Lancey had a perfect knowledge of his person. When the army of Howe was preparing to embark for the Chespeake, corps of riflemen was organized by drafting picked men from the different regiments, and was placed under the command of Major Ferguson, who had invented several improvements in the rifle, and who had acquired great skill in the use of that weapon. Of this corps, Mr. De Lancey was appointed the second in command. During the manoeuvres which preceded the battle of Brandywine, these riflemen were kept skirmishing in advance of one of the British columns. They had crossed some open ground, in which Ferguson was wounded in the arm, and had taken a position in the skirts of a thick wood. While Mr. De Lancey was occupied in arranging a sling for the wounded arm of Ferguson, it was reported that an American officer of rank, attended only by a mounted orderly, had ridden into the open ground, and was then within point blank rifle shot. Two or three of the best marksmen stepped forward and asked leave to bring him down. Ferguson peremptorily refused; but he went to the skirt of the wood, and, showing himself, menaced the American with several rifles, while he called to him and made signs for him to come in. The mounted officer saw his enemies, drew his reins, and sat, looking at them attentively, for a few moments.

A sergeant now offered to hit the horse without injuring the rider. But Ferguson still withheld his consent, affirming that it was Washington reconnoitering, and that he would not be the instrument of placing the life of so great a man in jeopardy by so unfair means. The horseman turned and rode slowly away. When the British army reached Philadelphia, Mr. De Lancey was promoted to a majority, in another corps, and Ferguson, not long after, went to the south, where he was killed, at King's mountain. To the last moment, Major Ferguson maintained that the officer whose life he had spared was Washington; and it is probable that the story in circulation has proceeded from this opinion. But on the other hand, Mr. De Lancey, to whom the person of Washington was necessarily so well known, constantly affirmed that his commander was mistaken. I have often heard Mr. De Lancey relate these circumstances, and though he never pretended to be sure of the person of the unknown horseman, it was his opinion, from some particulars of dress and stature, that it was the Count Pulaski.

Though in error as to the person of the individual whom he spared, the merit of Major Ferguson is not at all diminished by a knowledge of the truth. I correct the mistake only because the account is at variance with the probable situation of Washington at so important a moment, and because every circumstance connected with the history of that illustrious man, has great interest, not only with his own country, but the whole civilized world.

Yours, &c. J. FENNIMORE COOPER.

The same incident is described in the following letter of Captain Ferguson's quoted in *Two Scottish Soldiers* (by James Ferguson, Aberdeen, 1883 pp.66, 67):

We had not lain long when a rebel officer, remarkable by a hussar dress passed towards our army, within a hundred yards of my right flank, not perceiving us. He was followed by another dressed in dark green or blue, mounted on a bay horse, with a remarkably large cocked hat. I ordered three good shots to steal near to them and fire at them, but the idea disgusted me. I recalled the order. The hussar in returning made a circuit, but the other passed again within a hundred yards of us, upon which I advanced from woods towards him. On my calling, he stopped; but after looking at me proceeded. I again drew his attention, and made signs to stop him, but he slowly continued his way. As I was within that distance at which, in the quickest firing, I could have lodged half a dozen of balls in or about him before he was out of my reach -I had only to determine, but it was not pleasant to fire at the back of unoffending individual, who was acquitting himself very coolly of his duty; so I let him alone. The day after I had been telling this story to some wounded officers who lay in the same room with me, when one of our surgeons, who had been dressing the wounded rebel officers, came in and told us they had been informing him that General Washington was all the morning with the light troops, and only attended by a French officer in a hussar dress, he himself dressed and mounted in every point as above described. I am not sorry that I did not know at the time who it was. Farther this deponent sayeth not, as his bones were broke a few minutes after.

To which answers the author of *Memoires of his Own Time*:

"Whatever truth there may be in this relation, and whoever might have been the person in dark green and blue with the remarkable large high cocked hat, no one acquainted with the style of General Washington's costume during the war, or any other time, can suppose it to have been him, who was so generously dealt with by the Major. The General's uniform or military dress was blue and buff, which, it may be very safely averred he never varied, at least to an entire change of colours: neither was he ever seen in a hat of the description given in the letter. It is true, he wore a cocked hat, but, of a moderate size. It might, indeed, have been somewhat larger than those in fashion in America at the be-

51

ginning of the war but, it could by no means have answered to the co-
lossal dimensions given by the Major. The General had too correct a
taste in dress, to figure n the bully-like garb of a Bobadil or a Pistol; and
there was no inducement to such a disguise, being as much in danger in
green and blue with a large hat, as in blue and buff with a small one.
Major Ferguson, therefore, might have spared himself the self-gratula-
tion of 'not knowing at the time who it was, since, if justly described,
most assuredly it was not General Washington. -Ed.

Whoever had accompanied the officer in hussar uniform may be a
matter of speculation, but it seems probable that the man so attired was
Casimir Pulaski. He is usually shown in such uniform on his portraits,
though they are not contemporary, and such uniform is mentioned in
Reszta Pamietnikow Macieja Rogowskiego, (Paris, 1847), writen by
someone with an evident knowledge of some details.

It is interesting to observe that Pulaski and Ferguson were related
spirits and their fates were similar. I shall yet have an opportunity to
write about Ferguson so will not introduce him at this point.

About Pulaski's role in the Battle of Brandywine Paul Bentalou
wrote in his *Pulaski Vindicated* (Baltimore, 1824, p.27).

> He was at Brandywine, on the day of battle, with the Marquis de La
> Fayette and other distinguished officers, in the suite of General Washing-
> ton. At the time of our right wing being turned by the victorious en-
> emy pressing upon us, and the rapid retreat of the right and centre of
> our army became the consequence, Count Pulaski, proposed to General
> Washington to give him the command of his body guard, consisting of
> about thirty horsemen. This was readily granted, and Pulaski with his
> usual intrepidity and judgment led them to the charge and succeeded in
> retarding the advance of the enemy-a delay which was of the highest
> importance to our retreating army. Moreover, the penetrating military
> coup d'oeil of Pulaski soon perceived that the enemy were ma-
> noeuvring to take possession of the road leading to Chester, with the
> view of cutting off our retreat, or, at least, the column of our baggage.
> He hastened to General Washington, to communicate the information,
> and was immediately authorized by the Commander-in-Chief to collect
> as many of the scattered troops as he could find at hand, and make the
> best of them. This was most fortunately executed by Pulaski, who by an
> oblique advance upon the enemy's front and right flank, defeated their
> object, and effectually protected our baggage and the retreat of our
> army.

Johnson, a critic of Pulaski, disputes Bentalou's description of the
attack and the beneficial results flowing therefrom with such a small

force (pgs. 24-25 of his *Remarks Critical and Historical*), although, he acknowledges that the facts as presented by Bentalou "...has already gone the rounds of half the American presses; beginning, I believe, with the National Gazette." (p. 25 supra). Following this sentence, he attacks the American press for such reporting of what he labels a "tale" with the following comment: "What deplorable ignorance of our revolutionary history must prevail where such a tale could meet with such countenance! (p.25 supra).

The motivation for Johnson's denigration of Pulaski's service to the Revolutionary cause is clearly stated by him on page 24 of his article: "I will show that the story of his [Pulaski's] services in this country, is highly inflated and deceptive." Yet, Johnson pauses in his verbal rancor to acknowledge Pulaski's valor with these words: "Count Pulaski was a brave man, none braver, and merits our gratitude for the spirit with which he embarked in our Revolution." (pg. 9 supra).

While the above statement may seem like a grudging admission by Johnson, he was undoubtedly aware that his idol, Gen. Washington, had previously acknowledged Pulaski's bravery in his March 14, 1778, letter from Valley forge to Gov. Livingston of New Jersey, where Pulaski's cavalry had wintered at Trenton:

> I am pleased with the favorable account you give of Count Pulaski's conduct while at Trenton. He is a gentleman of great activity and un-questionable bravery, and only wants a fuller knowledge of our lan-guage and customs to make him a valuable officer. (*Washington's Writings*, Part II, vol. V, p. 279)

We may well ask why Johnson set out to denigrate Pulaski's services to the American cause. It is entirely possible that Johnson's anti-Pulaski attitude was triggered or set off by his impression (fallacious though it may be) that Bentalou was decidedly anti–Washington, for (on p. 15, supra), he categorizes Bentalou as follows: "...poor Bentalou is only made the mask of the assasin; of the deadly enemy and inveterate envyer of the fame of Washington." Even assuming, for the sake of argument, that this is so, why may we ask does he transfer his animosity towards Bentalou onto Pulaski's shoulders? In reviewing the writings of Pulaski, one might well understand or appreciate the loyalty of faithful Bentalou as a subordinate officer for his commander? So much for motives and would-be historians!

In 1825 from Charleston, Johnson, in keeping with his declaration that "I will show that the story of his [Pulaski's] services in this country, is highly inflated and deceptive." answers Bentalou with his version of Pulaski's actions at Brandywine in this fashion:

As to that of the thirty body guards at the battle of Brandywine, it can hardly be necessary to animadvert upon it. I have it in my power to ascertain facts from an eye witness, but I shall not trouble him with the inquiry. Pulaski may have been present, and may have requested to be entrusted with the body guards; improbable as it is that he, then having no commission in the American service, would be permitted to command them, I will not even controvert that allegation. But, that these thirty body guards, even with Pulaski at their head, should have brought ten thousand victorious men to a halt, is a tale only fit for the adventures of Amadis de Gaul or Baron Munchausen. There is not the least notice of any occurrence of this kind in the annals of the day, and surely it would have reflected too much honour on our cavalry to have passed unnoticed, if true. But it cannot be true. The fire of a single company would have prostrated the whole detachment, and the enemy would have passed on over their bodies.

The authentic records of the day assign the honour of checking the enemy and covering the retreat to adequate causes. And I cannot but think it unfortunate for this pamphleteer, that having to depend so much on his own credibility, he should have set out with so bold a claim on public credulity. His reviewer indeed, was ready to swallow any improbability; but, that in the eyes of the American public, forgotten although I admit our Revolutionary history so generally is, any writer should presume to appropriate to Pulaski the merit of having discovered, suggested and carried into execution the measures that saved our baggage, and covered our retreat at the battle of Brandywine, I pronounce to be nothing short of absolute effrontery. There cannot be a word of truth in it. And yet, most extraordinary as the fact is, this very tale has already gone the rounds of half the American presses; beginning, I believe, with the National Gazette. What deplorable ignorance of our Revolutionary history must prevail where such a tale could meet with such countenance!

So far as relates to the baggage, the tale admits of positive contradiction, and that from Genreal Washington himself, who writes to Congress on the 11th, the day of the action, "that the baggage having previously moved off, was all secure."(Letters, vol, II. p. 157—William Johnson "Remarks Critical and Historical on an Article in the Forty-Seventh Number of The North American Review Relating to Count Pulaski,"Charleston, 1825, pgs. 24-25. Johnson concludes with the assertion that the retreat of the American army was covered by

Greene's reserves, particularly by the reserve regiment of Stevens. (p. 15 supra).

In comparing the two versions, it is interesting to note that Bentalou speaks from personal knowledge, for he was a participant in the battle while Johnson was not. Bentalou was a 2d Lt. in the German Bn. which was assigned to Muhlenberg's Brigade of Gen. Greene's division. In addition to Brandywine, we must bear in mind that in the subsequent discussion on Germantown, Bentalou also fought there while Johnson did not. As a participant, it is only common knowledge that he had or acquired first hand information of the events. Johnson, not having been in the battle, acquired his information from various sources—from friends, some of which may have been eye-witness accounts or some hearsay, or from readings, although we know his skeptical opiniion of the 4th estate from his previous comment about the press: "What deplorable ignorance of our revolutionary history must prevail...."

William W. Gordon's study of Pulaski contains an interesting observation about Pulaski's personal combat style as a cavalryman:

> In the words of one of his comrades, "the Count in battle—how he
> seemed to fight as if enjoying a banquet; how, again and again, he
> would dash into the midst of the enemy, cutting his way on the right
> hand and on the left, as if the strength of ten men lay in his single arm;
> and then wheeling, cutting his way back again, and often without loss."
> (op. cit. pg. 226)

In the Johnson-Bentalou polemic on Pulaski's participation in the Brandywine battle, here are some points of interest for our discussion, examination, and cogitation:

(1) American press accounts (which even Johnson conceded) favorably reported Pulaski's battle behavior at Brandywine.

(2) Johnson claims "...to have it in my power to ascertain facts from an eye witness but I shall not trouble him with the inquiry." Any trial lawyer can claim a surprise eye witness to events but if he doesn't produce or depose him for the jury, of what validity is such a claim and what credibility does the lawyer have? The American jury of public opinion was entitled to hear all available witnesses and evidence but, aside from personal opinions, what real hard evidence does Johnson offer? Reader, you be the Judge!

(3) Johnson conceds that "...Pulaski may have been present, and may have requested to be entrusted with the bodyguards;"—end of concession. However, he continues that it was "improbable" that Pulaski "...would be permitted to command them...'simply because he

did not have an American Commission. What an avowed technocrat! What bureaucratic tape to interpose during a battle retreat! It was an emergency situation! It was a crucial moment in the swing of a battle! At such a critical time, would we expect Washington, so beloved by Johnson, to stand on technicalities and to "look a cavalry gift horse in the mouth," so to speak? Here was a battle-tested veteran of numerous cavalry engagements able to lead and ready to die. Washington certainly had nothing to lose in granting Pulaski's request. Under the battle conditions then and there prevailing, granting Pulaski's request would not have been unusual or unreasonable.

Clarence a. Manning, in his biography of Pulaski agrees with this analysis, saying:

> It was no time for ceremony and formality. The harassed Washington
> gave the permission and Pulaski jumped into action. With his usual im-
> petuosity and with his mixture of English, French, and Polish, he galva-
> nized the little troop into making an effective charge upon the enemy.
> His own example served better than his orders. The British had not ex-
> pected such a diversion, and the brief delay caused by the little band
> was effective for the American withdrawal. (*Soldier of Liberty Casimir Pu-
> laski*, Philosophical Library, New York, New York, 1945, pg. 215)

(4)   Bentalou insists that Pulaski's actions "...protected our bag-gage...'while Johnson essentially argues that there was no baggage to save bacause Washinton wrote to Congress "that the baggage having previously moved off, was all secure." Therefore, Johnson contends: "So far as relates to the baggage, the tale admits of positive contradi-tion...." Let us examine this issue.

Washington wisely did issue an order before the battle, to wit, on Sept. 1, 1777, as follows: "...it is now once more strictly enjoined that all baggages which can be spared both of officers and men be immediately packed up, and sent off this day to the other side of Brandywine..."(*Writings of Washington*, John C. Fitzpatrick, pg. 192). However, the officers were explicitly allowed to retain blankets, greatcoats, three or four shifts of underclothes, and the men were supposed to keep the clothes they wore, blankets, shirt and greatcoats if they had them.

The order then was not all inclusive, for it was only for baggages which could be spared. Deductively, there is specifically excepted baggages which could not be spared. Also, what of ammunition, supplies, necessary field equipment, quartermaster material, in addi-tion to the excepted baggage which could not be spared by both officers and men? Was it all hand carried or deposited in wagons sufficient to form a small train?

Johnson evidently interprets Washington's order and report to Congress on the baggages as proof that no baggage existed for Pulaski to save. A more reasonsable deduction from all this was that most of the baggage had been secured but that which could not be spared and any miscellaneous leftovers did in fact make up a small or limited baggage train for Pulaski to save. Johnson's logic is not convincing on the baggage issue.

This reasoning is substantiated and verified by Bentalou for in his reply to Johnson's "Remarks Critical and Historical," Bentalou states that "...enough light baggage remained to form a column of waggons. ..."

(5) Johnson spoofs that "...these thirty body guards, even with Pulaski at their head, should have brought ten thousand [sic] victorious men to a halt, is a tale..." Bentalou never claimed that Pulaski halted the advance of 10,000 men. With such a cavalier statement, he shows his ignorance of the order of battle. Yes, the British may have had 10,000 men but they were split into two forces with Knyphausen's group at Chadd's Ford on the west side of the river and Cornwallis'force on the opposite or east side of the river. The British attacks by these two forces sent the American right and center positioned forces into a retreat towards Chester.

At this time and place, retaining possession of the escape road to Chester is of crucial importance to the Americans. Enter Pulaski, say Bentalou! With permission "...readily granted...'by Washington and charges the advancing line of the one British column. He doesn't charge a line of 10,000 men as Johnson seems to think. He charges into a portion of one column, striking it at whatever width or spread that his small cavalry force encompassed or occupied. We don't know whether the charge is 4 abreast, 8 abreast or how wide is the British column and how much space between regiments, or whether there is a tight or loose formation. Details are lacking. In any event, it would appear that only a small portion of the British line is struck. The Americans are retreating and at times, are routed and fleeing. The British do not expect a turnabout and a cavalry charge. It is a surprise and is unexpected! That such an attack, even by a small force, can cause a momentary halt, confusion in the ranks, pushing back of men by horses, is understandable. Enough time could have been gained to permit the passage of the baggage train, which would not have been too long for the reasons previously discussed.

That it was not unusual for Pulaski to charge a large force with a similar small force as involved here is stated by Pulaski in a 1778 letter to his sister:

"I took part in many attacks...having only 50 dragoons whom I gathered. We were storming three times over one thousand of infantry."

After this episode, Bentalou states that Pulaski notices the British maneuvering for possession of the Chester road to cut off the American's retreat. Again, Washington allows him to collect as many troops as possible to counter this move. Although it is not reported, it is reasonable to assume that other responsible officers were also rallying the troops to control the Chester escape route. Once galvanized into action, Pulaski's battlefield conduct in this regard is easily understood, for he had the reputation of a dashing and vigorous cavalryman. For instance, in the joint Haddonfield venture with Gen. Wayne, they caught the British debarking at the ferry and Wayne reported to Washington: "Genl. Pulaski behaved with his usual bravery on the Occasion having his own with four Other Horses Wounded..." (Charles J. Stille *Major-General Anthony Wayne*, 1893, p. 131-32; Washington Papers, v. XXII pg.3)

In his rebuttal to Bentalou on this issue, Johnson presents no facts or evidence and asserts that this is a "Baron Munchausen tale." Name-calling or categorization is not a valid, responsive argument. Johnson was a lawyer, indeed a Supreme Court Justice, and may have been familiar with an old lawyer's maxim: When an advocate is bereft of all logical or factual argument and then stoops to name-calling, this indeed is the lowest form of argument! Amen!

The most convincing argument, which Bentalou could have offered that Pulaski's actions at Brandywine must have been meritorious and outstanding, was to cite the Congressional action a few days later in expeditiously approving Pulaski as commander of the Cavalry. Obviously some good reports about Pulaski had reached the Congress in order for them to reverse their prior negative vote for Pulaski. Johnson is silent on this Congressional issue and offers no explanation for the change in Congressional opinions or attitudes.

Clarence A. Manning also recognizes that Brandywine gave Pulaski a recognition factor amongst the Colonials and earned him a reputation as a fighter for he notes:

> The battle was over and lost and the period of recriminations started.
> Congress evacuated Philadelphia and retired to York. There were
> charges and cuntercharges. One officer accused another. The civilian
> leaders attacked everybody. But there was one thing certain. One man
> had acquired a reputation and that man was Casimir Pulaski. He had

shown that he was not one of the foreign officers who had come to the United States merely for increased pay and for political ambition. He had come to fight for American liberty. (supra, p. 215).

(6)   Of Pulaski's impetuous cavalry charge with a small force, Johnson emphatically says: "But it cannot be true. The fire of a single company would have prostrated the whole detachment, and the enemy would have passed on over their bodies." In those days, reloading a musket was a laborious, time-consuming task. We have no details as to whether the troops he charged had empty or primed muskets, or whether they were just advancing with bayonet, as the Hessians reportedly liked to do. I have seen no casualty figures as to how many of the chargers survived. For the advancing British, chasing a retreating force, an unexpected and surprising counter-charge could momentarily daze and confuse them. On the field of battle, anything is possible and military history is replete with amazing exploits and results. In commenting about Pulaski's success with small forces, William W. Gordon states:

> In all the military engagements of which we have record, he was distin-
> guished for his extraordinary personal bravery and for his handling of
> cavalry employing surprise and shock tactics by virtue of which he al-
> most invariably met with success despite the use of small numbers
> against greater forces. (*Count Casimir Pulaski*, the Georgia Historical
> Quarterly, vol. XIII, Sept. 1929, Number 3, pg.226)

(7)   Johnson summarily concludes his attack on Bentalou's Bran-
dywine report by insisting that "...any writer should presume to appropriate to Pulaski the merit of having discovered, suggested and carried into execution the measures that saved our baggage, and covered our retreat at the battle of Brandywine, I pronounce to be nothing short of absolute effrontery. There cannot be a word of truth in it." This is simply another example of rebuttal by blank denial. Johnson doesn't want it to be true, so he says it is not true. A lawyer's opinion does not make facts. Facts and relevant evidence should formulate opinion. Here again, motivation becomes crucially important to the reader in judging the accuracy and credibility of Johnson;s rebuttal to Bentalou, for Johnson has already succinctly declared his purpose in penning the rebuttal to be as follows: "I will show that the story of his [Pulaski's] services in this country, is highly inflated and deceptive." Here again, saying so doesn't make it so and denial, after denial does not make it true. The researcher and the lawyer searching for the truth, can only lament the failure to present pertinent facts and evidence to substantiate an argument.

CASIMIR PULASKI

The measure of a historian's respect and acceptance is his objectivity. Even if he grinds his axe wisely, a writer may achieve his goal if he can get the reader to believe in his objectivity. Johnson's use of such language as "But it cannot be true....I pronounce to be nothing short of absolute effrontery....There cannot be a word of truth in it....is a tale only fit for the adventures of Amadis de Gaul or Baron Munchausen," or that the American press has a "...deplorable ignorance of our Revolutionary history..." can only be classified as personal opinions, without any evidentiary basis, or simply name-calling, if not "wishful thinking." A trial lawyer does not present a case in this fashion. How much objectivity or impartiality can we attribute to Johnson in view of his stated motivation, his overwhelming desire to protect Greene and Washington from any criticism, and the manner in which he has presented his case throughout his writings? Since a lawyer or, indeed, any writer has to prove his case by a fair preponderence of facts and evidence, a fair judgment is that Johnson has not sustained his burden of proof.

So much for the Battle of Brandywine and the Bentalou-Johnson polemic skirmish, years after Pulaski's death. However, further polemics between these gentlemen will be discussed later in this book.

Bearing in mind that you can fool some of the people some of the time, but you can't fool all the people all of the time, Congress is the key to the truth. That Pulaski did in fact distinguish himself at Brandywine, when he was only a volunteer and had no official standing, is convincingly verified by the quick response of the Congress in reversing its prior adverse decision and in quickly approving his long-pending application for Command of the Cavalry with the rank of Brig. General. Approbation and acknowledgment of his battle behavior is further attested to and confirmed in a letter of James Lovell (who certainly and most emphatically was not a friend of the many foreigners who sought American commissions). Johnson should have been impressed by the flattering commendation and comment of Lovell.

James Lovell wrote to Gen. William Whipple on September 17, 1777: "...The foreign officers showed themselves to great advantage in the battle....Count Pulaski, who headed the Polanders, is now Commander of our Cavalry having first signalized himself greatly in the Battle of Brandywine..." (Omitted in Burnett's LMCC but given in Pen. Mag. His. V22, 1889, p.383).

Bentalou's account is accepted by most writers on Pulaski, including the scholarly expert and outstanding authority on Pulaski, Professor Wladyslaw Konopczynski, who repeated it on p. 347 of his book,

60

Kazimierz Pulaski. It is also accepted by Dr. Wladyslaw Wayda (*Kazimierz Pulaski w Ameryce*, pg. 17) who relies on Bentalou (who participated in the battle) and the commendation by James Lovell in his letter to Gen. Whipple. Lovell, in his official capacities, had access to the true facts as immediately reported after the battle.

Of the eighteenth century historians, C. Stedman noted: "... and two Polish noblemen exhibited in the Battle of Brandywine great proofs of bravery and attachment to the cause they exposed." (*The History of Origin, Progress and Termination of the American War*, London, 1794, vol.I, p.239).

David Ramsay said: "...Pulaski was a thunderbolt of war, and always sought the post of danger as the post of honour." (*History of the American Revolution*, vol. I, p.12).

William Gordon wrote: "...Count Pulaski, a Polish nobleman, with a party of light horse, rode up to reconnoitre the enemy; within pistol shot of their front..." (*The History of Rise, Progress, and Establishment of the Independence of the U.S.A., 1788*).

It is intriguing that Lovell and Stedman write about Polanders. I was not able to establish the presence of any other Pole at Brandywine but Pulaski. However, it is possible that it could be that half-mythical figure Rogoski or the quite real Ignacy (John) Zielinski.

★ ★ ★

Darkness saved the American Army before Knyphausen and Cornwallis could join their forces. Sullivan's division was routed and the rest of Washington's army retreated towards Chester According to La Fayette, Chester Road was crowded with masses of fugitives, cannon, and baggage carts even before the battle ended. The confusion at the scene was magnified by the roar of guns and the rattle of musketry in the background.

About 12 miles from the battlefield soldiers were stopped by the officers and Washington. However, Howe again failed to follow up his advantage. His army, supposedly, was too tired, and he had only three squadrons of dragoons for whom the terrain was too difficult.

Congress, in recognition of the bravery of the American troops, resolved that the Commissioner General would be directed to purchase (on the most reasonable terms) thirty hogsheds of rum, the same to be presented to the Army, and distributed among the soldiers in such manner as the General would direct as a tribute to the soldiers for their gallant behavior in the late battle with the enemy.

Reports of Pulaski's bravery on the battlefield and the effect of Washington's letter quickly influenced Congress to revoke its negative decision about Pulaski's command. On 15 September 1777 it was resolved: "That a commander of the horse be appointed with the rank of brigadier." The ballots being taken, Casimir Pulaski was elected the first American General of Cavalry.[18] He became the "father of American cavalry."

The British bivouacked on the battlefield on September 12th and 13th, sending forward detachments. The left wing of the British Army stayed at Dilworth while the right wing under Grant and Cornwallis reached Chester. Howe was restricted in his operations by having to take care of the wounded from both armies. He had to ask Washington for surgeons and occupied Wilmington. There he captured the Governor of Delaware, McKenley, with money and public papers.

Washington marched from Chester to Philadelphia, refitted the Army, secured ammunition and provision, and tried to get reinforcements. It seems that this time Washington put aside his Fabian habits and wanted to show at least a token resistance before abandoning Philadelphia to the British. The Army was not in condition for battle, being disorganized after the defeat, but Washington believed that the loss of Philadelphia would bring the most fatal consequences to the cause of the American Revolution.[19]

The following order may be a proof of his determination:

"The Brigadiers and Officers commanding regiments are also to post some good officers in the rear, to keep the men in order; and if in time of action, any man, who is not wounded, whether he has arms or not, turn his back upon the enemy and attempts to run away, or retreat before orders are given for it, those officers are instantly to put him to death..." (W.W 9, p.213).

No women, under any pretense whatsoever were to be with the Army but had to follow the baggage. The American Army halted on Lancaster Road close to a place then called Warren Tavern. According to Paul Bentalou, Pulaski's alertness saved the rebels:

Far from Washington being prepared to give his enemy battle, his army was then in a most deplorable condition, dispirited with defeat, but harassed with fatigue and hunger. The men were here served with rations of which they had been for a long time deprived. They wanted rest. Pulaski, who could not for a moment remain inactive, went out with a reconnoitering party of cavalry, and did not proceed very far before he discovered the whole British army in full march upon our camp; he retreated in full speed-went to headquarters-communicated the important intelligence to General Washington, who, received it with equal surprise and uneasiness- for, he had not the most distant idea of such a movement from the enemy. At his request, Pulaski expressed his opinion. It was that a detachment of about three hundred infantry, with his cavalry, would be sufficient to retard the approach of the enemy long enough to enable the Commander-in-Chief to make his dispositions to receive them. The command of that detachment was given to Brigadier-General Scott, of Virginia; and they were scarcely engaged, when a tremendous easterly storm came on...and which continued the whole night without interruption....However, great the sufferings of the Americans were that night, they were not the less fortunate-as probably this circumstance saved our army from total destruction. (*Pulaski Vindicated from Unsupported Charges*, Bentalou, op.cit. pgs., 25-29)

To which Judge Johnson answers that the movement of the British Army was:

Anticipated by Washington and which he was then manoeuvering to counteract; that he was resolved to meet the enemy and engage him in front; that there was no 'total surprise of' Washington, and that in broad daylight that Pulaski perhaps commanded one of the patrols and if so did only that which every patrol was bound to do, return and report. That to believe that Pulaski did all claimed for him; that Pulaski advises, Pulaski executes and leaves the Commander-in-Chief again, only the lean honor of conducting himself according to Pulaski's advice and under Pulaski's protection" is a reflection on Washington and that he was "incompetent without Pulaski's advice, to meet the crisis." (*Remarks, Critical and Historical...Charleston*, 1825, p.27)

Super sensitive about Washington's reputation, Johnson again defends by denial, denial, and denial. his announced motive is to show that Pulaski's services are " ...highly inflated and deceptive." (supra pg. 24)

An impartial view can be achieved by a careful examination of Washington's correspondence. On September 15th, he writes from the vicinity of Warren Tavern to the resident of Congress:

The main body of the enemy (from the best Intelligence I have been able to get) lay near Dilworth Town, not far from the field of action where they have been busily employed in burying their dead, which from accounts amounted to a very considerable number. We are moving up this road to get in between the enemy and the Swedes Ford and to prevent them from turning our right flank which they seem to have a violent inclination to effect by all their movements.

On the net day he writes to the same, from the camp between Warren and White Horse Tavern:

Sir: I arrived here last night with the Army and am now so far advanced as to be in position to meet the enemy on the route to Swedes Ford, if they should direct their course that way. Their situation, I believe, from the best information I have been able to obtain, is nearly the same as it was yesterday....

Further on Washington informs his correspondent, John Hancock of Massachusetts, that he ordered the troops to be refreshed as they were late getting to their positions. At the moment of writing, they were busy cooking their provisions. Hardly an urgent military occupation. Washington, by directive of Congress, was obliged to write his reports twice a day, so we can presume that this data was factual. It is obvious that Washington was showing every appearance of willingness to engage the British. He was well aware that they would probably take the route to Swedes Ford and was prepared to block their way.

But he was not prepared for Howe's movement towards him at the time Pulaski reported this discovery. That Alexander Hamilton would not like to disturb his tired or sleeping chief is also probable.[20] That Washington asked for advice is quite likely. It was common for him to ask the counsel of his officers, and Pulaski was more than an officer - he was a famous partisan and general. Again, Johnson seeks to minimize any praise for Pulaski, especially when it appears to him that it is a reflection on Washington. A fair reading of Bentalou's report does not reflect unduly on Washington but Johnson is ultra-sensitive about his idol, Washington.

It was a downpour of rain that prevented the engagement. Quite likely, this was very fortunate for the Americans. On September 17th Washington wrote to Hancock:

...Yesterday the enemy moved past Concord by the Edgemont towards the Lancaster Road with evident design to gain our flank right. This obliged us to alter our position and march to this place (Yellow Springs)...

And finally on September 19th he writes to the same:

...When I left Germantown with the Army, I hoped I should have had an opportunity of attacking them, either in front or on their flank, with a prospect of success. But unhappily a variety of causes occurred to prevent it. Our march in the first place was greatly impeded through want of provision which delayed us so long that the enemy were apprized of our motions, and gained grounds near the White Horse Tavern, with a part of their Army turning our right flank, whilst another part, composing the main body, were more advanced towards our left. We should have disappointed them in their design by getting on their left, but for the heavy rain which fell on that (Tuesday) evening....

Washington re-passed the Schuylkill River at Parker's Ford. Brigadier General Anthony Wayne was left on the other side of the river with the task of following and harassing the British rear. Generals Maxwell and Potter were to collaborate with him.

Howe asked Major-General Charles Grey to deal with Mad Anthony Wayne. Grey ordered the removal of flints from each musket in his force, so there could be no accidental discharge, and at night fell on Wayne's camp, killing 200 men, wounding 100 and capturing 71. The British lost 6 killed and 22 wounded. It was like a prelude to Pulaski's Egg Harbor.

From that day (September 21, 1777) Grey became known as "No Flint Grey." Since the British used bayonets, the weapon feared and hated by the Americans, the whole affair became known as the Paoli Massacre[21].

I have dealt with this incident because of its similarity to Pulaski's Egg Harbor misfortune in order to show that the best of generals could not win them all.

Washington wrote no official report of the matter to Congress because Congress was evacuating Philadelphia. Wayne was eventually court-martialled at his own insistence, and acquitted.

About that time one of Howe's foraging parties discovered and captured the American depot at Valley Forge. Among other things, there were lost 3800 barrels of flour, 25 barrels of horseshoes, several thousand tomahawks, kettles and tools, all of which would be badly needed for the winter at Valley Forge. The stores had been previously removed from Philadelphia to magazines in safer places. The Americans assumed that Howe had heard of this transfer, and that he knew about the value of supplies deposited in Reading.

On October 21st Howe's whole force was encamped about four miles west of the Schuylkill near French Creek. It looked as if they were headed for Reading. Washington re-formed and shifted his right in the same direction. Overnight, the enemy reversed its march, and moved down the river, crossing it unopposed at Fatland, and capturing six guns in one of the Continental redoubts. Washington was outmaneuvered, and on the 26th, the British entered the town where the Declaration of Independence was announced, to be greeted enthusiastically by the Loyalists. Joseph Galloway proudly accompanied the Loyalist troops, and their band played "God Save the King."

For the time being, the military situation was stabilized. There were skirmishes and some maneuvering on the American side, while the

British had the difficult task of reducing Billingsport, Fort Mercer and Fort Mifflin and clearing some artificial underwater obstacles known then as *chevaux de frise*. Howe established his headquarters at Germantown about five miles from Philadelphia while Cornwallis was occupied that city.

★ ★ ★

On 24 December 1776 Washington was authorized by Congress to raise a total of 3000 light horse, which was very unrealistic, especially if one remembers that there was no tradition of cavalry in North America and consequently officers and cavalrymen were lacking. Besides, the whole Continental Army in 1776 totalled about 47,000, according to General Knox who as Secretary of War compiled a report on this subject to Congress. Also there were short-time enlistments, desertions and unauthorized furloughs, so that Washington never had such a number at any given time at his disposal. It must be remembered that he took a desperate gamble at Trenton, for on 31 December 1776 he would be reduced to about 1400 men by expirations of enlistments. He was successful in his daring night attack on the drunken Hessianss. At that time, Washington had about 2,400 men and 18 cannons. General Ewing had a thousand militia and Col. Cadwalader about two thousand. They were supposed to attack from different directions, but were too late to take part in the engagement. Colonel Johann Gottlieb Rall, a veteran of the Russian war against the Turks, had under his command about 1,200 men. In the action the Americans had four killed and eight wounded. The Hessians lost 23 men, including Rall, and 918 were taken prisoner and paraded later through the streets of Philadelphia.

Washington was very realistic in establishing a cavalry force. In December 1776, he recommended Elisha Sheldon of Connecticut, who helped him in his retreat through Jersey. That gentleman was appointed a lieutenant-colonel, becoming the first commandant of a unit in the Continental Line. He had the rank and pay of a colonel of infantry, though later on, cavalry pay was slightly higher than that of infantry. Sheldon was from a good Hartford family.

Washington was authorized by Congress to appoint the other officers of the regiment but he assigneded this right to Sheldon, reserving unto himself, however, the power to reject candidates whom he thought unfit for the service. Washington had suggested to Sheldon that he should have only gentlemen for officers and those of good fortune, character and family, as such generally made the best officers.

In January 1777, Colonel George Baylor was authorized to raise a regiment of horse. Baylor could appoint his officers but Washington reserved for himself the appointment of the field grade officers, and the right of objection to any of Baylor's choices. Indeed, he withheld the nominations of the officers of troop to be commanded by his former aide, George Lewis, and solicited two lieutenancies for proteges of personal friends.

In January 1777, Colonel Stephen Moylan was also authorized to raise a regiment of light dragoons. In the same month the Virginia Light Horse under Colonel Theodoric Bland was accepted into the Continental Line.[22] These four regiments of cavalry comprised the new command of Gen. Pulaski.

Bland offered his troops to Congress in November 1776 but was accepted in January 1777. This made Sheldon the first senior officer of the U.S. Cavalry. Washington was instructed by Congress to settle the question of cavalry officers' ranks about that time.

In theory the cavalry unit, based on Sheldon's regimental organization, consisted of a colonel, a lieutenant-colonel and major as field officers, and a staff composed of a chaplain, a regimental quartermaster, a surgeon and his mate, a paymaster, a riding master, a saddler, a trumpet-major, an adjutant, four supernumeraries and six troops of 32 privates, armorer, captain, a lieutenant and cornet, a quartermaster-sergeant, drill-sergeant, a trumpeter, a farrier and four corporals.

After the organization of the first four regiments commenced, Washington, with his usual common sense, informed Congress that he was not going to constitute any more dragoon regiments until the first ones were horsed and equipped. However, no more Continental cavalry units were ever raised.

On paper, the cavalry represented a substantial force of about 1100 men and officers. It is interesting to observe that in a cavalry troop were 11 officers, non-commissioned officers and auxiliaries, and 32 privates. Roughly, in the whole cavalry, about one-third were not troopers.

The total number of cavalry troops in the Continental Army in December 1777 was 515, in January 1779 it was 632. (Charles Lesser, "The Sinews of Independence," Chicago 1976.)

According to a return in PC C Microcopy 239, the returns for cavalrymen and officers were in 1777, 630; 1778, 615; and in 1779 580.

No matter how impressive the cavalry appeared on plans approved by Congress, the reality was very different. According to the return of February 9, 1778 (Revolutionary War Rolls, National Archives, Washington, D.C.), Blands regiment had 10 company officers, 22 sergeants and corporals, 6 trumpeters a farrier, and 80 privates. Sheldon had 8 company officers, 20 sergeants and corporals, 6 trumpeters and farriers and 104 privates. Baylor had 6 company officers, 6 sergeants and corporals, 3 trumpeters and farriers and 96 privates. Moylan had 15 company officers, 17 sergeants and corporals, 7 trumpeters and 69 privates. Evidently none of the four cavalry regiments complained about a shortage of officers but privates were difficult to enlist.

So, there was a cavalry force of 475 men, of which troopers represented 349. The whole cavalry, counting field grade and staff officers, represented 539 which was only about half of its paper strength. Bland's regiment became so undermanned that its merged with those of Baylor's 3rd Regiment, this regiment being almost annihilated at Tappan in September 1778. Moylan had so few men and horses and they were so exhausted that during the Battle of Monmouth Court House in June 1778 they could do no more than scout the enemy and forward intelligence.

Had the cavalry been organized and trained as Pulaski wanted, based on his European experience, the War of American Independence would, perhaps, have ended much sooner.

The following letter from Washington addressed to the Board of War on December 30, 1777, explicitly shows the situation:

> Sir: Capt. Jones of Colo, Baylor's Regt. of Light dragoons, has a troop of Men inlisted and accoutrements complete; but not having been able to procure Horses, at the limited price, the Men are yet dismounted.
>
> I am informed, that there are a number of horses at Lancaster and Carlisle, which were purchased for the North Carolina light dragoons; but 'tis said, they have neither proper Arms or Accoutrements, if therefore those Horses could be delivered to Capt. Jones they would immediately render very essential service, for the regiments that have been upon duty the last Campaign, are so reduced, that they can scarcely furnish the necessary patroles for the security of the Camp. I am sending off all the worn down Horses to recruit, and I could therefore wish, that the Board would give orders, that the Horses at Lancaster and Carlisle may be delivered to Capt. Jones, except the North Carolineans, for whom they were intended, are ready to mount and take the Field." (W.W. vol. 10, p.226).

Who were those officers on whose co-operation the success of Pulaski's command depended, and who were the troopers?

The American dragoons were not so heavy as armored cuirassiers, though more solid than lightlancers or hussars who depended on sabers and lances. They were supposed to be armed with heavy sabers, broadswords and carbines, also called musketons, and be dressed in gorgeous uniforms. In civilian life, they were tailors, shoemakers, farmers and even mariners.

Even the famous Harry Lee was not quite free from the idea that horses were merely means of transportation of infantry and, discussing legionary corps, he wrote: "...this body might have been, when necessary, conveyed with the dispatch of horse by double mounting." (Henry Lee, *Memoirs of the War*, vol. 2, p.12).

The officers and men could be among the best riders in the world but they were not cavalry by European standards. Who were the regimental commanders?

The 1st Regiment of Continental Dragoons was composed of Virginian gentlemen volunteers. Their colonel was Theodoric Bland, a friend of Washington, and his ex-secretary. He was born in 1742 in Virginia, studied medicine at the University of Edinburgh, and for a time practiced in England where his slave Tom was sent from home Dr. Bland returned to America where he practiced his profession until ill-health forced him to become a planter. He was active in revolutionary politics and, being of literary inclinations, wrote articles against Governor Dunmore under the pen-name of Cassius.[23]

Born in 1740 into a prominent family, Elisha Sheldon, Commander of the 2nd Dragoons, had previously commanded a battalion of Connecticut Light Horse. Towards the end of the war, his unit was called a legionary corps. He was breveted Brigadier General in September 1780.

George Baylor was born in 1752 and was descended from the upper crust of Virginia society. He was recommended to Washington by Edmund Pendleton and became an aide-de-camp to the Commander-in-Chief. He carried the good tidings of Trenton to Congress together with the captured flag. He was thanked for his effort by that body, and Hancock wrote to Washington that Baylor should be promoted and given a horse. He duly got a horse and a promotion. (His role in the Tappan Massacre will be dealt with in Part Two of this book.)

According to the *Dictionary of American Biography*, his regiment was sometimes called the "Lady Washington Dragoons," which is confirmed by Jones. He was breveted a Brigadier-General on discharge from the Army.

Stephen Moylan was a colorful figure and, as he played a significant part in Pulaski's troubles with the cavalry, he can be described at some length. He was born in Cork in Ireland in 1737, the son of a prosperous Catholic merchant and of a Countess of Limerick (Martin

Griffin, Stephen Moylan, 1909, p.l). As the Protestant penal laws prevented the education of Catholic youth, he spent some time in Paris and Lisbon. He arrived in Philadelphia in 1768 and quickly achieved wealth and social prominence. He was a member of the Gloucester Fox Hunting Club, and president of the Friendly Sons of St. Patrick. Moylan early joined the revolutionary movement and became a muster master general of the Continental Army in August 1775. His duties included the fitting of the privateers. As an early advocate of independence he had hopes of being sent as an ambassador to Lisbon. He was a secretary to Washington, and became his aide which assured him the rank of Lieutenant-Colonel, though as yet he had not smelled powder.

In the *Dictionary of the American Biography*, he is described as dressed in a "very remarkable uniform consisting of a red waistcoat, buckskin breeches, bright green coat and bearskin hat." He was also a friend of Joseph Reed.

Moylan was married in Trenton in September 1778 to Mary Ricketts Van Horne, eldest daughter of Colonel Philip Van Horne. He was breveted Brigadier-General on the date when he left the Army, and Washington appointed him Commissioner of Loans in Philadelphia. Stephen Moylan died, leaving an estate valued at $800 and two daughters, one of which was supposed to be a fascinating beauty.

So, out of four colonels of cavalry, three of them were closely connected with Washington. Bland was a doctor and politician. Baylor a member of the upper echelon of Virginia society, of no profession and a willing but not very satisfactory secretary to Washington. Moylan was a businessman and only Sheldon seems to have had some cavalry experience, but all of them were important men.

Before I proceed to consider the state of the Continental cavalry on the eve of Pulaski's appointment, it must be observed that the position of its commander was not appealing to all men. Originally, Washington designated Joseph Reed for that function (he was respected in spite of his connection with Charles Lee). His main qualification for the post, it seems, was the capture on 30 December 1776 of twelve British chasseurs, who surrendered to seven horsemen, six of whom had never seen the enemy before.[24]

Born in 1741, Joseph Reed, not a friend to Pulaski, was yet another lawyer turned revolutionary. After practicing law in Trenton and developing good business relations there, he transferred his law practice to Philadelphia. In 1774 he was a member of the Committee of Correspondence and the next year he was president of the 2nd

Provisional Congress. Reed was critical of Washington's military abilities. In 1778 he was elected to Congress, and from December 1778 to 1781 he was president of the Supreme Executive Council of Pennsylvania. At the time of Pulaski's appointment he was with Washington as a volunteer without pay.

On January 22, 1777, Washington wrote to Congress: "...I shall also beg leave to recommend Colonel Reed to the command of the horse, as a person in my opinion in every way qualified; for he is extremely active and enterprising, many signal proofs of which he has given this campaign..." (William B. Reed, *Life and Correspondence of Joseph Reed*, p.295, Philadelphia, 1847.)

In the same letter Washington recommended that brigadiers from each state should be appointed to command the troops of that state. Congress elected brigadiers but did nothing about the separate command of the horse. On the 12th of May 1777, Reed was appointed Brigadier-General. On the 27th Congress resolved that Washington would be empowered to give the command of horse to one of the generals already appointed. On the very day Washington received this decision he wrote to Reed, "Congress, having empowered me by a resolve, transmitted this morning to assign one of the Generals already appointed to the command of the light horse. I mean that you should act in that line if agreeable to yourself, and I wish you in that case to repair to camp as soon as you can." (W.B. Reed, Joseph Reed, p.296).

Then on 14th June 1778 Washington urged Reed again;

> I sincerely wish that you may accept the appointment of Congress and the post I am desirous of placing you in and must beg to be favoured with an answer immediately on the subject as the service will not admit of delay. A general officer in that department would not only take off a great deal of trouble from me, but be a means of bringing the regiments into order and service with much more facility than it is in my Power, divided as they are, possibly to do. Mr. Peters waiting obliges me to conclude, and I do it with great truth, dear sir... (ibid p. 296)

However, Reed refused the appointment. Primarily he was offended by the indecision of Congress, and its passing responsibility for the appointment to Washington. He could, too, feel that he was not up to the task and being a clever man, he realized the present state of the cavalry. Reed's record of military service was blameless, but he knew that there was a difference between leading a cavalry squadron and being the chief of the whole force.

According to Bancroft, Reed was a trimmer of the most pronounced type. If that statement was true, and I do not vouch for it, then such a man was not likely to accept this kind of appointment, with no glory and all work.

Reed's opinion about the matter is expressed in a letter to a member of Congress:

> ...Upon my signifying to the General my intention of resigning, he proposed me to Congress for the command of cavalry. As that is line of service not liable in my opinion to the same difficulties as the other, I acquiesced in the recommendation and have been waiting the result. So much time elapsed, I think it probable that some difficulties may have arisen between the inclination of Congress and their complaisance to the General's recommendation, an embarrassment from which I ought to relieve them, as I am informed in no instance has any request or recommendation from him been slighted or refused... (*Life and Correspondence*, p.299).

It seems that after Reed's refusal of cavalry command no effort was made to fill that post, though Motin de Balme was appointed Inspector-General of cavalry on July 8, 1777, until Pulaski happened to come around, and Washington was practically forced into action by the Pole's solicitation and activity, and it is worthwhile to compare the tenor of the two following recommendations for the position.

About Pulaski:

> ...The Count appears by his recommendation to have sustained no inconsiderable military character...it is to be presumed this gentleman is not unacquainted with it (cavalry). I submit it to Congress how far it may be eligible to confer the appointment....He derives from hence a title to our respect that ought to operate in his favor as far as the good of service will permit; but it can never be expected we should lose sight of this ...

About Reed:

> I shall also beg leave to recommend Colonel Reed to the command of the horse, as a person in my opinion in every way qualified...

Indeed, Pulaski would have been much better off if his appointment to the command of American cavalry had been definitely rejected. Given a command of a brigade of infantry as La Fayette, Conway or Dekalb were, he would have had an opportunity to prove his military genius.

To realize what was awaiting Pulaski, and what material the Commander of Horse was supposed to shape into an effective fighting force, we have to review the history of the American cavalry prior to

Pulaski's appointments. Also, it is important to understand the attitude of the Commander-in-Chief for that branch of service, and of the second in rank after him, i.e., of General Charles Lee, and to remember that those people supporting the cavalry, and often Pulaski, were not always supporting Washington.

Before looking at the American cavalry as a whole, let us discuss some more Colonel Stephen Moylan of the 4th Continental Dragoons. As stated previously, he was a merchant and received his colonelcy without any military experience or education. His posts were administrative, but it cannot be denied that he possessed a maritial spirit and a Nero-like imagination. At the time of the siege of Boston he wrote to Joseph Reed; "It will be possible to bombard Boston; give us powder and authority, for that you know we want as well as the other. Give us these and Boston can be set in flames." (W.B. Reed, *Life of Reed*, 1, p.137)

Of all the military posts, Moylan most desired the command of cavalry, though he had no qualifications for such. Thus he wrote to Robert Morris on 7 January 1777: "I never mentioned my desire to the General of engaging in the Cavalry. Your letter, I believe, gave him the first intimation. I put it into his hands to show your gift of divination..." (Martin I. Griffin, *Stephen Moylan*, p.48)

On 21 January 1777 Stephen Moylan was commissioned to recruit a Light Horse Regiment. For this purpose he ventured to Philadelphia and Maryland and received about 42 thousand dollars for raising and equipping that troop. His men were supposed to be dressed in green coats trimmed with red, green cloaks with red capes, red waistcoats, buckskin breeches and leather caps trimmed with bearskin.[25]

According to Moylan, on April 14th a part of his regiment was well advanced in their exercises, though it is interesting to speculate who had trained them as previously Moylan modestly wrote to the President of Congress: "...Tho I have employed my spare time in studying the art of war and for fifteen past months have seen a great deal of its practice, my views were turned to the grand and extended parts thereof more than to the minutio. I do not therefore think myself capable of teaching a new regiment the necessary duties..." (M. Griffin, *Stephen Moylan*, p.41).

When he wrote that letter, Moylan was probably thinking of infantry and it is doubtful that he knew much more of cavalry.

A troop of cavalry was supposed to consist of 44 men. Captain Thos. Dorsey's troop in Moylan's regiment consisted of 43 men and women. The following note quoted in Griffin's "Moylan" is worthy of careful study: "Woodbridge (N.J.) 16th July 1777, Capt. Thos

Dorsey's troop of Col. St. Moylans Reg't drew 52 Rations for I Capt. 1 Lieut. 1 Cornet, 1 Ouartermaster, 2 Sergeants, 1 Farrier, 2 waggoners and 6 women, 30 Rank and File. Total 53 (Less) Retain 10 equals 43. Signed John Craig, L (Light) Dragoons." (p. 53).

That there was something wrong in Col. Moylan's regiment is demonstrated by the fact that around 21 July nineteen cavalrymen escaped from Moylan's regiment towards Philadelphia, either to desert or to get a pay settlement.

Sheldon conducted the court-martial and the sentences were severe, though mitigated by pardons, except for one Thomas Rannals. Altogether it was an unpleasant affair, not showing Moylan in the best light.

> Edward Wilcox, Quartermaster to Capt. Dorses 4th Cont. Dragoons, charged with desertion, taking a horse belonging to Col. Moylan's regiment and a trooper with his accoutrements found guilty and sentenced to be led round the regiment he belongs to with his face towards the horse tail, and his coat turned the wrong side outwards, and that he be then discharged from the Army...

The sentences for the privates were customarily more severe and thus:

> George Kilpatrick, and Charles Martin sergeants, Lawrence Brown and Enoch Wells corporals, Daniel McCarty, Patrick Leland, Philip Franklin, Jacob Baker, Thomas Orbs, Adam Rex, Frederick Grimmer, Daniel Cainking, Christian Longspit, Henry Whiner and Nicholas Walma privates in Col. Moylan's regiment of light dragoons, severally charged with "mutiny and desertion" found guilty of desertion and adjudged worthy of death...(pardoned by C.C.) Francis Fawkes and George House of Col. Moylan's regiment.... being charged with mutiny and desertion, are found guilty but some favorable circumstance appearing on their behalf, they were sentenced to receive twenty-five lashes on their naked backs....Thomas Rannals, of Col. Moylan's regiment sentenced to suffer death... (W.W. 9 p. 99).

As noted previously in this work, the Americans had no cavalry at the beginning of the revolution, except the Philadelphia Troop of about thirty men. But a strange apparation appeared and was noted:

> A few minutes past, (wrote John Adams to James Warren from Philadelphia in June 1775) a curious phenomenon appeared at the door of our Congress-a German hussar, a veteran in the wars in Germany in his uniform and on horseback, a forlorn cap upon his head, with a streamer waving from it half down to his waistband, with a death's head painted

in front, a beautiful hussar cloak ornamented with lace and fringe and cord of gold, a scarlet waistcoat under it, with shining yellow metal buttons-light gun strung over his shoulder-and a Turkish saber much superior to a Highland broadsword, very large and excellently fortified by his side-holsters and pistols upon his horse-in short the most warlike and formidable figure I ever saw. He says he has fifty such men ready to enlist under him immediately who have been all used to the Service as hussars in Germany, and desirous to ride to Boston immediately in order to see Burgoignes Light Horse. (Charles Francis Adams, *Studies Military and Diplomatic*, N.Y. 1911, p. 82. Also for the American cavalry see: Frederic Gilbert Bauer, "Notes on the Use of Cavalry in the American Revolution," *Cavalry Journal*, vol. 47, 1938).

I was not able to trace that hussar. Fred Anderson Berg said that in his *Eycyclopedia of the Continental Army* there was a record of hussars offering their service to Congress and that they had been accepted but never called to serve, at least not under the name of hussars. There were bills for raising hussars in Pennsylvania during the summer of 1775, but it is possible that such belonged to the Philadelphia City Troop of Light Horse.

However, it had occurred to the Commander-in-Chief that a troop of horse could be useful in a war, when a direct proposal was made to him by Captain John Leary, Jr., who wanted to furnish 40 horsemen at 8 shillings per day with their own horses and equipment. On June 21, 1766, Washington wrote to the President of Congress: "...such a corps may be extremely useful in many respects. In a march they may be of utmost service, in reconnoitring the enemy and gaining intelligence, and have it in their power to render many other important benefits..." (W.W. p.163). But the matter was evidently forgotten, though Washington mentioned it again in his letter of July 22nd.

* * *

On July 6, 1776, as it was later on reported in the daily order, the Honorable Continental Congress, impelled by the dictates of duty, policy and necessity, was pleased to sever the connection which existed between this Country and Great Britain by declaring the United Colonies of North America free and independent States. For the colonists it was the point of no return. At that moment, Washington was facing General Howe and the expected arrival of his brother, Admiral Howe. It was to be George Washington's first battle since he took the command of the Continental Army, and he was urgently asking for militia assistance. In the light of those circumstances the so-called Connecticut Light Horse incident is especially instructive.

Thus wrote Washington to Colonel Gold Selleck Silliman, the Commander of a Connecticut State regiment:

> ...you will readily conceive the necessity of our most vigorous and spir-ited exertions, and that there is occasion for all the men that can be pos-sibly got. But what to do with the Horse of this reinforcement (three regiments of militia Light Horse under Colonel Thomas Seymour), I am at a loss to determine. It will be impossible to support them, and even if it could be done the expense would be enormous. I cannot think myself at liberty to consent to the horses coming. At the same time I must request your exertions to prevail on the men. They may have it in their power to dismiss their horses, perhaps after bringing them almost here ...Recommending to your and their notice what I have said; and the alarming consequences that may result from not hav-ing sufficient and timely succour to repel the enemy.

However, Sir William Howe was not in a hurry to attack. Mean-while the Connecticut Light Horse arrived. Alexander Graydon in *Memoires of His Own Time*" (Philadelphia, 1846, p.155, 156) ridicules them in the following description:

> Among military phenomena of this campaign, the Connecticut light horse ought not to be forgotten. These consisted of a considerable num-ber of old fashioned men, probably farmers and heads of families, as they were generally middle aged, and many of them apparently beyond the meridian of life. They were truly irregulars; and whether their cloth-ing, their equipments or caparisons were regarded, it would have been difficult to have discovered any circumstance of uniformity; though in the features derived from "local habitation," they were one and the same. Instead of carbines and sabres, they generally carried fowling pieces; some of them very long, and such as in Pennsylvania, are used for shooting ducks. Here and there, one, "his youthful garments, well saved," appeared in a dingy regimental of scarlet, with a triangular, tar-nished, laced hat. In short, so little were they like modern soldiers, in air or costume, that, dropping the necessary number of years, they might have been supposed the identical men who had in part composed Pep-peril's army at the taking of Louisbourg. Their order of march corre-sponded with their other irregularities. It "spindied into longitude immense," presenting so extended and ill-compacted a flank, as though they had disdained the adventitious prowess derived from concentra-tion. These singular dragoons were volunteers, who came to make a tender of their services to the Commander-in-chief. But they staid not

long at New York. As such a body of cavalry had not been counted upon, there was in all probability a want of forage for their jades, which, in the spirit of ancient knighthood, they absolutely refused to descend from; and as the general had no use for cavaliers in his insular operations, they were forthwith dismissed with suitable acknowledgments for their truly chivalrous ardour. An unlucky trooper of this school had by some means or other, found his way to Long Island, and was taken by the enemy in the battle of the 27th of August. The British officers made themselves very merry at his expense, and obliged him to amble about for their entertainment. On being asked, what had been his duty in the rebel army, he answered, that it was to flank a little and carry tidings. Such at least was the story at New York among the prisoners.

But one should notice that the Connecticut Horse Militia were also described in the following manner:

...During the past week several of the newly-raised regiments of Connecticut Troops have arrived in town (New York), and appear to be as fine a body of men as any engaged in the present grand struggle for liberty and independence. Among them the Light Dragoons, between five and six hundred, who came to town yesterday (July 9th 1776) and paraded on horseback through the city, made a noble and martial appearance, and as this corps is composed of substantial yeomanry of a virtuous sister State, nothing could be more agreeable or animating to all true friends of their country. Some of those worthy soldiers assisted in their present uniforms at the first reduction of Louisburg, and their lank, lean cheeks and war-worn coats are viewed with more veneration than if they were glittering nabobs from India or Bashaws with nine tails. (*Force*, American Archives, 5, 1, p. 174).

Were those Connecticut men a different breed from the ones described by Graydon?

On July 8th, Major Thomas Starr arrived with fifty of his troops and informed Washington that the remainder were coming. The Commander-in-Chief sent him back to Colonel Thomas Seymour, with the repeated request that the men should be dismounted as there was no forage. It also seems that Washington was doubtful about their military prowess as he wrote: "...and their horses (must be) sent back otherwise the men can only be a check on the service as they cannot act as horsemen in case of action or if they could, forage would not be found to support them..."

It was on July 10th that Washington thanked the gentlemen of the Light Horse for the zeal and attachment they manifested on the occasion and informed them he could not consent to their keeping their horses but at the same time wished them to stay themselves.

However, about four or five hundred cavalry arrived and they agreed to bear the expense of maintaining their horses themselves and evidently were, as a reward, permitted to stay. Washington was praising their firm attachment to the Cause, but things went askew and on July 16th Colonel Thomas Seymour and other field officers of the Connecticut Light Horse received the following stern admonition:

> Gentn: In answer to yours of this date (New York, July 16, 1776), I can only repeat to you what I said last night, and that is that if your men think themselves exempt from the common duties of a soldier, will not mount guard, do Garrison Duty, or the service separate from their horses, they can be no longer of use here, where horse cannot be brought to action, and I do not care how soon they are dismissed... (W.W. p. 286)

On the next day Washington wrote to the President of Congress:

> ...the Connecticut Light Horse mentioned in my letter of 11th are now discharged and about to return home, having peremptorily refused all kind of fatigue duty...claiming an exemption as Troopers...Tho' their assistance is much needed and might be essential service in case of an attack, yet I judged it advisable, on their application and claim of such indulgence, to discharge them, as granting them would set an example to others and might produce many ill consequences. The number of men included in the last return by this is lessened about 500... (W.W. p. 295)

So by one stroke of bathos, Charles Lee would say, at a critical moment before the battle, about 500 cavalrymen are dismissed as a good example of discipline for an army where discipline at best was problematic. C.F. Adams wrote: "Yet only a month later, because of the lack of even a pretence of mounted service, Washington's advanced line was flanked, and the very flower of his army needlessly sacrificed. A thousand men were there lost. They represented the price of the keep of a few hundred horses for one month; while at that time the majority of the dwellers on Long Island were Tories, whose fields were heavy with forage." (Charles Francis Adams, *Military Studies*, p. 92)

S.B. Webb, aide-de-camp to Washington, wrote on July 18, 1776, to Governor Trumbull: "...It was only requested that they should mount guard, which they refused, on which the General was obliged to discharge them..." (Peter Force, *American Archives*, Ser. 5, vol. 1, p.

414). This note caused an angry reaction from Thomas Seymour who sent to the Governor a long report (for which see note [26]).

As has been stated, the Americans had no opportunity to use the cavalry in the French and Indian wars, and the only colonial war in which, perhaps, cavalry could have been effective was Bacon's Rebellion in Virginia. It did not, however, mean that they heard nothing about usage of cavalry in Europe, its espirit de corps and privileged position. It can be conjectured that because of that Seymour refused menial duties, giving as his formal ground that Connecticut law exempted them. ("...By the positive laws of the Colony of Connecticut establishing the Troops of Light Horse they are expressly exempted from staying in garrison or doing duty on foot apart from their horses.) The signatories were: Thomas Seymour, William Hart, Daniel Starr and Elisha Sheldon. (Force, Am. Ach p.371).

Whether the yeomanry of Connecticut were right or wrong in refusing fatigue duty, Washington's insistence on discipline and low regard for that branch of service cost him dearly at Long Island.

Besides, one should remember that cavalrymen had to take care not only of themselves but of their beasts and forage. Their horses needed to be brushed, exercised and their accoutrement taken care of. But most importantly those men were cavaliers who thought their main duty to be on the battlefield. The same idea was entertained by Pulaski when he proposed his corps of volunteers.

Speaking of privileges, let us note that riflemen, the darlings of the revolution, had privileges and consequently their rowdiness led to the mutiny on Prospect Hill, one of those numerous mutinies which plagued the American Army.

It is doubtful if the gentlemen riders turned into cavalry would have caused this kind of trouble.

In the same period Charles Lee, the second in command, thence commanding in the Southern Department, considered that from want of cavalry the Americans would have lost the capital, and only the enemy's dilatorines and stupidity saved them. He wrote to Gates: "...if I had a thousand of Light Horse I could protect these Colonies completely-urge the General to urge it-I am tir'd of writing on this subject." (*The Lee Papers*, N.Y. Historical Society, 1872, N.Y., p.97).

General Charles Lee had been in Poland (Haiman. op.cit. pg. 48 and Adam Zamoyski, *The Polish Way*, Franklin Watts, New York, 1988, pg. 240). Lee also wrote to Washington for 1000s cavalry on July 1st from Charlestown (op.cit., vol.2, p. 102).

For God's sake, my dear General, urge Congress to furnish me with a thousand of cavalry. With a thousand cavalry I could insure the safety of

these Southern Provinces; and without cavalry, I can answer for nothing. I proposed a scheme in Virginia for raising a body almost without
expense. The scheme was relished by the gentlemen of Virginia, but I
am told the project was censured by some members of Congress on the
principle that the military should not take the liberty to propose anything...

So a general of reputation was begging for cavalry. Without it he
had refused responsibility for the safety of his theater of war. But
Washington wrote in his report to Congress on 12 August 1776:

I would beg leave to mention to Congress that in a letter I received
from General Lee, he mentioned the valuable consequence that would
result from a number of Cavalry being employed in the Southern Department...*without them, to use his own expression, he can answer for nothing,
with one thousand he would answer for the safety of those states.* I should have
done myself the honor of submitting this matter to Congress before at
his particular request had it not escaped my mind... (W.W.5, p. 418;
author's italics)

Fortunately for the rebels, the British had no effective cavalry
either, though that which they did have terrorized the Americans to
such an extent that Washington in General Orders of October 27,
1776, offered a hundred dollars for each enemy trooper with his horse
and accoutrements and assured his soldiers: "...that in such broken
country, full of stone walls, there is no enemy more to be despised as
they cannot leave the road. So that any party attacking them may be
always sure of doing it to advantage, by taking posts in the woods by
the roads, or along the stone walls, where they will not venture to
follow them..."

During the siege of Boston the British landed one regiment of
cavalry, the 17th Dragoons. However, it was ineffective as many of
their horses died on the way. Later on this regiment merged with the
16th Dragoons, took the name of the Queen's Dragoons and served
under Banastre Tarleton in the South.

Had the British effectively used even the small numbers of cavalry
which they had or developed, the rebels would, perhaps, have lost.
Hardly any cavalry was used against Washington when he was
retreating through New Jersey.

On the contrary, the British pursued him with such a deliberate
slowness that it was said that it looked as if Howe calculated with the
greatest accuracy the exact time necessary for the enemy's escape.

The cavalry patrols would have prevented the surprise at Trenton
and cavalry pursuit after Brandywine would have been decisive.

Washington had no cavalry experience whatsoever, nor did he see it used effectively by the enemy and that had to be the main reason why he treated it so lightly. So his statement from a letter to Congress dated 11 December 1776 comes as a complete surprise.

In recommending Major Elisha Sheldon for Continental Service, he said: "...From the experience I have had in this campaign of the utility of horse, I am convinced there is no carrying on the war without them and I would therefore recommend the establishment of one or more corps (in proportion to the number of Foot)..."

However, he still did not have a clear idea of the full employment of cavalry as a tactical force. He knew, rather vaguely (probably from his reading) that it could be a formidable weapon, and had seen its practicable usage, though his experience was limited to horsemen, not cavalrymen.

Such was the situation, and the history of the American cavalry when Casimir Pulaski became its first chief. Making it into an effective and formidable weapon was to be his challenging task, and he needed all the support and understanding he could get.

★ ★ ★

Pulaski's nomination was announced in General Orders on September 21, 1777. The Battle of Germantown was destined to be fought on October 4th of that year.

Stephen Moylan was not the only person disappointed by Pulaski's appointment. Baron Dekalb wrote on 2 November, "as Congress has just made Pulaski Brigadier commanding the said cavalry M.de la Balme, being discontented at this preference, intends to leave..." (B.F. Stevens, *Fascimiles*).

Motin de la Balme had a long and reputable service in the French Army as a captain of cavalry, advancing to the rank of Lieutenant-Colonel. He made military discipline his speciality and wrote on that subject.

According to Deane, Balme could be of good service not only in the Army but also in those colonies which were raising and training cavalry. (Microcopy 247, 129, 703, 79, "Deane's Recommendation of de la Balme," 17 October 1776). He was also well recommended by Benjamin Franklin who wrote in Paris on January 20, 1777: "Capt. Balm strongly recommended as a very able officer of Horse and capable of being extremely useful to us in forming a body of men for that service." (M.P. 247, 108, 21)

On June 19, 1777, John Adams wrote to James Warren: "...We are much embarrassed here with foreign officers. We have here three capital characters, Monsr. de Coudray, General Conway and Monsr. de la Balme. These are great and learned men. Coudray is the most promising officer in France. Coudray is an officer of Artillery, Balme of Cavalry and Conway of Infantry..." (Burnett, L.M.C.C.2, 386)

Balme was appointed an inspector of Cavalry on July 8, 1777 (J.C.C. p.539) (Mon. Vallenois was on the same date appointed his aide I.P.C.C. 25 I.f. ll in James Lovell's writing.) But he resigned on October 3, 1777, writing: "In the Department I at present hold there still remained the hope of rendering your Cavalry fit for action, and ask of you, in case I should be happy enough to earn your approbation, a rank which would have given me the right to lead it to action; you would have known what art united with courage could have affected. But this hope, my only resource in this matter, you have entirely annihilated by giving the command of your cavalry to Baron de Polasky. After this, gentlemen, you will easily judge I cannot think of acting myself to form a corps which is to be under command of another person who has perhaps much less experience, less true zeal, and without doubt is less versed in this branch than myself..." (N.A. PCC 41, l, 142-144).

Evidently Balme regretted his rash decision as he asked Congress for re-employment. In his application on 15 December 1777 he stated: "...I have been concerned and ought to be when I saw I had orders to receive from a young man who (I daresay without any ostentation) is very far from the knowledge and experience I acquired about cavalry. I wish to be mistaken but you will see what shall become with a troop which might procure the greatest advantage against your enemies given me a leave..." (M.P. 247, 94, 78)

It is interesting to note that in his letter to Congress of October 15, 1777, Balme proposed to give on a request a memorandum containing essentials to raise, form, arm, exercise, clothe and discipline the troops to advance the revolution.

It is regrettable that such an officer should resign on Pulaski's appointment. (For Balme, see PCC and JCC).

Washington was not happy about Moylan's previously mentioned red regimentals because of the similarity with the British red uniforms. He wanted Moylan to immediately dye them a different color. He did not care what had to be done to the red uniforms as long as their color was changed.

However, on September 30th he evidently changed his opinion as witnessed by the following letter to Pulaski:

> Sir: Upon getting home, I found the inclosed from Genl. Reed. I there-
> fore desire you will immediately form a Detachment of at least fifty

Horse of which part are to be of Col. Moylan's, in their Red Uniforms, which will serve to deceive both the Enemy and Country people. I can give you no better directions than what are contained in Genl. Reed's letter, for the Route that the party is to take, I only recommend it to you, to put it under the command of a good Officer and to send them off immediately. (W.W. 9, p. 288)

It is doubtful whether Pulaski was pleased with this manner of deceiving the enemy and country people by putting on red coats. The Reed letter mentioned is not found among the Washington Papers and it cannot be ascertained what the mission referred to was.

John C. Fitzpatrick said in his annotation to Washington's letter to Pulaski: "...it seems possible from Moylan's letter to Washington (October l) that the purpose of the 50 dragoons was to surprise a small party of British light horse and foragers. Moylan's letter is in the Washington Papers."

On October 1, 1777, Pulaski sent Col. Bland the following order from Worcester: (*The Bland Papers*, p.69)

Sir,

Agreeable to his excellencie's order, you would detach fyftyne good horse to attend Generals Reed and Cadwalader upon special business, they will find General Reed at his quarters a mile or two to the right of Conner's house. Besides, Major Jimpson (Jameson) will select so many Light Horse as he can be ready to march with him to-morrow, 12 o'clock to the same hour all your regiment shall joigne at my quarter the other regimens of my brigade.

Pulaski, B.G. of Cavalry.

That special business was probably reconnaissance for the Battle of Germantown on the morning of October 4th. In his order of September 30th, Washington wrote to Pulaski to immediately form a detachment of at least fifty horses a part of which was to consist of Moylan's. Pulaski's order to Bland required fifteen horses, unless that was a linguistic error, to assist Reed and Cadwalader of whom there was no mention in Washington's order.

W.H. Richardson in his *Brigadier-General Casimir Pulaski* (p. 20) defends Pulaski, thinking that Moylan claimed that he had done the task allotted to Bland. But Richardson is right in pointing out that Pulask's order to Bland was characterized by William B. Reed, the editor of *Joseph Reed Papers* as curious and characteristic, which it is not, except for the spelling. Ater all, it was strange that Moylan on the same day wrote directly to Washington about such a small affair, and in his report there is no mention of Pulaski's name. Here is Moylan's letter:

> I set out last night between 11 and 12 o'clock, in consequence of General Reed's information that a party of the enemy's light horse had crossed the Schuylkill at Levering's Ford. I met him at Bonner's, and agreeable to his advice called at Levering's house, who had returned last evening; the party that seized him gave him his dismission on the hill leading to the middle ferry, one which he is very confident they crossed; as he is a Whig, I believe he would not deceive me, so that the expedition I set out on is frustrated. I shall send scouting parties from hence round the enemy's lines, and if any intelligence worth your notice can be picked up, shall transmit it to you; enclosed is a paper in German, which was put into one of my dragoon's hands by a friend; he says it contains the situation of the enemy at Mount Airy and Germantown; their picket is not strong at Mr. Allen's, a number of cattle in Germantown thereby guarded; the chief of their artillery is on the Schuylkill Road, their outpost there Vanderen's mill. I believe they are further advanced on that road, as I saw some Hessians this morning half a mile at this side of Vanderen's; they are collecting the grain from every farm as far as the eight mile stone, and are this day expected at Levering's on that business; their parties usually consist of eighty to one hundred infantry, and forty to fifty horse; the party that crossed Schuylkill yesterday were after horses and cattle, of which they collected large numbers.

On October 2, 1777, Pulaski received from Washington through the agency of Alexander Hamilton orders which Martin Griffin called contrary. However, the matter is simple and sufficiently explained in *The Bland Papers*, p. 71. Hamilton sent an order to Pulaski and Pulaski wrote his own order to Bland on the blank intervals which caused confusion in the appearance of the order, and to its present readers. Such a version is confirmed in volume I of *Hamilton's Papers*, p.336. The counter command referred to is Washington's to Pulaski.

Here are the orders (as printed in Bland's Papers, p.70):

> You will order to the men of my guard that I have send before you, to the same place, where you are, to follow you, and joigne me in the army. As soon as you meet the encampment, you will send me a orderly light horse to warn me of your poste."
> Peter Wentz, Worcester township, October 2d, 1777.

Monsieur,
Son excellence vous desire d'assembler toute 1a cavaliere, le plu-

tot possible, pres de ses quartiers, ou vous trouverez de place propre
pour les accommoder, ceux qui sont utilement employe excepte.
Vous informerez son excellence de le moment de votre arrive. Il n'y
a pas du temps a perdre. Je suis votre serviteur tres humble,

    A. HAMILTON.

I receive now contrarys orders of his excellency, as you will see, and
I pray you to joigne me, in the army, as quick as you can.

    PULASKI, General of Cavalry.

Sir,

    His excellency desires you immediately to collect all the horse, ex-
cept those on necessary duty, and to repair to some place as near his
quarters as you possibly can, consistent with the accommodation of
the horse. Inform him, when you have done this, and lose no time
in doing it. Yours,

    A. HAMILTON

★ ★ ★

On October 3, 1777, Washington's headquarters was at Worcester
Township. The army was informed about the success of General Gates
against Burgoyne. An appeal was made to arouse the ambition of every
man in the main army not to be outdone by their northern brethren.
"Covet my countrymen, and fellow soldiers, covet a share of the glory
due to heroic deeds. Let it never be said that in a day of action, you
turned your backs on the foe." Further on the soldiers were told that
as Howe's amnesty expired there was only conquest or death left.

    Lewis Fleury was appointed Brigade Major to Pulaski. He was a
distinguished and brave officer but was not of great help to Pulaski, as
most of the time he performed different duties than a Brigade Major
to the Commander of Horse. He then became attached to Steuben.[27]

    The first order of October 3rd was a prelude to the later order of
the same date. Here Washington decided to leave behind his Fabian-
ism and to finish Howe by one stroke of genius. The Delaware River
forts blocked British supply ships and Sir William Howe had to detach,
according to Washington's spies, about 3000 men to reduce them and
to escort supplies. The British forces were split in two parts with the
main body in Germantown, and the rest, under Cornwallis in Philadelphia about five miles away.

    Washington, even if he had decided for once on a risky action, was
cautious enough to seek the opinions of his general officers, and they
agreed that this was a favorable opportunity to launch an attack.
Smallwood, Wayne, Scott, Potter and Irvine wanted immediate action

85

while Sullivan, Greene, Stirling, Stephen, Armstrong, McDougal, Knox, Muhlenberg, Nash and Conway wanted to wait till reinforcements arrived from Peekskill. I was not able to find a mention of Pulaski's opinion.

The American Army had about 8,000 Continentals and 3,000 militia. The British forces were estimated at about 9,000.

As the Americans had been previously posted around Germantown, they had some familiarity with the area. In the complicated battle plan there are instructions for the cavalry: "The Columns of Cont: troops and militia to communicate with each other from time to time by Light Horse." There is no other written instruction for cavalry. (W.W. 9, p.308)

The Battle of Germantown is one of the controversial aspects of Pulaski's American career and must be discussed in some detail. Also there is, according to the author of *Battles of the United States*, Henrv B. Dawson, "a mystery connected with the Battle of Germantown and the confusion on the field has produced confusion in the several accounts of the battle which the commanding officers have left for our information..."

According to Washington's orders, the troops were to be ready to march out towards Germantown (about 12 miles) at six o'clock. The divisions of Sullivan and Wayne were to form the right wing and attack the British left. They were to move along Monatany (Manatawny) Road, while Greene and Steven (Stephen) were to march down Skippack (Shippack) Road and attack the enemy's right. Conway was to attack in front of Sullivan and Wayne, and assault the British left flank. Nash and Maxwell were to form a reserve under Stirling. "The Corps de Reserve" was supposed to pass down the Skippack Road. Armstrong and his militia were to move along the right to pass Wissahickon Creek and attack the British chausseurs left in flank and rear. MacDougall was to attack right of the enemy in flank, and Smallwood and Formand the right wing in flank and rear. Conway was to attack the left flank. Each column was to make synchronized assaults at five o'clock by attacking the enemy's pickets with bayonets.

However, Washington, writing to the President of Congress, presented a different picture. Sullivan and Wayne, flanked by Conway, entered Skippack Road and Armstrong went along Manatawny Road while Greene and Stephen, flanked by McDougall, were to attack the enemy's right, entering by the circuitous route of Lime Kiln Road.

The perusal of maps, especially of the excellent map in *Pennsylvania Magazine of History*, vol.1, p.366 in an article by A. Lambdin, "Battle of Germantown," shows that this plan was changed, probably at the last moment, and a new plan of attack was adopted for some unknown reasons.

If Sullivan and Wayne were to march by Manatawny Road, it was to attack the British left. As the attack was to be synchronized at about the same time McDougall was supposed to attack the right and left of the British force, and Greene and Stephen would then attack the center right. It seems to me that this put the Queen's Rangers (Loyalists) at the back of the British position. American militia, under Smallwood and Formand, received long and confusing instructions on how to follow their route, without naming streets: to "the White Marsh Road at the Sandy Run: thence White Marsh Church, where to take the lefthand road, which leads to Jenkin's Tavern, on the Old York Road, below Armitage, beyond the milestone half a mile from which turns off short to the right hand, fenced on both sides, which leads through the enemys incampment to Germantown Market House."

It seems that in the second plan, Stephen, Greene and McDougall were making an unnecessary circle and in effect the Americans were mainly attacking the British right and center, unless Washington believed that Armstrong's militia would be sufficient to deal with the British left.

Here is how it most probably looked in reality: Germantown was a village along a road two miles long. The British line of encampment crossed at right angles. The main street was called Skippack Road and was not straight. There were no lateral streets but several lanes ran from the main street to the parallel ones. The village could also be approached by Lime Kiln Road which entered by the Market House and by Old York Road. The fourth road was called Manatawny or Ridge Road and was located between the Schuylkill River and Wisahickon Creek.

By a successful and synchronized attack Washington hoped to push the British into the Schuylkill River.

According to the general order, the troops were to be ready to march out at six o'clock in the evening. As stated in Washington's dispatch to Congress, the army moved out at seven o'clock, although it was nine o'clock according to Sullivan and Howe; a report to Lord George Germain stated it was six o'clock. Washington's column (Wayne, Sullivan and Conway) did not reach Chestnut Hill, from where Shippack Road led straight down to the enemy camp, until sunrise.

According to Sullivan's letter to Mesheder Weare, President of the Council of New Hampshire Committee of Safety, dated October 25,

1777, describing that "successful affair," the British picket line was attacked at Allen's House on Mount Airy. The picket line was suddenly reinforced by the light infantry (2nd Light Infantry and 40th Infantry). Sullivan ordered Conway to form his brigade to aid attacking regiments and to repulse the light infantry. Wayne was dispatched to Sullivan's left, taking the position where Greene was expected. (Dawson, *Battles of the USA Documents*, p.326).

According to Wayne, he pushed the enemy nearly three miles and was in possession of their whole encampment[28] when a large body of troops advanced on his left flank and his men fell back, defying every exertion of their officers to the contrary.

Eventually the attackers were discovered to be American soldiers who were supposed to fight the British right wing. According to Wayne: "...The fog and this mistake prevented us from following a victory which in all human probability would have put an end to the American war..."

Meanwhile Sullivan pushed the enemy down the road but they stubbornly took advantage of every yard, of every hedge to slow down their retreat. In about an hour and a quarter, Stephen's division fell in with Wayne's on Sullivan's left, and soon after that Greene's firing was heard still further to the left. Maxwell's brigade moved to support Sullivan and was met with heavy fire from Chew's House which stood back on the eastern side of the main street. Lt. Colonel Thomas Musgrave took shelter in the house at the head of six companies and turned it into a fort.[29]

Washington, hesitant, asked for the counsel of his officers. A discussion started and Knox, a learned bookseller, turned by the Revolution into a general of artillery, informed the gathering that, according to the military rules of which he was a student, it would be very unscientific to leave a castle in the rear. Joseph Reed and Timothy Pickering opposed that opinion, but Knox prevailed.[30]

Stephen's division headed towards the sound of firing around Chew's House and from a study of a detailed map it is easy to understand how he went the wrong way instead of on Lime Kiln Road. The heavy firing around Chew's House was also heard by Wayne who moved back, assuming that Sullivan was being attacked by the enemy's left wing. Greene had been able to reach the Market House on the main street but was repulsed.

Suddenly, inexplicable panic burst among the American troops. General Sullivan says in his letter:

> ...My Division, finding themselves unsupported by any other troops,
> their cartridges all expended, the force of the enemy on the right col-

lecting to the left to oppose them, being alarmed by the firing at
Chew's House so far in their rear, and the cry of the light horseman on
the right, that the enemy had got round us, and at the same time discovering some troops flying on our right, retired with as much precipiation
as they had before advanced against every effort of their officers to rally
them...

Washington blamed the fog which caused the lack of communications and mistaking his own soldiers for the enemy, though it must be
said that the fog made for poor visibility for the British as well.
Washington states: "...In the midst of the most promising appearances,
when everything gave the most flattering hopes of victory, the troops
began suddenly to retreat, and intirely left the field in spite of the every
effort that could be made to rally them... "

The Americans were able to withdraw, and Howe, as usual, did not
pursue energetically. Gordon and, after him, Fisher say that Pulaski's
cavalry was attempting to check the British pursuing Greene, but was
forced back and rode into Greene's men, scattering and demoralizing
them. Notwithstanding the unfavorable context, C.F. Adams made
this observation about Pulaski's Cavalry: that as far as it appeared, it
was the first recognition of the mounted man as a distinctive branch
of the American Army organization.

However, as far as I know, no contemporary account, except
Gordon's, mentions Pulaski's name. Sullivan wrote about Colonel
Moylan's regiment of light horse which was sent to watch the enemy.
Judge Johnson stated it was Moylan who with three regiments of horse
steadily guarded the flanks of the retreating army. Lossing wrote that
Count Pulaski and his legion [sic]...covered Greene and Stephen who
were the last to retreat.

About the entire battle, Washington commented that the day was
unfortunate rather than injurious, though the Americans in fact had
152 killed, 500 wounded and 438 captured while the British casualties
were about 500.

Washington's opinion was not quite shared by all the members of
Congress, and his professional colleagues. If not Washington, then
Greene was blamed. Greene has found an enthusiastic defender in his
biographer, Judge William Johnson (1771-1834), the author of
Sketches of the Life and Correspondence of Nathaniel Greene, Major-General of the Armies of the United States, in the War of the Revolution,
complied chiefly from original materials, Charleston, 1822." This
work is an example of early nineteenth century historical scholarship
in two volumes, and is full of reflections of a moral and philosophical
nature-evidently a product of laborious effort. However, the author

chose to base his defense of Greene in the Battle of Germantown by blaming Pulaski for the defeat, and thus it deserves serious consideration. Johnson gave the account of the contest basically the same as the standard authorities, but he explained the failure of the American surprise attack as the fault of Casimir Pulaski. On page 83 of his work he said:

> ...The Americans are not a little at loss also to account for some events, merely because they write under the erroneous impression that the surprise was complete. Yet, the British assert, and on this point their assertion is not to be controverted, that their patrols had given them an hour's notice of the approaching attack. It is not to be wondered at that the Americans doubt this, upon the Supposition that the British patrol could not have approached the American Army without being discovered by their own. But it is a melancholy fact, of which few were informed, that the celebrated Pulaski, who commanded the patrol, was found by General Washington himself asleep in a farmhouse. Policy only, and regard to the rank and misfortunes of the offender could have induced the general to suppress the fact. Yet to this circumstance, most probably, we are to attribute the success of the enemy's patrol in approaching near enough to discover the advance of the American column.

It seems to me that Washington in his attack on Germantown attempted to imitate his famous success at Trenton. There was a pincer movement by three columns. Cadwalader against Donop at Bordentown, Ewing to cross almost in front of Trenton and about 2,500 best troops under Washington to cross above Trenton and come down to make the attack. If Washington was victorious at Trenton and Cadwalader at Bordentown the divisions would attack Princeton and New Brunswick.

In this plan timing and a synchronized attack were important, but it failed. Ewing and Cadwalader experienced difficulties in crossing the Delaware. Washington thought he would have about 3,700 men against 1,500 Hessians. He had only 2,600 but he succeeded.

However, in Germantown the similarities were superfluous. He had about 11,000 men against 9,000 British, but it was not Christmas Night, and the British were not drunk as the Hessians were, which seems confirmed by the tremendous number of prisoners, 918 (84 wounded) while 23 were killed, against an insignificant American loss of 4 killed and 8 wounded. Also Germantown was not isolated as Trenton was, as proved by Cornwallis's arrival.

Besides, Johnson himself wrote: " Thus it appears that the British commander omitted no ordinary precautions in posting his troops–for the purpose of guarding against surprise. Nor were his patrols neglected..."

The success of Washington's plan depended on commando–like precision. All the troops were to arrive within two miles from the enemy's pickets by 2 a.m. and wait until 4 a.m. At that hour they were to make their last dispositions and on the stroke of 5 o'clock they were to attack the pickets.

This could be achieved, perhaps, by trained commandos or Indians but not by ordinary eighteenth century soldiers. How could Washington suppose it would be possible to remove all of the pickets without causing any alarm? It should be mentioned that fog could help in such an enterprise but it was a factor hardly to be counted upon in military planning.

If Pulaski was really in charge of cavalry patrols, we do not know what his orders were, and as to sneaking up on the enemy, cavalry was obviously ill suited for such a task, especially in difficult and fenced terrain. Cavalrymen were easier to discover than infantrymen, and the noise of hoofs and horses whinnying were factors to be contended with,

According to Wilkinson's *Memoires* (p.363), it was Allen McLane and his light horse who rode in the van of the lead column and charged the first British pickets, killing two for the loss of one of his men and capturing some artillery pieces.[31]

Washington, who was with Sullivan's Division, claimed that the surprise was effectually achieved "so far as reaching their guards before they had notice of our coming." (Washington to John Augustine Washington, W.W.9, p.397)

General Armstrong wrote to Thomas Wharton, Jr.: "...My destiny was against various corps of Germans encamped at Vandering's or near the Falls. Their light horse discovered our approach a little before sunrise. We cannonaded from the heights..."

Would the British Army be sleeping while cannonading and musket fire was going on? So much for a surprise from that field of action. Greene, who was late, found the enemy fully alert.

It, therefore, appears that there was no surprise. This is confirmed in Howe's report to Germain; "...at three o'clock in the morning of the 4th, the patrols discovered the enemy's approach, and upon the communication of this intelligence the Army was immediately ordered under arms..."

The Rev. Henry M. Muhlenberg, who lived close to the American encampment, noted in his diary on 3rd October: "...There is a report that at daylight the British outposts at Barren Hill and Germantown will be attacked" (Collections Penna. Hist. Soc. vol:1, p.170)

Scouting parties approached the British lines and according to C.C. Pinckney, who most probably took part in the Brandywine and Germantown battles, the pickets were driven in for three nights by the cavalry under Pulaski (Hist Mag., N.Y. 1866, p.202).

Was Casimir Pulaski, the nominal chief of cavalry, supposed to patrol in person all the four roads leading to Germantown? Was it not possible that a single Loyalist could warn the British? Germantown was built along a long road and had a multiplicity of fences and roads. In such conditions a spy could easily observe the American Army and quickly and unnoticed make his report.

Anyway, to what extent were the approach and intentions of Washington's army secret? Thomas Jones, the contemporary Loyalist historian, states in his *History of New York*, N.Y., 1879, vol: 1, p.194: "...But the whole scheme was discovered to a Loyalist, and a lad was dispatched with the information to Sir William. He was an intelligent boy and gave the General a very particular account as to the number of men, the cannon, the road, the night and the time of night, in which the attack would be made."

According to Jones, Howe preferred the pleasures of the faro table to taking care of that business, and the American attack was a complete surprise. This version of a warning to Howe is supported by the contemporary British historian who served under Howe in the Philadelphia campaigns! "The neglect of the commander-in-chief in the action at Germantown was extreme. He was acquainted with the intentions of General Washington on the evening before the attack, and could provide against it." (C. Stedman, *History of the American war*, vol: 1, p.300).

From said sources, it appears that Washington's attack at Germantown did not surprise the British. There is no valid basis for Johnson's conclusion. If he wanted to defend Greene in his 1822 book, fine and dandy. However, a defense which attempts to shift the blame to someone else for the Germantown events, some 45 years after the battle, is not only ludicrous but unsubstantiated by sufficient and credible evidentiary material.

Next comes the question of whether Pulaski was really sleeping on duty. Here the question is not clear at all, and requires examination at length. As I said before, the Battle of Germantown has to be considered with all of its ramifications and for whatever impact it had on Pulaski's American career.

This accusation was discussed at length in a polemic which started after Paul Bentalou published his *Pulaski Vindicated.* Because of its importance to Pulaski's biographers I shall discuss in depth (not avoiding necessary repetitions) the chronology of this controversy, which resulted in publication of two important pamphlets by Bentalou.

Judge William Johnson published *Sketches of the Life and Correspondence of Nathaniel Greene* in 1822, which was sharply and severely criticized in an anonymous article in the October 1822 issue of *The North American Review*, vol. vi, p.416, et seq.

In the entire article there is no mention of Pulaski's name. The book reviewer discusses the antagonism between Rhode Island and Massachusetts, quotes some letters of Greene about the miserable state of the Army and the necessity to collect supplies by armed parties in order to subsist (not a surprising statement for any student of the American Revolution), discusses the cruelties committed between Tories and Whigs, and condemns Judge Johnson for partiality. He mentions the Newberg Letters and their authorship, ascribed by Johnson to Gouverneur Morris. The reviewer is not correct in his assertions that pompous, circumstantial and pseudoclassical language was particular to the Judge. He is not altogether condemning Johnson, finding something praiseworthy here and there, especially Johnson's condemnation of duelling. The closest the reviewer comes to Pulaski is the statement in the beginning of the article that: "We should observe here that most of the objectionable passages are to be attributed to an extreme anxiety to honor his hero." (Greene). There was also a critical review of *Sketches* in the *U.S. Magazine* for January 1823.

But as Greene was hero to Johnson, so was Pulaski to Bentalou. That old soldier, aroused by Johnson's attack against Pulaski, reached not for a sword, but for a pen, which was evidently a strange instrument for him. For help, Bentalou depended heavily in his criticism of Johnson on the above-mentioned magazines, and probably, on the assistance of Jared Sparks. To refute the allegation, he said it was impossible for a vigilant and battle eager Pulaski to sleep at such a time. As for the element of surprise, he claimed it was complete. Interestingly, he remarked: "Too many jealous eyes were fixed on Pulaski, for such an act on his part to remain confined to the knowledge of discreet few."

Bentalou asked Johnson who gave him the information. "Was it Washington himself-the only person on whose assertion he could safely rely?'

On this subject Bentalou says: "Although the Judge has not thought it expedient explicitly to state his authority, perhaps he intended to furnish a clue to it by the distinguished notice taken, in his work, of one who acted a conspicuous part in those scenes, and who is now no more. If so, had he known the bitter enemity which that person bore to Pulaski (from what motives, it is, at present, needless to tell) surely the testimony of so prejudiced and so decided a foe must have had little weight with him." (p.17 of the original, p.20/298 of Abbats reprint, Extra No. 8, *Mag. Hist.* N.Y. 1909). That person was Charles Cotesworth Pinckney (1746-1825) who was yet another lawyer turned revolutionary. However, unlike so many other lawyer revolutionaries, he had attended a military academy, and was probably at Brandywine and Germantown as aide-de-camp to Washington. The biographic material on C.C. Pinckney, with the notable exception of Marvin R. Zahniser's *Charles Cotesworth Pinckney* (University of Carolina Press, 1967), is not rich, and I was not able to find therein any record of animosity between the two men, except, of course, in the matter under discussion.

Bentalou said that no regard to the rank and misfortune of the offender could induce Washington to overlook such an occurrence, if in fact it had accurred in the presence of Washington. However, G.W. Custis (*Life of Washington*, Chicago, 1902, p. 195 & 320) said that Washington used to show clemency to first offenders, though there is no mention of this alleged incident in this connection.

Bentalou, first stating that he could not believe that Pulaski could have been asleep, for the sake of argument then suggests that the Commander of Horse, after first stationing his pickets, could relax. It must be remembered, as Bentalou would say in his second pamphlet, that Pulaski was not an a picket, or a leader of pickets, but the Commanding General of the Cavalry. It is quite humanly possible that due to many hours of continuous duty, he was fatigued and cat-napped. Many people experience beneficial effects from such a short rest, which was preferable to sleeping in the saddle. If Washington did find Pulaski asleep, and the conversation could take a similar turn as that with Gen. Adam Stephen: "You, sir, may have ruined my plans." Or an accusation could have been made in a more explosive manner by Washington as he did with Gen. Lee at Monmouth. Pulaski who, according to many authors, was quick tempered, could answer abruptly. On the other hand, some French interpreter could put his own meaning to Washington's words. Washington, even if he did not blame Pulaski for preventing the surprise, obviously would have lost his good opinion of him, which would in turn would have lead to animosity, and the lack of co-operation and understanding, which became evident in their later relations. However, this is only conjecture.

Bentalou, further on in his pamphlet, relates Pulaski's career in Poland which was correct in general, but not in every detail, and is remarkably similar to Sparks's story in the *American Biography*. Comments about Johnson are interspaced throughout the book. Bentalou tells how Pulaski at Brandywine at the head of 30 horsemen led the charge which retarded the enemy's advance, saved the baggage, and protected the retreat of the American Army.

Talking about Warren Tavern (Goshen), Bentalou describes how Pulaski saved the Army from a surprise and engaged the enemy in a delaying action, with the help of an infantry detachment under General Scott. About Germantown, the author says (the same goes for Pulaski's whole generalship of cavalry):

> On the day of the Battle of Germantown he was sorely disappointed and mortified. There were but four regiments of horse raised, and not one of them completed. Three of them only, such as they were, had joined General Washington's army, and on the day of the battle, guards were furnished out of those regiments, to attend on the commander-in-chief and on other generals–or employed in other service, so that Pulaski was left with so few men as not to have it in his power to undertake anything of importance. This was to him a matter of deep regret and bitter chagrin.[32]

It must be noted that neither the type of action nor the terrain was suitable for decisive cavalry action.

Further on, Bentalou relates the history of Pulaski's Legion and his comments will be referred to in the chronological order of the events.

Not only was Pulaski accused by Judge Johnson of misbehavior at Germantown, but in his comments about the Battle of Germantown, Johnson alludes to an anecdote in Graydon's *Memoires* (p.301) that Conway also was found in a farmhouse during an action, and refused to join his brigade on the grounds that his horse was wounded. The finders in that case were Reed and Cadwalader, but I have found no corraboration for this anecdote in my research.

Bentalous pamphlet was reviewed in the *North American Review*, No. 47, April, vol. xx, 1825, probably by its editor Jared Sparks, a noted American historian, but not always reliable. The review does not shed much new light on this matter, being chiefly an abbreviation of Bentalou's work, interspaced with long quotations from it. Remember that Bentalou participated in the Battle of Germantown.

There is one point mentioned in the article which is well worth raising: "...Whatever may have been the indulgence of Washington, it is not credible that the few who were informed, and who cannot be supposed to have had such motives of delicacy, should not reveal a fact, so well calculated to screen the American officers from the disgrace of a defeat, by throwing the burden on the shoulders of a foreigner just then arrived in the country." (Bentalou)

The review contains some details about D'Estaing's letter which will be revealed later on in Paul Bentalou's "Reply."

In the same year, 1825, the author of the *Sketches of the Life of Greene* decided to publish "Remarks, Critical and Historical on an Article in 47 Number of the North American Review," relating to Count Pulaski, addressed to the readers of the *North American Review*, Charleston. The portion of this article, dealing with Pulaski's actions at the Battle of Brandywine have previously been discussed.

The review of "Pulaski Vindicated" did not give Bentalou's name but there were some details about his life. Johnson thought that it was an old Polander who refrained from publishing his name as he was a mere straw man. As a matter of fact, Johnson assumed that the critics from the *United States Magazine*, the *North American Review* and the anonymous author of "Pulaski Vindicated" were somehow related or even the same person, the obvious suspect being Jared Sparks. It must be granted that Johnson had sound grounds for his suspicions.

Bentalou's second book was more difficult to find than the first one for it took me about two years before I found and read it. Meanwhile I was pondering over the same points as did Johnson about a hundred and fifty years ago—how to explain the old veteran's efficiency in using the pen, wondering why he wrote in such pompous style, quoting ancient writers and attacking Johnson's literary style, and why did he bring into the discussion the Newburg Letters affair, which had nothing to do with Pulaski?

Was someone writing for Bentalou or perhaps using his name or recollections? Meanwhile, I was able to ascertain that Paul Bentalou existed and that he was a Revolutionary officer, duly noted in Heitmans Register.

Reading microfilmed *Papers of Continental Congress* (247, Roll, 48, Item 41), I found Baron de Arendts recommendation of Bentalou dated at Philadelphia on February 22, 1777:

...At the same time begs (Arendts) leave to recommend to the Honourable Congress a Gentleman of good family and of many accomplishments, Mr. Bentalou. He has been strongly recommended in France to your...(illegible) who having since had much opportunity to get fuller acquainted with him, thereby convinced that he possesses a great deal of knowledge and takes pains to improve daily. He will certainly make a good officer. He has already served as a volunteer in French cavalry and understands a good deal of the business. He would become a humble suitor for an officer post in the Continental Army. He hopes by his good and brave behaviour in the same to recommend himself further...

In the collection of the Georgia Historical Society in Savannah, there is a very illegible letter of J. Meredith(?) dated 28 October 1884 and addressed to J. Lynah:

...I was very well acquainted with Col. Bentalou...I always understood that he had served under Pulaski and had done good service...He (Bentalou) enjoyed public confidence and had opinion for veracity. The officer who accompanied Pulaski was, I have no doubt, Bentalou, and I have a recollection of having heard that he was wounded during the war. I think his narration entitled to full credence.

William Abbats gives some interesting details about Bentalou in his foreword to the reprint of *Pulaski Vindicated*, but this information, of course, was not available to Judge Johnson.

According to Heitman's Register, Paul Bentalou was a 2nd Lieutenant in the German Regiment on 25 September 1776. This must be an error as Bentalou, according to Arendt, only arrived in America in November of that year, as is confirmed in Bentalou's second brochure. On April 12, 1778, he was appointed a captain in Pulaski's Legion, wounded at Savannah on October 9, 1779, and resigned in January 1781.

In peacetime the young warrior settled in Baltimore (where a street was named after him later on) and had some federal appointments under Adams and Jefferson. He married Katherine Keeports in 1780. In 1806 he visited France where he was promptly jailed but eventually released. He became one of the prominent citizens of Baltimore, and his death was a result of a fall in a warehouse in his old age.

Bentalou was a great and loyal friend to Casimir Pulaski and though a saber rather than a pen was his forte, he rendered a great service to history by publishing his two pamphlets. These, with William Johnson's *Remarks* and a study of cavalry by Charles Francis Adams, are, as of today, the most serious attempts to critically examine Pulaski's role in the American Revolution.

Johnson in his *Remarks Critical and Historical* questions why Bentalou waited two years before printing his defense of Pulaski. I shall attempt to proceed methodically in my review of the Brandywine and Germantown battles, since the rest of Johnson's arguments will be mentioned in their chronological sequence.

Johnson, in the above article, repeats his previous allegations about Pulaski. However, he advances a new claim. On page 6 of his article, he claims that Major-General Charles C. Pinckney was with Washington when they allegedly found Pulaski asleep in the morning or/and prior to the Battle of Germantown.

In the "Postscript" to his pamphlet, Johnson adds the following: "This pamphlet was put to press early in summer (1825). Its distribution was prevented by the Author being suddenly called from home. If Gen Pinckney's testimony to support the fact related about Count Pulaski should need corraboration, it can be further proved that Gen. La Fayette, when lately in Columbia, declared it to be true of his own knowledge."

To that visit the Judge refers by saying: "The time too for these concerted attacks was admirably selected, just when the tribute of gratitude so justly bestowed upon our early friends was raising to its highest pitch the public enthusiasm and gratitude for foreigners." Johnson was a lawyer. He knew that the best proof was to obtain sworn affidavits from Pinckney and/or Lafayette. Why didn't he do this?

In 1826, Paul Bentalou had published his second and more interesting pamphlet entitled: "A Reply to Judge Johnson's Remarks on an article in the North American Review relating to Count Pulaski." This time there is no doubt he published this rebuttal defense of Pulaski under his own name and gave his own biographical data. From a study of this brochure, one may learn that, indeed, the author used the assistance of a literary friend while writing "Pulaski Vindicated" and that person was gone. "A Reply" is written in much more lucid style than the first booklet, and relates more directly and specifically to Pulaski.

I have found no references to Pulaski's part in the Brandywine battle except those mentioned previously. It is interesting to note that Bancroft remarked that Pulaski at Brandywine had shown bravery, but no leadership qualities. As Johnson clearly stated, Pulaski then had no official status and no right of command.

As to the improbability of such a feat at the Battle of Brandywine as previously described, Bentalou did not argue with Johnson, limiting himself to a statement that it was indeed so. But similar feats were ascribed to the Philadelphia Troop of Light Horse (*Cavalry Journal*, vol. 47, 1938, F.G. Bauer, "Notes on the Use of Cavalry in the American Revolution," p.136) during Washington's retreat through Jersey. As to baggage, Bentalou said that while heavy baggage was sent away, enough of the light remained to form a column of wagons.

Talking of retreat, Bentalou gave a vivid account of his first meeting with Pulaski:

> ...For having halted, as was our duty, till the rest of the army had moved onwards, we at length took up our line of march. It was then long after sunset, but the night was beautiful, and the moon shone as bright as day. Pulaski with his horse, having performed his part of the duty of the day, overtook us before we reached Chester, and seeing from my appearance, as he moved slowly along our column, that I was a French officer, he relaxed his pace, and entered into conversation with me. Learning my disappointment in being unable to get into cavalry, he promised to send for me when occasion should offer. He took my direction at parting, and a few days afterwards redeemed his promise. I had the good fortune to please him, and when subsequently early in the spring of 1778 he obtained his independent legionary corps, he sent for me and appointed me to the command of the first troop of the light dragoons of the legion...

As to Pulaski saving Washington from surprise at Goshen, Johnson uses a combination of ridicule, sarcasm, and satire to scoff at Bentalou's defense of Pulaski, as follows: "'The Commander of the American Army within striking distance of his enemy is represented by them as about to sustain that last of military disgraces, a surprise, a total surprise, and that in broad daylight when a stranger, sent from Heaven as it were, interposes and saves him from destruction.

Then follows hasty unpremeditated preparation, and preparation which that stranger alone knew how to cover and secure. Pulaski advises, Pulaski executes, and leaves the Commander-in-Chief only the lean honour of conducting himself according to Pulaski's advice and under Pulaski's protection."

Bentalou points to an obvious truth that though Washington could have intended to give battle at that time, he was not prepared for it. Washington's propensity to ask for advice is well known and had Washington asked for such from Green, Johnson would probably have found it praiseworthy. The researcher can only wonder why the name of Pulaski is not mentioned more often in the protocols of the Council of War.

As to the Army not expecting the battle, Bentalou quotes two corraborating statements to this effect by Col. J.E. Howard and Gen. Samuel Smith.

Howard says: "...We had drawn provision and the men had been engaged in cooking, when about eleven o'clock a.m to the best of my recollection, an alarm was suddenly given, and the men were ordered under arms. By that time we heard the firing of the advance parties to our left, and, I think, on the lower road, which appeared to be at the distance of a mile, or a mile and a half. Some wounded horsemen came in..."

Smith says: "...I remember as well as if it had been yesterday that on the day you allude to our division was encamped east of the road from Philadelphia to Lancaster, and there was no idea of attack by the enemy, when I think about or after 12 o'clock the drum beat to arms..."

As to Goshen, we have Bentalou's statement. There is collaborative evidence to show that there was an unexpected alarm and it was probably given by cavalry which was commanded by Pulaski. It was one of the cavalry's duties to protect against such surprises and in this case no blame could be put on Washington.

Bentalou's "Pulaski Vindicated from an Unsupported Charge" was reviewed in Vol. 47 of the *North American Review*. Johnson took umbrage at the review and the reviewer. He states " ...that there were individuals connected with that Review, whose eternal enmity I had incurred..." He claims that the review would have been beneath his notice had it not contained what he considered to be two personal charges. The result was *Remarks Critical and Historical*. Here is the extract for the reader to judge (pg. 5 supra):

> Yet I should have deemed the Review as much beneath my notice as the pamphlet, did it not contain two most injurious personal charges, which I quote in the writer's own language.
>
> Under impressions like these it was with sincere regret that in this country we should find occasion given for any one to write a pamphlet with the avowed object of vindicating the fame of Pulaski from the injurious charge of an American historian; and surprise is mingled with regret when we learn that the charge is intended to throw a slur on the military character of a man whom the world has lauded with a unanimous voice, for his skill and bravery as a soldier. p. 378.
>
> The other passage is in these words: "These considerations alone are enough to destroy the force of the charge. It needs not be inquired whether Pulaski was found in a farm-house or what he did, or whether he did any thing at the battle of Germantown; it is enough to know that Washington was acquainted with all his conduct there, much better than any other person, and that he never lisped a whisper of censure for neglect of duty, but on the contrary aided his future promotion. In short, we doubt not that Judge Johnson has been deceived, and that the authority on which he re-

lied, from whatever source it came, *is not entitled to credit*; and every generous minded citizen of the United States *must lament* that he should have sanctioned by his name a charge calculated to reflect *no honour on Washington*, and to cast reproach on the memory of a brave man," &c.

How relevant is the issue of allegedly being asleep and the Germantown Battle? The Americans were hoping for a surprise attack, which was to commence at daybreak from all sides (Oct. 25, 1777, letter of Gen. Sullivan in Vol. V, page 464 of *Washington's Writings*). However, there was no surprise because British patrols had spotted Washington's army at 3 o'clock the morning of the attack. The American attack achieved sucess initially. The enemy was driven to Schoolhouse Lane in the center of Germantown, when the Americans found themselves unsupported by other troops. Their ammunition was gone. A fog hit the area but they could dimly see the British collecting in force, when they were suddenly made aware of British light horse in the area. They heard the firing at Chew's house, far in their rear. Believing themselves surrounded, they panicked and fled. (Lossing, *Field Book of the Revolution*, pg. 112). Indeed, one American writer describes the panic this way:

> A victory for the Americans was truned into a defeat by their sudden panic and precipitate retreat where it is alleged that they literally fled from their own victory. (William W. Gordon, *Count Casimir Pulaski*, vol. XIII, No. 3, Sept. 1929, pg. 186, the *Georgia Historical Quarterly*).

Lossing (supra, pg. 112) reports that the troops under Greene and Stephen were the last ones to retreat and they were covered by Count Pulaski's forces.

Whether or not Pulaski had in fact slept turns out to be completely irrelevant to the conduct and the outcome of the battle. There was no surprise but the initial American attack was extremely successful and would have been a great Washington victory, if not for the tragic fiasco and panic which occurred. Johnson knew this but nevertheless he makes a big deal out of it, even claiming that Gen. Pinckney was a witness and in the April 23 issue of the *Charleston Courier* "...volunteered to affirm the truth of the anecdote of Pulaski..."(Johnson, supra, pg6).

To paraphrase McArthur: "Old soldiers never die, they just get maligned long after they're dead." If the incident were true, and Washington could forget, couldn't Johnson have been as forgiving as his idol, Washington: the Reviewer (supra) hit the right note in stating:

...surprise is mingled with regret when we learn that the charge is intended to throw a slur on the military character of a man whom the world has lauded with a unanimous voice, for his skill and bravery as a soldier.

Hasn't the Bard given us a fitting title for this Johnson Production: "Much Ado About Nothing!"

In pages 18-22 (supra) Johnson presents his views on Poland, the Confederates of the Bar (of which the Pulaski family was one of the staunchest supporters), the Protestants, Catholics of the Orthodox faith, etc. He describes Pulaski's Confederates as a "...band of intolerant persecutors..." and scoffs at their claim of fighting against the Russians and for liberty with: "To represent such men, with such purposes, as combatting for liberty is a farce...'He accuses the nobles of "...bigotry, intolerance, and contempt of the lower classes..." One can easily and with much justification label Johnson as pro-Russian, anti-aristocracy, and anti-Pulaski.

Bentalou versus Johnson was not finished by this exchange of articles and pamphlets. *The North American Review* (v. 23, Oct., 1826) printed a review of Bentalou's "Reply." The Reviewer restated his position, this time somewhat humorously. Referring to the British accounts of the Germantown battle, he assumed that Howe was lying when he stated that his patrols discovered the American approach. However, the article quoted a lengthy and interesting letter of Colonel Timothy Pickering who said: "Sir, Nearly forty-nine years have elapsed since the Battle of Germantown; of course you may well suppose that many facts respecting it are beyond my power of recollection; while a few are indelibly impressed on my memory...I did not know at the time, nor do I recollect ever to have heard, that Pulaski was found asleep, until it was mentioned by Judge Johnson, in his *Life of General Greene*. Nor do I remember having heard him censured for any neglect of duty in the case referred to, the Battle of Germantown..." Pickering also said about Washington's habit of asking advice: "...The truth is that General Washington, not sanguine in his own opinions, was ever disposed, when occasion occurred, to consult those officers who were near him, in whose discernment and fidelity he placed a confidence; and certainly his decisions were often influenced by their opinions..."

Jared Spark also expressed the prevailing American attitude to Johnson's charge:

As no other writer has mentioned this circumstance, and it was never made known to the public till more than forty years after it is said to have occurred, and as it is proved by the whole course of life, that Pulaski's military fault, if he had one, was that of rushing with too much impetuosity upon the enemy, it seems both idle and unjust to entertain for a moment such a suspicion, especially when it is not pretended to rest on any better foundation than conjecture and hearsay. (*The Library of American Biography*, Boston, 1847, Little & Brown, pg. 421)

★ ★ ★

In due course Washington was thanked by Congress for his wise daring and hard-hitting concentrated attack upon the enemy near Germantown. Congress also resolved that Henry Laurens and Thomas Heyward would be added to the committee appointed to strike a gold medal honoring Washington for Boston. The Army was thanked too for their exertions at the Battle of Germantown. Washington hoped that the approbation of that honorable body, would stimulate them to still nobler efforts on every future occasion.

On October 6, 1777, the British under Sir Henry Clinton captured forts Montgomery and Clinton on the west bank of the Hudson. The news of this event reached Washington on the night of 12-13 October 1777. Next, he heard of the American success at Freeman's Farm, and remarked then about the loss of the fortress defenses on the Hudson: "The strike would have perhaps proved fatal to our northern affairs in its consequence had not he defeat of General Burgoyne so providentially taken place upon the 7th..."

According to C. Stedman: "In no instance during the American war was more invincible resolution exhibited than in this attack (against Fort Clinton)...Count Grabousky, a Polish nobleman, who had crossed the Atlantic on purpose to make a campaign as a volunteer with the British, likewise fell on this occasion. But his death was attended with circumstances which ought to be mentioned in honor to his memory. He had advanced to the storm in company with Lord Rawdon among the grenadiers but was separated from him among the felled trees, which forced every man to find a path for himself. Arriving at the foot of the work, he fell after having received three balls, When giving his sword to a grenadier, he conjured him, with his expiring voice, to deliver it to Lord Rawdon, and to assure his lordship that he died in a manner becoming one who had shared the dangers of such gallant troops."

An officer of the British Army noted:!"...The gallant count Gabrouski lately arrived from England has died of his wounds...." (Frank Moore, *Diary of the American Revolution*, 1858, vol.1, p. 509).

I wonder whether Pulaski heard about the valiant Grabouski [Gabrowski] or about Kosciuszko?

Fortunately, Burgoyne asked Gates for terms at Saratoga on October 13th, and the semi-official confirmation reached Washington in a letter from George Clinton on the 18th. Congress was kept in suspense until October 31st when James Wilkinson brought the good tidings and was rewarded by a thankful Congress with the brevet rank of Brigadier-General (the same rank which was given to Pulaski after the initial refusal and long delay) though it should be mentioned, that Wilkinson stated in his memoirs that the rank was given to him on Gates' recommendation for different services. Wilkinson's dispatches were addressed to the President of Congress, omitting the Commander-in-Chief.

The British Army moved to Philadelphia from Germantown and concentrated its main effort on reducing the river forts of Mercer and Mifflin in Delaware, which had stopped Howe's supply fleet. The forts were reduced on November 10th, thus securing the British in their possession of Philadelphia. Meanwhile, Washington had moved to White Marsh,

The French Court closely followed the course of the War. Washington's campaigns and maneuvers in the Philadelphia area and, especially the great victory at Saratoga, proved to them that the Americans were a match for the British forces. As a result thereof, the French-American alliance was signed in Paris on February 6, 1778. That was a great event, but meanwhile life for the first Commander of Horse became routine and he had more time and opportunity to shape and develop the four cavalry regiments into an effective traditional and tactical cavalry unit.

The first note of his presence and duties, after Germantown, was contained in a short command in the general orders for October 6, 1777: "Brigadier-Genl. Pulaski will make a return of the horse as soon as possible." On the previous day, all the detachments of horse had to be collected in one place, as close to the Army as possible, except for parties under Captains Henry Lee (First Continental Dragoons) and Charles Craig (Fourth Continental Dragoons).

Washington was well aware of the dangers of the approaching winter, and this is well documented in his correspondence. Soldiers had no shoes, blankets or spare clothes. The army was ill prepared for winter's onslaught.

Among others, Major Jameson of the cavalry received Washington's order to collect these articles from the inhabitants of Chester County. In the prosecution of his orders, Jameson was to differentiate between disaffected and well-affected. Jameson was also to procure horses for the cavalry.

That order, it seems, was given directly by the Commander-in-Chief to Jameson, omitting the proper chain of command (about which Washington was so sensitive when Gates wrote directly to Congress).

On October 17th a court-martial took place, the events of which were perhaps a reason for pique on the part of Pulaski. (W.W. 9, p.407)

"Lieut-Col. Byrd (Francis O. Byrd, Third Continental Dragoons) charged with 'Countermanding the orders Col. Bland gave two soldiers to fall into their rank, repeatedly on parade, and for disobeying the orders of Col. Bland, when directed to order the said men into their ranks on the night the Cavalry passed the Schuylkill. Col. Byrd admitted the justness of the charge. Whereupon the Court considered whether Col. Bland had, or not, a right to command Lieut.-Col. Byrd while a superior officer was present, and determined that he had not."

That superior officer had to be Pulaski because even if we take the officers in order of seniority, Moylan, who was at the top of the list, would not be the president of the court.

Let us restate the matter. Two soldiers were repeatedly falling out of rank. Pulaski saw it and did not react. On the contrary, in his presence Colonel Byrd countermanded Colonel Bland's order. It seems that either Pulaski did not understand the whole matter or the cavalrymen acted on his order, possibly forwarded by Byrd. Whatever were the facts of the incident, his role in it, though small, could not bring him popularity from those hostile to foreign officers.

Generally, the Colonials showed no great love and affection for the foreign volunteers. Theirs was a revolt against tyranny and taxation without representation. It was a war fought for humanity and principles (with the possible exception of Negroes, Indians, Papists, etc.) and foreign mercenaries were not particularly welcome, except specialists (like engineers), though strangely enough, Washington complained about the shortage of officers[33].

Meanwhile the camp gossiped about two men, Duche and another foreigner, Thomas Conway. On October 15th Mrs. Elizabeth Graeme Ferguson appeared in Washington's camp and delivered a letter to the General from the Rev. Jacob Duche, an ex-chaplain to Congess in 1774 and the author of an eloquent and patriotic sermon, which had been warmly received by the delegates.

Now, in 1777, he underwent a change of heart, and probably under Howe's persuasion, wrote to the Commander-in-Chief, attempting to convince him that he should influence Congress to open negotiations for peace with Great Britain. Characteristically, Duche was convinced that in this entire matter Washington's opinion was more important than that of Congress.

This is not so strange as in the future Washington was to over-shadow that much-maligned body and become Father of his Country, but in the revolutionary period, Congress was the symbol of the Revolution continuity and was its ideological and executive power. The duties of Congress were practically all-powerful, but their execution was made impossible or difficult by objective circumstances.

Many of Washington's apologists claimed that he could not co-op-erate with Congress and the revolutionaries without revealing to the British his notorious difficulties with supplies, deserters, recruitments, etc. However, Washington's difficulties were well-known to Loyalists and the British, because deserters were coming daily to Howe.

It is also said that Congress was a civilian body and as such was not able to comprehend the military arguments. In addition, Congress was almost as much afraid of a military dictatorship as the Polish "szlachta" (nobility) was afraid of royal despotism, though neither appeared in the history of the respective countries.

The American Army was basically a revolutionary force consisting of nonprofessionals whose leaders, however, longed for all the trap-pings and pomp and circumstances of military life. Graydon had remarked about ridiculous overuse of the title of general in the conversations of those gentlemen.

In the American Army the second in command, Charles Lee, was a professional but he was handicapped by being an Englishman. (His trial was different from the Moscow trials in that he most vehemently denied any guilt.)

The Thomas Conway affair was very involved and instructive. It should be studied by anybody interested in Pulaski for a better understanding of the army's background. T.Conway was born in 1747 in Kerry, Ireland. As the Catholics were persecuted by the English, Conway followed a regular military career in France, becoming a colonel in 1772. He was a specialist in training troops.

He brought with him good recommendations from Paris. He evidently made a positive impression on the Commander-in-Chief, as he recommended him to Congress in terms much more enthusiastic than for Pulaski, and he was made a Brigadier-General. He was assigned a regiment in Sullivan's brigade and he earned the respect of his chief who wrote about Conway: "His regulations in his brigade are much better than any in the Army, and his knowledge of military affairs in general far exceeds any officer we have."

The Fabian tactics of Washington were not winning the war, but at the same time his poularity was growing. Still he had many critics amongst the revolutionists. Even some generals sympathetic to him were keenly aware of Washington's propensity for hesitation and slow decision.

Timothy Pickering, Adjutant-General, remarked to Greene: "...Before I came to the Army, I entertained an exalted opinion of General Washington's military talents, but I have since seen nothing to enhance it."

General Kalb wrote: "Washington is the most amiable, kind-hearted upright of men, but as a General he is too slow, too indolent and far too weak. Besides, he has a tinge of vanity in his composition, and over-estimates himself. In my opinion whatever success he will have he may be owing to good luck and the blunders of his adversaries, rather than to his abilities. I may even say that he does not know how to improve on the grossest blunders of the enemy. He has not overcome his old prejudice against the French." (Freeman, G.W. p.496)

This opinion was seconded by Louis Duportail, Thomas Conway, Thomas Mifflin, and perhaps by Casimir Pulaski.

The following letter to Horatio Gates is characteristic of the climate surrounding Washington's critics since its author preferred to remain anonymous: "Repeated slights and unjustifiable arrogance combined with other causes to drive from the army those who would not worship the image, and pay undeserved tribute of praise and flattery to the great and powerful. The list of our disgusted patriots is long and formidable; their resentment keen against the reigning cabal, and their power of position not despicable...We have had a noble army melted down by ill-judged marches which disgrace their authors and directors...How different your conduct and fortune. In short this army will be totally lost, unless you come down and collect the virtuous band who wish to fight under your banner and with their aid save the southern hemisphere. Congress must send for you..." (Jared Sparks, *Writings of Washington*, Boston, 1834, p.484)

In Congress the most critical of Washington were Dr. Benjamin Rush, Lovell, Lee and Adams. Thus wrote John Adams in *Familiar Letters* (p. 322-23) about Burgoyne's capitulation: "...(it) was not immediately due to the Commander-in-Chief nor to Southern Troops" (were it due to him)..."idolatary and adulation would have been unbound so excessive as to endanger our liberties, for what I know. Now we can allow certain citizen to be wise, virtuous and good without thinking him deity or saviour."

James Lovell wrote to William Whipple on September 17, 1777: "as to the affair at Brandywine...I doubt whether you will ever accurately know whether Fortune alone is to be blamed or whether Sullivan and Chief should not share with her in the slanderous murmurs..." (L.M.C.C. Burnett, 2, 495)

There is an anonymous letter ascribed to Benjamin Rush, and quoted by Henry Steele Commager and Kichard Morris in *The Spirit of 1776* (p. 655): "The northern army has shown us what Americans are capable of doing with a General at their head. The spirit of the southern army is in no way inferior to the spirit of the northern. A Gates, a Lee or a Conway would in a few weeks render' them an irresistible body of men..."

But the scapegoat, the man whom Washington crushed, thus bringing the open opposition to an end, was a foreigner-Thomas Conway.

Conway, it seems, sinned mostly by his garrulousness which was described in this manner: "...Conway would say, 'No man was more gentleman than General Washington, or appeared to more advantage at his table, or in the usual intercourse of life, but as to his talents for the command of the Army'-and he shrugged as he spoke in that indescribable French way-'they were miserable indeed.'"

After Gates' victory Conway sent him a laudatory letter in which appeared the following sentence: "Heaven has been determined to save your country, or a weak General and bad counsellors would have ruined it."

On November 8th, Lord Stirling communicated to Washington that Wilkinson said to Major McWilliams that Conway said in his letter to Gates to wit the above remarks. That it was hearsay was obvious. By that time Washington was so vexed by his critics that he decided to bring the matter into the open. At once, he wrote to Conway, informing him in a curt manner that he knew about his letter to Gates. Conway attempted to explain it by an answer which could be taken either as very frank or very cunning. It seems that Washington and his friends preferred to accept the second evaluation.

Thomas Conway, offended, offered his resignation to Congress and asked Washington for leave of absence, so he could collect his effects before leaving for France. The request was willingly and immediately granted. But Conway's resignation was referred to the Board of War where the man most influential was Thomas Mifflin, who was not a friend to Washington. In December of that year Thomas Conway was made an inspector-general and advanced to the rank of major-general. To spare the delicate feelings of the native officers, Conway's promotion was on the staff and not in the line, so that he would have no command over American officers. Nevertheless his nomination was a blow to Washington's prestige. Already on October 18, 1777, in an almost virulent letter to Richard Henry Lee (W.W. 9, p. 387) about Congress's intention to appoint the Irishman a major-general, he denounced him in unusually strong words: "...General Conway's merit, then, as an officer, and his importance in this Army, exists more in his own imagination than in reality. For it is a maxim with him to leave no service of his own untold...I would ask why the youngest brigadier in the service...should be put over the heads of the eldest?'

Washington assured Lee that brigadiers would not serve under Conway, and remarked significantly: "I leave you to guess, therefore at the situation this Army would be in at so important a crisis, if this event should take place." Towards the end of his letter he clearly threatened his resignation: "To sum up the whole, I have been a slave to the service: I have undergone more than most men are aware of, to harmonize so many discordant parts; but it will be impossible for me to be of any further service if such insuperable difficulties are thrown in my way." Those words Pulaski could well use for his motto in his American service.

Washington eventually triumphed over his critics by bringing the whole matter of leadership into the open. Meanwhile Horatio Gates was indignant about the spying which he believed was going on in his headquarters. He suspected Alexander Hamilton.

When Thomas Conway appeared at Valley Forge in his new role of Inspector General he received from Washington a chilly but polite reception. Conway in dispatch of his duties proposed to prepare models, printed rules and regulations and give verbal instructions to officers but was snubbed on a technicality.[34]

Conway complained to Congress about being cold-shouldered and threatened resignation. But by that time he had lost his support in Congress and was sent away in connection with the Canadian expedition. But his story in America was not finished until his resignation was accepted by Congress and until Cadwalader put a bullet through the offending mouth. According to Alexander Garden, the garrulous Irish-Frenchman was still able to talk directly after that punishment (*Anecdotes*, p.90). Shortly after that duel, Conway sent Washington an apologetic letter (23 July 1778, Sparks, 5, p. 517). This epistle can be considered either as a confession of a dying and penitent man or as a clever move for reconciliation. Anyway Thomas Conway recovered, returned to Europe and followed a honorable career in the French service.

This was the moral atmosphere surrounding Pulaski after he took command of cavalry. I know of no evidence that Pulaski was involved in the so-called Conway Cabal, but it is evident that he and Washington did not see eye to eye on the training, capability, and use of the cavalry as a real fighting force. Pulaski was cited as being in the company of men critical of Washington, and Charles Lee, who had been in the Polish army, had a good opinion of him. Pulaski never become a member of the Washington military family or his protege for they were as different as any two men could be by virtue of birth, education, training, and prior military experience. However, Washington never disparaged Pulaski and praised him in his Congressional communications and correspondence.

Perhaps it should be mentioned that the critical appraisal of the performance, abilities and character of the Commander-in-Chief was not only a privilege but a duty of the political leadership of the Revolution, i.e., Congress which was ultimately responsible for its success or failure.

A secret plot against Washington or a conspiracy with a view to a military coup detat would have posed a different situation.

While this struggle for power was going on Congress reconstituted the Board of War and Gates became its president, achieving thus a position technically above Washington.

Pulaski experienced the first or his many difficulties with the Moylan versus Zielinski case. The following is taken from General Orders, October 31, 1777 (W.W. 9, p.472): "The Commander-in-Chief approves the following sentences of a General Court-Martial of the Brigade of Horse held the 24th inst.

"Colonel Moylan charged with 'Disobedience of the orders of Genl. Pulaski, a cowardly and ungentleman-like action in striking Mr. Zielinski, a gentleman and officer in Polish (sic.) service when disarmed; and putting him under guard, and giving irritating language to Genl. Pulaski.' The Court were of opinion that Col. Moylan was not guilty, and therefore acquitted him of the charges exhibited against him. Col. Moylan is discharged from arrest."

Some dragoons accused at the same proceeding were not so lucky in that court. For instance Archer Hinly, a private of Colonel Bland's Regiment, charged with plundering Wm. Lawrence, was found guilty and sentenced to run the gauntlet through a detachment of 50 of the Brigade of Horse. Judah Ludley, a private in Capt. Talmadge's Troop of Col. Sheldon's Regiment, charged with extorting money from John

Thompson and also for refusing to give himself up and attempting to escape from Capt. Richards and Francis Taylor and with attempting to draw his sword to keep them off, was found guilty and sentenced to run the gauntlet through a detachment of the Brigade of Horse consisting of 200 men. William Patterson, a private in Col. Sheldons Regiment, charged with plunderlng Wm. Lawrence...to run the gauntlet...of 50 men...(General Muhlenberg's Orderly Book, 1777, *Penn Mag. of Hist.* vol. 35, p. 165.)

Stephen Moylan was reprimanded by Pulaski and retorted with "irritating language." In this angry mood Moylan probably struck Zielinski who, let us remember, had no official status in the Army, being probably a volunteer attached to Pulaski.

As the court found Moylan not guilty, the inference was that Pulaski and Zielinski were wrong, but it is improbable that they would bring the case into a court unless the facts were basically true.

I was not able to ascertain whether at that period there were other Poles in Pulaski's suite besides Zielinski whose Christian name was uniformly given as John, although according to the Roll of Pulaskis Legion it was Ignacy.

Zielinski was the maiden name of Pulaski's mother and it may be presumed that it was he and not the mythical Rogowski who accompanied Pulaski on his voyage.

My inquiry at the Military Service Records, National Archives, Washington, D.C., brought me a copy of "Count Pulaski's Legion, Continental Troops. Register, p. 545, according to which Captain Zielinski's name appeared for the first time on March 19, 1779, but the time of service is counted as 10 months, 13 days.

According to Ed Dybicz, Polish-American historian (*Norristown Times Herald*, 11, 16, 71) Zielinski, who spoke good English, forwarded Pulaski's orders.

On October 25, 1777, Pulaski and all the dragoon commanders received the following circular from Washington. However it should have been directed to Pulaski as the commander of the Horse. The circular is self-evident, but raises the interesting point of how Pulaski was to distinguish between the friendly and the disaffected who could appear to him equally disaffected when their horses, blankets, clothes and fodder were requisitioned and paid for by worthless certificates. To abide by the rules meant in practice that the supplies on which the very existence of cavalry depended were not provided. The defaults in this respect are too well-known to students of the American Revolution to dwell on.

Sir: I am sorry to find, that the liberty I granted to the light dragoons of impressing horses near the enemy's lines has been most horribly abused and perverted into a mere plundering scheme. I intended nothing more than that the horses belonging to the disaffected, in the neighbourhood of the British Army, should be taken for the use of the dismounted dragoons, and expected, that they would be regularly reported to the Quarter Master General, that an account might be kept of the number and the persons from whom they were taken, in order to a future settlement. Instead of this, I am informed that under pretence of the authority derived from me, they go about the country, plundering whomsoever they are pleased to denominate Tories, and converting what they get to their own private profit and emolument. This is an abuse that cannot be tolerated, and as I find the license allowed them, has been made a sanction for such mischievous practices, I am under the necessity of recalling it altogether. You will therefore immediately make it known to your whole corps that they are not under any pretence whatever to meddle with the horses or other property of any inhabitant whatever, on pain of the severest punishment; for they may be assured, as far as it depends upon me, that military execution will attend all those who are caught in the like practice hereafter.

The more effectually to put it out of their power to elude this prohibition, all the horses in your corps, in the use of the non commissioned officers and privates, not already stamped with the Continental brand, are without loss of time to be brought to the Qr. Master General to receive that brand; and henceforth, if any of them shall be found with horses that are without it, they shall be tried for marauding and disobedience of orders.

I am fully confident, you will be equally disposed with me to reprobate and abolish the practice complained of, and will adopt the strictest measures to fulfill the intention of this letter, and prevent its continuance in future. (W.W. 9, p. 432, *Circular to Dragoon Commanders.*)

That the court-martial was instigated by Pulaski and not by Ignacy Zielinski may be verified by a note of Pulaski's in the Emmets Collection, Lennox Library (W. Kozlowski, *Pulaski w Ameryce*, p.344) where Pulaski had asked Bland to delay the proceeding as he had not yet prepared accusation and proofs against Moylan.

About a month later, Zielinski had sought justice on his own and in the presence of a French officer lambasted Moylan and dismounted him. Moylan had previously rejected Zielinski's challenge to a duel, retorting that he had not considered him either gentleman or officer, and that he would order his servant to cane Zielinski. This was said to Colonel Thompson. (*Letters to Washington*, vol. 21, fol.275).

La Fayette mentions the matter in his *Memoirs* on p.147, which I quote as it gives some idea about the common phenomenon of a court-martial in the American Army: "But the prejudges are not the same thing; for giving publicly the best of the dispute (for it here becomes trail for both parties) to an officer of the last military stage against one of the first, should be looked on as an affront to the rank and acquitting a man, whom one other man accuses, looked upon as an affront to the person. It is the same in Poland, for Count de Pulaski was much affronted at the decision of a court-martial entirely acquitting Colonel Molens. However, as I know the English customs, I am nothing else but surprised to see such partiality in a court-martial...How it is possible to carry a gentleman before a parcel of dreadful judges, at the same place where an officer of the same rank has been just now cashiered for a trifling neglect of his duty...When the judges are partial as on this occasion, it is much worse because they have the same inconvenience as law itself."

La Fayette was provoked into writing this by a court-martial decision acquitting some sentries whom he had found negligent. Probably this irritation caused that letter not to be as sycophantic as were most of La Fayette's letters to Washington.

The Americans were not the only dissatisfied ones. The foreigners were disappointed with the Americans. Duportail in a letter to Germain wrote that there was more enthusiasm for revolution in the cafes of Paris than in the whole of the United States. It was easier to be enthusiastic about revolution in cafes than around camp fires, and when the French had a revolution of their own, they had not fared too well. Anyway, the following opinion of Duportail, who became the French Minister of War in 1790, sounds strangely familiar: "To make short of the matter, it is not the good conduct of the Americans that enabled them to make a campaign sufficiently fortunate, it is the fault of the English." Dekalb wrote to Broglie: "I beg you to recall me as soon as possible."

Even hero-worshipping or cunningly knowing the art of flattery at such a young age La Fayette was disappointed. Previously he had remarked in a letter to his wife "...all the foreigners, I say, who have been employed here are dissatisfied, complain, detest others and are themselves detested...and I cannot understand why they are so much hated..."

Many foreigners, once enthusiastic either for the ideals of revolution or for the chance of advance and gain, returned bitterly home. But Pulaski had no home.

On October 29th a council of war was held, and among the questions asked of officers there was (1) whether it was prudent to attack the enemy and (2) where to take winter quarters. The council decided that it would not be prudent to attack the British and the question of winter quarters was deferred.

Among those noted as present was Pulaski and evidently he thought particularly about the winter quarters. On that subject, a council of general officers was held on November 30th, and Robert Hansom Harrison's summation, endorsed by Washington, shows: Greene, La Fayette, Armstrong, Smallwood, Wayne and Scott for Wilmington; Sullivan, Dekalb, Maxwell, Knox, Poor, Muhlenberg, Varnum, Weedon and Woodford in favor of the Lancaster-Reading line, Stirling for the Great Valley, Du Portail and Irvine for hutting in a strong position (W.W. 10, p.133 n) while Pulaski's opinion in sharp contrast to all the rest was as follows:

> I leave the choise of ground to those who are well acquainted with the country. I confine myself to considering the advantages which will attend a continuance of the campaign, and the inconveniences which will flow from retiring to winter quarters. Our continuing in a state of activity will give courage to our friends, be an antidote to the effeminacy of young soldiers and innure them to the fatigues which veterans undergo, keep them in exercise of their profession and entrust them, whereas the inactivity of winter quarters will ruin the Army, discourage the country, leave an extent of territory for the enemy to ravage and depopulate. Besides, how do we know what reinforcement the enemy may receive before the next campaign? For my part therefore I only think that the invalids in each regiment should be suffered to retire where they may, under the direction of proper officers, be refreshed and reunite. With all the rest collected I would make a vigorous attack upon the enemy as soon as the Schuylkill is frozen. In case winter quarters are determined upon I solicit his Excellency to allow me a body of cavalry and infantry to remain near the enemy's lines.
>
> —C. Pulaski   (P.M.H. XX 3, p.400, 1896)

Pulaski's wish to continue operations was "the Lone Voice in the Wilderness." The request to stay near to the enemy's line was granted not to Pulaski but to Captain Allen MacLane instead of to Pulaski who earnestly solicited it. He was obviously very disappointed because by temperament he was a man of action, if not in constant locomotion.

The winter quarters at Valley Forge were not the first winter quarters of the American Army. During the previous winter the Army suffered much from sickness, starvation, nakedness and lack of sufficient medications and medical care. Thus desertions became a great problem. Previously at least, soldiers had had some measure of protection in the houses of Morristown.[35] That in this winter the situation regarding clothes, shoes, blankets and food would be no better was obvious to Washington, but he had decided on Valley Forge, in spite of the fact that in Morristown his forces had melted to less than three thousand effectives, leaving him at Howe's mercy. Francis Dana wrote on 12th February that Howe could have destroyed the American Army had he enterprise. (Political Mag. vol:1, 1780).

Pulaski had not experienced winter in Morristown, but after years of partisan warfare, sometimes in the dead of winter in Poland, he knew what forced passivity would do to an insurgent army in sub–zero temperature. Had his experience and advice been heeded, much human suffering could have been avoided and the Army would not have been on the verge of dissolving, saved only by the enemy's commander.

Valley Forge has survived in legends and songs. It has been considered a forge from which the patriots' army emerged strengthened, invigorated and drilled in the best Prussian manner by the invaluable Steuben.

In fact the army of about 17,000 in 1777 had shrunk to about 5,000 in 1778. About 1,100 deserters had escaped to Howe in Philadelphia. It is unknown how many men simply walked away to home or died attempting desertion. In Valley Forge there were log huts for soldiers with insufficient straw to cover the floors, no soap, starvation rations and lice aplenty. Smallpox and typhus raged; there was no fodder for horses, and many died of starvation or were butchered for meat.

Washington was afraid that the Army would disperse or mutiny. The cry which sounded so ominously from the soldiers' huts in the evenings was: "No bread, no meat, no rum, no soldiers!"

But the dark days at Valley Forge were brightened by the presence of Washingtons wife, Martha, who arrived at the beginning of February 1778 under horse escort with Mrs. Nathaniel Greene, Lady Kitty Stirling and other ladies. Freeman says that Martha lightened long evenings and directed the entertainment. W. Herbert Burk says: "Knowing some French and being a woman of bright parts and a gay manner, she attracted to her husband's quarters La Fayette and the other foreign officers, including Steuben, Duponceau, DeKalb,

Fleury, Duplessis and the gallant Pulaski." (W. Herbert Burk, D.D., "The Valley Forge Guide," 1921, p.39).

These entertainments, however Spartan, were taking place when about 400 soldiers were dying per month and when almost naked men were rushing about huts, probably offending the modesty of the ladies, unless they kept to the officers' quarters which were mainly in the households of Valley Forge.

Before the outbreak of the revolution the only books on military exercise and regulations were the European manuals such as Bland's *Treatise on Military Discipline* (1727) or Windh's *A Plan for Discipline Composed for the Use of Militia of the County of Norfolk* (1759). It was in 1775 that Timothy Pickering of the Essex County Volunteers wrote *An Easy Plan for Discipline for Militia*.

Those books, of course, could not be the first regulamins for the Continental Army, and here the first set of regulations was written by Kazimierz Pulaski in 1777-78. He proposed new weapons, units and saddles, and elaborated on the tactics of cavalry and its role in an army. It was a few months before Baron Friedrich von Steuben wrote his regulations for infantry. If it had not been for his conflict with Washington, probably Steuben's role would have been played by Thomas Conway who was recommended by Silas Deane for his experience in training and disciplining troops. It should be noted that training of cavalry is more complicated than the training of infantry-men, for not only has the man to be schooled but his beast as well. He has to know how to take care of his horse and also how to use a broader variety of weapons, such as saber, pistols, carbine and lance. In civilian life he was a tailor, shoemaker, farmer or even seaman.

To digress about Steuben's training, it remains a puzzle for me how such beneficial and invigorating responses could be achieved by him from exhausted survivors of the grand army after the Valley Forge camp or with new recruits by the introduction of Prussian drill on men known for their independence of spirit, Indian tactics, etc. Also why did the Hessians so well trained in this drill, not have any spectacular victories in America?

While, no doubt, engaged in organizing the cavalry, its training and writing the regulations, Pulaski took part in such routine military tasks as skirmishing, foraging and patrolling which went on while Washington was hovering around Philadelphia and his main camp was moving pendulum-like between Whitpain and Whitemarsh. On November 12th Pulaski's name was mentioned as being in an action. Near Whitemarsh leading a troop of dragoons he encountered a British detachment, killed five soldiers and took two prisoners. The American losses were one killed and two captured. (*William Irvine Papers*, I, 101, Hist. Soc. of Penn.)

On the previous day, Captain Leigh with 16 dragoons attacked the British and captured 14, and about the same time a large troop of American cavalry attacked the British lines but was repulsed (H.H. Peckham, *The Toll of Independence*, 1974). There is also a November report about a patrol of cavalry under Major Gwyn retreating into Frankford in great confusion because Pulaski with a troop of cavalry had attacked them from the front and rear. They spread panic among the British troops there, who evacuated Frankford and made for Philadelphia. (Lossing, op. cit. vol. II, p. 42)

Further on I detail the whole of Pulaski's letters, setting forth the set of cavalry regulations. They should be read in consecutive order and they are of tremendous value for any military historian. Had the ideas there stated been promulgated and effectuated, an effective and disciplined cavalry force might have resulted. Such an effective cavalry force, soundly and tactically used, could have shortened considerably the war.

I do not know to what extent Pulaski was assisted in writing by Michael De Kovatch. It should also be noted that because of the crushed ambitions of de Balme, Pulaski had lost a man who could have been of the greatest assistance to him, if we are to believe Deane's recommendation.

I took my information concerning Kovatch's career prior to his getting a commission from Ed Dybicz's article in *Times Herald*, Norristown.

Michael de Kovatch accompanied Pulaski's cavalry at Swedesford, Gulph Mills, Valley Forge and then Pulaski's Legion. He was born in 1724 in Karczag, in Hungary, and said in his letter (Library of Philosophical Society, Philadelphia): ..."I am a free man and Hungarian. I was trained in the Royal Prussian Army and raised from the lowest rank to the dignity of a captain of the Hussars, not so much by luck and the mercy of choice than by the most diligent self-discipline and the virtue of my arms...The dangers and bloodshed of a great many campaigns taught me how to mould a soldier..."

In January 1778, Washington had agreed that Kovatch would be an exercise master of Dragoons (Steuben of Cavalry). His name is in Heitman's Register as a member of Pulaski's Legion.

My inquiry at the Military Service Records, National Archives (R50506) brought no record of his service, though his existence is documented well enough. (Ef. Emil Lengyel, *Americans from Hungary*, Lippincott, 1948.)on is not proof of non-existence.

About Kovatch, Joseph Johnson, the author of *Traditions and Reminiscences of the American Revolution*, Charleston, 1851, says: "...the second in command (Pulaski's Legion), a very experienced able officer...was Prussian by birth and had distinguished himself in the army of Frederic the Great of Prussia, from whose own hands he received a complimentary badge of honor..." (p.218-19).

However, Kovatch's influence on the following set of regulations still remains a matter for conjecture.

On November 23, 1777, Pulaski sent the following "Memorial relative to the Cavalry" to Washington:

My General:

The desire which I have of fulfilling my Duty, leads me to make frequent representations to Your Excellency of matters which regard the Service of the Cavalry.

What follows is my opinion, and if I am so happy as to find it agreeable to Your Excellency's Views, it will be necessary to carry my plan into execution as soon as possible.

As in all appearances it will be late before we retire to Winter Quarters I would have a detachment formed from the Whole Cavalry, composed of one Major, 2 Captains, 2 Lieutenants - 1 Cornet - 4 Serjeants - 10 Corporals and 120 Dragoons. The Remainder with the Colonels should repair to Winter Quarters at the place where each Regiment was formed and there the Colonels will endeavour to procure Recruits train them, and be ready against the beginning of April to repair wherever they shall be order'd to assemble. There they will gain some knowledge of the System formed by the most essential Manouvres.

When the whole Army enters into Winter Quarters the half of the remaining Cavalry may be dismissed to join the respective Regiments, the other half composed of Non Commissioned Officers and Dragoons may form the Bosnique armed with Lances - which I Undertake to train and perfect in their Exercise. The Augmentation of the Horses is likewise necessary. I spoke of it in a preceding note.

I would wish to form a Squadron of Bosniques consisting of 120 men. I answer for their Ability. The Form of this squadron should be - 2 Captains of which I desire to be the first, 2 Lieutenants - 1 Ensign -1 Adjutant - 1 Surgeon Major and 1 QuarterMaster - 2 Serjeants. 10 Corporals - 2 Trumpeters - 1 Farrier - 1 Sadler - 120 Bosniques. And as the Number of Cavalry even then would not be sufficient to fulfill all the Duties required in a large Army, I would propose to have 200 Militia men mounted who might serve ex-

tremely well for the less important Duties, and be a very considerable Relief to the Cavalry.

There is an intelligent Officer in the Horse Service who disgusted
by the Irregulities prevailing in his Regiment has asked for his dismission -his name is Henry Belhen his Office Adjutant of Moylens
Regiment - it would be a loss to the Cavalry if he should quit the
Service. I believe he might be retained by giving him the Commission of second Captain and continuing his pay as Adjutant he will remain with me in the mean time - as all our Officers need Instruction
he might be employ'd by me in seeing the Manouvres executed and
in exercising the Cavalry. There should be three other adjutants of
different ranks, who being out of the lines and having no concurrence with the pretensions of the others may be made very useful to
the Service.

I have repeat my Prayer that a speedy Decision may be had on
these points, as they respect the welfare of a Corps upon which the
Fate perhaps of the whole Army depends. (*Letters to Washington*, vol.
20, 1777, p.37)

December, 1777

Sir,

I make no doubt but your Excellency is acquainted with the present ineffective state of the cavalry. In this situation it cannot be appropriated to any other service than that of orderlies, or
reconnoitring the enemy's lines, which your Excellency must be persuaded is not the only service expected from a corps, which, when
on a proper footing, is so very formidable. Although it is the opinion
of many, that, from the construction of the country, the cavalry cannot act to advantage, your Excellency must be too well acquainted
with the many instances wherein the cavalry have been decisively
serviceable, to be of this opinion, and not acknowledge that this
corps has more than once completed victories. To this end I would
wish to discipline the cavalry; and I flatter myself by next campaign
to render it essentially serviceable.

What has greatly contributed to the present weak state of the cavalry was the frequent detachments ordered to the suite of general
and other officers, while a Colonel commanded, which were appropriated to every use, and the horses drove at the discretion of the dragoons.

The confidence, with which the Congress and your Excellency
have honored me, is a sure guaranty to the zeal I shall ever act with,
in the service of the United States. But, notwithstanding my great
desire of rendering the cavalry as useful as its first institution in-

tended, I find it impracticable, seeing it is deficient in its principal requisitions; my reflections on which, I have judged necessary to communicate to your Excellency, as a proof of my attachment to the good of the service, and desire of executing your Excellency's designs; hoping for an opportunity of deserving the favor conferred on me by your Excellency.

ARTICLE I. It is absolutely necessary, that the cavalry have a Master of Exercise, who should instruct the commissioned and non-commissioned officers in the rules of service, as, having the command, I am obliged to act with precaution; but this officer, actuated by different motives, would remove the bad habits and correct the defects of the superior officers. There is an officer now in this country, whose name is Kowacz. I know him to have served with reputation in the Prussian service, and assure your Excellency that he is every way equal to this undertaking.

II. That twenty-four dragoons be drafted from the different regiments to form a separate corps, who shall be taught the use of the pike or lance, of which two or three days will render them masters. For this purpose I must have chosen men.

III. A Quartermaster-General to the cavalry is essentially necessary to procure winter-quarters, stables, and provender, also to provide arms, accoutrements, and clothing. An intelligent officer, acquainted with the cavalry, should be chosen for this purpose. I would recommend to your Excellency, Major Blackden of Colonel Sheldon's regiment, a gentleman who has displayed his knowledge in the equipment of said regiment, and whom I think sufficiently qualified to merit this trust.

IV. It is full time the Quartermaster-General was sent to the place assigned for winter-quarters, in order to provide magazines, that the cavalry may be kept embodied and conveniently exercised and disciplined. The horse service has ever been respected. One third of the cavalry is generally on duty, often the whole. When it returns to camp, it should draw provision, and cook it agreeably to orders; but their full allowance is seldom granted. This I know by experience, being the worse served of any General in the service. To prevent this evil, a Commissary should be appointed to the cavalry. The cavalry in an army generally forms a separate division, and has greater privileges than the infantry, which the honor of the service exacts; but here I find it is the contrary. Not that I aim at a superiority over the rest of the army, but am desirous of having justice done the corps I command. It is my duty. For my own part I wish to be subject to your Excellency's order only, agreeably to my request upon entering the service, which is the limit of my ambition.

—PULASKI

(Jared Sparks's, "Correspondence of the American Revolution," *Letters to Washington*, p.53, et. seq.)

19 December, 1777

SIR, In my preceding representations, I have been particular respecting the present state of the cavalry, and the means by which it may be augmented and completed; but, on this head, I must necessarily know your Excellency's determination. The advantages that would arise from a superiority in cavalry are too obvious to be unnoticed. It may be further observed that, during this war, the country will daily become more open and clear of woods and fences, and consequently better adapted to the manoeuvres and service of the cavalry.

While we are superior in cavalry, the enemy will not dare to extend their force, and, notwithstanding we act on the defensive, we shall have many opportunitys of attacking and destroying the enemy by degrees, whereas if they have it in their power to augment their Cavalry and we suffer ours to diminish and dwindle away, It may happen that the loss of a Battle will terminate in our total Defeat. Our army once dispersed and persued by their horse will never be able to rally, thus our retreat may only be cut off, our baggage lost, and principal officers taken, and many other events occurr not less Fatal.

Your Excellency must be too much Occupyed to take Cognizance of the detail of every department-a Workman requires proper tools to Carry on his business, and if he does not use them in their place he can never be perfect. Your Excellency is undoubtedly acquainted with yours, therefore a person possessing your confidence and properly authorized is essentially necessary to answer decisively Such proposals as I have made in my late representations respecting the Cavalry.

I must not omit to mention here the dissatisfaction you have expressed at my seemingly inattention to your orders. Your Excellency may be assured that the good of the Service is my constant Study but the Weak State of the Corps I Command renders it impossible to perform every Service required. Nay my reputation is exposed as being an entire stranger in the country the least accident would suffice to injure me but notwithstanding, I cannot avoid hazarding every thing thats valuable in life.

—C. PULASKI, Genl. of Cavalry

If you think that my request is important and Right, and that you Would before expect the Resolution of Congress; I would be glad to be the bearer of Your letters to Congress. I hope to obtain sooner by that way their Resolved as we want so many things there is not time to be lost."

(J. Sparks's, "Correspondence of the American Revolution," *Letters to Washington*, p.57–58)

The following estimate and requisition for the Corps of Cavalry was endorsed on 19 December 1777.

1st. Let all detachments be called in, and a General review of the Whole Horse Arms and Accoutrements be appointed, and the Adjutant General or Majr of Brigade inspect into the state and Condition of the Horses and Arms. A Qur Mastr Genl into that of the Accoutrements. Let this review be continued from day to day until an exact return can be taken under the inspection of the Genl and Col's of the Condition of the Cavalry.

2nd. This being done let all the Horses to be branded, numbered and sized, the men also be numbered and sized, and all their Arms and accoutrements have No of the Regt troops and Man.

3rd. Let the Regts be divided into Squadrons, the Squadrons into Troops and let the troops into Squads.

4th. Let it be ascertained what number of men detached constitute such a command, and when any such number of men is detached from the whole or a Single Regt let the Brigade Major or the adjutant be obliged to keep an exact Roster; and detach every officer on Tour according to the strength of the Command.

5th. Let no Party of those be detachd except by order of the Commander in Chief, or the Commander of a division Wing of the Army; and that through the Order of the Genl of Horse or in his absence the commanding officer of horse present when the Brigade Majr or orderly adjutt shd keep a regular detail of the Parties detached, the service they go on, and be aswerable to the commander of Horse, that he be regularly apprized of the time for their detail.

6th. That all Guards and Pickets be relieved every 24 hours if within five miles, or every 48 if within ten and above five, and every four days if within twenty and above ten.

7th. That all Parties be considered as relieved when they return to the Regt of Corps and go on from that time in Ro with the others but if it shd be necessary to keep out flying partys that they be relieved once a week, and that the Officer commanding them before the time expires send an orderly man to Md Quars of Cavalry with information where he is in order to his being relieved.

8th. That when the Cavalry are not divided into Wings, but remain in one body, that a Picket from the whole be regularly mounted every day in the front of the Army, for relieving the Videttes, Patrolls &c. and that the brigade Majr of the day deliver to the officer of the Picket of those in writing the names of the posts to be relieved and a description of the situation and route.

9th. That besides the Picket for relieving Videts and Patrolls There shall be a certain proportion of the whole for doing the incidental duty, of carrying intelligence, reconnoitring parties, &c.

10th. When the Horse are divided on the Wings the Picket for each Wing and incidental Guards, to mount in front of their recruitive wing and be under the command of the officer commanding the Horse of their respective wing who shall appoint an officer of the day. Adjutant of the day &c and conduct the detail as above. The commanding officer of the Horse of each Wing to order out such Patrolls, and post such Videttes as the Genl officer of the Wing shall think proper, or he may find necessary. Receive and convey intelligence to and from the commander in Chief, &c.

11th. That All the Horse for Picket be warned the day before they mount, and that every Col. be obliged to see that the men, have at least one days Provision cooked and forage for one day, or assign the reason to the Genl of Horse through the Brigade Majr or the commanr of Horse through the Adjutt of the day, when the officer through whose neglect it happend shd be immediately called to acct and dealt with according to the nature of the offence.

12th. That Such Horses as are found unfit for Service be weekly reported, sold, or sent to recruit, and others purchased in Lieu of such as are beyond recovery for Service, and that some person be appointed to purchase Horses for the use of the dismounted Dragoons in Lieu of those that are Cast.

That Armorers and Saddlers be provided for the Horses, to keep their Arms and accoutrements in order.

On February 3, 1778, Pulaski sent again his Regulations for Cavalry to Washington as if wanting to remind him of the matter. The four articles at the end of the letter are repetitions of those from 19 December 1777. Pulaski again stresses his desire and conditions of service. Here is the beginning of his letter as per Sparks's *Correspondence of the American Revolution*:

His Excellency General Washington: I make no doubt but your Excellency is acquainted with the present ineffective state of the Cavalry. In this situation it cannot be appropriated to any other service than that of orderlys or reconnoitering the enemy's lines, which your Excellency must be persuaded is not the only service expected from a corps when a proper footing is so very formidable. Although it is the opinion of many that from the construction of the country the Cavalry cannot aid to advantage, Your Excellency must be too well acquainted with the many instances wherein the Cavalry have been decisively serviceable to be of this opinion and not acknowledge that this corps has more than once compleated victorys. To this end I would wish to discipline the Cavalry and flatter myself by next campaign to render it essentially serviceable. What has greatly contributed to the present weak state of the Cavalry was the frequent detachments order'd to the suite of general and other officers, while a Colo commanded, which were appropriated to every one and the horses drove at the discretion of the dragoons. The confidence with which the Congress and your Excellence have honored me are sure guaranties to the zeal I shall ever act with in the service of the United States, but notwithstanding my great desire of rendering the Cavalry so useful as its first constitutions intended I find it impracticable seeing that it is deficient in its principal requisitions, my reflections on which I have judged necessary to communicate to your Excellency as proof of my attachement to the good of the service and desire of executing your Excellency's designs hoping for opportunity of deserving the favor conferred upon me by your Excellency...

However, not all Pulaski's proposals and letters were without influence. Some echo of his correspondence can be seen in the following letter of Washington's to the Committee of Congress with the Army (Francis, Dana, Joseph Reed, Nathaniel Folsom, Charles Carrol and Timothy Pickering), dated January 29, 1778. (W.W.10, p. 362). However, in view of the desperate difficulties of the Commander of the Horse, the whole essay seems to be an exercise in futility, especially the part about the composition of officers and cavalrymen.

The benefits arising from a superiority in horse, are obvious to those who have experienced them. Independent of such as you may derive from it in the field of action, it enables you, very materially, to controul the inferior and subordinate motions of an enemy, and to impede their knowledge of what you are doing, while it gives you every advantage of superior intelligence and, consequently, both facilitates your enterprizes against them and obstructs theirs against you. In a defensive war as in our case it is peculiarly desirable; because it affords great protection to the country, and is a barrier to those inroads and depradations upon the inhabitants, which are inevitable when the superiority lies on the side of the invaders. The enemy fully sensible of the advantage are taking all the pains in their power, to acquire an ascendency in this respect, to defeat which, I would propose an augmentation of our cavalry, by adding a lieutenant, serjeant and corporal and twenty two privates to each troop. The establishment will then be as follows,

1 Colonel
1 Lt. Colonel
1 Major
6 Captains
12 lieutenants   All as usual except 6 additional lieutenants
6 Cornets
1 Adjutant
1 Qur Master
1 Sadler
6 farriers
6 Qur Master serjeants
12 serjeants
30 corporals
6 Trumpeters
324 privates

There are and will continue four regiments of cavalry, which composing a brigade, will require a Brigadier, Brigade-Major, Quarter master, Commissary and forage Master as usual. The Men for this service can easily be gotten: the providing horses and accoutrements will be found to suffer some difficulty, yet will not be impracticable. The procuring horses should be undertaken by judicious officers from each regiment, well skilled in them; and conducted, in such a manner as to occasion no interference with each other. Let Sheldon's purchases be confined to the Eastward of the North River; Moylan's between the North River and Susquehannah; Baylor's between Susquehannah and James River; and Blands to the Southward of that. The number of horses to be purchased by each, ought to be determined; and an average price limited, disclosed only to the purchaser, with a strict injunction to conceal it as much as possible; because, if once generally known, sellers would take advantages of it, and part with none under the limitation. The accoutrements to be provided in the same districts, and by the same persons; but as some of these districts abound more in manufacturers than others, all that can be engaged in each, in a certain stipulated time, ought to be secured, in order that the overplus, in one part, may supply the deficiency in another. And as these articles may be imported cheaper, and better, in quality, than they can be made here, I would advise that at least, fifteen hundred sets should be sent for to France, with directions to divide them in small parcels, and embark them in different vessels that we may have a probability of getting at least a part, and not run the risk of sustaining a total loss and disappointment, by adventuring the whole in one bottom."

Before Pulaski moved with the army to its winter quarters he most probably took part in the cavalry actions on November 21st when a large troop of American cavalry attacked the British but were driven off with loss.

He also took part in the "almost Battle of Whitemarsh," when General Howe left Philadelphia and marched ahead of a strong army to the entrenched American camp, and similarly to the Middlebrook affair in Brunswick where he decided that the place was invulnerable and returned to Philadelphia, thus ending the British campaign of 1777 there.

Washington, however, did not know that his position was too strong to be attacked and, expecting the battle, he drew two diagrams (W.W.10, p. 138).

On the first of them no cavalry is mentioned. On the second Sheldon and Moylan are on the left wing and Bland and Baylor are on the right one. Their task was "to watch (by small detachments) the movements of the enemy, give intelligence thereof and see that the enemy do not gain our flanks without their knowledge." Washington still has difficulty seeing cavalry as a striking, tactical force. W. Kozlowski quotes a fragment of a letter in the possession of the Historical Society of New York, from Armand de La Roueried to Washington who said that when the enemy attacked the American left wing he (Armand) started the action with a small troop of artillery until Pulaski arrived and took command.

In the *History of Philadelphia*, vol. I, p. 365, the following is written about Pulaski's activities around Philadelphia:

> ...Simcoe's Rangers patrolling the Frankford Road to enable the Buck County farmers to come in with their products had found plenty of skirmishing to do...But the Americans still prevented the market people coming down Frankford and often Pulaski's light horse beat up Simcoe's quarter in Kensington on the south of the city. Greene, with Potter and McDougall, kept equally close watch.
>
> As to the atmosphere of those times the correspondence on the subject of supplies for the British Army in Philadelphia carried on be-

tween Washington and John Lacey, a general in the Pennsylvania militia, is enlightening. (H. Niles, *Principles and Acts of the Revolution in America*, p.333 and W.W. vol. 10).

Thus on January 23rd Washington to John Lacey:

...I am well informed that many persons, under pretence of furnishing the inhabitants of Germantown and near the enemy's line, afford immense supplies to Philadelphia markets, a conduct highly prejudicial to us and contrary to every order, It is therefore become proper to make an example of some guilty one, that the rest may be sensible of a like Fate should they persist. This I am determined to put into execution, and request that when a suitable object falls into your hands, you will send him here, with the witnesses, or let me know his name, when you shall have a power to try, and if found guilty to execute; this you'll make known to the people that they may again have warning...

Lacey's order to his scouting parties, March 9, 1778:

if your parties should meet with any people going to market, or any persons whatever going to the city, and they endeavour to make their escape, you will order your men to fire upon the villains. You will leave such on the roads-their bodies and their marketing lying together. This I wish to execute on the first offenders you meet that they may be a warning to others.

Washington to Lacey from Valley Forge 20th March:

Sunday next being the time on which the Quakers hold one of their general meetings, a number of that society will be probably attempting to go into Philadelphia. This is an intercourse that we should by all means endeavour to interrupt, as the plans settled at these meetings are of the most pernicious tendency. I would therefore have you dispose of your parties in such a manner as will most probably fall in with these people, and if they should, and any of them should be mounted upon horses fit for draft or the service of light dragoons, I desire they may be taken from them, and sent over to the quartermaster-general...

This meant that parties of Light Horse and those soldiers who had clothes and shoes were being sent out to bring food for their starving comrades. Washington reluctantly used his dictatorial powers and ordered the requisition of grain, not distinguishing, it seems, between the well and badly affected whose mental attitudes, no doubt, were similar to that of the Russian and Ukrainian peasants when Bolsheviks requisitioned grain necessary to keep their revolution going.

***

The literature on Valley Forge is large and generally satisfactory, especially for those historians who read for facts. I especially recommend Dr. Waldo's journal in PMH 21.

Though the fortification of Valley Forge, built by Louis Duportail, impressed Howe so much that he judged it imprudent to attack it, it is described by Captain Thomas Anburey, who passed through the valley on his way to a POW camp in Virginia, after the Saratoga Convention was broken as:

> This camp was by no means difficult of access, for the right was attainable and in one part of the front the ascent was scarcely to be perceived. This is the only instance I ever saw of the Americans' defences having such slight work, these being such as a six-pounder could easily have battered down. The ditches were no more than three feet deep, and so narrow that a drum-boy might with ease leap over. (Thomas Anburey, *Travels*, p. 294).

Regardless of the strength of the fortifications, the soldiers were not strong enough to man them. For instance on December 22nd, Washington had received an intelligence that a body of enemy was about to cross the Schuylkill, but the division ordered to march and meet them was not able to move out. They had no shoes and no provisions, even for a short field operation. About that time some 2,800 men were unfit for duty.

The grand army arrived at the now famous Valley Forge on December 20, 1777. There is a small controversy as to where and with whom Pulaski stayed during his sojourn at that place.

According to an historian, Edward Pinkowski, Pulaski stayed with John Beaver, a fifty-five-year-old German immigrant and Quaker. (Edward Pinkowski, *Washington Officers Slept Here*, 1953, p.67 et.seq.)

There is a tragic story associated with his homestead. His son, Devault Beaver, was robbed by some soldiers. The youth walked across the street to the headquarters of General Anthony Wayne and complained. What he heard in answer sounded to him like "Shoot'em if they do not remain away."

The next morning Devault Beaver heard suspicious noises in the barn. He went to check it and discovered a soldier milking a cow, so young Beaver shot the culprit. He was tried by a court-martial and brought witnesses, including Wayne, to prove that he had orders to shoot intruders. Beaver was fined 1,000 bushels of threshed wheat.

Thus the man who wanted a drink of milk brought by his death food to his friends.

Another historian, Joseph Borkowski, stated that Pulaski was with General Enoch Poor (Joseph Borkowski, *Prominent Polish Pioneers*, Polish Falcons, 1975, p.32)

According to the maps of the camp site the two places seem to be different. The place given by Pinkowski is a bit closer to the stables.

I had inquired from the two distinguished authors, and Mr. Borkowski was kind enough to give me as his source a letter from the Valley Forge State Park Commission, dated July 9, 1971, which indicated that Pulaski had no private quarters but was staying with Poor. Mr. Pinkowski also informed me that Pulaski visited Valley Forge a few times, staying probably with Poor and other officers.

Writes Mr. Pinkowski..."On one occasion Steuben invited Pulaski to stay with him and his staff in his quarters, the one now known as Steuben's Quarters, which I had much to do with..." (A letter to the author).

According to Burk, Pulaski in Valley Forge became friends with Jedediah Huntington. On the subject of Pulaski's stay in that place, Ed Dybicz gives interesting information (*Times Herald*, Norristown, 10,29,75): "Locally the dashing Pulaski's exploits are traced to Valley Forge, Upper Merion, Swedesford, Germantown, Skippack, Plymouth, Whitemarsh, Tredyffrin, Towamencin, Lower Salford, the Norritons..."

Dybicz also wrote that Professor H.W. Kriebel, who had been interested in the Schwekfelder Church, made a discovery in 1927 of a letter written by Rosina Hoffman. The letter was in Perkiomen school library and it tells of Pulaski and some of his soldiers remaining for several days in the home of Balzer Hoffman, near his church in Salford in the vicinity of Mainland and Landsdale.

Schwenckfelders took their name from the Silesian nobleman Caspar Schwenckfelder, a religious reformer. This faith had adherents in Europe, some in Poland and Silesia.

It is possible that in the home of Hoffman, Pulaski could find hospitable welcome and perhaps understandable language. His later contacts with the Moravians show that he had been tired of being treated as an enemy by the local population, Whigs and Loyalists alike.

In Poland there were Loyalists (Adherents), Confederates, Russians and Neutralists, but Pulaski knew where he stood. There was always a considerable part of the population which considered him a hero and shared his ideas of patriotism. Here he was a stranger in a foreign revolution.

Pulaski's stay at Valley Forge was brief as on December 31, 1777, he received the following instruction:

You are to march the body of the Cavalry into Winter Quarters at Trenton, where you are to take the most effectual means for putting both men and horses in condition to act with vigour in the ensuing Campaign. Notwithstanding your distance from the Enemy and the apparent improbability of their forming any Enterprise against you, some degree of vigilance will be necessary to secure your Quarters from Surprise; this may be effected by such small patroles as will not make the Tour of duty come round too frequently, and break in too much upon the Repose of the men and horses, which is so essential to reestablishing them; the same Patroles may likewise be a safeguard to the Shipping laid up at Borden Town.

After you are well settled in Quarters, frequent Opportunities, in favorable Weather, are to be taken of perfecting the Cavalry in the most useful manoeuvres, even a Series of bad weather will not prove a total bar to the instruction of the men and horses, as they may at such times, perform the ordinary exercises of the Riding School, a proper house for which purpose you will provide immediately upon your arrival at Trenton.

This kind of discipline will not occasion any greater exercise than is conducive to the health of both men and horses.

The men are to keep their Arms in the best Order, and the Sadlers to keep the Saddles and Bridles in constant Repair; if any Regiment be without a Sadler the Commanding Officer of it is to procure one with proper Tools, upon the best Terms he can make.

The Colonels are commissioned to provide their Regiments with Cloathing and Accoutrements. All that can be done with respect to these Articles under your eye, is that the Officers require their men to make the best of what they have, by repairs.

You will have sufficient time for training a Troop of Lancemen, and the Lances may be made according to your directions on the spot. No pains should be spared to inspire the men with an affection for their horses, and make them perfect in the management of them. These important ends can only be gained by great attention and assiduity in the Officers. You must therefore strictly prohibit all Wandering from Quarters. (W.W. 10, p. 234)

It is intriguing to note that in this letter Pulaski is treated as if he were a subaltern instead of a general famous throughout Europe. He is instructed about the basics in cavalry and military service, and also warned about overfatiguing men and horses, which could only mean that Pulaski's zeal in training and maneuvering had already been noticed, though evidently not as praiseworthy as that of Steuben's.

The matter of introducing lances of the Polish cavalry is also mentioned.

The other dragoon officers were ordered to retire from their regiments to get horses, accoutrements and recruits for the next campaign. The equipment of dragoons was very expensive and desertions were to be avoided. They were to receive none but natives of the country or foreigners of approved fidelity in service or those who were particularly recommended.

From Trenton, Pulaski sent the following report to Washington dated January 9, 1778:

> I arrived here yesterday with the Cavalry where I expected to have found forage sufficient to subsist the Cavalry, at least for a few days, my Brigade forage master had been informed by Colo Biddle that such provision was made and that he would have nothing more to do than Issue the same, but, so farr to the contrary there was not a Load of Hay in Town. With the greatest difficulty we have been enabled to put our heads under Cover. I applied to the civil magistrates for directions relative to the forming a magazine, in the meanwhile the Horses must subsist. I am therefore obliged to divide them in several squads and send them out about two miles in the rear of the Town, untill the necessary provisions both for forage and Quarters can be made. It will be impossible for me to Quarter the Cavalry in this place unless the Galley men are removed, but they say they have an order from the Governor and Council to remain here and having prior possession, think they are entitled to hold it. I wait your Excellencys positive order in what manner to proceed and if in this Case, I must execute my first orders, It will be necessary the Galley men should receive orders to evacuate the Town, I have the honour to assure your Excelly that the Cavalry is in want of every article. It must be exercised and taught the service from the Colo to the private. Colo Kolatch is a man of great merit and deserves the Charge of Master of Exercises; he's an officer worthy of research and exclusive of a thorough knowledge of his abilities request his being employed by your Excelly. I can recommend him ans assure your Excelly will never have reason to repent your confidence in him, if this proposal should be agreeable to your Excelly, the sooner I am informed the better as he will be of infinite service to the Cavalry this winter in Quarters.
>
> I have met with an armourer who lives at Eastown, he undertakes

to furnish me with pikes, pistols, Carbines, &c., if your Excelly approves of him the Qr Mr General will take your orders on that head.

There are some excellent horses in this Country and as Colo Luterloh has received orders to press all horses fit for the service he may procure a number here, but this must not be delayed as I am informed many persons buy them for the use of the enemy."

(Jared Sparks, *Letters to Washington*, Boston, 1853, p. 64).

To which Washington answered by letter on January 14, 1778. There is a characteristic note of distrust of foreigners in connection with Kovatch, the Steuben of Cavalry.

Your Letter of the 9th Instant was delivered to me yesterday, and I immediately acquainted the Forage Master General with such parts of it as related to his Department. If proper Magazines for the subsistence of the Cavalry cannot be formed at Trenton, this is an insurmountable obstacle to their quartering there, and they must of necessity be removed to Flemingtown or some other convenient place in that neighborhood, where the proper supplies can be obtained. But if the only objection to Trenton, be a little difficulty that may at first occur, in procuring the most desirable Quarters for the Officers and Men, I would not have any time lost in seeking farther, the Barracks and the Town together will certainly furnish ample Quarters for the Galley Men and the Cavalry. The latter may with more propriety be billeted on the Inhabitants, in order to have their Horses immediately under their eye.

As so much has been said of the Character and abilities of Mr Crovatch, I have no objection to his being engaged in the capacity of Exercise Master for a few Months; at the same time I must caution you against a fondness for introducing foreigners into the Service. Their ignorance of the Language of the Country and of the genius and manners of the people, frequently occasion difficulties and disgusts which we should not run the risque of, unless it be in favour of extraordinary Talents and good Qualities. I shall give orders to the Quarter Master to employ the Armourer at Easton for the Service of the Cavalry, provided he has not been previously engaged in any other way, by the Commissary of Military Stores.[36]

I must postpone any decision with respects the Horses, until the arrival of the Committee of Congress, as I am in daily expectation of those Gentlemen. I hope you will not be long kept in suspense, if you can in the mean time, engage the Owners to keep their Horses on the spot, you will take every proper step for that purpose. I have no objection to your making Trial of the abilities of Mr Bedkin as

Brigade Major for the present; it will soon be discovered whether he is equal to the office. (W.W.10, p. 304.)

A. Hoyt Bill in *New Jersey and the Revolutionary War* (Princeton, N.J. 1964, p. 64) wrote about Pulaski in Trenton: "The town was soon further overcrowded by the arrival of the light cavalry that, owing to dearth of forage near at hand, Washington sent over from Valley Forge. Under the command of Casimir Pulaski, their scouting had been invaluable in the marches that followed battle at Chadds Ford, and they were now useful in keeping the country around Trenton clear of the gangs of Tories and outlaws that infested the Jersey side of the Delaware to the southward."

On his arrival at Trenton, Pulaski, realizing that the public relations are part of generalship, published the following proclamation in the *New Jersey Gazette*, (vol. 1, no. 8, Jan. 21, 1778):

To the Magistrates in Trenton,

Gentlemen-I have the honour to acquaint you, that having the command of a corps, which, from the fatigues of a laborious campaign, and the severity of the season, is under the necessity of taking shelter to recruit and re-establish itself in your State, am desirous of guarding against any attempts of the enemy which might bring distress upon the good people of this town and its neighbourhood, as you must undoubtedly be sensible that the seat of war is ever exposed to the fury and depredations of the enemy. Nothing on my part shall be neglected to prevent such evils; but all my vigilance may not suffice, without the assistance of the inhabitants, to render any quarters secure: I therefore request of you gentlemen, and the good people of this town, to give me the earliest intelligence of any movement of the enemy you may discovr towards this quarter, when, upon all such occasions, I shall take the most efficacious measures to exempt the inhabitants of this town from falling victims to the rage of a desperate and cruel enemy, and convince the publick that the zeal of the troops I command, will prove the justice of those inestimable rights they defend. I further request you will use your endeavours to procure me every convenience necessary for the subsistence of my troops while they occupy this post, in order that I may be enabled to make head against any incursions of the enemy. I expect that your patriotism will inspire you with the diligence and activity requisite to give satisfaction to those men, who from motives of honour, sacrifice themselves to a cause so righteous as that of liberty. These my requests may, if you judge necessary, be printed and handed to the inhabitants of this neighbourhood.

I have the honour to be, with respect, Gentlemen, your most obedient humble servant, C. PULASKI, Gen. of Cavalry."

Pulaski's difficulties with quartering and the system of favoritism and nepotism may be seen in an answer written to a young girl at Mrs. Roger's boarding school, who happened to be Nancy Shippen, daughter of Dr. William Shippen, the director-general of Continental hospitals: "...I have spoken to Mr. Barclay about Genl. Pulaski and am in hope no more troops or horses will be quartered on Mrs. Roger..." (Nancy Shippen, *Her Journal Book*, edited and compiled by Ethel Armes, Benjamin Blom, N.Y. 1968, p. 63)

Pulaski's efforts in Trenton were appreciated at least by the Governor of New Jersey, William Livingston, as it was indicated in Washington's polite acknowledgments as follows:

> I am pleased with the favourable account which you give of Count Pulaski's Conduct while at Trenton. He is a Gentleman of great activity and unquestionable bravery, and only wants a fuller knowledge of our language and Customs, to make him a valuable Officer. (W.W. 11, p. 80)

Previously, Pulaski had requested Jersey troops of horse to volunteer their services to the Continental Army. Livingston showed his appreciation to the Commander of Horse, saying that such a practice would be invaluable to his troops in acquiring skill and experience, which they could afterwards introduce into other squadrons. However, at the most, he could spare only one troop.

Meanwhile, Pulaski, who seems to be as much a man of the pen as of the saber, wrote still another of his numerous letters (Letters, MSS CC, vol. 21, folio 161). But before reading this letter one should know more of the epoch. In those times the use of alcohol and its appreciation was much more common than today. It was a popular way of purifying the intestines and almost a staple in the diet.

It was shortly before the Revolution that a young Quaker by the name of Jacob Lindley remarked at a meeting in Philadelphia that he was oppressed with the odor of rum coming from the breath of those who sat close to him. (Thomas Fleming, America 1776, *Readers Digest*, July 1976). Even school boys and students had beer and liquors included in their board. The prosperity of New England in a great measure was built on the rum trade. In the army in bad weather the soldiers received a half gill of rum and were cautioned against drinking new cider and stream water. (C.K. Bolton, *Private Soldier under Washington*, 1902, p.176).

Dr. Albigence Waldo's *Diary* is full of references to alcohol or its lack. And that he considered it to be a kind of medicine is evidenced by his note of January 3, 1778: "Fresh beef and flour make me perfectly sick, especially as we have no spirits to drink with it..."

It is noteworthy that Pulaski wanted to almost make a commando troop of the cavalry remaining in Trenton. His stressing of his good relations with Bland's officers is quite intriguing. Did he mean Theodoric Bland as well, for he was the officer who presided over the court which disgusted Pulaski by its acquittal of Moylan?

My General-

I have received your orders dated 14th Jany respecting quarters at Flemingtown. Previous to removing from hence I was desirous of informing myself whether this place might not be made suitable for us, but every one agrees that neither forage nor any other necessaries can be had in sufficient quantities for our use-on this account I am obliged to give Your Excellency notice that the Cavalry cannot otherwise be reestablished than by distributing it among the different houses in the rear of Penny Town 8 miles distant from hence. For my own part I intend to remain at Trenton, with a detachment from the whole Corps which cannot be very considerable because the men that I keep with me must be well armed and this is not the case with many. I hope in time to procure a sufficiency of forage to subsist 120 horse, if your Excellency approves of this step I will remain, otherwise receive new orders. I am exceedingly uneasy at not being able to establish with equal facility proper measures for regulating the Cavalry. I am employed in composing a Set of Regulations which I intend to send to you in a little time-if they are approved, I will have them printed and distributed among the Officers. It is almost needless to mention to you that I experience great difficulty in remedying different abuses. Two Dragoons of Moylens Regiment were wanting in respect to their officer call'd Tacssi, who arrested them and conducted them to his Ouarters; one of them attempting to come to me, the Officer seized the Sentry's Sword and gave the Dragoon two blows, which have maimed him. I have arrested the Officer for his passion and particularly because he used the Sentinel Sword, and I have imprisoned the two Dragoons. As I have reason to complain of the ill-will of the rest of the Officers, cannot but praise those of Blands Regiment who conduct themselves with the greatest propriety.

I would entreat Your Excellency to permit me to propose Capt Craig the Command of the Lance-men, he might be replaced by some other Officer as for instance by Capt Smith. There are many things here of which the Cavalry are in want, but the workmen raise the prices too much, I do not think it would be amiss to have them rated by the Magistrates. The articles which I allude to are Leather breeches &c &c the Inhabitants would willingly furnish us, but they complain that they have not received any money for the last years Receipts; on this account we cannot expect much willingness in them to serve us. Ye have not gained much by changing our Ouarters; in Camp the Cavalry received Rum from time to time-here we have none. I hope my General, that when you give orders for furnishing the infantry with means for making themselves merry, you will not leave the Cavalry in the dumps.

We are in want of Arms, and the Fusils which your Excellency ordered for us, are not yet arrived. You will pardon me my General for giving you so much trouble, in consideration of its arising from my anxiety to do my duty.

The Person whom I sent to examine Flemingtown reports to me, that two Regiments may be quarterd there and in its neighborhood-Baylors and Moylens Regiments will be placed there; Blands and Sheldons in Penny Town and its vicinity. I remain at Trenton with the Detachment that I have chosen and which I have been exercising in the meantime. I hope that we shall be furnished with Fusils and Pistols-there is a Merchant here who is desirous of contracting to furnish us with these Articles. If the Cavalry should be augmented I hope soon to receive your orders that the Officers may take their measures accordingly.

Trenton, 20th January, 1778. Received 22nd. Answered 26th. (MSS. CC. vol. 21, f. l6l)

To which Washington replied on 26 January 1778:

I can only repeat, what has been already written on the subject, that if the Cavalry can procure a sufficiency of forage at the quarters first assigned them, that situation is to be preferred, otherwise they must undoubtedly retire to the nearest place where this indispensable article can be obtained.

With respect to having the Prices of Articles necessary for the Cavalry rated, as it is a matter intirely of civil cognizance, it can only be done by the authority of the State. The scarcity of Rum is so great, that the infantry can only have it dealt to them on certain occasions; your men must therefore content themselves till times of greater plenty.

Your Officers complain that the Cavalry undergo severer duty now, than they did while they were in Camp. As rest and refreshment are two of the principal objects of your removal from Camp, I hope you will, by proper arrangements, give your Men and Horses an opportunity of reaping these benefits from their winter Quarters.

There is a large supply of Carabines arrived, at one of the Eastern ports, and orders have been given to bring forward a sufficient number to furnish the Cavalry. (W.W. 10, p. 352)

The scarcity of liquor was very real. On January 3, 1778, Washington wrote to Gen. William Smallwood: "...I am obliged to you for your promise of the prize wine...If the quantity should be anything considerable you must not be forgetful of the poor fellows who are exposed to the severity of the weather in very indifferent houses; indeed many of them are not yet under cover." And to Brigadier-General John Lacey, junior, on January 23, 1778, "...Your want of whisky I cannot remedy. We are in the same situation here, and nothing effectual can be done until the arrival of the Committee of Congress whom we expect every day..." (W.W. 10)

"A General Return of Provisions and Stores Issued in Camp to the Grand Army under the Command of his Excellency General Washington for the month of January 1778" (PCC, 192, f. 513) shows that Pulaski's troops received: 1,616 gills of spirits (rum or whisky), 33 pints of rice, 113 pints of salt, 4,979 pounds of pork, 2,847 pounds of beef, 8,203 pounds of bread and 5,214 pounds of flour. Altogether, 11,650 rations were due, 10,035 drawn and 1,615 retained.

On January 25, 1778, Pulaski wrote to Washington from Trenton:

My General-

I am altogether disappointed in my plans-not only the Country is laid waste, but there are people everywhere who have the right of first Comers. Magazines are formed to the right and left— the great quantity of Waggons belonging to the Hospital, make a great Consumption of forage the Inhabitants of themselves are not inclined to supply us as they are not paid. I send the Letter of Major Clough. The three other Regiments still remain here, but they will have subsistence for no more than five days at most. If your Excellency permits I will send the Cavalry towards Morris Town, there we may take proper measures. In the meantime we may form a Magazine here, and as the Campaign approaches, in the last month of our Winter Quarters, return her and continue the exercise which will teach us our Duty.

Pulaski was hurt by Washington's accusation of overtaxing the cavalry and relaying the complaints of officers about "severer duty." He wrote that it was false and that those who lied should be punished. He was explaining the obvious truth that cavalry training was more

time-consuming than that of infantry, as not only the soldiers but also the beasts had to be taught. He was spending a lot of effort to train cavalry, but if all the dissatisfied were finding Washington's ear it would be better if Pulaski should quit than tolerate disorder and laziness, or create dissatisfaction. That was the kind of language Washington had not heard as yet. (*Letters to Washington*, vol. 21, fol. 215).

However, it was not only such things as training and equipping the lancers which were irritating Pulaski. The affair with Clumm is a prime example of legal entanglements and problems with civilians which arose:

Pulaski to Washington, January 31, 1778, from Trenton:

> I have the honor to inform your Excelly of three Troops of horse belonging to the state of New Jersey well accoutred and their horses in best order, and the Gentln are very desirous to go down to the lines.
>
> I received a letter from Major Jameson that the party of men now under the Command of Capt Craig is to be relieved; as I have send of(f) all the Arms and accoutrements of the Cavalry to be repaired and the men are badly Clothed, should be Glad if your Excellency would write a few lines to Govonor Livington as the Officers and Gentleman in the Different Troops are willing to take that duty for a few weeks, which would recruite the men and horses now on Command Very much.
>
> I must not omit mentioning a Circumstance, though of the most Trivial nature, yet a little embarrasses me, A waggoner belonging to the Brigade an honest inoffensive Countryman, having undesignedly taken a mainger from the Stable of (one Clumm) to feed his horses, the latter maliciously without informing me of the matter, took a writ against the waggoner and put him in jail, by which means his Team was neglected the gears lost, on being informed of the affair, I took the waggoner into my costody where he remains a prisoner. My Ignorance of the Civil Law induced me to referr the Matter till I could be further advised. (*Letters to Washington*, vol. 21, 220.)

It was probably at that time that: "Count Pulaski exercised his legion of cavalry, and his dexterous movements were the wonder and emulation of the officers, many of whom were considerably injured in attempts to imitate his feats. It is related that among other feats that a daring horseman would sometimes, while his steed was under full gallop, discharge his pistol, throw it into the air, catch it by the barrel and then hurl it in front as if at enemy. Without checking the speed of his horse he would take one foot from the stirrup and, bending over toward the ground, recover his pistol, and wheel into line with as much precision as if he had been engaged in nothing but the management of the animal." (B.J. Lossing, *Pictorial Book of the Revolution*, N.Y. 1851, p.310).

This story seems to be repeated from Samuel W. Eagers, *An Outline History of Orange County*, (N.Y. 1846, p.337). Eager, however, mentioned it only marginally without giving the source, while describing the horsemanship of Dr. Joseph Whalen.

Such tales of horsemanship were nothing unusual in the contemporary literature. Among others, Patrick Ferguson, Pulaski's alter ego, was an accomplished horseman.

But Pulaski was not only a warrior in the saddle but also a brilliant cavalry leader.

Returning to the much-quoted Lossing story, the whole incident had to occur either in a different place or time. It must be added that in the vicinity of Philadelphia there were two Morris houses and Norristown.

In his letter the Commander-in-Chief was reprimanding Pulaski for overfatiguing the cavalry, while not such a long time ago he had asked the Commander of Horse to exercise them. In the future Washington was to rebuke Moylan for not training his men. Meanwhile it is perplexing to note that the Commander-in-Chief was undermining the authority of the Commander of Cavalry by listening to complaints of officers about their being overworked, and evidently agreeing with them.

At that period Pulaski seemed to be preoccupied with his idea of creating a shock troop of crack cavalry armed with lances. He proposed Ignacy (John) Zielinski as a lieutenant, informing Washington that Zielinski had served in a similar formation in Poland. As to the Moylan affair, Pulaski stated that Washington should comprehend the matter as a man and soldier who understood the question of honor. (Compare lukewarm letter of Kosciuszko on the same matter in Haiman's *Kosciuszko*, p. 197.)

To COUNT PULASKI, Head Quarters, February 4, 1778.

Sir, I have received your two Letters of 29th and 31st of last Month. The forming any considerable deposit of Forage at Trenton, while you have so small a Force to protect it does not appear to me advisable, as the Enemy may, with the greatest facility, destroy it.

My approbation of Capt. Craig's appointment, was signified in my last Letter; I cannot at any rate consent to your giving Mr. Zelienski the Commission of first Lieutenant; his character has not yet been cleared from a charge of a very serious nature, brought against him by Colo. Moylan, and this circumstance apart, which is of itself a sufficient reason for at least suspending his appointment, there may be a concurrence between him and other Officers who may have better pretensions. A court martial ought immediately to be held for the Trial of this Gentleman in pursuance of the order given long since. I am not at Liberty to take notice of any ex parte relation in affairs of this nature, whatever evidence you may have in favour of Mr. Zelienski, will properly come before the Court, and when I am furnished with their proceedings I shall be able to judge of the matter.

The Committee have now under consideration, the means of re-cruiting and remounting the Cavalry, their determination will be transmitted for your government, as soon as it is made.

You will be pleased to transmit me an exact Return of the Cav-alry immediately, and hereafter to continue to make accurate Weekly Returns. I am desirous of submitting your Pattern Saddle to the in-spection of the Committee, you will therefore send it to Camp with-out delay.

As Mr. Worsham is so well recommended by the Officers of his Regiment, I have no objection to his filling one of the vacancies in it. I am, etc.

P.S. Inclosed is a Letter to Govr. Livingston relative to the three Troops of Jersey Horse. The bearer will deliver one thousand Flints for the use of the Cavalry." (William Worsham, quartermaster-ser-geant of the First Continental Dragoons. (W.W.10, p.413. He was made cornet, February 4, 1778; lieutenant in 1780; served to No-vember 1782.)

Washington to GOVERNOR WILLIAM LIVINGSTON, Head Quarters, Valley Forge, February 4, 1778.

Sir: Brigr. Genl. Count Polaski informs me, that there are three troops of Jersey Horse who would enter into the Continental Service for a short time, if they could obtain your Excellency's consent. They will be a very great relief to our Horse, if they can be spared and will answer another very valuable purpose. We find that our common Dragoons are not proof against the bribes offered to them, by the people who are con-stantly carrying provision to the City of Philadelphia, so that instead of cutting off the intercourse, they encourage it, by suffering many to pass who pay them for it. If it is agreeable to you, that the Horse above men-tioned should be taken into the service, be pleased to signify it to me by a line. (W.W. 10, p. 420)

Washington's letter to Pulaski is written in a very overbearing manner. Pulaski's ideas, proposals and complaints are ignored, and the affair between Zielinski and Moylan blown out of all proportion. Pulaski is reminded that he is supposed to transmit the exact returns, a matter more important than lancers or the training of cavalry.

On the same day Pulaski wrote Washington a letter which he considered to be his first in English, evidently forgetting about the "Plan of a Corps of Volunteers" presented to John Hancock in August 1777.

TRENTON, 4 Feby 1778.

Sir-I join the letter from A prisoner, Je'wil determined mi answer. The Cavalry is Placed according to Instruction from Colonel Bidle. I remain hier with the detachment of Lenceurs. I mean If Your Excely approved of, to March toward Borlington in this time. Our Magazin will be form sufficient for to furnish the Whole Cavalry fifteen Days by Soch Time we shal biguin the Genl Exercise. I Report further, that in Eastown the Murchents and treatsmen ar not wiling to deliver the Necessaris wanting for want of Money. I hope Your Excely wil order to Satisfy'd them, If you recollect the first letters I wrote, particularly the Article of the Horses and about the Commission for Colonel Kowaer with Authoryty to Comend a detachement as a Colonel hi will bi of more service in an attack as in other duty.

10th February, 1778.

I send your Excellency one of my Lancemen, he is completely equip'd. I find people here who are willing to serve, if you approve of it my General, I will advance them money for (blank in the MS.) The Governor is here and promises to give me an answer as soon as a Council shall have been held, which will happen in a few days.

Whatever is to be done for us I hope will be done without delay, our time is short and I suppose the Campaign is to be opened by the Cavalry, it will not be for want of attention in me, if they are not in condition to do it. I send Your Excellency the proceedings of two Courts of Inquiry, one respecting the Dragoons who are said to have robbed an Inhabitant, the other respecting Mr. Zelienski. A Court-Martial cannot be held on this affair, on account of Colo Moylan's absence, and in consequence of the officers being so scattered-even for the affair of the Dragoons I could collect a sufficient number to hold Court Martial.

Your Excellency may have them tried according to the report or order them to be sent to the Galleys, this is an exemplary punishment, and would be useful to the public, as the Fleet is in want of men. There are some persons here who are desirous of serving with me as Volunteers with arms and accoutrements. (L. to W. 21, fol: 272, Feb. 10, 1770)

To which Washington sent the following reply:

Headquarters, February 14, 1778

Sir: I have received your Letter of the 10th Instt. with a Schedule of expences for Clothing and equipping the Cavalry, and have submitted them to the consideration of the Committee of Congress, these Gentlemen will by no means consent to a Plan, which appears to them so extraordinarily expensive, as each Colonel has undertaken to provide for his own Regiment, and the Lance Men are to be draughted, the men who compose this Company must take their chance for Cloathing &ca. with the rest of the Dragoons.

You are at Liberty to raise as many Recruits as may be wanted, provided it can be done upon the Terms allowed by the Continent; that is, twenty Dollars bounty, to men engaging for three years or during the War, but I do not approve of your giving encouragement to Volunteers, as the trouble which they occassion, generally overbalances their service

With respect to the deposition in favor of Mr. Zelienski; as the whole proceeding is exparte, I can take no notice of it, and must refer you to what I said on the subject in my last Letter.

Among the Articles of Charge alluded to above, that of the Sheep Skin Saddles, is particularly extravagant, perhaps this may be owing to the Lining, you will be so good as to inform me at what rate you can contract for the Tree of the Saddle alone, the Skip Covers may be procured from the public Butchers, without being an Article of additional expense.

Inclosed is a Letter for Commodore Hazelwood, which forward. (W.W. 10, p. 458.)

In America the type of saddle generally used was the flat British saddle, not too different from the present–day English saddle. There were also French saddles which had padded seats and higher padded cantles and pommels. The skirts were fuller than in English ones, square and provided with straps on the offside for attaching spare horseshoes. (Harold L. Peterson, *The Book of the Continental Soldier*, Stackpole, 1968, p.210).

It seems that Casimir Pulaski tried to introduce a saddle of Polish design, i.e., of the strong Oriental influence where the rider had a strong back support which enabled him free operation of lance and saber. Similar types of saddles were also used in Hungary.

Pulaski's Legion had such Hungarian or Hussar saddles covered with sheepskin, the best for this purpose.

Pulaski's project was duly forwarded to a committee of Congress which rejected it.

Angrily Pulaski wrote to Congress on February 19:

Gentlemen: I have the mortification to see my best projects frustrated by some circumstance or other, which I attribute to the climate of this country, that so far influences its inhabitants as to make them differ in sentiment with me, though upon our mutual agreement depends the success of my intentions. After numerous obstacles, I have got everything in a fair way; procured workmen to undertake everything necessary for the corps I command. Still I cannot be understood by those to whom I look for aid and countenance. My plan for forming a groop of lancemen I find has not been approved of by you gentlemen, owing to the sum it would cost to equip them. This shall be no objection, as I will undertake to equip them at the sum you will please to allow. Let me know what it may be, and send me the money, and will equip forty men. It is true, with this number I may not greatly contribute to the gaining of a battle, but the disadvantage of their not being augmented shall appear evident. Then I shall not be refused the equipment of as many as I may demand.

I have the honor to acquaint you that the English have succeeded in augmenting their cavalry. They purchase horses from their friends at any price; from others they take without payment, while we are waiting to be supplied at a price they are not to be purchased at. I have bought three horses for my own use, one of which cost me $1,000, and the two others $1,200, neither of them too good for a dragoon. The price of horses is sufficient to ruin a man that is desirous of being properly fitted for the service. For this reason I am under the necessity of demanding my pay as general of the cavalry. I should not have asked it for any other use than the appropriating it to the equipment of the corps before mentioned. I therefore request you will order me to be paid from the time of my appointment till August next. I hope you will consider at the same time the extraordinary expense a general of cavalry is at, compared to one of the infantry. I have experienced it already, and in all other countries a considerable distinction is made in every respect."

Pulaski was not the only person in the Continental Army guilty of looking towards Europe for an example. The learned General Brigadier Knox, in his letter to Washington of 15 June 1778, wrote: "...In all considerable armies in Europe, a General Officer has the command and direction of artillery, and the preparation of everything pertaining to the ordnance department appropriate, and of all species of arms offensive and defensive belonging to a soldier..."

Casimir Pulaski's letter was sent to a proper body. Congress was afraid of the possibility of the military dictatorship and attempted to control the continental army by its committees sent directly to headquarters. The members of the committee in question were Francis Dana, Joseph Reed, Nathaniel Folsom, John Harvie and three members of the Board of War, Horatio Gates, Thomas Mifflin and Timothy Pickering. The committee, in concert with Washington, had full powers among others to determine the reinforcement of cavalry.

However, Pulaski's memorial shared the fate of the numerous other ones by being duly pigeon-holed, and the Commander of Horse had some bitter reflections about his American service. I quote here the letter to his sister published for the first time in Leonard Chodzko's *Zywot Kazimierza na Pulaziu Pulaskiego*, p.216:

24 February 1778, Trenton.

It will be enough for you, Dear Sister, to know that I am in good health. My fortune varies as it is usual in the time of war. Here, I am commanding the whole cavalry, and I took part in different attacks successfully enough. I do not intend to stay here long. The native customs cannot agree with my temper, and additionally, my service here is a waste of time. I cannot do anything good. People are very jealous, and everything is antagonistic. But the next campaign I shall be here. In future, if it would be possible, I shall become a merchant which is here the most useful.

And on the same day he wrote to Ruhliere.

I have written to you several times, not knowing whether any of my letters had reached you. I am the chief of cavalry here but am not too satisfied. I puzzle how to perform well my duties and get used to the rest but it is impossible that I would do it. If I would describe what I feel, you would have too much to read, so I abbreviate everything, telling you that I find in America the image of Asia. But the English are different from the Russians. They are less active.

Our cavalry is still dispersed in few parts and when it is necessary to fight, everything is reduced to zero. I have proposed to raise the number of cavalry because of the service to the Army. The English have number superiority and better weapons and have more horses. I took part in many attacks but in spite of the best intentions I could not shine, having only 50 dragoons whom I gathered. We were storming three times over one thousand of infantry. If I had a sufficient number I would be successful. I see no advantage in remaining here. The people here do not like foreigners who are tolerated rather than considered to be necessary. So I plan after the next campaign to return to France and take care of my own affairs. We have a project of attacking the English in Canada and the Marquis La Fayette is the commander. All the Frenchmen are with him. Militia in New England had orders to join him. Many of the Canadians are waiting for this joining. There is a probability that it will be successful. I must say that not only God but all the circumstances are favorable for American success, otherwise they would be not able to stand.

We had disorder in Poland, but would we have favourable circumstances similar to those which Americans have we could continue struggle against all the European powers. So we can believe that Tories, as Royalists are called, will not receive support, and the English would leave the American continent.

And to his friend in France:

Our army is dispersed. In the next campaign maybe it will be increased to 16,000 and the English will have only 12,000. I am with my corps cut off and the English are worrying me occasionally. To resist them I have no more than 60 cavalrymen but the English when they get out have at least 2000 infantry and 200 cavalry. That is a difference but nonetheless we are not afraid of them. It happened one day that my five dragoons took some waggons of their rearguard. I do not intend to use services of others as I sent them to equip. In the next campaign I want to do a heroic deed.

Apropos Mr Beumarchais he forgot about me completely. He did not mention me even by one word, he had not even sent me a letter. Would I have money with me I could get 9 louis in paper for one of gold. I had to borrow some money, no more than two for one. What a difference. Good-bye. I have not got paper enough. It is time to finish.

My regards for the lady I liked. I forgot the name of that lady you introduced me to at Champs Elysees. Please do not forget also Count de Qyville. (*Correspondance du General Casimir Pulaski avec Claude de Rulhiere*, Institute Historique et Literaire Polonaise, Paris, 1948).

Those were bitter but private letters but also on the same day Pulaski wrote to Washington an official letter (*Washington Papers*, vol. 22, p. 77).

It had been caused by the enterprising Anthony Wayne who had swept the district between New Salem and Mount Holly, burning Loyalists' hay (he had no waggons to remove it), and driving their cattle and horses with the thoroughness which earned him the nickname of "Drover."

He had asked for Pulaski's co-operation. Washington had previously written to the Commander of Horse in this matter (*Letters to Generals*, MS, B vol. 5, p.104). But before the message reached Pulaski he had received an abrupt order from Wayne.

.. General Wayne has joined General Washington again. He ordered Brigadier-General Pulaski, who was then in Trenton, to follow him at a moment's notice... (Major Baurmeister, P.M.H. vol. 60, p. 163).

Anthony Wayne was appointed Brigadier-General on February 21, 1777, so his seniority over Pulaski was about half a year. Pulaski forwarded Wayne's order to the Commander-in-Chief, explaining that he refused the request, having only 18 men necessary for the local duties. This is confirmed by Pulaski's letter of January 31st where the Commander of Horse reported to Washington that he had sent all the weapons and accoutrements of the cavalry for repair and had asked the militia to take over for a few weeks.

In the present letter, and most importantly, Pulaski asked whether he would be obliged to obey all the senior officers (i.e., infantry generals) or be dependent only on the Commander-in-Chief. Evidently, joining the American Army, Pulaski thought that similar to most of the European armies, cavalry would be treated with preference. The question of the right of command of cavalry appeared frequently in Pulaski's correspondence, (*Washington Papers*, vol. 22, p.77) and perhaps Lovell's negative answer was never communicated to him. There is no annotation on the document which would indicate it was ever sent to the person concerned.

If Pulaski was obliged to accept orders of some 50 generals who had seniority over him, the idea of cavalry as a separate branch of the service would not be practicable, and Pulaski's reaction and behaviour were not only the question of hurt ambitions but of a workman requesting proper tools.

After sending Washington a letter to say that it was impossible to assist Wayne, Pulaski changed his mind. This can be seen from his letter dated 28 February, from Burlington (L. to W 22, p.100), but this epistle also contains a formal resignation.

I have the honor to report to you that having assembled all the Cavalry of the Regiment Blan(d) and of the detachment which I have had with me, I have found 44 Troopers, 5 Sub-ordinate Officers for the Service, and although they are not in the best condition, I have marched with them against the Enemy, but as the road is insupportable, I am forced to Pass the night at Burlington.

To-morrow, I count on reconnoitering the Enemy, and I shall act accordingly. I shall see Gen. Wayne, and I shall concentrate (join) with him. I shall neglect nothing which the good of the service shall require, but I do not expect to be under his orders. Nevertheless, I shall serve to my own prejudice the Public interest.

Neverthe less, I shall try, My General, to diminish Your embarrassment on my Account by resigning from my charge, with which Congress has honored me by your recommendation.

I sent from here two armed bateaux on Ancokes (Rankokas) Creek to observe by the River the approach of the Enemy, who were found two Hours after mid-day on four different vessels at the passage which is called Sene (i.e., Sein) Merise (Maurice Bay?). I repeat to Your Excellency the very great necessity of attending to the needs of the Cavalry. They lack everything. I should have desired to equip well, at least, the Regiment of Blan(d) with the Lancers, but as this is forbidden me, it is necessary to employ other measures, without trusting too much to the Colonels, who certainly will be in no Condition to accomplish their objects.

It is not for myself that I speak; I do not count on having the honor of being at the head of this Corps in the coming Campaign, but, as I shall always be a friend to the interest of the Americans, I am forced to tell my way of Thinking; moreover, if after me the Command shall be given to Col. Moilen (Moylan), all the Cavalry will be in the same Condition as his Regiment. Colonel Blan(d) is an active Officer. He will suit this command, and Monsieur Moilen (Moylan) can be contented with something else. I say what I believe to be necessary.

Going south, Pulaski joined Wayne and approached Haddonfield, close to Camden. He sent the following report to Washington (*Letters*, 22, 102). It seems that Pulaski wanted to withdraw his resignation. Probably battle action improved his temper after months of inactivity and struggling with red tape.

My General-
We have given Battle to the English but the infantry arrived a little late and in small Numbers, so that the English boldly marched upon (us) with the 3 pieces of cannon and 600 Infantry which I have seen myself; our infantry and the Cavalry attacked in the beginning and afterwards defended themselves resolutely and always giving

ground returned to the charge. Four of the Dragoons Horses were killed, three totally disabled, and three others slightly wounded.

In this affair, I too lost my horse, which cost me a good deal and was excellent; he lost his leg as the result of a shot. You will permit me, my General to choose for the time being another horse from among the Dragoons until I find one to my liking. I have the honor to say to Your Excellency that the Dragoons accomplished wonders. They are good Soldiers, but they lack everything, they will lose the desire to do good Service.

In pursuit of the enemy, I took 7 Prisoners, among whom is a Captain of a Vessel, who, being a Scout to reconnoiter our maneuvers at close hand, fell within the lines. All the others are Sailors who were beating the woods, and were captured by our Cavalry. The Night before this attack I alarmed them so that they retreated precipitately at the same time from Hatienfield (Haddonfield), and my patrol, in pursuit of them took a prisoner, who avowed that they were 1200 with 4 pieces of Cannon. There are the details.

In regard to General Wayne, I gave him to understand that he has abused his authority and that he knows that his orders do not concern me in view of the special Order which I had from Your Excellency and, moreover, that I ought to be exempt from all other orders, as the Commander of the Cavalry and (as one) who had entered the Service under no other condition than that of not being in subjection to any other than the Chief of the Army, but that my Zeal for the service surpassed this point of Honor and that after an Agreement I would do everything that he should find advantageous to put in operation. I have acted accordingly, and I cannot complain of the General in any other respect; on the contrary, according to his way of doing (i.e. Characteristically), he was too frank for me to do him justice. I repeat to Your Excellency that the horses are (all) too necessary; this drove which is with me can do no more because of the bad road; also, if I shall find a good horse anywhere, I shall impress him, General Weyne has some 20; I do not like them at all. Awaiting orders.

P.S.-In the pursuit of the enemy, I took some live Stock, and I had a Part of His Hay burned. (*Letters*, XXII, 102, translation.)[37]

Here is how Anthony Wayne reported the same action (*Major-General Anthony Wayne* by Charles J Stille, 1893, p.131, 132):

General Wayne to General Washington. HADDONFIELD 4th March 1778

Sir,-Soon after I wrote your Excellency from Mount Holly-I recd

Intelligence that the Enemy had Detached themselves in small parties and were Collecting Cattle forage &c in the Vicinity of Haddonfield, Coopers, and Timber Creeks. This Intelligence Induced me (altho' my Numbers were few) to make a forced March and Endeavour to drive in or cut off some of their parties-At nine o'clock at night I arrived at one Capt. Matlacks about four Miles to the South East of this place where I was soon after joined by Gen'l Pulaski with about fifty Light Horse-Col. Ellis with two Hundred & fifty Militia, being the Whole of his Command, took post at Evesham Meeting at the junction of the Roads leading to Egg-Harbor and Mount Holly-At Ten O'clock Genl. Pulaski attempted to surprise the Enemy's advanced post at a Mill a half a Mile Out of Haddonfield-he failed in the attempt-but Col. Stirling who Commanded the Enemy having in the fore part of the Evening Rec'd Intelligence of our March,-and our Numbers being Exaggerated to thousands-moving in three Columns-the one to his Right an Other to his left and the third in front-the North Briton thought it prudent to Retreat under Cover of the Shipping, he accordingly Decamped at Eleven at night and Arrived at Cooper ferry before day-Destroying some Spirits and leaving Waggons Horses Cattle &c behind which he had stolen from the Inhabitants who have since Claimed and Rec'd their property-

The Troops being much fatigued-I could not follow before late next Morning-I advanced with Gen'l Pulaski to Reconnoitre their position-and on coming near the ferry found that they were there in full force, the Wind being too high to admit the Boats to pass-however they were too well posted to do any thing with them-being covered and flanked by their shipping-About the Middle of the Afternoon the Wind lulled when they threw over about 36 head of poor Cattle the whole they had been able to save from the Numbers they had Stolen.

On Observing that they were about Retreating over the River-& Gen'l Pulaski anxious to Charge-I ordered up Capt. Doyle with his Company consisting of Fifty men-who lay three miles in advance of the Rest, directing the Other part of the Deatchment to follow as fast as possible. About the same time I Rec'd Intelligence of a fresh body of Troops having crossed from Philad'a who were Marching up Cooper's Creek and seemed pushing for our Rear-Col. Ellis being posted with his Militia on that Route I ordered him to Advance and Receive them-

About this time Capt. Doyle Arrived-near the Enemy's Covering party-whose numbers appeared to be about three times as many as ours when joined by the Horse-but as they were approachable on each flank & the Center being favourable for the Cavalry Gen'l Pulaski & Myself were determined to attack them-In Order to gain time for the main body to come up, as well as to Amuse and prevent that party of the Enemy from proceeding further up Cooper's Creek-We soon Obliged the Covering party to give way-when Mr. Stirling advanced in full force to support them-this answered my expectations and wishing to lead them from under Cover of their shipping-I Ordered the Infantry to keep up a Constant fire falling back by slow degrees until they should be joined by Col Butlers Detachment-About the same time the Hessian Grenadiers attempted to force over Cooper's bridge in face of about 100 Militia under Col Ellis-but they soon gave up that idea-finding it Impracticable.

The fire of the Enemy from their field pieces shipping and Musketry became General-however they could not be drawn out-but night coming on, and Col Butler not being able to get up until too late to see-the Enemy Effected their Retreat to Phila-before Nine at Night but not without some loss attended with Circumstances of Disgrace. Genl. Pulaski behaved with his usual bravery on the Occasion having his own with four Other Horses Wounded-The fifty Infantry being the only part that had an Opportunity of Engaging-behaved with a Degree of bravery that would have done Honor to the Oldest Veterans-Mr. Abercrumbie who Commanded the Detachment that went to Salem-hearing that the Militia were Collecting in great Numbers-and that we were advancing from Mount Holly-also took the Horrors and Embarking on board His boats &c got safe to Phila-three Evenings ago leaving all his Collection of Cattle &c &c behind.-Thus ended the Jersey Expedition which has not been attended with that Advantage that those North Brittons expected of their first Arrival."

"The Toll of Independence" notes dryly: "Near Cooper's Ferry, N.J. a British foraging party under Lt.-Col. John G. Simcoe was moving waggons across Delaware River when attacked by Americans under Gen. Pulaski. After inflicting some casualties Pulaski retreated." (*Proceedings of New Jersey Historical Society*, XlV, 3rd Series, 1929, p. 154, narrative of Thomas Stokes).

And here I quote fragments of a letter from Major Baurmeister to Von Jungkenn, March 24, 1778 (PMH, 60, p. 161 et.seq., 1926) which shows the view from the other side of the conflict:

On February 15th General Wayne advanced to Bristol in Jersey with 400 men and on March 9th penetrated still deeper into the province from the bank of the Delaware in order to burn grain and forage and collect horses and cattle. He assembled at Haddonfield 350 Jersey Militia under Colonel Ellis, from which an alarm watch has been detached as far as Cooper's Ferry opposite this city. General Wayne has joined General Washington again. He ordered Brigadier General Pulaski, who was then in Trenton, to follow him at a moment's notice with the eighty dragoons and one hundred continental troops under him. General Washington's army, exceedingly weakened by desertion and disease, is prepared to approach Lancaster. The whole country around Valley Forge is devastated on the 17th a detachment of light infantry surprised a troop of rebels on the Westfield road the other side of the Schuylkill, killing four and taking eighteen prisoners. As usual, detachments are being sent out on the evening before a market day to protect the country people who venture everything to bring fresh food to the city. Enemy parties always search for these people and maltreat those they catch and take their goods away. Often the farmer pays them for safe conduct, in which case the food is sold for that much more in the market. On this day three rebel staff officers escaped from prison. The following morning fifty-seven were removed from this building and put into the new city prison. Furthermore, they were no longer permitted to walk about, under escort, for about an hour each day. On the same day, eight provision ships arrived from Ireland, having made the voyage from Cork in fifty-one days. At the Gulph Ferry Mill, fifteen miles from here, is a strong enemy outpost detached from Valley Forge. On the night of the 19-20th this post sent out a party of sixty men, who crept up close to the Schuylkill opposite the 10th redoubt, where they collected some cattle and set fires. The wing adjutant, Captain von Munchausen, with forty mounted Hsian jagers under Lieutenant Mertz was so fortunate as to catch up with this party the following morning just before they reached the Black Horse. He captured one officer and ten men and killed and wounded several more. The rest of the rebels were lucky to be able to hide behind a swamp. The jagers had only one horse killed. Since the rebels are devastating the land and carrying off everything, a train of waggons covered by 150 light infantry went to Chestnut Hill and Germantown on the 21st to collect leather and forty hogsheads of vinegar and bring them into the royal stores of this city. The owners were paid the real value of the merchandise.

At retreat time on the 6th, 200 dragoons under Major Crewe of the 17th Regiment of Dragoons were detached to Chestnut Hill by way of Germantown in order to surprise some continental troops who, coming from Fatland Ford via Norriton, had roamed that far in an attempt to raise militia and burn forage and food. They consisted of 250 men whom General Wayne had turned over to Governor Livingston before leaving Jersey on the 24th of February. On the 4th of March they had crossed the Delaware near Burlington with twenty-five of Pulaski's dragoons and proceeded to Fatland Ford on the Schuylkill, whence they advanced to Chestnut Hill terrorizing the country people. However, when they heard of the approach of the British dragoons, they assembled on the right bank of the Wissahickon, followed the footpaths along this creek to Schuylkill Falls, and crossed the river without our dragoons being able to pursue them. Our troops killed five men and captured one officer and seventeen soldiers."

On March 1, 1778, Washington wrote this uncompromising letter to Pulaski.

My General, I have received your letter of the 27 ultimo and in answer to your question respectively the right of command in officers of equal rank in the Infantry and Cavalry. I am to inform you that those is no other preeminence in our service than what arises from seniority. The officer whose commission is of prior data commands all those the same grade indiscriminately whether horse or foot. You will afford General Wayne all the assistance in your power and the rather as the service in which he is engaged is of great importance, a sufficient number to furnish men for keeping a look-out and preventing any sudden enterprise of the Enemy against his parties is all that is requisite.

Here Washington confirmed that which was clear and obvious for him from the very beginning of American cavalry existence. It was an inferior auxiliary branch of service and there were no privileges in its service, contrary to European custom. Already on August 15, 1777, Washington had written a stern letter to officers of the Fourth Continental Dragoons (W.W.9, p.68) in which he said "...I am not conscious of ever having said, or done anything that could lead to a belief that the rank of a Lieut. of Horse was to be equal to a Captain of Foot, for the obvious reasons that neither justice nor usage would authorise it..." (W.W.9, p. 68).

In a letter of August 17th he repeats: "...nor did I see any reason why superior rank should be given to officers of Cavalry but where commissions are equal, the commands should be ascertained by priority of date..."

Those men who had such unconventional ideas about cavalry were:

William Bird, Richard Dorsey, John Craig, Nicholas Ruxton Moore and George Gray.

Thus, writing to Pulaski on March 1, 1778, Washington was merely repeating his former convictions, and the rather stiff form of letter was perhaps influenced by the hope that Pulaski would resign his command. That Washington wanted this is witnessed by his letter to the Committee of Arrangement of October 6, 1778, which will be discussed in Part Two of this book.

So it may be assumed that it was with relief that Washington dictated the following letter to the first American Commander of Horse:

> Headquarters, March 3 1778. Sir. I have received your favor of the 28 n, informing me that you were proceeding with a part of Bland's Regmt to join General Wayne. You will have received my instructions relative to the service which you are to render. Your intention to resign is founded on reasons which I presume make you think the measure necessary. I can only say therefore that it will always give me pleasure to bear testimony of the zeal and Bravery which you have displayed on every occasion. Proper measures are taking for completing the Cavalry and I have no doubt of its being on a respectable footing by the opening of the campaign." (W.W.11, p. 20)

But Col. John Laurens wrote: "The dislike of some of his officers to him as a stranger, the advantages they have taken of him, and their constant contrivance to thwart him on every occasion, made it impossible for him to command...." (Laurens, John, *Army Correspondence*, p. 41, N.Y. Bradford Club, 1867.)

Colonel Stephen Moylan probably experienced a feeling of deep satisfaction when he perused the following order:

> As Count Pulaski has left the command of the Horse, never, I believe, to return to any general command in it again, I have to desire that you will repair to Trenton and take on yourself the command of that Corps until Congress shall determine further on this head. You will use your utmost endeavors to have the Cavalry belonging to the four regiments (not in New Jersey) put in the best possible order that they may take the field with some degree of eclat. (W.W.11, p. 115)

On the same day the colonels of cavalry were informed by the Commander-in-Chief that: "As Count Pulaski will, I believe, quit the command of Cavalry and is now absent from that Corps and at York, you are to receive your orders from Col. Moylan."

These orders signified the practical dissolution of the Continental

Cavalry, closing at the same time the first chapter of the American service of Casimir Pulaski.

But the Count, far from being disgusted with the service, was led by his thirst for glory and zeal for the cause of liberty to solicit further employment.

That was to be the Pulaski Legion, and the history of that corps and of its creator will be the subject of Part Two of this work Also the reader will find there the full assessment of Pulaski's role in the military course of the American Revolution, and of his character.

PART TWO

PULASKI AND HIS LEGION

CASIMIR PULASKI

All those who desire to distinguish themselves in the service of their country are invited to enlist in that corps which is established on the same principle as the Roman Legions were. The frequent opportunities which the nature of the service of that corps will offer the enterprising, brave and vigilant soldiers who shall serve in it, are motives which ought to influence those who are qualified for admission into it to prefer it to other corps not so immediately destined to harass the enemy; and the many captures which will infallibly be made, must indemnify the legionary soldiers for the hardship they must sustain, and the inconsiderable sum given for bounty, the term for their service being no longer than one year from the time the corps shall be completed. Their dress is calculated to give a martial appearance, and to secure the soldier against the inclemency of the weather and season..."

The above advertisement appeared in the American press in April 1778 rather inconspicuously in the classified sections, among notices of runaway servants and slaves, houses, ships, Negroes and Negresses for sale, etc. But Jared Sparks,the American historian says: "The scheme of independent legions seems to have been first suggested by Pulaski; and it proved of the greatest importance in the subsequent operations of the war, and above all in the southern campaigns. Lee's and Armand's legions were formed upon a similar plan." Vol. 4, *The Library of American Biography*, Jared Sparks, Boston, 1847, Little & Brown, p. 426.

The corps in question was to consist of infantry and cavalry and to be led by General Count Pulaski.

Three years before this advertisement was printed the news of Lexington reached New York, starting a riot. Since that time an indecisive war had been dragging on. The British who did not know how or did not want to use their advantages were now sending peace feelers, but the French recognition of the United States encouraged the Americans to fight on for freedom and independence.

In spite of promises, allusions to the Roman Legionary principles, and appeals to patriotism and avarice, the task of Col. Kovatch, Major Count Montfort, Major Betken, Captain De Segond, and other officers, recruiting for Pulaski's American Legion was not easy.

The people were tired of war, The situation foreseen by Casimir Pulaski, soon after his arrival in America, was by now fully realized. The eager Whigs were already fighting in the Continental Army or had lost their enthusiasm for the military brand of democracy and deserted or had been killed in action or died of starvation and cold, sickness, wounds or had been taken prisoner. Up to that time 2316 Americans had been killed, 3251 wounded and 10,835 captured since

1775, while the totals for 1777 were 1389 killed, 2253 wounded and 2169 captured. (*The Toll of Independence*, ed. Howard H. Peckham). And according to General Knox's report the number of regular Continental troops in 1777 was 34,850. The peak of enlistment was 46,891 in 1776, and the lowest 13,292 in 1781.

Large numbers of men were avoiding military service or fighting on the King's side, By the end of 1778 there were about 75,000 Loyalists under arms, serving the Royal cause. It will be of interest to compare the following advertisement with Pulaski's:

> All Aspiring Heroes have now an opportunity of distinguishing them-
> selves by joining the Queens Ranger Hussars, commanded by Lieuten-
> ant Colonel Simcoe. Any spirited young man will receive every
> encouragement, by immediately mounted on an elegant horse, and fur-
> nished with clothing, accoutrements, &c, to the amount of forty guin-
> eas, by applying to Cornet Spencer, at his quarters, No. 133 Water
> Street, or his rendezvous, Hewett's Tavern, near the coffee-house, and
> the defeat of Brandywine, on Golden Hill. Whoever brings a recruit
> shall instantly receive two guineas. Vivant Rex et Regina."

This appeared in the autumn of 1777 in Rivington's *Royal Gazette* in New York.

Lord George Germain boasted that more Americans enlisted under the British than were to be found in the whole Continental Army, and that the British could recruit men in America for five or six pounds (but evidently not for Simcoe's corps) while Continental Congress could not get them for less than 250 dollars.

At the same time Washington was putting ads in the independent Press to ask deserters to "please come back home. Everything for-given."

In addition to the general difficulties of recruitment for the Continental Army there was stiff competition from the states. Boun-ties of land and cash were generously offered. At first the bounty was ten dollars for three years of service, but in 1779 it jumped to a thousand dollars, plus a suit of clothes and 100 acres of land. In 1779 the State of Virginia was offering four hundred dollars and 300 acres of land to every volunteer. As the galloping inflation was making paper dollars almost worthless, the state of North Carolina, to raise a corps of riflemen for two months, tempted the volunteers with the reward of a cow and a calf. Generally service in the militia was more attractive as the militiamen stayed in their states, and the time of their service was short. The competition for recruits was made stiffer by the existence of state quotas of soldiers for the Continental Army.

Pulaski's recruiting activities was broad in scope: Colonel Kovatch was at Easton, Major Montfort at Lancaster, Captain Segond at Baltimore, Captain Pashke at Boston, Captain Bedkin at Jersey, Lieutenants Woolf, Palmer and Welch in Virginia, Lieutenant Bompell in Pennsylvania and Major Dubuis in Albany.

Pulaski was always on the move, supervising recruitment and training.

Such a range of recruitment was made possible by the following resolve of Congress, dated April 6, 1778:

> Resolved that if any of the states in which Brigadier General Pulaski shall recruit for his Legion, shall give to persons existing in the same for three years or during the war the bounty allowed by the state in addition to the Continental bounty, the men so furnished, not being inhabitants of any other of the United States, shall be credited to the quota of the state in which they shall be enlisted, (*Journals of the Continental Congress*, Gaillard Hunt, ed., Washington, 1904).

Pulaski had probably been thinking for some time about creating an independent corps, as the command of the cavalry only brought him disappointment and frustration. He was able to achieve the formal approval of the Commander-in-Chief, and Washington wrote to John Hancock on 14th March the following letter:

> Sir-This will be presented to you by Count Pulaski, who, from a conviction that his remaining at the head of the cavalry was a constant subject of uneasiness to the principal officers of that Corps, has been induced to resign his command. Waving a minute inquiry into the causes of dissatisfaction, which may be reduced perhaps to the disadvantages under which he labored, as a stranger not well acquainted with the language, genius, and manners of this country, it may be sufficient to observe, that the degree of harmony, which is inseparable from the wellbeing and consequent utility of a corps, has not subsisted in the cavalry since his appointment and that the most effectual as well as the easiest remedy is that which he has generously applied.
>
> The Count, however, far from being disgusted with the service, is led by his thirst for glory, and zeal for the cause of Liberty, to solicit farther employment, and waits upon Congress to make his proposals. They are briefly, that he be allowed to raise an independent corps composed of sixty-eight horse and two hundred foot, the horse to be armed with lances, and the foot equipped in the manner of light infantry. The former he thinks he can readily fill with natives of good character, and worthy the trust reposed in them. With respect to the

other, he is desirous of more latitude so as to have the liberty of engaging prisoners and deserters from the enemy.

The original plan for the lance-men was to have drafted them from the regiments of horse. But, as this method would produce a clashing of interests, and perhaps occasion new disturbances, the Count prefers having a corps totally unconnected with any other. My advice to him, therefore, is to enlist his number of cavalry with the Continental bounty; and if it should be found consonant to the views of Congress to allow his raising the number proposed over and above the establishment for the horse, then he would have them on the footing of an independent Corps; if not, he might at all events have them as Drafts, as in this case there would be no grounds for complaint. With regard to the infantry, which the Count esteems essential to the success of the cavalry, I have informed him that the inlisting of deserters and prisoners, is expressly prohibited by a late Resolve of Congress. How far Congress might be inclined to make an exception and license the engaging Prisoners in a particular detached Corps, in which such characters may be admitted with less danger than promiscuously in the line, I could not undertake to pronounce.

I have only to add that the Counts Valor and active zeal on all occasions have done him great honor, and from persuasion, that by being less exposed to the inconveniences which he has hitherto experienced he will render great Services with such a Command as he ask for, I wish him to succeed in his application. It is to be understood that the Count expects to retain his rank as Brigadier and I think is intitled to it, from his general Character and peculiar disinterestedness on the present occasion." (*Writings of Washington*, John C. Fitzpatrick, ed. vol. 11, p.82).

How sincere Washington was in his praise of Pulaski and what he thought was the main reason for his recommending the Pole to the command of the corps may be judged from the following letter to the Committee of Arrangement from Congress:

Head Quarters
Fish Kill, October 6, 1778.

Sir: I had the honor of receiving, three days since your letter of the 30th of September; and should have answered it at once but was delayed by being separated from my papers, a recourse to which was necessary to assist my memory.

I recollect, that in a conference with the Committee of arrangement on the subject of inlisting prisoners and deserters, I gave my

CASIMIR PULASKI

opinion explicitly against the practice; and that a letter was written by them to Congress, agreeable to this idea, though I am not equally clear, as to the precise contents of the letter, or whether I understood the scope of it to comprehend Pulaski's corps. It may have happened in the perplexity of business, that the peculiar circumstances of the establishment of this corps did not occur to me; otherwise I should have conceived myself bound to make an exception in its favour. A compact made between the publick and the Count, when all the inconveniences of engaging such characters had been fully experienced would have restrained me from recommending a measure, which was a direct breach of it, and might give just cause of complaint. The principal motive for authorizing the Count to raise his corps, was to induce him voluntarily to relinquish the command of the cavalry, with which the officers under him were in general dissatisfied; and it was thought better to submit to the defect in its composition, than either to leave the cavalry in a state, which occasioned a total relaxation of discipline, and destroyed its usefulness, or to force the Count out of it, whose zeal and bravery entitled him to regard, without compensating in some way that might reconcile him to the sacrafice, he was required to make. When he proposed his plan to me, I informed him of the objections to it and even avoided flattering him with the concurrence of Congress. You will perceive by the inclosed extract of my letter to them on what footing the affair was placed. Their resolve of the 28th of March which sanctioned his raising a corps left the point of engaging prisoners and deserters undecided, but empowered me to dispense in that instance with their resolve against it, if I should deem it not injurious to the service. The reasons before assigned determined me to consent to the Counts views so faas to permit his composing a third of his infantry of deserters.

When the Board of War consulted me on the propriety of permitting this corps to join the army, recurring to the original principle of its formation, my opinion naturally favoured its coming forward, if agreeable to Congress. After all the trouble the Count has given himself to raise and equip the corps, he could not but esteem it a singular hardship to be deprived of the benefit of his exertions from considerations of inconvenience, which existed before they were undertaken and had been in a manner precluded by Contract.

The circumstance of the Count's having exceeded his establishment was a matter to which I did not advert. There would certainly be no injustice in reducing the extra number. But whether as the men are raised and clad and the expence already incurred, it may

161

not be as well to risk the additional disadvantage which may attend bringing them into the field is a question which Congress will decide.

I am extremely sorry, if any misconception in me should have been the cause of the least embarrassment to the Committee; and I hope the explanation I have now given will remove every difficulty. With the greatest esteem etc. (W.W. p. 42)

★ ★ ★

Details of Pulaski's project are contained in his letter probably sent to Horatio Gates though given by Sparks as written to Washington:

Sir Yorktown, 19 March, 1778

Without going into a detailed history of my life, which would be too long, it will suffice to say to you, in the language of an old soldier and of a citizen, that, in coming to America, my sole object has been to devote myself entirely to her welfare and glory, in using every exertion in my individual power to secure her freedom.

I think the nation was satisfied of my sentiments when it saw that I accepted the post of Brigadier-General of cavalry, though a long service, and my former rank of Commander-in-chief of the army of Poland, had given me a right to expect a higher position. But the sole desire to distinguish myself by my zeal in the cause of the United States, has disposed me to sacrifice my repose and my life to its support, at all times, and in whatever position. I venture to flatter myself, Sir, that my conduct at the head of the cavalry has proved this to the complete satisfaction of the people and the Honorable Congress; happy, General, if I may now be assured of that confidence, on your part, to which I aspire, and if, as I hope, you will honor with your approbation a plan which I have conceived with a sole view to the public good. Here it is, just as I have conceived it to be best adapted to benefit the army and the public.

The corps placed under my command shall be independent, and formed of the two companies of cavalry and of six companies of infantry. If the Board of War, on which it will depend, shall see fit to enlarge it, on seeing, by experience of its courage and conduct, that it might be thus made of greater utility, it will be for them to decide.

The duty of the Commandant-in-chief of this corps will be always to observe, very close at hand, all the movements of the enemy; to take upon himself different enterprises, of the nature of surprises, ambuscades, affairs of posts, rear-guards, protecting flanks, &c., and to advise the Commander-in-chief of the army, and the Board of War, of every thing which he shall find to be of interest. It is easy to see that the whole system of the Commander of such a corps is simply one of active operation. So that, without enlarging on the advantages to be derived from it, it is easy to see that a corps which shall have no other object than to surprise the enemy, to watch them incessantly, and attack them at all points by continual surprises, must be of great utility.

The corps will be recruited from the people of the country, from deserters, and from prisoners of war, agreeably to the letter of General Washington.

I would propose, for my subaltern, an experienced officer, by name Kowacz, formerly a Colonel and partisan in the Prussian service. And as my plan is to employ all the other officers whom I personally know to be capable of serving with distinction and honor, after obtaining the consent of the Honorable Congress for the execution of the plan, I shall have the honor to mention them.

The muskets for the infantry, the pistols for the lancers, the sabres, and the horses, to be furnished me as soon as possible. I will undertake to execute the rest; and as it is difficult to find leather for boots, saddles, &c., I request an order upon the Commissary of Leather to furnish it to me, and upon the different Commandants where my recruits may be, for quarters and rations.

I hope that the instructions may be such, that one third of the cost of equipping the corps may be furnished at once; another third, in proportion as the corps is filled up; and so on.

You enjoy, General, the most distinguished, estimation in our army. I reverence your virtue and your valor; and your military knowledge gives me a confident hope, in presenting this view, of the success of a plan which is only interesting to me through my desire to make myself useful to the nation.

I hope, General, that you will do me the favor to obtain a prompt decision.

C. PULASKI.(Sparks Jared, ed. *The Correspondence of the American Revolution* Being Letters of Eminent Men to George Washington, Boston, 1853.)

Pulaski's proposal was considered favorably by the Board of War which was headed by Horatio Gates. It seems to me probable that Gates inquired about Pulaski from Thaddeus Kosciuszko who had to be familiar with Pulaski's leadership in the war of the Bar Confederacy in Poland, and from Gen. Charles Lee who, though nominally a British prisoner, enjoyed a considerable amount of freedom of movement and communication. It is also possible that R.H. Lee and Adams were supporting the project.

The following letter from Gen. Lee is worth carful scrutiny as it should be rembered that Lee was Stanislaus August Poniatowski's protegee and was in Poland during the Confederacy of Bar war, and his opinion of the Confederates was that they were banditti.

This letter seems to be an answer to somebody's inquiry about Pulaski and was written after Monmouth. It contains a well defined opinion of Pulaski's abilities very different in tone to the lukewarm apprisal of Washington.

> Count Pulesky is certainly a good soldier or He is not -for my own part I believe him a very good one in the first place He is a Polander whose genius is adapted to the light of expedite war-in the second place he has had much practice in the best schools-is undoubtedly brave and enterprising-if He is not a good soldier as his corps is expensive He ought not to be retain'd-therfore it is expedient either to send him about his busyness entirely or to make the proper use of him-but on the supposition that He knows his trade, I wou'd propose the following scheme-that his legion shou'd be immediately compleated to (twelve) hundred men-four hundred Cavalry and eight hundred light infantry -for these eight hundred infantry that a draft shou'd be made without loss of time from every Regiment of the Continent entirely of natives, not so young as to be unable to resist the fatigues of this sort of service, and but still of the proper age for violent exercise and forced marches-Major Lee who seems to have come out of his mother's womb a soldier, shou'd be incorporated in this Legion with the rank of Lieut. Colonel and to command specifically the whole cavalry-if Major Lee's corps (for I know their strength) will (not) added to the Cavalry Pulesky already has, compleat 'em to four hundred-let their be a draft made from the other Regiments of Cavalry-Moilands Blands and Sheldon's all Natives and the very youngest men because on Pulesky's principle of exercise (which I verily believe to be the best in the world) none but very young men are capable of being trained to the manoeuvres-but (as) it is not certain that either Count Pulesky or Major Lee understand the detail of Cavalry (on which so much depends) let some Ouarter Masters or Serjeants who have served in the British Cavalry (and there are many on the Continent) be found out, encourag'd with rank and emolument and employed-a Corps thus composed with brave and understanding Officers at their head, such as are Pulesky and Lee with a few subordinate officers knong in the detail will render more effectual service than any ten Regiments on the Continent-it wou'd likewise put a stop for the future (or it ought to put a stop) to that odious pernicious practice of picking the best men from every Battalion on what are call'd extraordinary occasions-which practice has absolutely no other effect than disgusting the

greater part of the Officers of the Army and rendering the whole dispirited and unfit for actions I cou'd quote a strong instance of the bad consequences of this custom-Some days before the affair of Monmouth, General Scott was detach'd with a Corps of pick'd men and officers to the no small disgust of those who were left behind, who cou'd not help considering it as a sort of stigma on their characters-after this the Marquis of Fayette was detach'd with another (force) of one thoushand pick'd out in the same manner-this Body now consisting of twenty five hundred men instead of falling on the Enemy's flanks did from some fatality absolutely nothing at all. I was afterwards order'd to march to sustain 'em with three scanty Brigades compos'd entirely of the refuse, and of this refuse I was under the necessity of forming my own guard on the day of the action of Monmouth-for the pick'd Corps by the blunders committed were so fatigued that They cou'd scarcely move their legs. (*The Lee Papers*, New York Historical Society, 1874, vol. 3, p. 286.)

On March 19, 1778, the Board of War considered favorably Pulaski's proposal and this favorable report became the basis of the March 28th resolution of Congress.

From its very inception, Pulaski's Legion was plagued by troubles. The original resolve allowed enlistment of prisoners and deserters, but it was soon changed. On 30th March Henry Laurens wrote to Washington:

... At reading the journal this morning, Congress reconsidered the Act of the 28th for authorising Count Pulaski to raise a separate Corps and expunged the words "Prisoners and" which stood in the last sentence and your Excellency will receive within the present Inclosure a Copy of the Act as now amended... (*Letters of Members of the Continental Congress*, ed. Edmunt C, Burnett, vol. 3, p. 146).

Congress had resolved on February 26, 1778 that: "Whereas experience hath proved that no confidence can be placed in prisoners of war or deserters from the enemy, who inlist into the continental army; but many losses and great mischiefs have frequently happened by them; therefore, resolved that no prisoners of war or deserters from the enemy be inlisted, drafted or returned to serve in the continental army."

The whole matter concerning Pulaski's right to enlist deserters and prisoners of war is mysterious. The resolve of 28th March is in amended form and the Journals for 30th March do not contain any mention of amendment.

The report of the Board of War, March 19, 1778 (PCC, Item 147, folio 557-558), consisting of Horatio Gates, Timothy Pickering and Richard Peters, none of them too friendly to Washington, said:

> That the Count Pulaski retains his Rank of Brigadier General in the Army of the United States and that he raise and have the Command of independent Corps to consist of sixty-eight Horse and two hundred Foot, the Horse to be armed with Lances, the Foot equipped in the Manner of Light Infantry. The Corps to be raised (?) such Men as General Washington shall think expedient and proper and if it shall be thought by General Washington that it will not (?) the Service, that he have Liberty to dispense in this particular Instance with the Resolve of Congress against enlisting (Prisoners-struck out) Deserters (*Papers of the Continental Congress*, Item 147, folio 557-58).

This document which became the basis for the Congress resolve of March 28th is illegible and blotted. Somebody evidently tampered with it but it is clear that originally the Board allowed Pulaski to recruit deserters and prisoners.

Pulaski, as usual impatient for action, did not allow Congress to take its time. Its resolve of March 28th was prompted by Pulaski's letter of the same date (PCC, 164, 1). Though it looks strange to a English reader being written in a phonetic Polish spelling it closely resembles English sounds:

> Gentil Men-
> My Zeal for Your Servyce is veriwell known. It don't deserve to be rejected. I beg as a favour to permit me to serve You or If my proposal disples You let me no. The answer for wich I am expecting sinse ten dais. wich the honourable Congress well give me, shal be the recompens of my gud willing to conduct the Publick interes. I expect it, And I remain with respect
> Gentil Men Your Most humbl Servent
> Cr Pulaski, Gl.

The computerized index to "Papers of the Continental Congress listed on the same date, i.,e., 28 March 1778, Casimir Pulaski as the author of 'Thoughts re enlisting the enemy." As was explained to me by the most helpful Alan F. Perry, Archivist of the Center for the Documentary Study of the American Revolution, the document was indexed as Pulaski's on Worthington C. Ford's asumption.

Obviously Pulaski, who never served in the Prussian Army, could not be the man who penned these "Thoughts." However, as said Mr. Perry, its author could be Friedrich von Steuben, with whom Pulaski perhaps discussed his ideas about the Legion, or Michael Kovatch.,

The arguments contained in this document are in accordance in with military practice and theory at those times:

> Thoughts about the Objections made against Inlisting Deserters of the Enemy.
>
> I take the King of Prussia as being a Master in political and military business. He keeps a large army in a little Dominion by encreasing his army so much as possible with Deserters from all the nations without distinction and he sends his own people from the Army in to the Country to cultivate it. So he did in the War from 1756 to 1763 in which time I served in the Prussian Army. After taking the whole Saxonian Army as prisoners, he send many thousands of his own Soldiers from the Camp to their houses. Everyone know how his Prussian Majesty's Dominions were covered with his Enimys so that only a few fortifications were in his power. His Army was then not otherly composed but with Deserters and prisoners of war and as I know by experience not only whole Companies but Regiments deserted from our Army that could not hinder the King of Prussia from filling up his Army again with Deserters and prisoners of war, and not only he defeated very often his Enimys and retook his Dominion but he forced his Enimys to offer him peace.
>
> I take only Deserters for my object and I say a Deserter will fight better than another one, because he fears to be taken and punished with death. He is an learned and good Soldier, if he is well treated and kept under Disciplin, and the Damage caused by a Deserter to the Enimy is compensated by a Deserter from the Enimy bringing arms and cloath with him." (PCC, Item, 147, folio 549)

Americans were not always so much against enlisting the deserters. In 1776 they thought the French Canadians would desert His Britannic Majesty's colors to join the struggle for independence and were quite disappointed when the inhabitants of Canada somehow preferred the tyrant George III to the tyrant Louis XVI.

When the Hessians cast a shadow of terror through the American continent a committee was appointed to devise a plan to encourage them and other foreigners to desert the British service. It was resolved by Congress on August 14, 1776,that:

> ...these states will receive all such foreigners who shall leave the armies of His Britannic Majesty in America, and shall choose to become members of any of these States: that they shall be protected in the free exercise of their respective religions and be invested with the rights, priviliges and immunities of natives as established by the laws of these States: and, moreover, that this Congress will provide, for every such

person 50 acres of unappropriated lands in some of these States to be
held by him and his heirs in absolute perpetuity...

And guess who entertained dignitaries on the first anniversary of the
revolution?

Last Friday, the 4th July, being the anniversary of the independence
of the USA, was celebrated in this city (Boston) with demonstrations
of joy and festivity. About noon all the armed ships and galleys
which were in the river were drawn up before the city, dressed in
the gayest manner with the colours of the United States and stream-
ers displayed. At one o'clock, the yards being properly manned, they
began celebrations of the day by a discharge of thirteen ships, and
one from each of 13 galleys, in honour of the 13 United States.

In the afternoon an elegant dinner was prepared for Congress to
which were invited the President and Executive Council and Speak-
ers of the assembly of this State, the General Officers and Colonels
of the Army and strangers of eminence and the Members of the several Continental Boards in town. The Hessian Band of Music, taken
in Trenton on the 26th December last, attended and heightened the
festivity with some fine performance suited to the joyous occasion,
while a corps of British deserters, taken into the service of the continent by the State of Georgia, being drawn up before the door filled
up the intervals with feux de joie. After the dinner a number of
toasts were drunk, all breathing independence and a generous love of
liberty...

Each toast was followed by a discharge of artillery and small arms
and a suitable piece of music by the Hessian Band. (*The Boston and
Country Gazette*, July 28, 1777).

The Hessians, the bogeymen of the Revolution, and a corps of
British deserters entertaining guests on the first anniversary of the
Independence Declaration! It must be kept in mind that desertions
were a common phenomenon of the age and deserters were not
treated with contempt. The Eighteenth Century wars in Western
Europe were not wars of ideology or national survival, excepting the
Bar Confederacy Insurection.

As to Washington's and some Congress members' fears about
unreliable foreigners, it must be noted that treachery was not limited
to foreigners. On March 25th, Joseph Galloway sent the Earl of
Dartmouth a report on soldiers and galleymen who deserted Washington and took the oath of allegiance to the King in Philadelphia.
Soldiers born in England numbered 206, in Scotland 56, in Ireland
492, in Germany 88, in Canada 4 and in America 283; while

galleymen born in England numbered 69, in Scotland 22, in Ireland 157, in Germany 16, in France 15 and in America 65. (B.F. Stevens, ed., *Facsimiles of Manuscripts*, London 1889, vol. 24, Nos. 2093 & 2094). And what about Benedict Arnold?

In addition to all the recruiting troubles, Congress and Washington belatedly tried to raise cavalry which made Pulaski's task even more difficult by intensifying the competition for cavalry recruits.

Probably the Board of War was more realistic about the problem than Washington and Congress.

On May 27, 1778, Tim Pickering signed the following document addressed to William Atlee and all other Commissioners of Prisoners in the Service of the United States:

> Sir, Although tis prohibited to inlist prisoners or deserters into the common battalions, yet tis understood that for the purpose of completing Genl. Pulaski's independent Corps he should be permitted to inlist both. You will therefore offer the General officers, having his Orders to recruit such of the Hessian prisoners in your district, not Shoemakers or Tailors, who are not married in Europe, nor have wives in the enemy's possession. We are so desirous of compleating speedily this corps that you will oblige us; as well as serve the publick by facilitating the enlistment of such Hessian prisoners as do not come under the above description as far as shall be in your power. (P.C.C. 78, 1, 177)

On May 29, 1778, the President of Congress, Henry Laurens wrote to Atlee:

> I received by the hand of Count de Montfort your favor of the 26th. After some conversation with that Gentleman he took leave fully convinced that his attempt to enlist prisoners of war had been contrary to the Resolution of Congress under which he was authorised to act. Your opposition was consequently well founded and your conduct commendable. (L.M.C.C. Burnett, vol. 8, p. 266)

To which Atlee replied on June 2nd, his letter being referred to the Board of War.

> Sir, I am honoured with your favour of the 29th of last month by the post approving of my conduct and mentioning the propriety of my opposition to the Count de Montford's enlisting the prisoners of war here. I am happy in the approbation of Congress, but from the tenor of your letter, fear I have since that acted contrary to this sentiment. The Count on the 29th of last month on his return from York brought me a letter from the War Office dated the 27th, of which the inclosed is a copy directing me to suffer Genl. Pulaski's officers

to recruit such of the Hessian prisoners as are not Shoemakers or Tailors, who are not married in Europe, nor have wives in the enemy possession, and desiring me to facilitate their inlistment as far as my power. This letter being brought by the Count, I concluded Congress had referred the matter to the Board of War and that it contained all the answer I had to expect to my letter to you. I therefore in obedience to it not only encouraged the Hessians to inlist but gave the Count a certified copy of it, that he might meet with no opposition from the Commissaries of Prisoners in other places. He engaged several here and will doubtless meet with success elsewhere.

I am at a loss to know whether to put a stop to their further inlistment of prisoners here or not. It is a measure which seems to me not quite agreeable to the will of Congress, but if it is countenanced by the Board of War who desire me to further it all in my power I shall always be happy in discharging the duty of my appointment to the satisfaction of both those Honourable Bodies. And tho' it gives me uneasiness to be thus troublesome to Congress, my duty to them and myself obliges me to mention these matters and puts me under the necessity of asking their positive directions which I beg to be honoured with... (PCC 78, 1, 173)

To which the Board of War answered on June 5th, 1778:

Sir, Your letter to Congress of the 2nd instant has been referred to the board with the sense of Congress intimated at the same time, that prisoners of war should not be inlisted into any corps in the service of the United States. The licence given Genl. Pulaski to inlist prisoners is to be considered as recalled. The licence was founded on a supposed intention of Congress to permit the inlistment of prisoners into that particular corps. Prisoners were in fact included in the resolve (as originally drawn up) as well as deserters; and tho' the former were finally struck out, yet the information given to the board led them to the determination mentioned in their former letter to you on the subject...Tim Pickering. Junr, (LMCC, 279)

On the same subject wrote Thomas McKeane, and let us note that his and Joseph Reed's name can be found frequently associated with documents not favorable to Pulaski:

Upon receipt of your favor of the 26th ulto, I applied to some of the members of the Board of War respecting the Instructions they had given to General Pulaski for inlisting prisoners of war, and was told they had given such and had wrote to you about it. This made me think it unnecessary to write to you, but upon examining the Acts of Congress on this head I found the Board were wrong, and that no prisoners of war can be inlisted in that Legion, or in any other Corps. Congress decided accordingly yesterday of which you will be informed by the President, Tho' we have surplus of privates of the Enemy at present after exchanging our own, yet they have Citizens and may take more prisoners. Besides, from my knowledge of the human heart, I am convinced that if these prisoners of war were to come to a close and hot engagement with the enemy, the fear of the latter in case of their being made prisoners would induce them to seek safety in flight." (op.cit, p. 280)

Thus as it happens, ideology triumphed over common sense, and the prisoners of war who, especially Hessians, would fight equally well or badly on anybody's side were to rot in the POW camps.

Wrote Robert L. Hooper, Jr., to Elias Boudinot from Easton, on June 13, 1778: "..General Pulaski has enlisted 16 of the British prisoners of war and detains them, and about thirty died since I received your Orders to confine them in a close gaol..." (P.M.H.B. vol. 40, p. 497)

Nevertheless on June 25, 1778, Charles Armand Tuffin, the Marquis de la Rouriere, was authorized to recruit from the enemy's foreign troops, Frenchmen and others not owing allegiance to the King of Great Britain (JCC p. 642).

Pulaski, the future leader of the independent corps, was being closely watched by various officials. This is evident from Washington's letter dated May 1, 1778:

Sir, I am exceedingly concerned to learn that you are acting contrarily both to a positive resolve of Congress and my express orders, in engaging British prisoners for your Legionary Corps. When Congress referred you to me on the subject of its composition, to facilitate your raising it I gave you leave to inlist one-third deserters in the Foot and was induced to do even that from your assuring me that your intention was primarily to take Germans, in whom you thought a greater confidence might be placed. The British prisoners will cheerfully inlist as a ready means of escaping, the Continental bounty will be lost and your corps as far as ever being complete. I desire therefore that the prisoners may be returned to their confinements, and that you will for the future adhere to the restrictions under which I laid you.

The Horse are to be, without exception, natives who have ties of property and family connexions. I am sorry it is not in my power to grant your request relative to drafting four men per regiment for your corps, as this would be branching ourselves out into different corps without increasing our strength, and men cannot conveniently be spared from the line at present... (*Writings of Washington*, John C. Fitzpatrick, editor, vol. 11, p. 337)

It was obvious that Pulaski needed those men, not for strengthening his own corps, but as cadre for training purposes. Previously, he had received two privates for each horse regiment and a sergeant for that purpose. (W.W.ll, p. 213)

While still on the subject of deserters, it must be noted that even before Pulaski's Legion was completed, it was troubled with desertion. Perhaps the first deserter was the man whose genial description appeared in *The Maryland Journal* and *Baltimore Advertiser* of April 28, 1778:

> Deserted from General Pulaski's Legion a certain William Taugard. An Englishman, about 24 years old, 5 feet, 3 inches high, he is a thick-set man, has black hair, brown complexion, large mouth, laughs very often and has on such occasions hollows in his cheeks. Had on when he left a blue coat and white breeches, but was destitute of jacket. Whoever apprehends him and effectually secures said deserter shall be freed from any military duty for one year, according to section 13 of an Act of Legislature of Maryland. De Segond, Captain.

This advertisement was followed on August 18th by a list of 18 names, mostly English and German, and the Hon. Gen. Count Pulaski promised to pay 20 dollars for each captured deserter.

It must be observed that advertisements for deserters were quite common in the Press.

Pulaski experienced less difficulty enlisting officers than privates, as did most army units. On April 9, 1778, Washington wrote to the Committee from Congress the following letter:

> Gentn: By a Resolve of Congress the appointment of Officers to the Corps which Brigadier General Count Pulaski is authorised to raise, has been referred to your decision in conjunction with me. As I know the superior confidence which a Commander places in Officers of his own choice, I have given him my approbation of the Gentlemen whom he has nominated. It remains with you to decide in their favor or have other substituted... (WW,11, p. 230).

This letter was sent by the committee to Congress, and on May 1, 1778, Pulaski sent the following letter to Henry Laurens:

BALTIMORE, May 1, 1778

SIR: I have had the honor to mention the necessity to appoint many officers. I recommended to the Congress the Knight James de Segond to be captain. He hath now in my corps more deserts, than any other; his company is already completed and filled up. The other is Mr. Bedkin, captain of spearsmen. He hath served already two campaigns. He is American born, and good officer. He was my brigadier-major in the cavalry. The third, Mr. Bentalon, for captain. He hath served two campaigns, too, in German battalion; Frederick Pashke for captain; Emperic Wena for second lieutenant; Abraham Boemper for second lieutenant. Those three last were in your service late in the same rank, one in German battalion, the other in the disabled-soldier battalion, and the first was under the QuartermasterGeneral in the camp. The General Washington let me entirely the choice of my officers. I sent his letter to the delegates. Thus I don't find any objections to settle this matter, and the good of the service requests a sudden decision. The commissions ought to be dated from the very same day that you delivered to me the first one.

In some weeks I expect my corps shall be complete and joined here, and then I should be able to send to the Congress an exact account of my expenses. You know that the sum of $50,000 is not sufficient enough to buy the horses, whom they ask the foolish price everywhere.

I represented already that to the Congress, and I should desire you in this instant to grant me $10,000, for I think that the Congress included such sum (in the $50,000 granted to me), having delivered the ditto three days before the last resolved.

I beg you as a favor to help me in raising, completing, and putting in the best foot possible my legion, who, protect by you, will be (torn) get you great deal of honor. The officer who is desired with this letter ordered to go in Easton: thus I expect your answer by the first opportunity. I delivered up the money to Mr. Francis Hopkinson. I send his answer wherein his return I should be very glad to be sure if the matter whom I was told by you will go in, and when it will be performed and begun. I can upon your answer take the proper dimension.

I sent back again my commission to Mr. Duhon, because the time of my service was not mentioned in. You know that I came over here in the last June, and I was appointed in your army little while after, and then I should be glad that you will mention that in my commission.

Sir, I am your most humble servant,

C. PULASKI, General

To the honourable Henry Laurens, esq., President of the Congress, at Yorktown.(Indorsed:) Letter from General Pulaski, Baltimore, 1 May, should be June; read June 4, 1778. Referred to the Board of War.(PCC 164, f.9)

The opinion of Nathanael Greene is here quoted to show the conditions in which Pulaski, a foreigner, had to work.

...Horses were wanted to mount our dragoons. They could not be procured but by virtue of impress warrants...Some mistakes and several abuses appear to have happened in impressing stud horses instead of geldings, but those mistakes arose from the necessity of mounting our dragoons in such a manner as to give us an immediate superiority over the enemy, as well as in the quality of the horses as their number. The people complained...

The rights of the individual are as dear to me as to any man, but the safety of a community I have ever considered as an object more valuable. In politics, as well as in everything else, a received and established maxim is that greater evils should in every instance give way to lesser misfortunes. In war it is often impossible to conform to all the ceremonies of law and equal justice, and to attempt it would be producive of greater misfortunes to the public from the delay than all the inconveniences which an individual may suffer...

Nothing but light horse can enable, with the little army we have to appear in the field, and nothing but a superiority in cavalry can prevent the enemy from cutting to pieces every detachment coming to join the army or employed in collecting supplies. From the open state of this country their services are particulary necessary, and unless we can keep up the corps of cavalry, and constantly support a superiority, it will be out of our power to act or to prevent the enemy from overrunning the country and commanding all its resources.

...if horses are dearer to the inhabitants than the lives of subjects, or the liberties of the people, there will be no doubt of the Assembly persevering in their late resolution...

(George Washington Greene, *The Life of Nathanael Green*, N.Y. 1867:3, p. 288)

And Signer, W. Paca wrote thus to Governor Johnson:

Dr Sir,

I shall be much obliged to you to forward the enclosed by some safe hand to Harford County.

A Mr. Rudolph an officer of the Light Horse with a Sergeant paid me a visit a few days ago they were in pursuit of Horses and demanded some of me. Mr. Rudolph shewed no Authority from Major Lee to press all horses between Chesapeake & Delaware that would suit for Light Horse. After reading his Authority, I told him if he attempted to seize any of my horses I would blow his brains out and if he did not leave this State or cease to exercise such power I would issue my warrants and commit him to Jail: he declined seizing my horses and gave me to understand his power was only in Ten.

He and the Sergeant went to Talbot & there attempted to seize a Horse but were baffled by a Spirited resistance. They made a like attempt since & Mr. Rudolph got a severe whipping. He has since gone off, before he came to me he called at Col Ed Tilghmans & seized a horse off young Neds which he carried off. I knew nothing of it till too late.

My love to Charles & family. I Am glad to hear that my Brother Judge done his duty.

Wye Island Yrs truly

11 June 1778 Wm Paca

(Archives of Maryland, 1778, p. 131)

Pulaski was mistaken in appealing to Laurens for protection, and assuming that the President of Congress would help him to make the Legion truly independent. Laurens during the Conway affair behaved equivocally, until he actively helped Washington. His connection with the Adams-Lee group was occasioned by a common hatred of Silas Deane. About the time Pulaski was writing to him, Laurens strongly supported Washington's military authority, even above Congress.

Philadelphia was a principal supply center for the Continental army and Pulaski was authorized to draw upon Continental stores, after he exceeded the 130 dollars allowed by Congress for furnishing one recruit. There are a number of receipts from that area and period in the National Archives.

But Maryland took good care of its legion as shown by numerous numerous entries in the Archives of Maryland *Journal and Correspondence of the Council of Maryland* (Baltimore, 1901).

Monday 18 May 1778

...Commissry of Stores to deliver to Capt. Bailliry 2 pairs of Shoes and 4 pairs Stockings for two Recruits charged to Gen. Pulaski's Legion.

Wednesday 27th May 1778

...Ordered that the Armourer deliver to Capt. Segond of Pulaski's Corps two Horse Trumpets...

Tuesday 9th June 1778

...Ordered that the western shore treasurer pay to Capt. Segond of Pulaski's Legion sixty pounds the allowance on ten Recruits per Acct by the AG.

...Ordered That Capt. Keeports deliver to Capt. Segond of General Pulaski's Legion as many Camp Kettles as he may have occasion for allowing six men to a Mess...

That the Commissary of Stores deliver to Capt. Segond two Drums.

9th June 1778
To G. Keeports
Sir,

Capt. Segond has applied to us for Linen for Shirts and Overalls for the Recruits inlisted in this State for Genl. Pulaski's Legion. We are not able to furnish it here nor probably shall be till our galley return with the Linen from below. The Capt. says you and Mr. Calhoun have Linen. If either of you have, we wish these Recruits to be supplied with those Articles, as the other Recruits of the Quota of this State...

Monday 9th June, 1778

...That the Commissary of Stores in Baltimore deliver to Genl. Pulaski's order 4 Rifles and 40 Canteens for his Legion.

That the Armourer deliver to Capt. Segond 5 pairs of Pistols.

...That the said Commissary of Stores deliver to Capt. Segond Oznabrigs 60 pairs of Overalls and Linen for 200 Shirts to be charged to Gen. Pulaski's Legion.

13 August 1778
Council to G. Keeports
Sir,

Col. Baron Bose of Genl. Pulaski's Legion has applied to us for an Order on you for a piece or two of blue or gray cloth for the use of himself and his officers. If you have such as will suit, we request you to deliver...

Council to Delegates in Congress, 26 March 1779

...for those of Count Pulaski's Legion inlisted in this State, of whom we never had a Return, they were more than 100...

★ ★ ★

While organizing his corps, Pulaski found relaxation and perhaps welcome in Bethlehem, a settlement of Moravian brothers and sisters in Northampton County, about fifty miles from Philadelphia.

According to Lossing, it was there that Pulaski visited Lafayette who was recuperating from his Brandywine wound. Lossing as usual does not give his source, and I found no confirmation of the visit. It remains as much a matter of conjecture as the Kosciuszko-Pulaski meeting at Trenton at Christmas 1777, or Pulaski's visits to Haym Salomon in Philadelphia. Lafayette lodged close to the Sum Inn at the Frederick Beckel house, where he was nursed by Beckel's wife and daughter, Liesel, on whom he made a deep impression. Since his wound was slight, however, his stay was not long. He arrived on September 11, and left on October 22. (W.C. Reichel, *History of the Bethlehem Female Seminary*, Philadelphia, 1858, pp. 179 and 183). That period saw intensive maneuvering around Philadelphia, and the Battle of Germantown, so it is doubtful whether Pulaski found time to visit Lafayette.

The Moravians-Unitas Fratrum-originated in the territory now known as Czechoslovakia and were a splinter group of the Hussites. They found asylum in Poland, famed in those days for religious tolerance. There they were known as the Czech Brothers. This tolerance, however, was gradually replaced by Catholic activism, and the country underwent a period of internal and external troubles. The brothers moved to Herrhut in Saxony where they enjoyed the protection of a noble, Nicolaus Ludwig Zizendorff, who eventually was ordained with the written permission of Bishop Siatkowski from Poland.

The first group of Brethren landed in Georgia, in the vicinity of Savannah, where they did not stay long before moving to the more congenial atmosphere of Pennsylvania, where the Quakers professed the same principle of not bearing arms.

The Moravians were industrious people and built an impressive settlement with commodious buildings, many workshops, and even a brewery. Their numerous skills were widely known and the Moravians were probably "discovered" by Colonel Kovatch during his travels in search of accoutrements and clothing.

The Moravians were mostly Germanic in their ethnic composition, but years of connection with Poland, the presence of the Czechs, Slovaks and Poles amongst them, and the probable understanding of the Polish language and customs made their village a pleasant place for Pulaski. Even a hill at the settlement was called "Niski" which means "the low one" in Polish.

The Moravian diaries noted the presence of Pulaski and his officers on a few occasions:

January 24, 1778- "The famous Col. Kobatsch, a Prussian officer of Hussars in the late war, arrived from Easton to see whether we could aid him, equip and mount a corps of Hussars, which he is recruiting for Congress. He found, however, that we were unable to assist him, as our saddlers, glovemakers and founder had no stock for their trades."

(But as the receipts show in National Archives (N.A.17730) on July 21, 1778, Col. Kovatch purchased from a certain Abraham Clark of Bethlehem, 50 pairs of leather gaiters at 10 dollars each and 100 pairs of shoes at six dollars each.)

April 16- "Gen Pulaski and Col. Kobatsch attended the meeting this afternoon."

May 17 (Sunday)- "At the English morning service, there were present Samuel Adams, Delegate from Massachusetts, and Genl. Pulaski, with some members of his corps, in full dress uniform."

July 31- "Heard heavy cannonading in the forenoon. Col. Kobatsch and the equipped members of his corps recruited in Easton passed through en route to Baltimore."

January 2 (1779)- "A troop of Pulaski's cavalry passed through on the way to Lebanon for winter quarters."

(The Moravian Diaries as quoted in John E. Jordan's *Bethlehem During the Revolution*, Penn Mag. Hist., vol. 13, 1889)

And another diarist from Nazareth, Pennsylvania, notes:

December 31, 1778- "The long-expected Light Horse came to stay overnight–about 80–and later Col. Kobatsch. We arranged that some of them should go to Friedenstahl and 20 with their horses to Christian Springs, where we have more stalls. Only a few remained here at the inn."

February 18- "Later we had another not so pleasant a visit of 150 infantry of Gen. Pulaski's corps, and 20 of them were billeted in the Hall. As they were Germans and nearly all of them Lutheran or Reformed Church, they requested a sermon which the Rev. Lembke preached for them on I Tim. 1:15. They and their officers were very attentive and orderly." (P.M.H. v. 38, p.309)

Bethlehem, while comparatively in the interior, was close to the line of operations and was the seat of a large agricultural and peaceful community. It was also a thoroughfare for troops. The buildings originally constructed for the communal living were large and solid, so it was not strange that it was chosen twice for a military hospital and had to accommodate prisoners of war. In addition, the heavy baggage of the Army and its ammunition, and also the private baggage of Washington were located there at times.

Perhaps this place in the text is as proper as any other to mention the little-known fact that while Washington refused his Commander-in-Chief pay, he was receiving table or subsistence money of 1500 dollars per month. For comparison, a Major-General received 160 dollars per month, Brigadier-General 125 dollars, Dragoon 8 1/3 dollars, and Infantryman 6 2/3 dollars. (PCC 247,41)-Estimate of the Gen. & Staff Officer Pay and Estimate for Regiment of Cavalry and Partisan Corps, 1781, PCC 247,41)

Naturally the Moravians experienced bad times during the Revolution, especially since the sympathies of their elders were with George III. Once General Charles Lee threatened to ransack the Brethren's Bethlehem, but was prevented from doing so because the British captured him. The Moravians paid in the last three months of 1777, 1500 dollars to the American Army which did not include an exorbitant fine for being conscientious objectors. The buckwheat and fence around their fields were destroyed, as were acres of Indian corn, turnips, cabbage, flax, 594 cords of wood and tons of hay. Let us here remark that among the culprits were Bland's and Lee's dragoons even before Pulaski took over their command.

In addition, there were threats from the neighborhood militia, and the pacific brothers heard bullets whistling close to their heads from accidentally discharged rifles. Altogether, life was not too easy for that religious community in spite of having friends among the delegates and the fact that Henry Laurens was their protector. The following document bears testimony to the times.

Bethlehem, September 22, 1777
Having observed a diligent attention to the sick and wounded,
and a benevolent desire to make the necessary provisions for the relief of the distressed as far as the power of the brethren enables them,
We desire that all Continental officers may refrain from disturbing
the persons or property of the Moravians in Bethlehem; and, particularly, that they do not disturb or molest the houses where the
women are assembled,
Given under our hands at the time and place above mentioned.

John Hancock	Richard Henry Lee
Samuel Adams	Henry Laurens
James Duane	William Duer
Nathan Brownson	Cornelius Harnett
Nathaniel Folsom	Benjamin Harrison
Richard Law	Joseph Jones
Eliphalet Dyer	John Adams
Henry Marchant	William Williams
Delegates to Congress	

(Cit. W.C. Reichel, *History of the Bethlehem*, Philadelphia, 1885, p.180)

John W. Jordan notes in his article (PMHB,1889) that Pulaski, while stationed at Bethlehem with a detachment of his troopers, always placed a guard at the Sisters' House during the passage of the troops through the town. In grateful acknowledgment of the protection thus offered them, the superintendent, Sister Susan von Gersford, suggested making a banner or guidon. The design of the work was entrusted to Rebecca Langly and Julia Bader (the daughter of a pastor of the congregation during the Revolution). In their work they were assisted by a number of their friends, especially Anna Beam, Anna Husey and Erdmunth Langly.

John Hill Martin, in his "Historical Sketch of Bethlehem," Philadelphia, 1873, quotes the *History of Lehigh County*: "Count Pulaski was complimented for his gallantry by a presentation of a banner embroidered by the Single Sisters as a token of their gratitude for the protection he had afforded them surrounded as they were by a rough and uncouth soldiery."

That supposed event became an inspiration for a poem by Henry W. Longfellow, "Hymn of the Moravian Nuns" (in fact not nuns but single women and widows), which did much to perpetuate Pulaski's memory. But Jordan, after a careful examination of Moravian diaries, finds not the slightest reference to such presentation as described by Longfellow, who, as the poet wrote himself, was inspired by a simple passage in the *North American Review*: "The standard of Count Pulaski, the noble Pole who fell in the attack on Savannah during the American Revolution, was of crimson silk, embroidered by the Moravian Nuns of Bethlehem, Pa."

The banner issue remains unresolved. Was it a gift of the grateful Bethlehem sisters or was it a simple business transaction, as claimed in the Pennsylvania Archives (2nd Series, vol. xi, 1880, p.153), though no sources are cited for this authoritative statement?

Paul Bentalou, referring to his polemist, Judge Johnson, gives still another version:

> Our author appears very much disposed to an awkward jest on the exhibition of the flag of the legion, on Lafayette's entrance into Baltimore. This relick I had, with an old man's feeling, kept locked up in my house forty-five years, and there probably it had remained, had not the return of the soldier of freedom to our shores drawn from concealment every memorial, however trifling, which it was thought might recal to him the grateful recollection of the period and the companions of his early toils. Among the rest, the standard was displayed by a company of volunteers in this city, who requested it of me for this purpose, and to whom I was induced to grant it by the consideration I have just spoken of. When the occasion was answered, it was deposited in the Baltimore

Museum, as a "relick of old days" interesting to Baltimore at least, which, when a village, had been the cradle of the legion, and whose women, with a touch of patriotism, had caused this standard to be made and presented to the young corps. (P. Bentalou, Reply, etc pp.38,39)

The Moravian women were famed for their embroidery, and I surmise that Pulaski could have ordered the banner and the sisters intended to present is as a gift, but Pulaski insisted on paying for it. This matter, however, is of importance since there is an intriguing Masonic design on the banner. If the banner was a gift, Pulaski might not have known anything of the design. However, if he ordered it that would be significant.

The banner is about twenty inches square and was attached to a lance. On its right side there is an all-seeing eye in a triangle. There are yellow rays around the eye, and an inscription reads: NON ALIUS REGIT-No Other Governs. On the reverse side are letters US (supposedly used for the first time on a flag) and around them the words UNITA VIRTUS FORCIOR [sic]-United Valor is Stronger. The banner was of crimson silk with yellow threads, and the Latin inscriptions were greenish in color. (This banner is on display in the Maryland Historical Society Museum, Baltimore, and a replica is in the possession of the Polish National Alliance in Chicago.)

Professor Wladyslaw Konopczynski points to the fact that Pulaski was probably a Mason, and directs attention to the presence of that Masonic symbol on the flag. He also suggests the possibility that Pulaski joined a lodge in France, or at least had some Masonic friends who supplied him with letters of recommendation.

Konopczynski cites as a significant fact that during his stay at Bethlehem Pulaski stopped at the Sun Inn, held by Matthias Schropp. In fact Matthew Schropp (spelled Mattheus by J.H. Martin) was a steward of the Bethlehem Economy who had applied for an inn license. The first innkeeper was Peter Worbas, the second Jasper Payne, and during the Revolution Just Jansen and his wife Mary jointly occupied that position. ("The Old Moravian Sun Inn," the *Pennsylvania German Society Publication*, vol. 16, October 16,1895) Perhaps Professor Konopczynski mistook Sun Inn for Sun Tavern (correctly Tun Tavern) where Masonic meetings were held in Philadelphia.

The Sun Inn was the largest establishment of its type in Bethlehem and was, according to Aubury, equal to the first tavern in London. It is not puzzling then, that under its roof slept almost all the patriots who signed the Declaration and the generals of the Revolution who were only partially enumerated by John Hill Martin in "Historical Sketch of

Bethlehem,"Philadelphia, 1873. That there were Masons among them has no more significance than that a ferry at to Easton on the Delaware River was used by the same set of men.

More valid is a fact revealed by R.W. William M. Stuart, then District Deputy Grand Master, Grand Lodge F & M, New York, in his book *Masonic Soldiers of Fortune*, Macoy Publishing, N.Y., 1928, who wrote: "In view of the fact that the banner had a Masonic design, it would seem likely that Pulaski was a Mason at this time. However, the Master Mason of Washington, D.C., recently printed an item to the effect that Count Pulaski was made a Mason in a military lodge in Georgia shortly before his death. The Grand Lodge of Georgia laid the cornerstone of a monument to his memory in Savannah on March 21, 1824, General Lafayette presiding at the ceremonies. (op. cit., p.149).

Leonard Chodzko in *Zywot Kazimierza na Pulaziu Pulaskiego*, Lwow, 1869, gives a report on Masonic ceremonies connected with Pulaski's Monument at Savannah, while William R. Denslow in his extensive compilation of *10,000 Famous Masons* writes:

> There is no proof of Pulaski's Masonic membership. All references to it stem from after 1824, when the cornerstone of the monument was laid with Masonic ceremonies and Richard T. Turner, high priest of the Georgia Chapter at Savannah, reported to his chapter that they laid the cornerstone of the monument to "Brother Pulaski." Other sources say he was affiliated with the Maryland Line. Casimir Pulaski Lodge No. 1167, meeting in Logan Square. Masonic Temple, Chicago, is named in his honor, and a brochure issued by them states in part,"Casimir Pulaski was raised to the subleme degree of Master Mason in Gould Lodge of Georgia on June 19, 1779...was buried with Masonic honors." d. Oct.11, 1779.

The Masonic issue is not entirely clear. Gould was an early Masonic writer, not a lodge, and there is no known documentary proof of Pulaski's membership in the Masonic fraternity. Such a membership would mean a change in his ideology, for the Bar Insurrection, of which he was the chief leader, was almost fanatical in its Catholicism. Morton Deutsch, a known Freemasonry researcher, told me during a telephone conversation that Pulaski was not a Mason, but his research was not available to me.

However, Stanley F. Maxwell, Sovereign Grand Commander of the Supreme Council 33 AA Scottish Rite, wrote to me: "There would appear to be ample evidence, if not actual proof of his (Pulaski's) membership in the Masonic Fraternity," and I am inclined to agree with this opinion.

★ ★ ★

Not everything was proceeding smoothly during the Legion's organization. General Smallwood suffered acutely from an oversupply of officers and shortage of privates. He did not take kindly to his soldiers deserting to Pulaski's Legion, and complained bitterly to Washington and the Maryland Council. Washington ordered Pulaski to return immediately recruits belonging to Maryland to General Smallwood or any officer of Maryland troops. The order was complied with and a "List of Deserters and Men Given to the 3 Maryland Regiments from Gen. Pulaski's Legion" is in the National Archives. (N.10 Pulaski's Legion, Dec. 10, 37488974, 1897).

Also, the Legion's soldiers somehow fell into conflict with members of the Invalid Corps created about the same time as a result of a complaint of a very serious nature lodged by Captain Woelper concerning the abuse of a guard and a prisoner under his care. Washington ordered on June 24th that such mutinous disposition should be immediately inquired into and if it was as represented, proper punishment imposed and measures taken to prevent such behavior in the future.

The corps of invalids was created to perform guard duty and as training schools for young gentlemen in the arts of war. Even their officers were encouraged to sacrifice a part of their wages for the maintenance of a library. However, the invalids could be quite troublesome. For instance, as published by Horatio Gates, the invalids audaciously demanded to pay the same price for butter and some other articles as they were priced some years ago. It must be explained that due to inflation, the price of food went up, so that the population was starving. Price control had to be established, and commissaries appointed who were selling and giving food to the wives and children of soldiers.

It was probably because of troubles of this kind that Pulaski on June 6, 1778, wrote to Washington: "The duty of the service keeps me from presenting myself to your Excellency. I send for this purpose M. de Sigoine. He will have the honour to tell you what I want–their effect will depend upon your Goodness." (MS. Pa His. Soc)

That Pulaski had the command capability is demonstrated by the following incident. During the Revolution, the Continental Navy was practically non-existent, but privateering flourished.

American privateers took about 600 British ships during the years 1775-83, which included 16 men-of-war. The prize money was estimated at $18,000,000. In acute competition with the state armies and Continental Army for men, privateers generally had the upper hand.

Pulaski dreamed about sea power for his Legion. He learned that some brig offered for sale was a bargain and he wrote to Thomas Johnson, Jr., the following letter:

Sir

As I have a mind to Establish My Legion upon a Solid Condition, I Don't think there is a Better Expedient for that purpose, then to associate all my people together, and to Detach often a Couple Dozens of them at Sundry times for to Go to Sea.

I have several prospect to Execute that project, the first, is to assure of my self of my Soldiers, By the advantage they'll perceive in the said Society, and as Every one of them Shall have a Share according to the money they'll Lay to the mass in the attempt, that I want to make, I Dont Doubt But this will Engage them to Serve with Great deal more Zeal for the public Cause: for that purpose I want to purchase a Vessel, I understood, -here Lays a Brigantine which is to be sold By orders of your Excellency. I then Do Send Mr Baldesqui Bearer of this Letter, to Deal with the persons appointed for that matter. I hope Sir you will be Kind Enough to Befriend me in this project which I am Certain will Become most usefull for the unitate State. I will tell you more about my prospect. I do foresee that the Britons will necessarely be obliged one day, or other to Evacuate this Continent, at that time the marines will Surely be more useful then the Original land troops; my Soldiers must then be instructed soon, and be Like the Roman troops which were obliged to make their Service Everywhere.

The Vessel that I intend to have fitted, shall at present be fitted out Like a privateer, but Calculated for to Carry a Great many things Necessary for the want of my Legion, which the Congress don't Chuse to Supply it with, Considering the Great Expenses that would occur upon the Number of my Soldiers.

If I am Lucky Enough to succeed in this first Expedition, I intend with the Benefit of it, to have a frigate Built, and then after, I'll try to do some thing Better. I am most persauded that my Good intentions for your Country will interest your Goodness for me.

I am with Respect, Sir
Your most humble and Very humble Servant
C Pulaski Gn
Baltimore June the 10th 1778.
(Archives of Maryland, *Journal & Correspondence*, ed. W.H. Browne Baltimore, 1901 p. 129-130.)

However, the following answer of the Council shattered Pulaski's dreams of marine exploits and it was Feliks Miklaszewicz, a deserter from the British Army who came too late to join Pulaski, who imitated in a small way the feats of Admiral Krzysztof Arciszewski in the American waters.

In Council Annapolis
10th June 1778.
Sir,
Mr Baldesqui has been so obliging as to deliver your Letter and be the Bearer of this. It is very desirable that the Brig at Baltimore should be employed, but the Claim of her former Owner Capt Stone, has hitherto prevented any Thing being done with her, she wants expensive Repairs and, as he is prosecuting a Suit at Law, if he recovers the Vessel, the Repairs must go with her. The Assembly desirous of having the Matter setled on the same Principles of Justice as prevail between private Men, gave us special Powers for that End, but Capt Stone's Obstinacy or, at least, his Difference, in Sentiment from us, has occasioned him to reject every Proposition. We wish to sell the Brig but, as we would not assure the Title, it is but right to apprise any Person who might be inclined to purchase, of her Circumstances, nor can we advise you, who must be a Stranger to our Rules of Property, to invest your Money in a Dispute which will at least, give you much Trouble. General Count Pulaski's Defence of the Liberties of Mankind in general and his attaching himself specially to the Interests of America, intitles him to our attentive Regard and we should have been happy in having it in our Power to sell him the Brig without any Incumbrances on her; he will justly impute his Disappointment to the cause we have intimated.
General Count Pulaski.
(Archives of Maryland, p.128; Miklaszewicz cf JCC, p.1400 & 1406; PCC, 41, 6, f. 63; 78, 15 f. 619.)

In spite of all the obstacles Pulaski was able to complete his Legion in July and the Maryland and Baltimore Advertiser for August 4, 1778, reported, "On Wednesday last (July 29) the Hon. General Count Pulaski reviewed his Independent Legion in this Town. They made a martial appearance and performed many Maneuvres in a Manner that reflected the highest Honour on both officers and privates."

Though it was a flattering description, it did not differ much from equally glorious portrayals of other contemporary troops of the Revolution.

The equipment and appearance of Pulaski's Legion can be reconstructed on the basis of fragmentary descriptions from the various contemporary sources and bills in the National Archives, Washington, D.C.

An article by Donald W. Holst and Marko Zlatich in *Military Collector and Historian*, vol. 16, No.4, winter 1964; and Harold L. Paterson's work *The Book of the Continental Soldier* were of great help in this reconstruction.

Pulaski's ideas about the uniforms are probably reflected in an estimate in French, dated March 1778, ascribed to him by the Manuscript Division of the Library of Congress (Estimation des furnitures dicides pour l'habilement de 500 hommes avec revers et parements d'une couleur que l'habit, Miscallenus Papers, US Revolution). But had he in mind the larger force?

12,500 annes of royal blue cloth
2,500 annes for the facings and lapels of which 500 is scarlet,
    500 green, 500 crimson, 500 duffle or white, 500 yellow or orange
25,000 annes of blue shalloon to line the coats
7,000 annes of linen to line the breeches, pockets and the like
10,000 dozen white coat buttons
10,000 dozen small white vest buttons
10,000 annes of linen for shirts
5,000 blue caps
10,000 sticks of colored twist for collars and pockets
10,000 pairs of shoes

According to the partial descriptions and also to the list of the Legion's deserters who made away with clothes and accoutrements, a typical dragoon had a coat, a skin jacket, skin breeches, boots, a black stock and buckle, a shirt, stockings, a sword belt, swivel and belt, a carbine, sword and sling, a pistol, a greatcoat, cap and blanket; while the Legion infantryman had a coat, woollen jacket and breeches, linen jacket, shoes, a black stock with buckle, shirt, stockings, cap, knapsack, bayonet belt and firelock but no greatcoat.

Both Foot and Horse wore a cap of which a black turban with a metal star and white feathers seemed to be the basic elements. The dragoons' coats were trimmed with fur.

It is interesting that a company of Legionnaires was supplied with the trade marks of the American Revolution; hunting shirts, tomahawks and rifles. The cavalry had French rifled carbines, lances, and sat in the Polish or Hungarian-style saddles which resembled the modern cowboy saddles. The buttons of all the ranks were white and had the letters USA, but to judge from the large number of such buttons returned to the Cloathier General (19480, Aug. 21, 1778, John Miller, ACG), some other style was also used, perhaps with the letters PL standing for Pulaski's Legion. There is in existence such a silver button (Calver and Bolton, *History Written with Pick and Shovel*, N.Y. 1950, p.141).

A weathervane figure supposed to represent Pulaski (now in the museum of York County, Pennsylvania Historical Society) is attired in a uniform similar to that of an American dragoon.

The swords were of English-American style as opposed to the scimitar-like Polish-Oriental style.

The following items contained in the general account of expenses made by General Count Pulaski for his Legion give further information on the Legion's uniform, equipment and arms:

(R.W.R. N.A.M.P.M. 246.116)

For the Making of 560 Coats

 30 leather waistcoats with sleeves
 90 woolen breeches
 222 Jackets
 150 OverHolls
 85 Hunting Shirts
 24 Shirts
 426 pairs gaiters
 200 cloth portemantels
 50 Baggs
134 1/4 Blue cloth
 130 yards Silver Lace for the non-Commissioned officers &
  trumpeters coat
4000 yards of binding for soldiers coats
 60 yards Green laces for the trumpeters coat 90 yards strings
  for the Trumpeters
 35. for painting 20 overpack saddles, to d 355 canteens
 36. to washing & mending 57 pairs leather breeches
 37. to repairing 45 pairs of boots
 39. to 232 Lather jackets with Slewes
  82 leather breeches at 20:0:0
  40 dat 24:0:0
  furskins to treemer the Dragoons coat
 40. 360 Pairs knee buckles
  24 pairs sisars
 41. 50 Lather gaiters
  20 pair gaiter top
  100 pair Boots at 10/

50 ditto at 11/5
2200 Nails for Shoes & Boots & mending of them
150 pairs Boots Buckles for the Standarts & two pennants
42. 64 Leather caps at 100/
   61 ditto 16.D
   50 ditto 20.D
   100 Knap sacks
   30 pack saddles & knapsacks
   120 Dragoon's saddles complete @ £14
   78 ditto @ £17
   120 Sheep Skin to cover the Saddles
   144 Bridles & Bits
   34 halters
   98 Cartridge Boxes
   126 Sword Belts
   60 Swiffles & belts
   To Repairing of Caps
   54 Riffles Pickers
   21 covers for the Carabinez
   100 pair pistol holsters
   200 halters Rupes
44. 50 yards of Black cloth to put around the Soldiers capes (sic)
   450 feathers
45. 40 Carabines
   50 Pairs Pistols
   400 stars for the Soldiers caps
   20 Rifles
   100 Lances
   62 Swords
   100 Sword Slings
   152 Hatshes caps
   400 Combs
   12 Blankets
46. 220 Little Hatshes
47. To fifes and the teaching
49. To have the trumpets teached
52. for three french horns.

(*Military Collector & Historian*, No.4, vol:16, p.100 & R.W.R.M. 246)

According to a contemporary witness, a certain Mr. Miller, the uniforms of Pulaski's men were nearly white. The Legion was formed mostly of Burgoyne's army prisoners, Germans and others (Towsend

Yard, "The Germantown Road and its Associations," *Pennsylvania Magazine of Biography and History*, vol. 6, p.10)

According to accounts printed in the Ex. Doc. No. 120, 49th Congress, 2 Session, Message from the President of USA, p.40 et seq., it was ordered on April 1, 1778, that a warrant be issued on the Treasurer "in favor of Count Pulaski for 10,000 dollars for the purpose of purchasing horses and recruiting his corps."

Altogether Pulaski received from the Treasury in 1778 for his Corps $87,768. The total charges against Pulaski as on February 1779 amounted to $138,186. According to a letter from the Treasury Department Register's Office, dated February 24, 1887, "diligent search of the books and records of this office fails to show that any payments or compensations has ever been made to Count Casimir Pulaski, Brigadier-General of the Army of the United States, for services rendered by him in the years 1777, 1778 and 1779...except as shown by the transcript herewith which shows no balance."

The transcript, evidently for the expenses of the Legion, does not show that any wages were ever paid to Pulaski. As for the claim that Pulaski spent one hundred gold livres for the corps, the Register's Office had no record. There is a possibility that Maurycy Beniowski could have spent that sum from Pulaski's Polish funds for recruitment of Hussars. Puraski's estates were confiscated but not that of his mother. Also his sister had funds.

An account of Count Pulaski's Legion, Continental Troops, Revolutionary War (sine anno) contains the following memorandum: "Captn. Baldesqui as appears by the (within) Abstract, is accountable only for 43.500 Dollars which amount was paid him for the arrearages of the Legion-the remaining sum of 90,000 Dollars Genl. Pulaski is to account for J. Carleton." Also Cf. R.W.R.M. 246.116.

The whole complicated question of accounts involved Pulaski and his paymaster Baldesqui in long and humiliating proceedings which echoes even today. Not being competent to give a professional analysis of the accounts, I may remark only that Pulaski took good care of his soldiers, equipment and horses, that inflation was raging and there was scarcity of goods of all sorts.

Pulaski's Legion consisted of Staff, 1st Troop, 2nd Troop, 3rd Troop, Company of Chasseurs, Company of Grenadiers, 2nd Company of Infantry, 3rd Company of Infantry, and Supernumerary Company. An "Account of Count Pulaski's Legion" gives the number of soldiers on the payroll as 357. However, this number included some who deserted.

Richard Spencer in his article "Pulaski's Legion" (Maryland),

Historical Magazine, vol. 13, No.3, p.241 et seq.) gives the number of Pulaski's Legionnaires as 330.

The names of officers in the Legion reconstructed chiefly on the basis of PCC, Item 59, vol:2, folio 123-131 are as follows: General Casimir Pulaski, appointed 18 April 1778, Colonel Michael Kovatch, appointed 18 April 1778, Lt. Colonel Charles (Baco) Baron de Bose, appointed 1 May 1778, Major Count Julius de Mountford, appointed 18 April, Captain of 1st Troop (Lancers) Ignatz Zielinski, appointed 18 April, Cornet George Elholm, 1st Troop, appointed 1 September 1778, Captain of 2nd Troop, Paul Bentalou, appointed 20 April 1778, Captain of 3rd Troop, Henry Bedkin, Lieutenant Francois de Roth, Infantry; Captain of 1st Company Jerome le Brun de Bellecour, also Aide de Campe, appointed 30 of April 1778; Lieutenant John Seydelin of 1st Company, appointed 23 of April; Captain of 2nd Company, James Chevalier de Segond, appointed 22 April 1778; Lieutenant of Second Company Francois Antoine de Troy, appointed 1st of June; Lieutenant of Second Company, Joseph la Borderie, appointed 1st of September 1778; Captain of 3rd Company, Friedrick Paszke, appointed 29 of April 1778; Lieutenant of 3rd Company, James de Bronville, appointed 21 of April 1778; Captain of Supernumerary Company and Paymaster, Joseph Baldesqui, appointed 10 May 1778; Lieutenant in the same William Palmer, appointed 11 May 1778; Lieutenant in the same, William Welszh, appointed 15 May 1778; Lieutenant of 3rd Troop, Jean Stey, appointed 15 of May 1778.

All those officers were certified by Pulaski as appointed by him and commissions were confirmed by Congress on October 5, 1778. The matter was urgent as Pulaski's Legion was to meet the enemy and in the case of officers taken prisoner the commission was of great value in their subsequent treatment and possible exchange.

A certain Captain Baitting, or Bailling, is mentioned in the Maryland Archives, Council Correspondence, vol. 21, pp.67,90,111, as being of the Legion.

On December 10, 1778, Congress affirmed the following commissions: Kotkowski, Captain; Charles Frederick Bedaulx, Lieutenant-Colonel; and on February 1779 Gerard de St Elme, Brevet Major, Louis Celeron, Major Patrick Vernier; on March 1, 1779, Alexander O'Neill, Captain of Infantry; Baptiste Verdier, Lieutenant; Beaulieu Louis, Andrew Carlevan; Baron Charles de Frey, Captain.

Besides those there were the following officers in Pulaski's (later Armand's) Legion: Joseph Bohan, Captain, Chevalier de Crenis, Elliot, Peter Faulkner, Christian Mancke, Matthew Irvin, Israel Schrader, Louis de Segournier, Claudius de Bert, Abraham Boemper,

William Butler, Lewis Celeron, Cicaty Beraud, Colerus Krystyn Lebrun, Crenis, William Richardson Davie, Desconture, Dubois, Foot, Gerard (Girard), Thomas Glascock, George Guthrie, Hovenden, Carlos Jullien, Ludemann, Le Charles, Jacob Leon, John Baptista Lomagne, Howelman, Cristin Mancke, Charles Markle, Samuel Sulina, de Maubon, Meres David, Benjamin Moses, William Murdock, Pettit, Reidel Henry, de Pontiere, Roth Wilhelm, Seegern Fryderick, Seibert Henry, George Shaffner, John Sharp, Ludwick Sigournier, John Baptist Ternant, John Felix Texier, Enoch Walsh, Noulff, Emerick Wenn and Wohlfest. This list was compiled from various sources and may not be complete. Variations in spelling occur and duplications of names spelled differently do happen. For instance, Pulaski spelled Sullivan as Sulima or Suliman, Pashke as Paszke or Paszki, and many names are almost illegible on handwritten lists. The name of Joseph Baldesqui was, for example, often spelled by Pulaski as Baldeski which led Mieczyslaw Haiman to claim in *Polish Past in America* (Polish Museum, Chicago, 1974, p.43) that he was a Pole. However, "Polacy w Walce o Niepodleglosc Ameryki" said that his nationality was unknown but if he were a Pole his name could be Beldowski or Americanized to Baldesqui. Italians claimed him as Baldeschis. (G. Schiavo, *Four Centuries*, Vigo Press, 1852) But there is no mystery about Joseph Baldesqui. He was a Frenchman. In a memorial to Congress read on December 11, 1779, and referred to the Board of Treasury he stated:

> For fear of being too tedious I shall not insert into this Memorial a Narration of all the Misfortunes which have sprung from my attempt to form a connection with, and to serve your States. I beg leave to Mention in short to your honours, that I was taken with a very valuable vessel and cargo, my own property, rich I had fitted out destined for these States, and carried to New York, where I was a prisoner for five months in the most loathsome and distressing confinement on board a prison ship, from which I made my escape by swimming to the Jersey Shore.
>
> It was at that time that I met with General Count Pulaski, with whom I had been acquainted in France. He desired me to accept a commission in his corps, and I consented with much pleasure as it gave me an opportunity of proving my Zeal to Render myself useful to your Country, as well as my own, whose alliance with your States was already proclaimed... (PCC 41, vol. 1, pp. 266-271)

The above statement somewhat clarifies Baldesqui's nationality. The matter of accounts will be referred to in the later part of this book.

The Sullivan mentioned was a quartermaster, while Bellwile was probably the man who claimed to arrive in America via England with Pulaski, Dr. Nicholas Belleville, surgeon, John Texier, surgeon, James Lynah (Lynch), surgeon, Lunn, Surgeon Mate, Fred Sander, surgeon's mate, Godfroid Leopold, riding master, and Joseph Caleton, paymaster, are others mentioned.

Of the officers Zielinski and Kotkowski, to judge from their names, were Poles, but I was not able to find anything about their Polish background.

Cezary Augustus Cristin Elholm could have been Polish, Danish, French or German. In the Wisconsin Historical Society, there is a letter in the Drapers Collection (9DD5O) by an unknown member of the Tipton party which says: "As to Major Elholm, there need be no more said of him than that the cause of his coming to America was his joining to depose the King of Poland for his granting a free toleration in religion to his subjects, that he sacrificed his native country, his fortune, and his friends to his ambition once, and therefore is not to be trusted..."

If this were true, in spite of the author's intention, it conferred a highly honorable testimonial on Elholm's patriotism and idealism. Some more details of the subsequent career of Elholm are given in Samuel Cole William's *History of the Lost State Franklin*, and Mieczyslaw Haiman in *Polacy w Walce o Niepodleglosc Ameryki*.

Another Pole was probably Frederick Pashke, later on connected with the Society of Cincinnati—a good and brave officer who perhaps served with Pulaski in the Bar Confederacy.

According to a letter from Mrs. Stefania Gros de domo Marckiewicz, published by the Polish weekly *Gwiazda Polarna*, (No. 22, 1976) Fryderyk Pashke was the grandson of Mateusz Paszke, a patriotic leader from Tyszowiec. The name Paszko could have originated in Eastern Poland, being similar in origin to a name such as Kosciuszko. In the Papers of the Continental Congress (247, 78) we read that Fredrick Pasche was a Premier Lieutenant in the regiment of von Graszwirski in the King of Poland's service, and in the last war he was a cornet of Horse in the King of Prussia's service.

Leon Orlowski said that it was probably Paschke who accompanied Beniowski in his later expedition to Madagascar. (Maurycy August Beniowski, Warszawa 1961, p.214)

For Paschke, see Mieczyslaw Haiman, *Slady Polskie w Ameryce* and Edgar Erskine Hume, "Poland and the Society of Cincinnatti, *The Polish American Review*, No. lO, 1935, Chicago, and numerous memorials in PCC.

According to Thomas Balch's *The French in America During the War of Independence* and William Abbott's introduction to *Pulaski Vindicated*, Charles Baron de Bose was Polish. This sounds doubtful as first of all the title of Baron was not known in Poland, and secondly no such name could be checked by me in the registers of nobility. Besides, Poles in America generally preferred to appropriate the title of "Count."

Jerzmanowski, Kraszewski or Krassowski, Kozlowski, Karol Litomski, Maciej Rogowski, Terlecki and Lozvinski are all persons of doubtful existence, though their names are often mentioned in the popular press and books and even serious historical works such as those of Lossing, Bach, Boleslawita and Haiman.

Maciej Rogowski is the hero of *Reszty Pamietnikow Macieja Rogowskiego*, which was published in Paris in 1847 by the poet Konstanty Gaszynski. This is a well written book reminiscent of Jan Chrysostom Pasek's memoirs.

However, it brought a good deal of confusion into historical research. Its assumptions and descriptions popped out all the time, but nowhere did I find collaborating evidence, except in the well known contemporary works of Gaszynski.

Loszwinski is one of the protagonists in *Les Amours du Chevalier de Faubla* by Louvet du Courrai, and the similar-sounding Baron Lovzinski of *Interesting History of the Baron de Lovzinski*. With a relation of the most remarkable occurrences in the life of the celebrated Count Pulaski, well known as the Champion of American Liberty, and who bravely fell in its defence before Savannah, 1779." This was republished in 1929 by Charles H. Thompson of Plattsburg, MD, as *Historical Facts in the Lives of Count Pulaski and Baron de Lovzinski*.

There is also a book of evident fiction by Samuel L. Knapp, *Polish Chiefs* (N.Y. 1832), where are mentioned the following personages: Petros Polandski, Father Ziski and Kazimierz Pulaski's son [sic] Skrzynecki.

However, it must be mentioned that the Revolutionary War Records are not complete, and the various material is dispersed through numerous collections and archives all over the States. It is regrettable that the monumental work of Peter Force was not finished.

In retrospect, one can speculate that some of the persons mentioned really existed, especially Kozlowski. While still in Poland I met people of that surname claiming him as one of their ancestors and Pulaski's companion.

According to Mieczyslaw Haiman there was a Revolutionary War soldier called Maciej Loughaski, and to some people this name might resemble that of Lovzinski. Haiman, doing a research on Polish presence in the Revolution, had found over 110 names which were thought to be possibly Polish. His list is not fully confirmed but reflects his thoughts after a lifetime of research. In any event, Haiman's list is the only one available and is a starting point for the young scholars of today and tomorrow. The Polish presence in the U.S. dates from the first settlement at Jamestown, Virginia, in 1608, prior to the Pilgrims' arrival. Thereafter, it was a small trickle with increases during the periods of the Polish uprisings, with the mass immigration towards the end of the 19th century and continuing to the WWI era.

What offering did Poland place on the altar of American Revolutionary freedom? To evaluate the Polish contributions, let us briefly examine the conditions then and there prevailing in the Colonies. The Americans challenged one of the finest, if not the best, armies in the world. The colonies were hopelessly divided, not only regionally, but split between Patriots and Loyalists; there was a marked disparity in economic and military wealth among the adversaries; and the war lingered and lasted exhaustingly for so many years, that it truly tried the hearts, minds, and souls of the Colonials. There were many disappointments and defeats, some victories, raging inflation, intense cilvilian suffering, and a plethora of seemingly plaguing and insurmountable problems that simple survival and the ultimate victory were a monumental tribute to the John Wayne type of "true American grit."

In this broad, graphic context, the slightest achievement, the smallest deed, the tiniest proffer of aid, the token helping hand—these all took on an aura of significant importance and value, of magnified and magnificent proportions far beyond their actual material worth. This was expecially true in the field of engineering and cavalry which the Colonials needed. The French provided invaluable engineering services as did Gen. Thaddeus Kosciuszko, while Pulaski was famous throughout Europe for his cavalry expertise and exploits. Therefore, by comparison with others, Poland's contributions to the American cause may have been quantitatively small but qualitatively important. Could America have won without French support and aid? It is doubtful. Washington's campaigns around the Philadelphia area and Saratoga undoubtedly convinced the wavering French that the Americans were a match for the British and Hessian forces. The French alliance was a great morale booster and the beginning of the end for the British.

Saratoga was essentially a victory of defense tactics, for all the onslaughts and attacks of British and Hessians could not penetrate the formidable American fortifications. Pulaski's countryman, the engineeer Kosciuszko, had selected the Bemis Heights defense area and was responsible for the fortifications of the American lines, which were impenetrable and resisted all attacks. Gen. Gates,the victor at Saratoga reported to congress that Kosciuszko "...chose and entrenched the position..." When a friend congratulated Gates on the victory, he replied: "the hills and woods were the great strategists which a young Polish engineer knew how to select with skill for my camp." (M. Haiman, *Poland and the Revolutionary War*, Chicago, 1932, p.18)

Since Washington's Philadelphia area campaigns and Saratoga convinced the French to join the American cause, and since the help of France was instrumental in achieving the final victory, Kosciuszko's contributions to the Saratoga victory and Pulaski's service in Washington's campaigns take on added luster and importance in evaluating Poland's contributions to the American cause.

In the rolls and records of Pulaski's Legion, which I was able to check, I found no Polish name among the privates. However, Haiman gives the following: Jozef Gabriel, a Bar Confederate soldier in the Legion, Tomasz Snaughder (Schneider) a Bar Confederate soldier in Pulaski's Legion, Bogumil Niemerich (Neimrich or Niemirycz), Kogai Samuel (Kokogai, Kokoski, Koogey or Kolodziej?) in the Bar Confederacy, serving as a musician in the 4th Continental Artillery.

Jakob Knias (Kunias) and Joseph Chalupetzky (Chalrnpecki) served in Pulaski's Armand Legion, while Jan Laski (Laskey) was a sailor on the *Massachusetts* in the period when Pulaski arrived on her in America. (Mieczyslaw Haiman, Polacy w Walce o Niepoleglosc Ameryki).

In the light of this information on privates and officers in Pulaski's Legion, its name often given in the popular press as the "Polish Legion" is not based on numbers of Poles but on the Polish origin of the Legion's commander, Pulaski.

But, regardless of its composition and name, the Independent, American or First Legion was ready and its commander spoiling for action. However, some people were anti-Pulaski. In order to slight him, they were doing their best to harass and hinder the Legion's efforts to take the field as soon as possible.

Pulaski wrote to Henry Laurens on July 5, 1778, and this letter again shows his grasp of general strategy.

> I hasten to thank you for the remembrance with which you have honored me. I received your letter by an officer, and am sorry to appear, at present, backward in military operations. It is my wish to be ready and active, and to show all my zeal for the service of the

United States. I believe that this campaign will be very instructive. The enemy may make different movements on the left; they wish to engage us in a general battle, but our interest is to avoid it, and not abandon to the fortune of war the interests which, being already on a solid footing, may be reversed. You know that there are some reverses of fortune, and the battle being lost, the conquest of all the Jerseys may follow. Philadelphia may be re-taken and New-Jersey re-occupied, and the junction with New York cannot then be avoided.

It may be that General Clinton will not be so active, but it is certain that the English must risk every thing for the present, or entirely abandon America. I believe it then necessary that our great object should be not to risk every thing on the fate of one general engagement, and by many detachments, observe the movements of the enemy, disconcert them whenever possible, cut off their divisions at favorable opportunities, rather than to attack them with our whole army.

My plan would be to send, with all haste, the best engineers to fortify the forts which are at present destroyed; to throw forces into them; construct chevaux de frise, and in such quantity that they would better obstruct the approach of the English fleet. Otherwise, it might happen that the enemy having succeeded in Jersey, will re-take Philadelphia, establish their posts in detached places, so well fortified, as to resist our most vigorous attacks.

I could not finish my arguments, as I wish to explain myself more fully on these subjects. I know the prudence of our general, and doubt not that he will do all for the best. Present to him my respects, and believe that I am ever his.

I beg, as a favor, that you will let me know if you in Congress are preparing for the conflict. I shall arrive with all despatch, and though, perhaps, with a small force, I may not be useless. Adieu,

Very truly, your friend and servant,

C. PULASKI.

My compliments to the General Marquis De LaFayette, Baron De Steuben, and to all the family of the general. You may say to the Marquis De LaFayette that I have written twice to him, without having received an answer. (Joseph Johnson, *Traditions and Reminiscences of the American Revolution*,Charleston, S.C. 1851, p. 243) Original of the letter is in possession of the Georgia Historical Society.

It is characteristic that Pulaski sent the following letter of complaint to Richard Henry Lee, the mover of the resolution for a Declaration of Independence, Foreign Alliance, and a Plan for Confederation, altogether perhaps the most influential person in Congress.

Wilmington, August 13, 1778.

Sir; I arrived here two days ago with all the cavalry and expecting the infantry in four, will present myself with my corps to Congress to pass the review in the end of this month and pursue the enemy immediately after. I should have been very glad to be ready sooner but I hope everybody shall be persuaded that it is not the business of one day to raise and form a Corps. However I heard the Honorable Congress don't seem to be much satisfied with my application. I can't guess what may be the reason for it, for I always did all my power to prove them that honour and a true desire of distinguishing myself in defence of Liberty was the only motive which fired my breast for the cause of the United States. I do trust myself enough in your knowledge to be in hopes that you will be kind enough to support me against the false pretentions which might have been made against me. (R.H. Lee, *The Memoir of the Life of Richard Henry Lee*, 1825, vol. 1, p. 296)

Probably among those "false pretensions" (accusations) was a petition from a certain Henry Baron Essich which was read in Congress on August 12, 1778, and it was ordered: "That it be referred to a committee of three to be empowered and directed to inquire into the facts therein set forth, and to grant such relief as they may think expedient into the state of the legion commanded by Count Pulaski, and report thereon; the members chosen, Mr. Penn, Mr. Marchant and Mr. Chase."

I was not able to find out who Henry Baron Essich was, and my inquiry to Mr. Alan F. Perry, Archivist, Center for the Documentary Study of the American Revolution, National Archives, Washington, D.C., brought me an answer that Essich's petition was not located in PCC, the printed journals, or in the index to the Library of Congress's collection of Washington Papers.

On September 11, 1778, the delegates from Delaware laid before Congress a letter of the 8th from Caesar Rodney, Esq., President of the State of Delaware, with sundry papers enclosed relating to a complaint against Count Pulaski. It was ordered that the same be referred to the committee directed to inquire into the state of the Legion commanded by Count Pulaski.

In the *Boston Gazette* on September 28, 1778, the following account was published: "Congress having been pleased some time since to order a corps to be raised (and styled a legion) to consist of a body of light horse and light infantry to be commanded by the Count Pulaski (a Polish officer of distinction) that gentleman has excited himself in the above business so effectually that on the 7th instant above six hundred horse and infantry marched through the city of Philadelphia. The uniformity, regularity and martial appearance of the corps reflects great honor on the Count."

Also in September (JCC p.939) a motion was made by Mr. Joseph Reed to appoint a suitable person to proceed immediately to Trenton, or wherever the legion under the command of Count Pulaski may be, and cause the said legion to be mustered, selecting such non-commissioned officers and privates as should be under due inquiry be found to be prisoners or deserters and that such noncommissioned officers and privates be not permitted to proceed but return to Philadelphia and deliver up their horses, arms and accoutrements to the quartermaster general and commissary of military stores, the men to be disposed in the manner as Congress would decide.

The passage of this motion would have practically disbanded Pulaski's Legion. One may easily guess at the situation from the following comment from Washington: "...In respect to Lieut-Colonel Dirk (Jacob Gerhard Diricks [Dirks]) I do not find that there is any necessity for granting the prayer of his Petition. We have already too many Officers, and I do not apprehend the interest of the States would be much promoted in his appointment. If he could make up two or three Companies, they would be of Prisoners and Deserters..."

Quotes William G. Whitley, the author of *Revolutionary Soldiers of Delaware* (p.19): "When the Sheriff of New Castle, John Clark, was trying to enrol in a militia recruits for the flying camp in 1777, out of 63 men only 22 proferred themselves willing and ready to march. Some of the negative answers sounded: 'Will not march, I'm damned if I march, family in distress, I never will march.' So much for revolutionary fervor and that was for service in the militia generally for short terms only."

Fortunately for Pulaski and the American cause Congress was too busy considering Deane's case to follow through on the motion.

★ ★ ★

On 19th September 1778 Michael Kovatch wrote from Germantown the following letter to Henry Laurens:

> Honorable Sir. As I have at present the honor to serve the United States and my late Expeditions against the Indians has brought me upon the thoughts to take the Liberty to make certain proposition to the Honor-

able Congress concerning a durable future Security against the Indians, and other bad fellowes; my long service abroad in the Hungarian and Prussian Service as Huzzar Officer has given me a sufficient knowledge to be a proper judge of such Regulation as I intend to propose and the Letters I have from the Honorable Board of War will be a proof that I executed the orders with approbation against the Indians but this has given me a certainty that under my Plan such security as mentioned would be made if the honorable Congress will honor me with the Regulation of it-which I shall faithfully execute, and glory in the honor of such a command which will also give me an Opportunity to show my attachment and Fidelity for this country's cause. I shall be glad to have the honor of an answer before I march with the Corps, having the honor to be with great respect. Your Most Obedient and Most Humble Servant, Michael de Kowats, Chevalier of the most Honorable Order Poor Le Merite of the King of Prussia and Colonel of the American Legion of Graf Pulaoski. (PCC, 247, 97, 13, 487)

The handwriting is different to "Thoughts about the Objections made against Inlisting Deserters of the Enemy," but this proves nothing as some letters were written on behalf of their authors.

I was not able to find many details about Kovatch, but it is of interest to note that Leon Orlowski, an excellent biographer of Beniowski, supposed that Kovatch could be a companion of Beniowski in his famed escape from Siberia, and expedition to Madagascar. (*Maurycy August Beniowski*, p. 171)

Among others, Duer, Chase, Harve and R.H. Lee voted in favor of the motion. Also, Congress in September ordered that John Hooper and James Murray of Pulaski's Legion be charged with robbery of James Chandler. They were to be delivered to the magistrate to be dealt with according to law, and Pulaski was to give orders for carrying out the punishment.

On September 30, Count Pulaski, with his Legion and all Continental soldiers fit for service in and near Philadelphia, was directed to repair immediately to Princeton, there to await the orders of General Washington or the officer commanding in New Jersey.

However, the previous plan was to send Pulaski's Legion to South Carolina. On September 19th Washington ordered Pulaski to join the main army at Fredericksburg. What the Commander-in-Chief thought about the Legion is clear from the following fragment of a letter to the Board of War, dated at 200 West Point on September 19th:

...With respect to the Count Pulaski's Corps, as the Campaign is yet open and there remain Two Months in which the Enemy may act in the field if they incline, I think it will be best for them to join the Army, if Congress should concur with me in sentiment. This will be agreeable to the Count's wishes and ideas of all parties when he was authorised to the Corps. His Horse may be of use on the advanced posts and his infantry can be kept with the main body of the Army or drawn in and be othervise employed if they discover a disposition to desert. (W.W. 12, 470)

What the Count thought about all the bickering and delays in ordering him into action can be seen from his letter of September 17, addressed to Congress:

Gentlemen: Do not be surprised at the liberty I take in announcing to ye the loss in the retard...expedition of those who are actuated with every sentiment propitious to yer use. I am a republican which the love of glory and the honour of supporting the Liberty of Union drew hither. I blush tho to find my self languishing in a state of inactivity animated with the zeal of servir ye. The request I now make is but my due, ye permited me to rease a corps of partisans, my priviledge is to be directed by my experience for the most useful measures. Ye order that I shall wait near Philadelphia until the opinion of the General in chief of the army be known with regard to me. Why cannot I be admitted to go on and receive his advice on my march since nothing here ought to detain me. The accounts of the detail belong to the Treasurer, it will not be embaressing for me to acquit anything which shall appear superflous as I have expended 16,000 dollars at least of my own. The revue is passed, there remain but for me to aske the payment of the soldiers and commissions for the officers with permission to march for the enimy. That is what I take the liberty to request in waiting yer answer. Philadelphia le 17 7bre 1778. -Endorsment: Count Pulaski. 17 September 1778. Read in Congress when Treasury business was called for. (JCC 164, 13)

A whole set of orders of a rather confusing nature was issued in regard to Pulaski. First of all, Congress decided that he was to march to Trenton with his Legion without delay, to await there the Commander-in-Chief's bidding. Meanwhile Washington wrote from West Point on September 19, ordering Pulaski to join the army in Fredericksburg, Congress willing.

On September 30 Washington wrote from Fredericksburg to Pulaski: "You are to proceed immediately upon receiving this with the whole of your corps, both Horse and Foot, and put yourself under the command of Major-General Lord Stirling, who will be in the neighborhood of Paramus. As the enemy are out in considerable force in

New Jersey near Hackensack, you will make particular inquiry of their situation as you advance lest you should fall with their parties."

Woodford's and Maxwell brigades, Pulaski's Corps and the militia were to be united under the command of Stirling.

All those points of destination were in the vicinity, but Pulaski, perhaps, found the orders confusing or was hoping to go south and delayed on purpose. On September 30, 1778, Pulaski was in Philadelphia and Congress ordered him, his corps and all the Continental soldiers fit for service to proceed immediately to Princeton to await Washington's orders.

Let us review some of the events which took place while Pulaski was training, organizing and taking the field with his Legion.

France had recognized the American independence, thus practically securing it. The mere act of recognition thinned the British garrison in North America as other outposts of the Empire, especially the West Indies, had to be defended too.

The British had been seeking reconciliation with the Colonies, but Congress rejected all peace feelers. Lord Howe who, it seems, sabotaged the British military effort was replaced by Sir Henry Clinton.

Friedrich Wilhelm Augustus von Steuben arrived at Valley Forge and had been recognized instantly as almost a saviour of the American Revolution because his Prussian drill was supposed to change the free citizen soldiers into ideal fighting machines in Friedrich the Great style.

Conway had been totally discredited because of his criticism of Washington and in a duel had a bullet put through his offending mouth.

During an extravaganza farewell for Howe in Philadelphia Captain Allen McLane spoiled the fun, perhaps much to the envy of Pulaski.

Clinton, after evacuating Philadelphia, marched towards New York, pursued by the American army. On June 28 an indecisive battle took place without American cavalry participation since the cavalry was reduced by attrition after Pulaski's departure. Charles Lee was accused of disobeying orders. Rebuked by Washington, he took offense and got involved in a dispute with Washington which he, of course, lost.

At the beginning of July, Major John Butler, with 900 Loyalists and allied Indians, swept Pennsylvania and Wyoming Valley, and Joseph Brant and his Indians raided New York State.

In Charlestown, South Carolina, which some writers credited Pulaski with saving from the British the next year, fights raged between the Rebels and the Loyalists with cannon and small arms. In Boston a monument was built to a French officer killed by Americans.

On September 28, Major-General Charles Gray surprised and butchered Baylor's Third Continental Dragoons at Old Tappan in New York, and this incident was considered one of the major atrocities of the war.

According to a graphic description in William Gordon's *The History of the American Revolution*, Gray caught Baylor's horsemen asleep and naked in a barn. A summary execution took place and men were dispatched with the bayonet without quarter. Only one of the light infantry captains ventured to disobey the order, thus saving the whole fourth troop. If that version were true, it seems that the British had more mercy for rebel officers as a number of them were captured, among them Baylor and Clough, left on parole at Orange Town.

Washington blamed Baylor for negligence. Anyway, the Third Continental Dragoons disintegrated, seldom to be heard of again.

★ ★ ★

The Committee of Arrangement wrote to George Washington on September 30, 1778:

When the Committee of Arrangement had the Honour of conferring with you on the Affairs of the Army it appeared to them that it was your Excellys. Opinion that no Prisoners or Deserters should be inlisted, and farther that such as had been inlisted should not join the Army: The Treachery of Armand's Corps about that Time having too fatally demonstrated how little Dependance could be placed on such Characters. In Consequence of which the Committee whose Sentiments perfectly corresponded with what they supposed to be yours wrote to Congress representing the Necessity of putting an immediate Stop to such Inlistments and also of purging such Corps as were proceeding to join the Army under your Excellencys Command. In this Representation they did not expressly point out the Count Pulaski's Corps, but as it comprehends a considerable Number of those exceptionable Characters we fully intended to include it in the Reform we then recommended.

This Letter the Committee forwarded to Congress about 2 Weeks after their Arrival at Camp having first shown it to your Excelly. and received your Approbation of its Contents. Upon their Return to This City they found nothing had been done with Pulaskis Corps, but our Letter had inadvertently been referr'd to the Board of War who also mistaking the Nature of the Reference had wrote to your Excelly. for your farther Opinion on this subject. This Letter your Excelly. has answered so as to leave it doubtful whether for some Reasons not express'd you do not mean that Count Pulaski's Corps should go forward as it is, one half of which at least is composed of Deserters and Prisoners, and We are inclined to think that upon a strict Scrutiny there will be found a much greater Proportion. If this is the Case we presume your Excelly. has altered your Opinion at least with Respect to this Corps, either upon farther Consideration or upon some particular Circumstances not attended to when we had the Honour of conversing with you on this Subject. Your Excelly. will see by this State that the Committee find themselves in an aukward Situation as having represented the Necessity of a Measure founded upon your Opinion, in which some Gentlemen who favour the Employment of Prisoners and Deserters think we were not sufficiently warranted. And of Course the proposed Scrutiny of this Corps has been delayed and will in all Probability finally fail, unless some farther Advice is received from your Excelly. on this Head.

We must serve that in all Probability if the Corps should be purged there will remain sufficient to compose the original Establishment of 68 Horse and 200 Foot, As the Count has extended his Numbers far beyond it, by adding what he calls supernumerary Troops and Companies.

The Committee are sensible of the Value of your Excellys. Time but as the Determination of this Matter will probably lead to the Settlement of other Corps of like Character, and they are attended with a very heavy Expence, we trust you will not think a few Moment's unusefully employed on the Subject.

With the most respectful Sentiments and very sincere

Regard We are Your Excellys. most Obed Hbbl Servt,

JOS: REED

Chairman

(L.M.C.C. p. 432)

The letter from the committee of arrangement to Congress referred to in this letter to Washington was doubtless that of Sept. 3, read in Congress Sept. 7, and referred to the board of war and quoted at the beginning of this part of the book.

Before Pulaski marched out to meet the enemy he was involved in an unpleasant incident. We learn from the *Journal of Continental Congress* that on October 2, 1778, a letter from Chief Justice McKean was read, whereupon Congress came to the following resolution:

Whereas complaint has been made to Congress that Brigadier Count Pulaski has resisted the civil authority of this State, it is resolved that the Board of War do require his personal attendance at the War Office at 9 o'clock to-morrow morning and that he continue in Philadelphia until inquiry can be made therein, and until further order of Congress, it being the fixed determination of Congress to discourage and suppress any opposition to civil authority by any officer in their service.

On the next day a letter of October 2nd from Brigadier-General Pulaski and one of the same date from the Board of War was read, whereupon it was ordered that the Board of War be directed to inquire into the claim made against Brigadier Count Pulaski.

In which he had been lately arrested, and if such claims arisen for the articles furnished to his Legion that the Board of War should pay what would appear reasonable and if not accepted the Board would provide the bail to suit. The Board was directed to inform that it was the duty of every military officer in the service of these States to yield obedience to any process issuing from any court, judge or magistrate within any of the United States.

Resistance by the military to the civil authority was not all that unusual during the Revolution. It may be argued that the total subordination of the army to the civilians would have extinguished the Revolution swiftly. I have yet to hear of a revolution where due process of law was observed. The most conspicuous cases of officers in trouble with magistrates were of Colonel Carrington, Hooper and General Stark. Also Light Horse Harry found himself in a similar predicament.

In those times, even as an apologetist for the Revolution admits: "...It was only by the greatest exertions and occasional recourse to the severest measures that the necessary supplies could be obtained..." (George W. Greene, *Life of Nathaneal Greene*, Boston, 1864, p. 79).

I have attempted to find the nature of the charge against Pulaski to no avail. Mr. Alan F. Perry, Archivist in the Center for the Documentary Study of the American Revolution, informed me that Pulaski's letter of October 2, 1778, was not located in the Papers of Continental Congress. Nor is it listed in the index to the *Washington Papers*.

Neither did a routine search of McKean's papers in the Pennsylvania Historical Society bring any results. In an authoritative work, *Thomas McKean-Forgotten Leader of the Revolution*, by John M. Coleman, there is not even mention of Pulaski's name. Dr. Wladyslaw Wayda wrote in his *Pulaski w Ameryce* that he found in the index to

Congress protocols that the case had been connected with grain (p.65). However, Item 29, folio 199 of the PCC contains a committee report on provisioning.

It is my belief that the whole case against Pulaski was engineered by Joseph Reed who for a long time had been acquainted with McKean. In fact, there was at that time a feud between the State and Congressional authorities, and it is worth mentioning that McKean's persecution of Arnold was an important factor in his betrayal decision.

Thomas McKean was one of those lawyer revolutionaries, a delegate from Delaware and Chief Justice of Supreme Court in Pennsylvania. Altogether a formidable opponent.

At that time Pulaski's Legion was quartered in Germantown, where, shortly after Pulaski's death a section of the town was named Pulaskitown (Joseph A. Wytrwal, "Memorials to General Casimir Pulaski," *The Georgia Historical Quarterly*, vol. IV, Sept. 1960, No3, p.245).

This was probably at Taggarts Field where the British previously were camped.

The Legionnaires, as is almost uniformly mentioned by writers, were a rough lot, and it seems that they took whatever they wanted. Pulaski was always energetic in defense of his soldiers and got arrested as a reward.

Samuel Adams wrote to James Warren the following on this subject:

> ...I will finish this scrawl with an anecdote. Not many days ago a sheriff of the County of Philadelphia attempted to serve a writ on the person of the Count Pulaski. He was at the head of his Legion and resisted the officer. A representation of it was made to Congress by the Chief Justice who well understands his duty and is a gentleman of spirit. The Count was immediately ordered to submit to the magistrate, and informed that the Congress was determined to resent any opposition made to the civil authority by any of their officers. The Count acted upon the principle of honor. The debt was for the support of his Legion, and he thought the charge unreasonable as it probably was. He was ignorant of the law of the land and made the amend honorable. The Board of War afterwards adjusted the account and the creditor was satisfied. (L.M.C.C.3,459)

Such an experience would be humiliating for anyone, and much more so for Pulaski. The pride of a Polish squire was as sensitive as that of a hidalgo, and Pulaski was ambitious, melancholy and retrospective. He remembered that shock to the last days of his life.

On October 3 Pulaski was still in Philadelphia, but it seems that after listening to the rebuke from Congress, he proceeded to Trenton as Livingstone wrote to Stirling on October 5: "...Count Pulaski is at Trenton...I hope your orders will hurry him as I heard two days ago of his being here..." And on the following day: "I had directed your Express to Count Pulaski at Trenton. I was then in hope that he would have been upon his march today to join you..." (Wayda, p.XLI)

On October 10, Moore Furman of Pittstown complained bitterly to Joseph Reed that first Bland's dragoons and then the remainder of Baylor's took his forage and Pulaski sent his quartermaster for the same purpose (PCC 247,95,9,85).

★ ★ ★

In Sir Henry Clinton's words: "The rebels had considerable salt works at Egg Harbor, and a large depot of Naval stores for supplying the privateers that usually rendezvoused there and from its vicinity greatly infested New York Harbour..." (Henry Clinton, *The American Rebellion*, ed. William B. Willcox, New Haven, p.105 n.)

The British Rear-Admiral, James Gambier, ordered Captain Henry Collins of the *Zebra*, with the *Vigilant*, *Nautilus*, some galleys and small armed vessels, with the army furnishing 300 men under the command of Patrick Ferguson, to destroy the nest of rebel pirates. As William S. Stryker in *The Affair at Egg Harbor* (Trenton, 1894) said, local lore claimed that at one time as many as thirty armed sloops had been lying in wait for some heavy-laden vessel, which had been sighted off shore. Late in that summer of 1778, two valuable prize ships, the *Venus* and *Major Pears*, were in the harbor.

(Lord Cornwallis's expedition into Jersey, in addition to foraging and getting fresh provisions, was a diversion to draw American attention away from Egg Harbor.)

The British squadron sailed off on September 30th, but due to unfavorable winds could not get off the bar at Little Egg Harbor Inlet until 5th October. Before the arrival of the British Expedition, three captured privateers, with six or eight guns each, and an armed pilot boat had escaped. All other vessels were sent about twenty miles up the creek to the village of Chestnut Neck.

Captain Ferguson, who had under his command men of the Fifth Regiment, British Foot and of the Third Battalion, New Jersey Volunteers, loaded them on the galleys and armed boats and started up the creek. He landed at Chestnut Neck and without difficulty dispersed the militia and destroyed vessels, storehouses and settlements. On the 7th Captain Ferguson destroyed some principal salt works and also "some stores and lodgements belonging to the people

the most notorious for being concerned in the privateers; and destroying and oppressing the peaceable and moderate part of the King's
subjects which was likewise accomplished without any loss." (Ibid,
p.27)

While the British squadron was hoverng at the entrance to Egg
Harbor and the Americans having had intelligence several days
preceding their arrival, Pulaski was being arrested, detained and
explaining the matter of some requisitioned grain.

It was only on October 5th that Congress resolved that the Legion
under the command of Count Pulaski be ordered to proceed immediately to assist in the defense of Little Egg Harbor against the attack
now being made by the enemy on that fort. The Board of War was
directed to communicate that order to Pulaski immediately.

Pulaski arrived at the village called Middle of the Shore on
Pothacong Creek (later named Tuckerton). His force consisted of
three companies of light infantry and three troops of horse. According
to Ferguson's report of October 15, 1778, the Legion had a detachment of artillery and one brass field piece. I believe it was a local militia
detachment or Proctor's company, as Bentalou said in his "Reply."

The question of officer appointments was not completely in
Pulaski's hands. Congress considered that commissions in the Legion
were sometimes suitable rewards for some individuals, and thus it was
thought that as a certain Jeunesse had not been properly rewarded for
his service it might be expedient to appoint him to Pulaskis corps.
(J.C.C. Nov. 12, 1778, p.1124). And on February 23 in Congress the
Board of War in considering the case of Capt. R. de Celeron reported
that there was no way of providing for him but in Pulaski's Legion. In
that case Congress determined that Verney was to be appointed over
Celeron at Pulaski's request.

But in Pulaski's Legion there was also a certain Charles Juliet
referred to him by Congress and the Board of War. In *Papers of
Continental Congress* (Item 147, vol. 2, folio 251-2) there is a report of
the Board of War dated September 2, 1778, with present Dana, Peters
and Pickering:

> The Board have considered Genl. de Kalb's letter relative to Lieut.
> Charles Juliet, referred to them by Congress; they have also conversed
> with Mr. Juliet and find that Genl. Pulaski would receive him as a vol-
> unteer in the infantry of his corps. But he has not the means of subsist-
> ing himself in that character, yet from Genl. de Kalb's recommendation,
> and because encouragement has been given for foreign officers to quit
> the enemy's service, we are of opinion he should be employed. If his
> services are approved, he may have a commission hereafter either in the

legion, or the corps of German volunteers, as Congress shall please to order; the board being of opinion that Lieutenants Fuhrer and Kleinschmit already reported to Congress are sufficient to make the experiment of recruiting for the latter corps. The board therefore beg leave to report that Lieutenant Charles Juliet be permitted to serve as a volunteer in the infantry of Genl. Pulaski's Legion, and have the pay and subsistance of a lieutenant for his support..."

And that was confirmed by an Act of Congress on Sept. 3rd.

The Legion encamped in the vicinity of James Willet's farm, where Pulaski made his headquarters. A few hundred yards from the farmstead and closer to the harbor but behind the trees, were troops of horse, artillery and some infantry. Further down the island road were more infantry under the command of Baron de Bosen, the second in rank and command in the Legion. The British squadron in the harbor was prevented from putting to sea by contrary winds.

As the British partially achieved their objective and there was small probability that they would land again, and behind Pulaski's camp were stationed Proctor and militia of the country, all that, perhaps, gave to the legionnaires a false sense of security. Suspicions were not raised when Charles Juliet organized a fishing party on the afternoon of October 13th and then disappeared. It was supposed that he had drowned. Perhaps Baron de Bosen, with whom Juliet had quarrelled, sighed with relief. According to Bentalou, their quarrel was of a matter of honor as de Bosen despised a man who deserted his colors. If this were true, de Bosen would not have been able to function in Pulaski's Legion, which consisted in great measure of deserters.

Ferguson gave Juliet the name of Bromville, an officer commissioned on October 5, 1778, but evidently the double deserter used that name to avoid responsibility for his former desertion. However, William S. Stryker quotes a letter printed in the *Historical Magazine*, vol. IV, p.136, which said: "In the fleet from Long Island arrived several Hessians, among them Lieutenant Juliet, of the Landgrave Regiment, who deserted to the Provincials when the island was besieged by them and then went back to New York. He is under arrest." (also quoted in Draper's *King's Mountain*).

So, it is possible that his betrayal did not bring him immediate forgiveness, assuming the quoted letter was true. Why should Juliet reveal to the British his real name?

Anyway, the true James Bronville was discharged honorably from the Legion as was attested by Pulaski publicly in the *Boston Evening Post*, Nov. 28, 1779.

It seems probable that Juliet gave not only the exact description of the position of the corps but of de Bosen's lax security.

At night on October 14, 1778, Ferguson, accompanied by Juliet, landed with British soldiers, Jersey Loyalists and some marines at Osborn's Island and secured the dwelling of its owner Richard Osborn, Junior. Osborn's son Thomas was, it seems, forced to serve as a guide. The expedition marched across the island, came to a narrow defile and then to a bridge over the ditch on Big Creek.

An account of what had happened at Egg Harbor is usually based on one of the following sources-Bentalou, Ferguson or Pulaski. I quote here all three of them to present a full picture.

As to Egg Harbor, the story runs thus:-In the autumn of 1779, a small British fleet, with some land troops, was sent from New York to the coast of New Jersey. To prevent their depredations, Pulaski was ordered thither by the Board of War, with his legion, a company of Proctor's artillery, and a body of Jersey and Pennsylvania militia. On our arrival, the enemy reimbarked, and their ships remained at anchor near the shore. Pulaski formed his camp in front of the enemy, placing the infantry of the legion, under the command of Lieut. Col. Baron De Bosen, at some distance on his right: the first troops of light dragoons of the legion, with the militia, formed his left, under the command of the captain of the troop. During the preceding winter, three Hessian officers had deserted to us from the enemy, and the youngest of these men, (who certainly deserved neither reception nor countenance) was sent to Pulaski by the Board of War, without a commission indeed, but with orders to let him do the duty of a sub-lieutenant in the legion. This man was treated with such severity by De Bosen, whose high sense of honour led him to despise one who, though a commissioned officer, could be guilty of deserting his colours, that he determined to revenge himself in a manner that could not have been foreseen or imagined. Under pretence of fishing, he one day left the camp, with two other men, and as they did not return, and it could not be supposed he would have the hardihood to return to the enemy, they were thought to be drowned. It seems, however, that he ventured to go back, and the enemy, under his guidance, and the cover of the night, landed and penetrated, before break of day, to De Bosen's quarters. On the first alarm, the Lieut. Colonel rushed out, armed with his sword and pistols; but though he was a remarkably stout man, and fought like a lion, he was overpowered by numbers and killed. The instant the news reached head quarters, the cavalry went full speed to the spot; but we had the mortification to see the enemy ready in their boats, on their return to the ships, with the exception of a few stragglers, whom we made prisoners in numbers greater than our own loss. The principal object seemed, indeed, to have been De Bosen. The voice of the deserter was distinctly heard exclaiming, "this is the Colonel-kill him;" and De Bosen's whole body was found pierced with bayonets. That the Colonel did not sufficiently consult his own safety, is very probable; but what mighty disgrace attaches to Pulaski or his legion from this surprise, is not so obvious. The fault belongs, if any where, to the Board of War, who sent the traitorous Hessian to Pulaski. (Paul Bentalou, *A Reply to Judge Johnson's Remarks*, Baltimore, 1826, p.36-37.)

The incident was thus reported to Sir Henry Clinton by Captain Ferguson. The report was originally printed in the *London Gazette*, December 1, 1778, and reprinted in the American press, among others in the previously mentioned *Boston Evening Post* and is quoted in numerous books as in Stryker, Ferguson, Wayda, Griffin and New Jersey Archives, 2nd series.

Little Egg Harbor, October 15, 1778.

Sir:...We had information by a captain and six men of Pulaski's Legion, who had deserted to us, that Mr. Pulaski had cantoned his corps consisting of three companies of foot, three corps of horse, a detachment of artillery and one brass field piece within a mile of bridge which appeared to me easy to seize and from thence to cover our retreat. I prevailed upon Capt. Collins to enter into my desire and employ an idle day, in an attempt which was to be made with safety and with a probability of success. Accordingly at eleven last night, 250 men were embroiled, and after rowing ten miles landed at four this morning within a mile of the defile, which we happily secured and leaving 50 men for its defence pushed forward upon the infantry cantoned in three different houses, who are almost entirely cut to pieces. We numbered among their dead about 50 and several officers among whom, we learn are the Lieutenant Colonel, a captain and an Adjutant. It being a night attack little quarter could, of course, be given, so that there are only 5 prisoners; as a rebel colonel Proctor was within two miles with a corps of artillery two brass twelve-pounders, one three-pounders and the militia of the country. I thought it hazardous with 200 men, without artillery or support to attempt any farther, particularly after Admiral Gambier's letter. The rebels attempted to harass us in our retreat but with great modesty so that we returned at our leisure and reimbarked in security. The captain who has come over to us is a Frenchman named Bromville. He and deserters inform us that Mr. Pulaski has, on public orders, lately directed no quarter to be given and it was therefore with particular satisfaction that the detachment marched against a man capable of issuing an order so unworthy of a gentleman and a soldier. Patrick Ferguson, capt. 70-th Regmt.

P.S. We had an opportunity of destroing part of baggage and equipage of Pulaski's Legion by burning their quarters, but as the house belonged to inoffensive Quakers who, I am afraid, may have sufficiently suffered already in the confusion of the night's scramble the injury to be thereby done the enemy would not have compensated for the sufferings of these innocent people. (W. Stryker, Egg Harbor, p.30)

But to judge from Pulaski's reports, one would almost conclude that the skirmish was a victory for the Americans. In this respect Pulaski's report was not much different from Washington's after Brandywine. However, Pulaski was voted neither thanks nor rum for his Legionnaires.

On the other side, for his action at Egg Harbor, Patrick Ferguson was commended by Clinton to Germain. Ferguson during the northern campaign of 1779 had been engaged in the action along the coast, and on the Hudson. He had been ordered to improve the defenses of Stoneypoint, but was then dispatched south before he could check the effectiveness of his engineering. In spite of being crippled in a hand due to the wound suffered at Brandywine, Ferguson took a distinguished part in the operations in South Carolina where he commanded the American Volunteers.

Patrick Ferguson died a heroic death at the Battle of King's Mountain in October 1780. He was one of the greatest partisans of that war and his career reminds one of Pulaski.

Here is Pulaski's account, as printed in Ex. Doc. No. 120 49th Congress (2nd session) Senate. (Original: P.C.C. M247.181)

Pulaski to Congress.

Read 17th. Committed to the Committee of Intelligences.

OCTOBER 16, 1778.

SIR: For fear that my first letters concerning my engagement should miscarry or be delayed, and having other particulars to mention, I thought proper to send you this letter.

You must know that one Juliet, an officer, deserter from the enemy, which was given me by the board of war to be at the suite of my legion, deserted two days ago with three men which he debauched and two others whom they forced to follow them. The enemy, excited without doubt by this Juliet, attacked us the 15th instant at 3 o'clock in the morning with four hundred men. They seemed at first to attack our pickets of infantry with fury, who lost a few men in retreating. Then the enemy marched to our infantry. The colonel, the Baron de Bose, who headed his men and fought vigorously, was killed with several bayonet wounds, as well as the Lieutenant de La Bordorie, and a small number of soldiers and others were wounded. This slaughter would not have ceased so soon if on the first alarm I had not hastened with my cavalry to protect the infantry, which then kept a good countenance. The enemy soon fled in great disorder and left behind them a great quantity of arms, acoutrements, hats, blades, &c. We took some prisoners and should have taken many had it not been for a swamp through which our horses could hardly walk. Notwithstanding this we still advanced in hopes to come up with them, but they had taken up the planks of a bridge for fear of being taken, which accordingly saved them. However, my light infantry, and particularly the company of riflemen, got over some of the remains of the plank and fired some volleys on their rear. The fire began again on both sides. We had the advantage and made them run again, although they were more in number. I would not permit my hunters to pursue any farther, because I could not assist them, and they returned again to our line without any loss at that time. Our loss is esteemed, dead, wounded, and absent, at about twenty-five or thirty men and some horses. That of the enemy appears to be much more considerable. We had cut off the retreat of about twenty-five men which have retired in the country and the woods, and we can't find them. The general opinion is that they are ccealed by the Tories, which are very numerous in the neighborhood of this encampment.

None but the legion were engaged. Major Montfort had been sent to the Forks to gather and bring the militia, but half of them were gone home and the remainder found so many difficulties that they almost mutinied against Major Montfort, and I am informed that even the colonel, who commanded and lives at the Forks, wanted to use him in a cruel manner.

I must add that I am continually alarmed by parties of Tories who seem to make a sport of it, and who in all appearance make use of all opportunities to injure us. Two men who guided the enemy and were taken in that occupation I have ordered to Trenton, with some prisoners and arms.

Count Montfort has assured me that the inhabitants towards Lead Point are good Whigs, and are attached to the common cause, and are about 250 militia, all inhabitants. At Big Egg Harbor there is 400 militia. I shall be at last forced to search the houses and take the oath of fidelity from the inhabitants, otherwise I shall be continually exposed. I shall endeavor to discover those who conceal(ed) the enemy whose retreat we cut off, although it will be dangerous, for the Tories have sometimes fired on my patrols; my orderly sergeant even liked to be killed by the Tories last night, but be assured I will neglect no means to contain them and at the same time stop the enemy.

I have, &c.,

PULASKI.

P.S.-The enemy attacked only my post at Little Egg Harbor. I beg you would order the militia to be obedient, or take them away entirely, for they are so ill inclined that they will only spoil our affairs; besides, they disperse and retire when they please, and particularly when they are wanted to face the enemy.

On October 18th Laurens wrote Pulaski the following:

...Sir, I have yesterday the honor of presenting to Congress your letter of 16th which is the only one yet came to my hand. While we regret the loss of Colonel the Baron Bose, Mons. de Bosdirie, and ? who fell with the brave officers in the late night attack by the Enemy, the Escape of the whole and the retort made upon the assailants is ascribed, Sir, to your animated and timely exertion. Congress wait to hear from you the particulars of this affair...there is much propriety in the disposal of the two guides. With respect to the Tories and that conduct of the Militia which you complain of, attempts are daily made for obtaining reforms in both, but in infant States such evils ? not to be removed in a moment. (Mis PCC, 247, 23, 117)

Pulaski to President Laurens.

STAFFORD, October 19, 1778.

SIR: It is not surprising that you have not received my letters; they were directed to the Board of War, and as they have not communicated them to you, I believe they have not been delivered, and that we have been badly served by our expresses.

Here follows the detail of our affair:

The desertion of Mr. Jelliot is the only cause, for he was their guide with the Tories, who are very numerous here.

I took my precautions in consequence of his desertion, and gave my records to my colonel of infantry.

The night of Wednesday to Thursday the enemy landed at Osborn's Island and crossed the bridge; the sentinel, who was advanced, fired, on some men who were advanced, and retreated to the first picket. The signal of alarm being given, every one got under arms. Patrols were sent on all sides, but no one were discovered. The colonel imagined that his sentinel had fired on some other object than the enemy, so that he returned to his first position; the enemy, two hours after, finding everything quiet, fell on our first guards without firing a musket. Several of our soldiers fired on them, which alarmed the rest. The colonel headed those he could immediately gather, and was killed with another officer and several soldiers, for the English were in a much greater number. They made so great a resistance that they gave me time to come with my cavalry to their assistance and rally them. The enemy were so terrified with the noise of my horse that they fled and retired in so great a disorder that they abandoned arms, accoutrements, &c.; part of them dispersed in the woods. I pursued the rest, and would certainly have prevented their embarking if I had not found an obstacle in a bridge, which the enemy had cut. Not able to pass it with my cavalry, I sent my chasseurs with some of my infantry, who met the enemy again. The firing began again on both sides, and they fled again. I ordered my men back and reviewed my legion. The numbers of the dead may be computed at 10, the wounded 12, and some prisoners. I cannot positively say how many are dead, because those poor wretches have dispersed, and every day we find some killed or wounded, but by my review I find thirty missing and several horses.

We have this day heard a cannonading from morning until night. I imagine it to be an engagement of some vessels.

I expect no assistance from the militia, for they have abandoned me. I remain alone, but notwithstanding, if I can be informed of their landed, shall endeavor to prevent their re-embarkation; if, on the contrary, I am informed of the departure of the enemy, I shall join Lord Sterling.

I have the honor to be, with respect, yours, &c,

C. PULASKI.

At ? o'clock at night the 19th October.

I am just informed that the enemy had made some movement and that they may land this night. For fear of surprise I shall wait for them under arms.

8 o'clock in the morning, 20th October

We have had an alarm last night occasioned by the English who had been routed who could not get on board. The militia had seen them and thought they were landing. We were assured of this by the general, who went to reconnoiter himself. As they were concealed, and favored by the Tories they found means to re-embark, and the enemy certainly waited for them to get under way, for this morning their fleet sailed.

I shall conduct all my force towards Barnegat for fear that the enemy may burn as they go on.

Pulaski to President Laurens

LITTLE EGG HARBOR, October 21, 1778.

SIR: As the enemy are going away from this and are only detained to save one of their frigates that ran on shore, I have directed Colonel Proctor to return to Philadelphia twenty-four hours after they are gone. I shall stop at Barnegat until they are passed; if they don't stop there, I shall as soon as possible join Lord Sterling.

My corps is very much fatigued and require some days' rest. I could wish to carry them to Trenton. My infantry have mostly lost their blankets in the last surprise; one hundred would be necessary; I beg them, and I hope by your assistance to procure them.

I send you the signatures of several inhabitants who have taken the oath of allegiance; they ought all to take it, and they are numerous. I inclose you the commission of one of my lieutenants, who thought proper to deliver it to me. Mr. Girard can give you a good account of all that has happened. I shall always endeavor to convince you of the respect with which I am your excellencys most humble and obedient servant,

C. PULASKI.

This moment the frigate run on shore, is burning, and all the rest will sail immediately, in my opinion.

A Son Excellence Monsieur le President de Laurens. Philadelphie, Pres. Mos. de Girard.

(Indorsed): No. -. Letter from Count Pulaski, 19 October, 1778. Read 23. Referred to the Board of War Ordered sixty blankets. (Ex. Doc. 2-365).

The above documents, except Laurens's of 18 October, were printed previously. However, the following letter addressed to Congress I have seen only in Papers of Continental Congress (247,181, p.36) and it makes an interesting addendum to the Egg Harbor affair. It is dated October 19, and its author was Gerard de St Elme:

Sir, By the letter you have wrote to our General which he communicated to me, I am not surprised that you did not receive the letter directed to the Board of War, and particularly these I wrote your Mr. Gerad and several other persons whom I informed of all that happened. Our General has charged me to answer your letter and give you an account of particulars of our affairs. I have done it on my own knowledge and information of those who were present. We are betrayed on all sides, we can't take a step but an hour later the Enemy is informed of it, and know where we go, so that we are extremely fatigued, particularly since the last lesson the Enemy gave us. We shall be again under arms this night, because we know they are to land. As to me I think they aim at our General because he opposes them much, and they would end advantageously if we should be obliged to remain alone in this unworthy country because you know the number of the Legion is too small and in too ungrateful a country to undertake anything. If anything new happen I shall have the honour to inform you.

Gerard de St. Elme.

As I am to encounter the Enemy without a commission and am as much exposed as any officer of the Legion I recommend myself to...(?) If you comply with my demand I beg it may be as soon as possible.

The British prisoner, guide Thomas Osborn, came out of hiding when the battle was over and told his story but was not believed, and the officers saved him from the soldiers' revenge with difficulty. His father was arrested and both men conveyed to Trenton jail. However, no treason could be proved, and the two Quakers (almost the whole settlement was of that faith and the Middle of the Shore was referred to as Little Egg Harbor Monthly Meeting) were allowed to return home, bearing the following pass:

Permit the bearers, Richard and Thomas Osborn to pass to their homes at Egg Harbor; they being examined before the Judges at Trenton, and not found guilty are therefore discharged and at liberty.-By order of Gen. Pulaski, Le Bruce de Balquoer, William Clayton, Justice of the Peace, Hugh Rossel, Jailer Trenton, Oct. 30th, 1778 (Stryker, p. 21).

So the Osborns under Pulaski fared better than Carlisle and Roberts under McKean. But Pulaski forced a number of Quakers to swear a loyalty oath to the United States. Some signatures were the crosses of illiterates, others put by an awkward hand, and still others in flourishing characters. The form of declaration ran: "I do swear before God the Supreme that now being persuaded [by Pulaski] of the justice of

216

our cause in the Defence of our Liberty to be always faithful in fulfilling the will of the United States of America, their orders issued by the honorable Congress and also Endeavour all in my power to render our Country Independent...So help me God. And: I do solemnly Declare and Affirm that I do not hold myself Bound to Bear Faith and Alliegance to George the King of Great Britain. I will most solemnly Declare and Affirm that I do bear faith and true Alliegance to the United States of America and I will do all in my power to support the Laws established under the Authority of the People. (PCC, 164,33).

Whether those oaths had more importance than the oath which, as Pulaski claimed, the Russians forced on him was a matter of conscience.

Pulaski had suffered greater setbacks in his career than at Egg Harbor, though Rivington's *Royal Gazette* incorrectly reported on October 24th that his Legion had been almost totally destroyed. He realized that fortunes of war were changeable. There were everyday affairs which had to be taken care of. He wrote from Trenton on October 24th to Laurens, requesting a commission for his quartermaster Sullivan and recommending for bravery three volunteers: Halesar, Clause and Barre. (PCC, 247, 181, 46)

But on October 26th from the same place he wrote Congress a very characteristic letter full of bright ideas:

GENTLEMEN: My duty is to perform whatever orders you give me, and also to communicate to you with sincerity on whatever may occur and circumstances may offer. I think that a flying corps placed near King's Bridge might take possession of that post and perform some advantageous enterprises. If I was destined for that purpose and sent that way I would neglect no means and seize the first opportunity of undertaking something favorable for this purpose. I should have three hundred infantry, and with this re-enforcement I might pursue my views to public advantage. I think that General Sterling's division is more than sufficient to defend that country, and take possession of Staten Island when the enemy evacuates it, and even for that purpose General Maxwell's brigade might be employed. To-morrow I shall set off to join General Sterling's division; if there is nothing to do there, I beg you you will permit me to cross the river, march forward, and take the orders of the General of the Army. I shall wait for yours, gentlemen, on this head, and act in consequence.

My infantry and two companies of cavalry will set off in two days after me; therefore I shall receive your answer at Elizabethtown.

You must not refer me to the General of the Army, as it would be so much time lost, and the motions of my corps cannot influence on his projects; besides the corps of a partisan is of little use when its commander has not the power to seize the favorable opportunities which may offer. I have explained myself and am ready to submit to whatever you'll please to direct.

I include the declaration of some Quakers; if I had remained a few days longer I should have converted every one.

I am, with great respect, gentlemen, your most humble, obedient servant,

C. PULASKI

I beg earnestly you will dispatch Captain Bardesky as soon as possible, as he is very necessary here; he waited to deliver my accounts.

Mr. Girard, who was full of ardor to distinguish himself in the last affair, merits the regard of the honorable Congress.

His excellency President Laurens, Philadelphia. (Indorsed:) Letter from Casimir Count Pulaski, read 27th October, 1778. (Ex. Doc. N. 120 49th Congress, Senate)

Again Pulaski wrote as a strategist and gave them to understand that he would prefer to take his orders from the Honorable Congress rather than from a certain "General of the Army." The ex-commander of horse also lectured the lawyers, merchants and other civilians of that body about the importance and tactics of a partisan corps. His letter read on October 27 would have had no influence whatsoever in all probability, but Congress had already decided that Pulaski should proceed to Sussex Court House, about 30 miles from Trenton, to await Washington's pleasure. President Laurens, merchant by profession, was requested to remind the super cavalryman Pulaski that the cavalry had to stay in a place where forage could be easily supplied. And talking about horses, it was about that time that Kovatch, Col. Command of the American Legion, advertised a reward for two horses strayed or stolen in Trenton, both branded "IL," Independent Legion or First Legion. The newspapers of those times were so full of advertisements for strayed horses that one has to suspect that most of them were stolen. Horses during the war were in constant demand, not so much for cavalry as for wagons and artillery. As a matter of fact, good cavalry horses were a rarity in America in spite of the fact that this continent claimed the world's first Jockey Club. Consequently good riding horses were bringing tremendous prices, and Captain

Segond valued his horse killed at Egg Harbor for £200, i.e. the price, as said Washington, even a rat of a horse would fetch.

It seems that the officer who was sent with this letter, perhaps Gerard, brought to the Legion's commander intelligence of anti-Pulaski friction as he wrote a very bitter letter:

Trenton, October 27, 1778.

Gentlemen: It is most useless to try of Justifyng my Self since to the prejudice of my Corps composed only with men of Honnour ye Look so fund of Hearing the Complaints of men only jealous of others' Reputation, besides all I could say would be Contradictio by their falsehood, and I know perfectly well their Right will always be above them of foreigners. My only prospect in this is to take the Defence of my camrades which surely Deser...not to be insulted. I have been in ye service sixteen monts ago and certainly ye never had a man more Devoted and perhaps more able of being usefull to ye but as far as I can see I would do all the best things in the world they should always turn to my Disadvantage in the mind of Such Bad persons which on pretext of taking the publick's interest are only thinking to their own and which Look's with Inland Eye anything above their merit. We come near the time in which all noise against foreigners shall be over in being separated with your Republick it is nevertheless very Hard to Cary away with us the Regret of not Having pleased you in a time our intentions was never others that to sacrifice our selves for your welfare. I am acquainted with the complaints ye have had against my corps. I beg of ye Gentlemen to be kind enough to Examine the matter and I am sure ye'll recover the wickedness of our accusers. Now I will begin from the Time I was authorized by ye Gentlemen to Raise this Independent Corps in the month's of April I did send the officer Here after mentioned to Recruit viz. at Easton Colonel Kowats, at Lancaster-major Montfort, at Baltimore capt. Segond and Bailtune, at Boston capt. Paskee, in the Jersays capt. Bedkin, in Virginia Lieu. Woolf Palmer and Welch, in Pennsilvania Lieutnant Bompell, at Albanie major Dubuis and on Berlin inhabs at Easton as for me I went from one place to another to Look at Every think to get all the Recruts together get them Dressed and Exercise them. I was never informed of any bad conduct of the persons under my command without givinall the satisfaction in my power. I have not been always used so far from it I have been abused by some of the Justice of this country. The Last affair I had in philadelphia and the insult I had in particular by one of this members will never be advantageous to the reputation of this country. I just come from doing all in my power to fullfil the Difficult Expedition I was sent and I am told my corps is accused of misconduct Because I suppose some of my soldiers has taken some triffles or others for which they were punished most severly tho' they wanted Every things which they could not be supplied with for their money being amongst Torys that Looks upon us worse than their own Enemies. They fired several times in the night upon my patrols and centrys and I was obliged to force them to show me the Road to the Enemy in the last action I had...the Retreat to 30 men which was Hidden by the said Torys and when my soldiers were seeking for them they were fired at without knowing where it came from; now do ye think Gentlemen such conduct from the inhabitants of that place could get them the friend ship of my soldiers who did behave so well for sake of their welfare, now to compleat their Badness they told ye the English would have hurted them less than we did And I suppose you believe them. I shall say no more about that matter it is sufficient I think to make you perceive the Injustice of our calumniator You say my corps behaved ill in Baltimore. I will send you the certificate I have from the Justice of that place about the contrary. I show you also the certificate of the Q.M. and furage master of Trenton of whom I heard you had complaints. Colonel Hupper from Easton can also give you an account of the Behaviour of the Corps when he was Laying there, in fine M. Suliman bearer of this will tell you further I desire nothing Gentlemen So much as being Justified in ye minds and Having once fulfilled my Duty carry away along with me you Good opinion. I hope also Gentlemen you'll Grant me two favors the 1st to give me oppotnity to make you acquainted with the valor of my soldiers, the second is to settle my accounts with capit Baldesqui and Reimburse him the Money I Have Laid out for the Legion, if ye chuse at the same Time for your own interest to Deliver a Commission of Capt. to Mr. Suliman who will be appointed Q.M. to the Legion you'll oblige me as to...I am...C. Pulaski de Corvin. (PCC.164, f.54-7)

To that letter Laurens sent by Colonel Direks the following answer on 3rd November, 1778:

Sir, I had yesterday the honor of presenting to Congress your letter of the 27th October.

Had the Gentleman who alarmed you with an history of Complaints delivered my sentiments in terms which I meant to convey them to him you would have felt no chagrin but rather satisfaction on that account. A detail of particulars at this time would be unnecessary and troublesome-numerous complaints it is true have been heard from various persons of irregular and unproper conduct of the Legion but none since that which took its rise in Germantown have been laid before Congress, therefore such do not amount to a charge.

I labored to explain to the Gentleman above-mentioned that neither Congress nor any of its Members as far as I learnt imputed blame or censure to Count Pulaski, and that from the regard I had for him it made me unhappy to hear that he was censured anywhere for the disorderly behavior of his Men, or the unwarrantable menaces of any of his officers, and I must impute that Gentleman's deficiency in the information which he gave, to his imperfect understanding in the English Tongue, although in justice to myself I must observe I took some pains to impress upon his mind the high sense I entertained of Count Pulaski's Merits.

Your letter above-mentioned lies before the Board of War where I presume this of 26th respecting Monsieur Molion now before me will be transmitted. When a report from that Board comes before the House, you will be further informed... (PCC 13, 2, 146-7, *Letterbook of Henry Laurens*)

That was a nice letter, and Pulaski, not used to sincere compliments from Congress or Washington, was evidently touched as he wrote from Minnesink on November 25th the following:

SIR: This moment I receive the letter you honored me with the 3d I know your kindness, and am persuaded that the evil reports of some private persons will not prejudice your mind against me, and I am also persuaded the honorable Congress will do me justice. I am sorry, however, I cannot convince them more effectually of my zeal for their service. I have wrote to General Washington, to Congress, on what relates to my quarters, and wait with impatience for their answer.

I demand to be employed near the enemy's lines, and it is thought proper to place me in an exile which even the savages shun, and nothing remains but the bears to fight with.

I thould have less grief, however, if the earth produced a sufficiency to feed my horses, but they will starve, and it will be said it is my fault. The patrol I am obliged keep on the other side the river completes their ruin, and my security requires it against the enemy's attempts, but I believe my precautions are proof against all they may undertake.

I have now only to assure you of the respect with which I am, &c,

PULASKI.

P.S.-I have the honor to report Mr. de Monfort has received his dismission, and I am in absolute want of a field officer, and in consequence I beg Congress to send me without delay Mr. Bedan Q. Colonels. I have a good opinion of him, and I believe he will be useful to the corps.

I inclose you Mr. de Montfort's commission.

(Indorsed:) No 13. Letter from Brig. Count Pulaski. Nov'r 25, 1778. Read I Dec'r. 2d Dec'r referred to the board of war. (49th Congress Second Session Ex. Doc. 120)

However, before Pulaski received Laurens's letter he had sent to Washington a letter which looked as it were following a letter of resignation:

I have the honor to send you my Rapport by Mr Gerard. I did wish to do it myself but the Indisposition in which I am since several days hinders me.

I am here without forage. If that is to last long the horses will suffer great deal.

I should wish before my departure for Europe to be of some Service; if it will please you, my General, you may furnish me with the Occasion.

I expect here your Orders-

Sussex Court House, November 6. (Letters to, Washington Papers 28, 263).

Perhaps, the indisposition mentioned by Pulaski was of a diplomatic nature, and I detect in the usage of the word "occasion" the Polish meaning of occasion "noble battle."

Ironically he was sent to fight Indians at Minisink:

Poughkeepsie, November 10, 1778.

Sir: Your favr. of the 6th. was delivered to me at Fishkill by Mr. Gerard. I am sorry your indisposition deprived me of the pleasure of seeing yourself.

Upon consulting Govr. Clinton, of the State of New York, upon a position, in which your Corps can be employed to advantage, and at the same time be plentifully subsisted in the Article of Forage, he advises the Minisink settlement upon Delaware. You will therefore be pleased to march immediately for that plate, and take your Station as near Cole's Fort as you conveniently can. Let your Cavalry and Infantry be quartered as near together as possible, that you may, in case the Indian Enemy make any attempt upon the settlement, draw your force quickly together. I must beg you to make use of all means to keep your Corps from marauding or in any way distressing the Inhabitants, who will cheerfully contribute everything to your support if properly demanded. There are two Gentlemen of particular influence in that Country, Mr. Depui and Mr. Van Camp, who will assist you very much in procuring Forage and other necessaries. I am &ca. (W.W.13, p.220)

Washington, properly, was concerned about Pulaski's state of health but there was not a word about his intended departure for Europe, only admonition about the Legion's marauding. It is hard to believe that in 1778 Washington was naive enough to think that inhabitants would cheerfully contribute anything if properly asked. (Vide the Letter of W. Paca and special Congress permission for Harry Lee to requisition horses.)

★ ★ ★

Before proceeding further with this study a word or two about those "inhabitants," mainly Quakers, with whom Pulaski was constantly in trouble, and the Indians, would not be amiss.

The Quakers, whose official name is the Society of Friends, originated in England in the middle of the 17th century. George Fox was their outstanding leader. In the beginning they were persecuted for the tenets of their faith, which required them not to remove their hats before superiors, nor to bear arms or take oaths. In America they were also persecuted. Bringing a known Quaker into the colony of New England was punishable by a fine of five hundred dollars and the exactions of bonds to carry him back. Such a "known Qu'aker" was to be whipped twenty times and sent to the House of Correction until shipped out. Defending Quakers' views was punishable with a fine and eventually with banishment. A male Quaker could lose an ear on the first conviction and the other one on the second conviction. On the third conviction male and female Quakers were to have their tongues bored through with a hot iron. In 1658 the death penalty was enacted.

Quakers had established their haven in Pennsylvania, thanks to William Penn, the Quaker King, who had obtained from the Crown a royal charter for a province in America in settlement of a claim due to his father, Admiral William Penn. After gaining the support of the Indians and founding the city of brotherly love-Philadelphia, he returned to England after appointing a commissioner to govern Pennsylvania according to a charter of liberties.

His grandson, John, changed Penn's policy towards the Indians. Around 1764 (the time of the Pontiac uprising) in the city of

Philadelphia, he issued a proclamation offering the following bounties for the capture of Indians or for their scalps: every male above the age of ten captured–151 dollars, scalped (killed) 134 dollars. Indian women and boys under ten brought their captors 130 dollars each, while Indian women's hair was worth 50 dollars per head.

In Pennsylvania the Quaker held a dominant position, but when it came to armed conflict with the British, their love of order and adherence to the principle of non-resistance brought them only trouble. Besides, according to their "Testimony," they abhorred every measure tending to break off the normal connection of the people of these provinces with Great Britain.

To the many members of Congress and other revolutionaries, Quakers were evil opponents of the Revolution. They were equivalent to the "reactionaries" of the Stalin era of more modern times.

Pulaski, for whom the subtle religious differences and political shades were strange, was severe with them and the Loyalists. They retaliated by making numerous complaints to Congress.

For the time being, Pulaski was leaving Quaker country to proceed to Indian territory. Minisink was one of the oldest settlements in Orange County in the State of New York. It had a small stockade fort, a mill and some houses. The inhabitants cultivated land, bred cattle and had orchards. Since its beginning the history of Minisink had been full of conflict with the Indians. Finally, after Pulaski left, Minisink was attacked in 1779 by Joseph Brant, with his Indians and Tories, and burned. Several people were killed, and the pursuing party of militia and volunteers was ambushed.

Pulaski probably had heard about the Indians and their manner of conducting warfare. He was not enthusiastic about his mission. Indians fought by ambush and surprise. They tortured prisoners, scalped both the dead and living and did not spare women and children. To Pulaski, brought up in the tradition of chivalry, where the word knight was an everyday expression, such an opponent was not inviting, especially as the frontiersmen, on whose collaboration he would have to depend, adopted their enemies ways and manners. Although he did not know it then, even Indian warfare passed him by, for after the massacre in Cherry Valley in New York on 11th November, there would be no military activities until the spring, when the Americans started punitive expeditions against the Indians. The whole Indian force terrorizing the Americans consisted of 1,500 braves. It is doubtful whether Pulaski would have derived any satisfaction from burning Indian villages and destroying their cattle and fields.

As mentioned before, the British, in consequence of the French-

American alliance, transferred troops to the West Indies and other weak spots of the Empire. Thus, the British force was reduced from 34,000 in August 1778 to 22,500. With such a dearth of men, the Indians, with unfortunate results, played a more important part in the British operations.

Perhaps Washington's order to Pulaski to defend the frontier was not such a slight, though Col. Philip Van Cortland, it seems, could stay there, as well as the Legion.

On November 15, 1778, an impatient and discouraged Pulaski wrote to Washington, asking him for leave to resign:

> Sir, According to your instruction I will march towards Coles Fort but will stop at Rosegrantz to refresh the horses which suffered very much because of lack of forage at Egg Harbor, and did not fare well before. On the other side of Delaware all is burnt by Indians close to the Fort. If you want me to attack them you must give me time to recover and gain intelligence, then I can act. If you are concerned only with quartering, this place is unsuitable. I represent you, General, that in the vicinity of Rosegrand my Corps could be well kept and ready to punish Indians if they would invade, otherwise being fatigued I should be not able to do anything.
>
> I shall await the orders of your Excellency at Rosengranz and obey you if you ask me to cross the river. I hope that after returning the Legion to its place and bringing it into good order I shall have your permission to go to Philadelphia. It is necessary in order to arrange the embarkation. My ambition cannot be satisfied by the command of the Corps at quarters or battling the enemy not worth fighting, a victory over whom brings no honor.
>
> I only wish to leave the Legion in such a state that it might remind by its services my name to the citizens of this country. I shall be always glad to think that I contributed, though in a very small degree, to your attempts at establishing a new republic. I hope, your Excellency, that my zeal and disinterestedness which were driving me in the service under you would give me your respect, and that is all which I want.
>
> P.S. I have honor to present to you one of my compatriots Mr. de Kotkowski. He has served in Poland in one of my divisions. I know him as a brave and useful officer for the American Service. I would like to have him placed in the Legion with the rank of captain and pay of lieutenant whose duties he will do till he would find an opportunity to show his talents and receive other employment. (*Letters to Washington*, 29, 4).

225

Kotkowski had also Dean's and Franklin's recommendations. It is entirely possible that Pulaski's Legion was to be the vanguard of an expedition to be commanded by Gen. Edward Hand, a former physician. In the meantime, there was nothing to do. Hence, Pulaski sent Washington the following letter dated November 23, 1778, from Minisink:

> Dear General: Agreable to your orders to me while at Sussex Court House I marched the Legion to the Place. I find the Indians Enemy have retired near one hundred miles from there, from which it appear, that there will be nothing for us to do. One examining the country I find it will be impossible to support the Cavalry with forage many days. The Persons appointed for that purpose haved delivered me enclosed address which will account for the matter. My reasons for not marching to Coles Fort the place pointed out by you are that there is neither inhabitants nor forage for our subsistance and the Gentlemen to whom you refer me for assistance in this country lives 30 miles below the Post. I have not procur on Look of Hay or Bushel of grain, the People from the Back Country having filed to their settlement among their friends. Our stay Here will greatly distress the whole. I therefore should be glad your Excellency would remove my corps to some other Post, in the meantime should be glad your Excellency Leave of absence to Philadelphia to settle some accoumpts of the Legion. I should Likewise be glad of an answer to the letter I wrote You some time ago. (Letters-B. VII-106).

Pulaski sent the same letter to Laurens with the following change towards the end: "...Therefore should be glad you will remove my corps to some other place. Bristol, I am told, is a good post and plenty of forage too. If you dont think proper to send me there I should be glad to go to Brunswick. I have sent that thro' Col Suliman who, having been on the spot, can if you choose, inform you of more particulars. (PCC 247, 164, 62)

Pulaski, assuming that his words would not be believed, enclosed the following certificate:

> Minisink, 22 November, 1778. May it please your Honor. We thy subscribers being inhabitants of the place above mentioned hope your honor will consider the situation of many distressed people, who are the inhabitants of this place in humanity taken into our habitations-and maintain at our expense, being driven from the homes by the Indians and lent them cattle grain. Hope your Honor will consider the above. At the same time we are willing to assist any of our soldiers struggling in this our glorious cause -we therefore think that it will be in our power from the above circumstances to support the cavalry more from this

date-furthermore we, thy subscribers, have examined the inhabitants
and made every possible means to assist your troops-and find our efforts
in vain to support the cavalry longer than the time above mentioned...
(PCC,164,66).

At the end of this document are signatures of militia officers mostly
illegible.

Washington finally replied to Pulaski's letters on November 24,
giving his consent for Pulaski's trip to Philadelphia and expressing his
appreciation for Pulaski's "...merit...services...and principles."

Head Quarters, Fredericksburgh, November 24, 1778.

Sir: Your favour of the 15th by Count Kolkowski, I received a few
days since. If I have a right idea of your situation at Rosecrantz it
will fulfil the object intended. Coles Fort appeared a good position
for covering a considerable part of the frontier; but any place in the
vicinity of it, will answer the purpose as well; and as the circumstances you mention, make that particular spot inconvenient on the
score of subsistence, you will either remain where you are or choose
for yourself such other position in the neighbourhood as appears to
you best adapted to the accommodation of your corps.

The motives which incline you to leave this country, at the present juncture, are laudable. When you have arranged the affairs of
your corps, you have my consent to go to Philadelphia as you propose. I assure you, Sir, I have a high sense of your merit and services
and the principles that influenced the part you have taken in the affairs of this country. The disinterested and unremitted zeal you have
manifested in the service gives you a title to the esteem of the citizens of America, and have assured you mine.

I gave Count Kolkowski a letter to Congress in which I communicated your request.

I have ordered Col. Spencer with his regiment, Colo. Armand
with his corps and Captn. Schot with a party under his command to
join you as speedily as possible; The more effectually to enable you,
or the Officer commanding to repel any attempts of the enemy in
the quarter where you are.

As you have signified to me your intention to return to Europe
immediately, I have ordered Brigadier Genl. Hand to repair to Minisink and take the command. I am, etc. (W.W. 13, p. 322)

What could those laudable motives be which made Pulaski want to
leave America? First of all, he was sick of intrigues, persecutions, petty
harassment and lack of scope for his ambitions. Unable to convince

the Americans of the European tactical use of cavalry as a strike force, he had opted for a small Legion to imitate his famous hit and run tactics so successful against the Russians, only to be frustrated again. Neither he or his Legion were trained for Indian fighting, which was best left to the frontiersmen. The area was "...unsuitable..." and lacked forage for the horses. Militarily, it was the wrong mission for the wrong unit. He considered the Indians "...not worth fighting..." and even a victory over them would bring "...no honor..." He was too restless a fighter to do garrison duty or protectionist defense. He had come to fight the British, to hit, to strike, and strike again in the manner of cavalry warriors. He was a dashing cavalry leader with no place to dash in the Minisink forests. We could liken him to a George Patton, caged in England, while the allies landed and expanded their Normandy beaches without him. In any event, in such a mood of despair and frustration, Pulaski saw no future in continuing.

Writing to Laurens and Washington about his intention to return to Europe, he might have thought that they would remonstrate and ask him to remain, thus improving his bargaining position. Whether this was all a ploy, is a matter of speculation! His objective was to have an opportunity to prove his military talents. Unfortunately, there was a temporary lull in the war and many generals and politicians thought that after France entered the conflict Great Britain would be forced to recognize U.S. independence in a relatively short time.

There was a war of the Bavarian Succession going on in Europe and Professor Wladyslaw Konopczynski speculated that Pulaski wanted to participate. That war between two greedy rulers, Joseph II of Austria and Frederick II of Prussia, was a typical dynastic and territorial war of maneuvers called also the " Potato War," as its main purpose was to cut off the enemy fom supplies.

It could hardly involve Poland, though, of course, both monarchs recruited cavalry and infantry in Poland, especially in the partitioned territories. However, Pulaski was persona non grata as a regicide in both Austria and Prussia. This conjecture by Konopczynski would seem to have little merit.

On the other hand, there was also a war between the Porta and Russia, and there Pulaski could participate, though his experience previously in Turkey was highly disappointing.

Most likely Pulaski received a letter from his brother, Antoni, who tried to arrange a pardon for Kazimierz through the Sejm (Diet). Antoni achieved Pulaski's rehabilitation posthumously.

Antoni, the youngest of the three brothers, was taken prisoner by the Russians while 18 years old, and sent to Kazan. There on the

Tsarina's side he fought against the Pugatchev rebellion while some of his comrades joined that peasant uprising. After the Bar Confederation failed, Antoni was rewarded by being allowed to return to Poland, where he became a colonel, and a member of Parliament (the Sejm). It is interesting to note that Antoni was responsible for the reform of the Polish cavalry.

★ ★ ★

Kotkowski, whose name is given in the documents in a variety of spellings, took part in the Bar Confederation Uprising. He approached Silas Deane in 1776, but left France in July 1777. Lord Stormont noted: "...M. Katskoeski has no rank, but has recommendations...'in this report about the French officers going to America. (B.F. Stevens's Facsimiles, No 176). Among those was Vel Croissant who served in Poland. It must be observed that this annotation does not prove that Kotkowski really left France at that date. Beniowski, in a letter to Franklin, mentioned a young man he was sending to his friend (Pulaski), and it could have been Kotkowski. (The Franklin Papers, vol. VII, No.53, American Philosophical Society, Philadelphia, Pa.)

For the first time officially Kotkowski was mentioned in Pulaski's letter to Washington, dated 15 Nov 1778. What Kotkowski was doing until then is a matter of speculation. I think that after his arrival, he joined Pulaski and participated in the Battle of Brandywine as contemporary witnesses wrote about "Polanders,"and Pulaski, Kotkowski and Zielinski could have been those Polanders. Not being able to obtain a commission in the cavalry, Kotkowski might stay with it as a volunteer at Pulaski's probable expense or he could try to find military employment somewhere else. Pulaski was a Commander of Horse practically in name only. Even Zielinski only got his commission after Pulaski became the Chief of the Legion. Kotkowski then applied for a post with Pulaski who recommended him to Washington. Kotkowski also had very good recommendations from Franklin and Deane (PCC 247,129,703,79 & MP 247, roll 108,33).

As Deane's original recommendation of Pulaski is not traceable, the following sentence from Kotkowski has to suffice. "...The Count Polouski whose character is established as one of the first in Europe..." This was the opinion of Franklin who, recommending Kotkowski, stated: "...Count Pulaski, who was a general of the confederation and who is gone to join you, is esteemed one of the greatest officers in Europe..."

Both diplomats also warmly praised Kotkowski. Such a letter was nothing unusual coming from Deane, but Franklin was careful with his support and apologized for giving the letters of recommendation to foreign officers, but Kotkowski's zeal was not to be disappointed. Besides, he could speak English.

Baron de Frey was a commanding officer in Minisink who was commissioned as a captain at large in July 1778. It was probably no secret to him that Pulaski intended to resign. Consequently, Kotkowski found himself without a protector. I am not certain of the date when Pulaski made de Frey the fourth officer instead of the first, for which reason de Frey moved to Moylan's camp. Had it happened before Kotkowski's arrival, it could explain de Frey's attitude towards the newcomer and protegee of an ex-boss. Had it happened afterwards, it could explain de Frey's shift from number one to number four.

Anyway, in Minisink Kotkowski was involved in an unpleasant and mysterious incident resulting in his court martial. The proceedings in two versions (in what seems to be the same handwriting) are enclosed in General Edward Hand's letter of January 15, 1778, to Washington (Washington Papers, Library of Congress). (Spellings of names as per documents.)

> Captain Baron de Fry, being sworn, stated that at 7 p.m. on 9th January Westfall and his wife came into his quarters crying and told him that Lieutenant Cotoosky threatened to kill all in their house. So Baron de Fry went to the house and told Cotoosky that he behaved very ill. Cotoosky answered that the landlord was a rascal. Baron de Fry told Cotoosky that he was not in Poland and could not take such satisfaction. Cotoosky immediately drew his sword and Captain de Fry asked what he was going to do, at which Cotoosky lifted the sword. De Fry wrestled the weapon but was caught by the hair by its owner and shouted for help. Cotoosky then went to the second room to fetch a rifle. Not finding one he returned and hit de Fry in his face.
>
> De Fry behaved calmly, trying to argue with Cotoosky and became a victim of an attack.
>
> Westfall deposed that Cotoosky rode to his house, ordered the door opened, and rode through the house with drawn sword, swearing and cursing, knocking chairs and other things down. In a foreign language he ordered soldiers to open the cellar. Westfall then escaped.
>
> Frederick Cook, a soldier, deposited that:...'Cotoosky rode into Mr. Wesfall's house with his sword drawn and tried to ride on a bed where the woman of the house lay, and made a pass with his sword at another woman that was in the house...

According to Westfall, provisions and some other things were stolen from the cellar, and Peter Snyder, a soldier of infantry, confirmed the truth of these events.

The proceedings did not explain what Kotkowski was searching for, with a sword in his hand, and breaking the lock to the cellar. Only his answer to de Frey that he was doing the right thing, was quoted. There is something more missing in this description.

Every newcomer who had the experience of being told, "Don't behave as if you were in Poland" knew the feeling of impotent fury. Kotkowski had a sword in his hand when he was provoked. His behavior, if not justified, can be understood.

Edward Hand wrote to Washington:

...Inclosed I send you Copy the proceedings of the General Court Martial ordered for the Trial of Lieutenant Catoosky, or Kokowski, of Count Pulaski's Legion. In the morning of the 11th that gentleman waited on me and tendered his commission which I did not think proper to accept of he. The next night he deserted and has not been heard of. Probably he expects to visit or write your Excellency before you hear of his late behavior and by that means be allowed to resign without disgrace...

On February 7, 1779, Washington wrote to Hand:
...Count Kokowski arrived in Philada. before the proceedings of the Court Martial held upon him. He has, I believe, returned or is about to return to Europe, and consequently you will have no more trouble with him. I fancy had he staid he would not have been able to have made the man he abused any reparation for his damages ... (W.W. 14, 75)

Kotkowski pleaded not guilty but did not, evidently, put much trust in the justice of the court, and disappeared.

I was not able to establish what happened to Kotkowski. Heitman does not give the date of termination of his service. According to Joseph Borkowski, he re-entered the American service, although the court martial sentence was that he be cashiered from the Army and barred from re-entry. He was also to make good damages to Westfall

As of December 3, 1778, Pulaski still intended to return to Europe and is quite bitter about his American career.

Pulaski to Congress:

Menesing–December 3 1778.

Gentlemen: Seeing the time of my Departure from America coming on,

I was sorry that in the course of my Service I not could obtain that Intimaci wich could have given me an opportunity to answer to that opinion by wich Others has gained by some lustre a Preference to wich, I have a Pright to be jealous. During this Instance it has pleased the commanding General to reinforce my corps and thereby to enable me to do some thing for the publick. I am therefore intended to make an Invasion in the Deserts of the Savages who, as I am informed by prisoners, prepares themselves to some new Mischief upon our frontiers. I will trie to prevent them and if the circumstance will allow to make them less dangerous to the Inhabitants of this country. It is the faults of some gentlemen who neglect their Duty that make me intreat you with thing of smal value. I am in want of all Instruments necessary in the surgery. I have been directed from one to another and the end has been that there was none to be got, it is very necessary article I hope to get them by your kindness. I am informed, Gentlemen, that one seeks to make different difficulties for capt. Baldesqui about my accounts, I can assure you that in spite of all me articles whatsoever they may seem to be there, rest very much upon my own expence for which I neither can nor will charge you. I am not very rich although I could have been it, but surely it is not upon your Expenses I shall enrich my self. It is very hard to give himself all possible trouble to serve you well and to be rewarded with such disagreement. It is necessary for Mr. Bedeau who I have recommended to Lt. Colo to join his corps since on must make particulars use of the winterquarters for exercising the soldiers.(PC.C. 247, 164, 76).

But on the very next day he changes his intention diametrically:

Gentlemen: I suppose Colo Sulliman has informed you of the impossibility to keep the horses longer upon this place for want of forage, all what I can do is to support them until the Time of Expedition directly after on must quarter them elsewhere. I am get obliged to make my representation to you concerning the appointment Mr. Klein as Lt. Colo in this Legion. It is not because I have any prejudice against his abelities which are unknown to me, but I am persuaded he cant be fit for a corps of Partisans whose sudden movements craves a body of a handy disposition. I have given my reason to the General of the army for wich I had a Mind to depart for Europe, but this is not at this Time whem I am in some activity. I love my profession, and I can not employ this better as in the cause of freedom. But it is therefore I must assure me of Men of whose character and abelities in the service I am acquainted of. I have chosen Mr. de Bedeau and bear the necessary trust to him and certainly I can not but the praised for the acquisition I give you of a so good officer. Gentlemen! I am sorry that the Circumstances frequently compels me to intreat you with complaints: on informs me in this moment of several Chicannery who they suffers there are charg'd with my accompts, after the exactes Inquisitions and clearest prows of the expences, the Resolution is taken to send them bag where they were. After a tree monts trouble must begin upon new. This is not the way, Gentleman, to reward the pain we take to serve you wel, pleading is not my study I only beg you without Delay to finish the Matter upon any manner. I claim, Getlemen, for your Generosity, the is the appenace(?) of noble minds it becomes a peopel who expones their lifes in threwing of. The Yoke of Tyranny let me ungo oppression and you will oblige me. Gentlemen, your most... (PCC.247,164,80).

It should be noted that Pulaski had no prejudice against the Germans. On the contrary, in connection with the de Maubon commission it was noted "General Pulaski wants German officers and offered a Lieutenancy in his Legion to Count Maubon" (PCC 247,181,58), and "The Hessian troops are extremely disliked by the Americans. Most of Pulaski's cavalry are Hessian deserters."(P.M.H.B. vol. 65, p.91, 1941).

Pulaski wrote to Washington asking for ammunition and artillery and received the following conditional refusal:

Paramus, December 7, 1778.

Dear Sir: I had the pleasure of receiving yours by Captn. LeBrun (Capt. Lebrun de Bellecour) at this place. The spare ammunition of the Army having gone on with the park of Artillery to Pluckemin, I have given an order to have a proper supply sent on from thence. I have likewise given an order upon the Cloathier General for one hundred shirts. We have already made a distribution of what Blankets were upon hand. The Board of War are taking measures to procure a further quantity when you shall have a proportion.

The badness of the Roads at this season will render the transportation, of even a very light piece of Cannon, difficult. I have therefore declined sending it up at present; but should any offensive operation be determined upon, and it should be thought practicable to carry a piece or two of light Cannon thro the Woods, they can be sent up with more convenience when the Roads are hardened by the Frost.

I have directed the German Battalion to be stationed at Easton, with a view of ordering them to the Frontier should their assistance be needed. I have thought it better to let them remain there until wanted, than to send them up to consume your stores which I imagine are not very ample. I expect by the time this reaches you General Hand will have arrived. I am, etc.

P.S. You will be pleased to be as careful as possible of the ammunition, delivering it out only when wanted, and ordering frequent examinations of the quantity delivered to see that there is no unnecessary waste by the soldiery. (W.W. 13, 373)

General Edward Hand had arrived in Minisink on December 17th and found the situation as described by Pulaski. He confirmed it in his report to Washington (W.L. 29, 263 MSS); who evidently had not believed Pulaski, as can be seen from a letter to Nathaneal Greene:

Head Quarters, December 15, 1778.

Dear Sir: His Excellency is not a little surprised to hear that Count Pulaski's legion has got back to Easton, from whence he will remove them the moment he knows where to send them. Colo. Moylans Regiment is certainly to remain at Lancaster so they cannot go there, and it will not do to send them to Frederick town upon the chance of that place being vacant. If there is a possibility of subsisting them at or near the Minisink His Excellency would order them back, he thinks their coming down is only a pretence to get into more comfortable quarters. Be pleased to enquire of Colo. Biddle whether he has had any representation of the state of Forage in that Country. If he is of opinion that they really cannot be subsisted there, let him name any place where there are no Horse at present and they shall be instantly ordered thither. All our Compliments wait upon Mrs. Greene. I am, etc. (W.W.13,397)

The Commander-in-Chief did not know the whereabouts of Pulaski as he addressed his communication of the next day to the officer commanding Count Pulaski's corps. He asked him to remove the cavalry from Easton and to follow the orders of Deputy Quartermaster General Colonel Robert Lettis Hooper. Pulaski's infantry remained for time being in Minisink.

On January 4, 1779, Pulaski's presence in Philadelphia was confirmed by his signing references for Alexander O'Neil, an Irishman who served under him in the Bar Confederation Uprising. (PCC,41,7,216)

Congress, having a grateful sense of Mr. O'Neil's service, could not accept the said offer. However, on March 1st he was appointed captain of infantry in the Legion. About that period Major Mountfort resigned as his private affairs obliged him to retire. (Deane Papers, III, 364).

On January 19, 1779, Washington ordered Pulaski to move the cavalry and all the supernumerary horses to Wilmington where proper directions would be lodged for their future progress by Mr. Wade. The reason for this was the scarcity of forage, but, according to the Quartermaster, the counties of Kent and Sussex were the best place for cavalry wintering.

It seems that Washington did not consider that the Legion would be in action before spring, as he ended the letter by saying: "...You will, of course, give instructions to the Officer Commanding to preserve the strictest discipline on the march and in quarters, that the inhabitants may have no reason to complain of licentious conduct in the Soldiers... (W.W.14,24).

On January 27, 1779, Pulaski's cavalry was not yet at Wilmington as Frank Wade wrote to Greene: "I have not heard of Gen. Pulaski or any of his Legion." (Greene Corrp. II, 82 Am Phil. Soc.)

Pulaski was only partially right in believing that the war was approaching the end. That basically was true about the Northern Theatre but not about the Southern one, for Sir Henry Clinton, in accordance with the wishes of George III, shifted the operations to the South where the Loyalists were in force.

Colonel Archibald Campbell captured Savannah from Robert Howe (who was much more heroic suppressing mutinies) with the loss of three men killed and nine wounded, while taking 451 prisoners, 48 cannon and a large quantity of supplies.

General Augustine Prevost took command of British operations in the South, and began an offensive, taking Fort Morris. Campbell as easily seized Augusta, and Georgia was shortly overrun by the British and Loyalists.

Henry Laurens became a casualty in the Arthur Lee-Silas Deane battle and John Jay, a lawyer, was elected President of Congress. General Charles Lee was at that time in Philadelphia, and Gates was still considered as a possible successor to Washington who then spent about six weeks in Philadelphia.

There were several factors which could strengthen Pulaski's position. Changes in the personnel of Congress, an opportunity to visit his influential friends, perhaps news that his brother Antoni in the autumn of 1778 arranged for a safe conduct for Casimir to come to Warsaw and answer the charge of attempted regicide.

I assume that if Antoni got a safe pass for Pulaski, he had also arranged for his exoneration. Stanislaw August Poniatowski, though a weak king, was magnanimous towards his enemies. His hatred of Casimir Pulaski was probably the result of a firm conviction that Pulaski was his only really dangerous enemy, the man who would not hesitate to push him from the throne. Now that Pulaski was helpless and in changed circumstances, there was no further need to fear and hate him. Returned, Pulaski would become one of the first magnates in the Polish Republic.

On February 2, 1779, it was resolved that: "...Count Pulaski be ordered to march with his Legion to South Carolina and put himself under the command of Major-General Lincoln, or the commanding officer of the Southern Department." (JCC)

Whatever the reasons for his hardened attitude, and it must be noted that the Legion were the only Continental troops immediately available for the succour of the South, Pulaski put forward some conditions before going there.

Philadelphia February 4 1779.

To President of Congress. Brigadier General Count Pulaski finding himself most honnoured by the confidence which the Hon. The Congress are pleased to put in him in sending him to the Southward, desire to know their answer upon the following Artikles which he has the honor to lay before them. 1. He desires to be commanded by nobody but the commander in chief of Southern Department though there might be in that Department some superior officer and he desires also to be authorised to make use of the Cavallery and of the Independent Legion of the Chief Commander or in some private or separate Department. 2. He desires to be authorised to change on his March the Horse of his Corps which by fatigue or otherwise might be unfit for service for which purpose the Quarter Master should receive orders from the Board of War to assemble some proper horses and all the necessary fourage from a place to another 3. He desires to be authorised to augment his if he could find any proper recruit on his March and also that the Company of capt. Shott be joined with his corps as it has already been ordered by his Excellency General Washington. The expence for the above mentioned augmentation should be paid by the states. 4. He desires that before his departure the accounts of the Legion be settled here, as the bad health of capt. Baldeski, Paymaster of the Legion wont allow him to go to the Head Quarters to meet there with the Auditor General. It would be necessary that the Committee of War should examine and settle those accounts. The General being present could give all necessary information. 5. As since Legion has been raised several officers have been discharged, the Vacant place should be filled as follows: Mr. Vernio as major, Mr. O'Neill as capt. Verdies as capt, Beaulieu as Lt, Kertevan as Lt, La Close as Ltn These officers being appointed Count Pulaski desires the Honorable Congress to give him leave to fill the other vacant places by capable officers as he might find them in time. As he is informed that there is a nber of soldiers recruited by the Ltn. Colo Kleyn to the number of twelve or there about who are not fixed to any Corps yet, he desires to be allowed to take those soldiers in his legion. —C. Pulaski, gen. (PCC, 247, 164, 84).

To avoid any misunderstanding the Board of War wrote on 6th February to

General Benjamin Lincoln:

Sir, By a late resolution of Congress General Pulaski is ordered to the Southern department with his Legion. We would request that the General and his Corps may be so employed that he will not be subject to the direction of any officer inferior in rank to the Commander-in-Chief of the department. This will be extremely satisfactory to the Count, and we conceive it to be the spirit and meaning of the resolution of Congress. We are, sir, with great respect, your most obedt servants, By order of the board: Tim. Pickering. (LMCC p.59)

★ ★ ★

Congress proved to be a better strategist in this case than Washington. They foresaw that now the South would become a war theater, and General Lincoln was sent there by a resolve of September 28, 1778, which gave him command in the Southern Department. Pulaski was ordered to the same place.

Pulaski's ideas about the size of his corps are clear from the Board of War report of February. It is probable that he did not make any secret about his intentions. On February 4th, Congress, it seems, in full knowledge of Pulaski's plans resolved: "That the Commander-in-Chief be directed to give the necessary orders for recruiting the corps commanded by General Count Pulaski and Colonel Armand respectively, to their full complement of infantry, to be enlisted for the war, and to receive the Continental bounties granted to the rest of the infantry."

What Pulaski had in mind was a full establishment. Evidently some influential person became alarmed and Congress on February 12 ordered that they meant only the original establishment.

Pulaski's opinion on the matter is expressed in the report of the Board of War, February 15, 1779:

At the instance of Gen. Pulaski we beg leave to represent to Congress that he is dissatisfied with the present situation of his corps on account of its numbers being to small for a command equal to his rank or to answer the purposes required by the plan which induced him to apply for

237

the raising of it. He says that on his agreing to leave the command of the Horse he proposed to raise the Legion on the footing it was established by Congres but that it was not intended he should only command this number of men in that corps. He was to do detached duty with this corps but a sufficient number of light troops from the army was to be sent him from time to time to enable him to act with his legion in the partizan way and to support his enterprizes. That it was intended he should have under his command all foreigners particularly and with this addition he should have had a respectable and useful body of troops. But as he is now ordered to the Southward this plan cannot take effect and therefore it will be necessary to augment his Infantry to the number of a regiment, at least, as he cannot possess the advantages to the Southward he would have had...He says too that he has officers sufficient for the command of a regiment and therefore it will not be more expensive to the public on the score of officers had he permission to encrease the number of privates. We have only related Gen. Pulaski's representations to us and to save time if Congres should think these are sufficient reasons therefore-we beg leave to submit the following resolution: That Gen. Pulaski have permission and he is hereby directed to augment the Infantry of his Corps to the number of a regiment and for this purpose and also to enable him to re-enlist the men of his corps whose times are about expiring a warrant of the Board of War, for the sum of...to be paid to the Gen. Pulaski or to his order from time to time, as the Board shall deem expedient. He to be accountable from such sums and shall be paid him or his order. (Signed) Root, Lee, Pickeng, Peters. (PCC 147, III, f. 55).

A regular regiment was 728 men and officers, but it could be 1000. Congress, however, did not change its decision which was expressed on February 13, as follows:

That Brigadier-General Pulaski be authorized, as casualties happen, to recruit men to keep up the infantry in his corps to its original establishment, and that a warrant for $50,000 be drawn in favor of the paymaster master of the Board of War, to be paid to Brigadier-General Pulaski, or his order, from time to time, for the purpose before mentioned, and to re-enlist during the war the men of his corps whose times are about expiring, he to be accountable for the sums he shall from time to time receive.

Resolved, That all the men, inhabitants of these States, who shall be recruited in the corps of General Pulaski and Colonel Armand, in any of the United States, shall be credited to the quota of the State in which they shall be enlisted, they not being inhabitants of any other of the United States.

Resolved, That Brigadier-General Pulaski and Colonel Armand make returns to the Board of War and of the recruits they shall enlist; and in such returns the places of nativity and settlement, and the State wherein they were enlisted, shall be particularly mentioned; and the Board are hereby directed to transmit to the respective States the names and numbers of such persons inhabitants thereof as shall be so enlisted.

It would seem from the following letter of Pulaski that he had no bad feelings towards Hand in spite of his treatment of Kotkowski:

Sir, I have the honour to communicate to you the order which I've received from Congress to march with my Legion to the southward. I return my heartful thanks for all the kindhess you have treated my Corps with, during the time they have been under your command. The Bearer, Lt. Colonel Bedaulx, shall pay for the advance you have had the goodness to make for the payment of my infantry, and settle all accounts at the Menesinks. I beg the favor you would give him proper directions for the march of the infantry and give him your assistance if the occasion would require it. I would be very glad to find any opportunity to show and convince you of the regard and esteem, with which I am, Sir, etc.

Philadelphia, February 7, 1779.

(MS. in the possession of the Polish Museum in Chicago)

★ ★ ★

On February 8, 1779, Washington sent the following letter to Pulaski. As Pulaski had achieved so much that he was receiving direct orders from Congress, the letter is expressed in a very polite manner:

Middlebrook, February 8, 1779. In consequence of the resolution of Congress of Febr. 2-nd directing your Legion to South Caroline, to act under the command of mjr.-gen. Lincoln or the commanding officer of the Southern Department I have ordered the Infantry of your Corps, which were stationed at the Minisink, to march immediately to Lancaster, Pa. You will be pleased to inform yourself of the nearest route to your place of destination and put the troops in motion as soon as possible. I make no doubt but that you give such orders as may seem best calculated to facilitate the march, without over fatiguing the men or rendering the horses unfit for service as well as do everything in your power to keep the men together and prevent the destruction of property. Congress by a resolve of the February 4, direct the recruiting of your corps of infatry to its full complement. But for power and money for this purpose I must refer you to that Hon. Body. When you have obtained these, you will proceed in the execution of the business. The present established bounty is 200 dollars to every man enlisting for the war and Land and Cloathing after passing muster, besides the usual allowance and 20 dollars to officers for every man recruited under this description. To this is added 3 dollars per day to the officer on the service as compensation for extra services.

The detached corps under Captn. Schott cannot be spared at this time. You will be pleased to give orders to the Horse of your Legion to proceed with your Infantry. I am etc.

P.S. You will disencumber the troops of all baggage which you can spare and carry only such as cannot be dispensed with. (W.W. 14, 78)

Previously the Board of War had recommended that the corps of the late Baron Ottendorf, now commanded by Captain Schott, should be incorporated with Count Pulaski' Legion.

A similar letter to the one to Pulaski was sent to Lieutenant-Colonel Charles Armand Tuffin, the Marquis de la Rouerie. There was, for some time, talk of incorporating his corps with Pulaski's but Armand was so much against it that he preferred to go to South Carolina as a volunteer. The idea had occurred to Washington when both Armand and Pulaski declared their intention of quitting the States.

Armand's corps was taken into the Continental Service in June 1778. It consisted of infantry, there having been difficulty in recruiting, and in August of that year had only 121 privates, mostly German deserters. In January 1779, Armand's corps had a troop of 42 dragoons, 2 companies of fusiliers of 46 men and a company of chasseurs of 80 men. (*Memorandum* 247 169-229)

In the beginning of February Pulaski's Legion was at Yorktown, Pennsylvania. Charles Pettit, the assistant quartermaster general, planned the following route, formed on the advice of the Honorable John Penn, Member of Congress for North Carolina, and Mr. Avery, the Attorney General of that state, from Yorktown in Pennsylvania to Savannah in Georgia: from Yorktown to Winchester to Staunton, Virginia, Digg's Ferry, to Guilford Court House to Salisbury to Charlotte, North Carolina, Campden to Congaree, to Purrisburgh, South Carolina. (Greene Corsp. Am Phil. Soc IV,80). Not only was it supposed to be the shortest route but the one which most likely afforded the necessary supplies of provisions and forage.

Mr. Avery recommended that assistance from the country was needed and that the officers should apply to: Col. Nathaniel Hart and Col. John Williams of Caswell County, Charles Bruce and Mr. Lindsay, Members of the House of Commons in Guilford County; Mr. Montgomery at Salisbury, Mr. James Brandon and Mrs. James King of Rowan. They were also to inquire of Mr. Matthew Lock for a proper person to apply to at Mechlenburg.

On the same day, i.e., 11 February 1779, Colonel Clement Biddle, Forage Master General wrote to Greene:

> Pulaski's Legion are collected at Yorktown, and we are waiting for the money from the Treasury to send a person off to supply them on the road. I shall also write to the DQM in Georgia relative to the Forage Department (ibid).

Then Pettit wrote to Greene on February 15:

> Considering the Route I find it necessary for Genl. Pulaskie to take, I think it expedient to send a person to proceed him as quartermaster and forager the whole of the way. But as this person must act independently of the Deputies, going through an entire new Country he must have a sufficient supply of money with him and cannot set out till that is obtained.

Again on February 21 Pettit wrote Greene:

> Count Pulaski is yet at Yorktown waiting to settle his accounts as he alleges he is considerably in advance of Congress. I have, however, sent off Mr. Faicet with money and instructions to provide for the Legion. I was much at pains in settling the Route and plan, and at length concluded on what I thought clear conviction to send them by way of Winchester and between the Mountains (ibid).

Pulaski thought in advance of the needs of his Legion and wrote to Congress on February 12:

> Gentlemen, General Washington refers me to Congress to settle all the affairs concerning my corps. It should be necessary that I should Recruit as much as possible for them instantly. I shall give an account of the money I shall receive for that purpose to any persons ye will direct me at my Destination. I shall want at my arrival at Charleston a letter for the province to the end that I might Draw of the stores all the necessary cloathing for the use of soldiers of the Legion according to the climate of that place. I want some caps which may be found here in the continental stores, some Rifles for the Riflemen, a few saddles to replace these that may be spoiled during the road, and all those things may be found in the continental stores. Likewise, twenty Lances which I can

find at Lancaster. I want also a couple of ammunitions Waggons. I have also the honor to Represent to the Hon. Congress that my Expedition should be made as soon as possible. I wait for that matter nothing but the end of the settlement of my accounts and the answers on the subject above-mentioned. (PCC.247,164,88)

Philadelphia, February 16, 1779.

Gentlemen: I will truble you no more with my Representation for I think the publick interest is a sufficient motive to induce you to put an end to the affairs which Detaints me here. You have seen already my first petition even as my letter to the Board of War on the subject of increasing my infantry I hope you will take about that matter the more solid way for your interests and the more satisfactory for me. I am forced at the same time to Let you know that the Expenses I am at During the Time I am obliged to stay in this town will necessarily trouble me if too Long. I am most always Reffused what is granted ordinarly to the generals and obliged to keep my Horses at my own expenses I would Reely very glad to be out of all those trouble some and to find the occasion of convincing you that I am with the greatest Regard and respect. (PCC 247, 164, 90)

Philadelphia, February 18, 1779.

Gentlemen: I would have been very glad to settle the accounts of my Legion before my Departure but as I see that would detain me too long here, that my presence becomes necessary to my corps and that it is Essential for me to set out as soon as possible for the South Expedition. I will be obliged to you to Let me have fifteen tousend dollars which are the Ballance of my account. I would not ask for that money if the considerable Expenses I have made since I am in this country did not put me under the necessity of wanting it. Capt. Baldesqui who will not be able to set out as soon as me by Reason of his bad health, shall present you my accounts when ever you please. I would also be glad that you should determine the number of my infantry it would be necessary it should be composed at Least of 600 men and that you should deliver me a sum for the Recruits, I will make on my way to compleat it. I then beg of you Gentlemen to Dispatch me as soon as possible one way or other I wait to set out only for your answer. (Papers 247, 164, 94)

Congress acted on the same day on Pulaski's letter of February 18, resolving:

That the Board of War inform Count Pulaski that Congress direct him to join the Southern army without loss of time, and enable him to do so, that the sum of 15,000 dollars be advanced to him out of the money lodged with the Board of War for the use of his Legion; for which he is to be accountable. That the paymaster of the said Legion repair to the main army and settle the accounts of the said Legion with the auditors and then proceed to join his Legion. That the Board of War also advance to Count Pulaski bounty money to recruit the Legion to its full complement of infantry, and Count Pulaski make report thereof to the Board of War, that Congress may then if necessary give orders raising an additional number of recruits to be added to the said Legion.

The unending matter of accounts still kept Pulaski from going South and before he could proceed he was to hear from his old enemy Joseph Reed who wrote to the Board of War on March 8, 1779:

Col. Smith has also represented in very strong Terms the Abuse & Distress of the Subjects of this State by Gen. Pulaski's Corps. Is Pennsylvania to be forever scoured by that undisciplined & irregular Corps without Redress? or must we be drove to actual Violence & resistance. They forage indiscriminately & take whatever they want from the poor terrified Inhabitants, many of whom strongly impressed by the Terrors of military Violence in Europe, submit to the spoiling of their goods & Insult to their Person without complaining, while others resent it in open Clamour & Complaint, & will soon probably redress themselves.

We had some Complaints some Time ago that this Corps which we suppressed upon assurance from Gen. Green that they should be removed from this State, & they were actually on their way, when General Pulaski countermanded them. We do not know the Reasons nor are they material, but we are resolved to submit no longer to such insupportable grievances.

We expect your Board will take effectual Measures for our Relief & which we do not apprehend can be done but by removing them out of the State, as Gen. Green promised.

I am, Gent.,

Yours, &c.

Letters are carried down to your own Offices upon this subject which we understand correspond with the above Relation.

To which the Board of War promptly answered the very next day:

Of that part of your Excellency's letter relative to General Pulaski's corps, a copy has been taken & inclosed to him this day in a letter from the board on the subject, a copy whereof we have the honour to send you herewith. The Count some time since received orders

243

to march to South Carolina, in consequence of which he has collected his corps at York Town from whence he will in a few days
proceed on that route. The board have an equal abhorrence with
your Excellency & the honble Council of the abuse of military
power complained of as exercised by that corps, and will on all occasions, to the utmost of their power, discourage and prevent such irregular & oppressive practices.

Your Excellency's other letter respecting the sounding the river
has also been recd. You and the honble Council will permit us to express our regret at the intervention of any obstacles in the execution
of a business so highly interesting to the United States in general,
and to this State in particular. But you say you will consider farther-
we impatiently wait the result of your deliberations, as Gen. du Portail will soon return to camp.

As to the map lent to this board, we perfectly remember its being
soon returned to us by Col. Laumoy, the engineer who used it, as
not answering (or but in a small degree) the purpose for which it was
borrowed; and we are also well satisfied from our recollection, that it
was sent back to the Council, or their secretary. Nevertheless, we
shall very readily communicate to your honourable board General
du Portail's map as soon as we are furnished with it, as we will with
every other matter in our power which we think will be useful to
the State, or which you may request.

We have the honour to be, with great respect your Excellency's
most obed. Servants,

By order of the board, TIM. PICKERING.

Indorsed,
    From Colonel Timothy Pickering by order of the Board of War
with a copy of a letter to Gene Pulaski.
    Directed,
    His Excellency Joseph Reed, Esq., President of the Supreme Ex-
ecutive Council of Pennsylvania. War Office.

BOARD OF WAR TO BRIG. COUNT PULASKI, 1779.

War Office, March 9, 1779.

Sir,

We have the honour to inclose you a copy of our letter, & an extract of another, relative to the conduct of your corps in your absence. We hoped that all such grounds of complaint, had long since
ceased. But as those mentioned correspond with former reports we

cannot avoid giving some credit to them. The complaints are of such a nature as to demand a strict enquiry, at the same time they should lead you and your officers to maintain a stricter discipline in the Corps. This the peace & quiet of the Citizens of these States as well as the honour of the Corps indispensibly demand. You will suffer us Sir, to suggest the necessity of European officers divesting themselves of European Ideas, while they serve in America. The Inhabitants of these States are unused to the severe exertions of Military power, they expect protection, and not violence and oppression from troops raised and supported at their own expense. It must give you pain, as it does us, to find the Legion followed with the execrations of the People among whom they have been stationed.

We are sensible that some irregularities happen among all troops, but no charges are so pointed as those against the Legion, from whence we cannot but conclude their conduct to be more reprehensible. We regret Sir, that there should be occasion of mentioning matters that must unavoidably give you uneasiness, but the duty we owe the People, and the respect we bear to you, Oblige us to do it.

We do not mean however to delay the Legion on these accounts, Its services are wanted at the Southward, whither we desire it may be marched with all possible dispatch. But we wish past complaints may engage the Corps to more cautious and regular behaviour in future, this we conceive necessary if the Legion would recover & preserve its honour, or even wish to remain in existence.

We have the honor to be very respectfully your most Obet Servants, By order of the Board, TIM. PICKERING.

Directed,

Brig. Gen. Count Pulaski.

Not satisfied, Reed complained still further:

The imprudent Behaviour of some Officers stationed in the Country also contributes to increase the Mischief. The Inhabitants of Lancaster County actually embodied themselves agt Pulaski's Corps and Colonel White's Conduct at Lancaster has not lessened the Disquiet. He without any Provocation or as appears since a mistaken one the other Day beat the Aty Genl with Circumstances of great Indignity-this the 3d Time that Officer of the Govt has been so treated by Continental Officers.

(Pennsylvania Archives Philadelphia, 1853, Vol. 7, p.230 et. seq.)

When Washington dared to suggest to Reed in his letter of April 27, 1779 (W.W.14,453), that the northern frontier had been defended by Spencers, Pulaski's and Armand's corps he received the following answer:

> As the Idea of our receiving any Protection from Amand's & Pulaski's Corps must have arisen from some Misapprehension or Mistake, we beg Leave to assure your Exclly that we never derived the slightest Benefit from them, but on the other Hand are still smarting under their Abuse & Desolation, the Complaints of which we suppressed, & the Complainants perswaded to bear with Patience their Losses & Sufferings. (ibid)

Perhaps Pickering was justified in complaining about the Legionnares, though neither the Continentals nor the Militia were angels. To judge from the contemporary diaries, the opinion of Christopher Marshall (Extracts from the *Diary of Christopher Marshall*, New York, 1969, p. 213) was fairly typical-"a parcel of thieving fellows". However, it should be remembered that Pulaski's soldiers stood out in their new white uniforms and, being mostly foreigners, were easy to pick upon. They were heartily disliked by Tories and Whigs alike, having no local friends and supporters. Perhaps in their requisitions they were not able to recognize the subtle nuances between friend and foe or between the haves and the have-nots. However, let us remember that the Moravians, and the inhabitants of the South had a much better opinion of the Legion. (Records of the Moravians in N. Carolina, Adelaide L. Fries, ed.)

As a result of all the delays Pulaski was still at Yorktown on March 28, 1779, from where he sent the following letter:

> March 28, 1779.

> Gentlemen: My march has been stopt at my arrival in this town by the absence of the Q.M. who was appointed by colonel Petit to provide and pay the forages for the Legion along the Road. However my Infantry went away from here the 18th of this month and I have sent to the Board of War a copy of the orders and Instructions I gave to be observed during their march. I will set out this day with the Cavalry which number is no more so considerable as it was having turned part of it to the infantry. 336 men, officers, non commissioned officers and Privates are at Present the full number of my Legion. I have sent three of my capts to Recruit three companys and compleate the others with the number above mentioned. Instead of 50,000 dollars you have ordered to be Delivered to me to Reinlist the men of my Corps and Recrut some others when possible I Received but five and thirty. 168 of my men which was inlisted for one

year only are at present Reinlisted during the war, then you can see very easily the thirty five thousand dollars I Received cant be sufficient to supply me for the future, according to the Bounty granted by the Last Resolve of the Hon. Congress. I then beg of you, Gentlemen, to order 15,000 dollars more to be delivered to capt. Baldesqui Bearer of this, who has already advanced to me part of this money. Events are, Gentlemen, most always uncertain but should the fate of arms answer to the good Dispositions of all the military persons which composes my corps I ought to belive I will have the satisfaction of announcing to you some good news from the field I am going to and I hope also time will shew if I deserve the confidence you have honoured me with.

Nine hundred pounds of the money printed 20 March and 21 April was amongst my officers and privates. As that money could be of no service to them, and as they will surely want it in the Long Journey we are going to, I desired Capt. Baldesqui to give them some other instead of it, being most Persuaded, you will be Kind Enough to order that money to be charge back again to him by the Treasury. (PCC 247, 164, 98)

The Continental money, besides being enormously inflated, was also being counterfeited. The issues of May 20, 1777, and April 11, 1778, were withdrawn from circulation by resolve of Congress on January 2, 1779.

Pulaski, evidently remembering a pleasant welcome in Maryland, stopped at Annapolis around April 9th to try to recruit some more soldiers for his Legion. Most of his legionnares signed only for a period of one year. In 1778 the Assembly by its resolution of April 21 put recruits for Pulaski on the same footing as their own.

On April 10, 1779, Pulaski sent the following letter to the Council:

Annapolis the 10th April 1779.

Gentlemen,
I came down to have the honour of presenting my Compliments to you; in the mean time call for your assistance in my recruiting. Congress having ordered my Legion to Georgia authorised me to the same right of inlisting Soldiers, for undouptely or by sikness or desertion I'll lose some of my men on the road, which lost added to the one I made in the last Campaign could hardly be repared in the southwad the white people being very scarce there, that granted I should be very much indepted to you, would the Capt Segond who I leave behind, find the same protection and support which the Council granted to him last year.

I clame Gentelman for your steem and amity, calling my legion, Maryland legion I'll endeavour my self to have that name for ever honoured by our friends and respected by our enemies, and that way reach to the glory whom I and my officers are found off.

I am Gentelmen with the greatest consideration
Your most humble and obedient Servant
    C. Pulaski.

(Archives of Maryland, p. 341)

On the same day Pulaski wrote to Johnson:

Annapolis April the 10th 1779

Sir,

Twice I came down in Hope to see you and get your Acquaintance, I was twice dissappointed, and unlucky Enough to find you out the town. you will hear I am in my way to Georgia; Give me Leave to take my farewell, and in the mean time to beg for the Continuation of your kindness for my Legion. I left a Request to the Concil on that Purpose: I flater myself you Will favour me with the influence you have among the Gentlemen of that Board, the Capt. Segond who stay behind, is desired to Return you thousand thanks, and Let you Know all the Chagrin, and sorrow I had of having not the honour to see your Excellency, and shew my self the Greatest Consideration with Wich,

I am Sir
Your most Humble
Most Obedient Servant
C. Pulaski L.

(Archives of Maryland, p. 342)

Leaving De Segond behind, Pulaski proceeded to Charleston where already on April 5th, Tho. Bee, a lieutenant-colonel of South Carolina, was impatiently expecting him, though fearing he would arrive too late or be too weak after the journey to be of any service (PCC 247, 72, 485).

On April 23 William Finne of Williamsburg, Virginia, wrote to the President of Congress, John Jay, the following letter concerning Pulaski's recruiting activities:

Brigadier-General Count de Pulaskie having left in this city a recruiting officer desired me at his Departure to purchase a number of horses to be in readiness for recruits to follow him to the Southward without loss of time; But not knowing whether I might be practicable in doing so and besides having no money by me for that purpose on indeed any public money at all in my hand I request Congress to advise me how I am to act in this Business and if horses to be purchased to order money to be sent me as soon as possible. (PCC 247, 95, 78, p.253).

In Baltimore the Council refused to co-operate inspite of Pulaski calling his forces the Maryland Legion. De Segond received the following letter:

Council to the Chevalier De Segond de la Place

In Council 20th April 1779

Sir,

The Assistance given in this State last year, towards recruiting Genl Pulaski's Legion, was in Consequence of a particular Resolution of the General Assembly, from the Terms of which, the Intention of the Assembly seems to have been, that the Liberty of inlisting within this State for that Corps should only continue 'til the Number of Men then appointed to be raised by a proportion on each County should be compleated. In the last Session, the General Assembly came to another Resolution for recruiting the Maryland Quota of Continental Troops, a Copy of which we inclose you, this enables recruiting for the Maryland Continental Regiments only. We have no Discretion in this Business, the Direction of the Assembly is the Rule of our Conduct, from which we are not at Liberty to deviate. (Maryland Archives, p. 354)

★ ★ ★

It took 29 days to reach Charleston (W. Kozlowski, *Pulaski w Ameryce*, p.169). There were some ramifications of Pulaski's journey. Benjamin Todd wrote that General Lincoln was reinforced by Pulaski's Legion and some troops from North Carolina. Sickness raged in the British army, with desertions rampant. They were in great want of bread. (PCC 247, 169, 369). A newspaper report noted that Pulaski's horse was killed with 14 balls. (*The Boston Gazette*, May 29, 1779)

The war was not going well for the Continentals. General John Ash was completely routed at Brier Creek because of his incompetence. According to the British he lost 150 killed in action, and many others were drowned while trying to escape. Brigadier-General Elbert, 27 other officers and 200 men were taken prisoner. The battle lasted about five minutes.

The British losses were supposed to be 5 privates killed and one officer and 10 privates wounded.

Undaunted, General Lincoln, with two thousand light infantry and cavalry, set off for Augusta. General Moultrie was eventually left at Purrysburgh, north of Savannah, with some militia and the second and fifth South Caroline Regiments, altogether about a thousand men. General Prevost attacked him at Purrysburgh and Black Swamp, pushing towards Charleston. Only at the beginning of May was Lincoln convinced that it was not an enemy feint and marched from Silver Bluff, in the vicinity of Augusta, to the relief of Charleston.

According to a contemporary historian (Captain Hugh M'Calls *The History of Georgia*), Lincoln: "sent three hundred light troops and the legion of Pulaski, which had been stationed at the ridge, forty-five miles north-east from Augusta, to re-inforce Moultrie." (p.418)

But from Moultrie's Memoirs, and from the letter of an officer of Pulaski's Legion (mentioned by a very reliable historian, W. Kozlowski, and confirmed by Bentalou) it would seem that Pulaski arrived with his cavalry at Charleston on May 8, 1779, and his infantry arrived on the 11th. Under the date of the 10th, Moultrie noted: "The remainder of the 2nd regiment with General Pulaski's infantry to occupy the half-moon in the center as a corps de reserve; and to sally out upon the enemy from time to time, as the service may require, without breaking the line: Gen Count Paulaski will be kind enough to take upon himself the charge of posting the army according to the above plan; and also the daily inspection of the whole during the siege." (p.413, 414).

However, in a different place, Moultrie gave the 11th as the date of the infantry's arrivals Pulaski had under his command also a troop of local volunteers, the Racoons.

According to Moultrie, the Americans on 11th May had "advice that the enemy were near our lines. Genl. Count Pulaski paraded his legion about one hundred and twenty and some militia, and attacked the advance of the British troops a little beyond the old race ground in sight of our advance guard; but he was soon overpowered. In this skirmish, he lost Col. Kowatch killed and most of his infantry, killed and wounded or taken prisoners; and it was with difficulty that the remainder got in with our advance guard. Gen Provost's army soon appeared before the town gates, at the distance of about a mile..." (William Moultrie, *Memoirs of the American Revolution*, New York, 1802, p.424, vol. I).

The above attack described by Moultrie was represented in the contemporary press and private letters and diaries as a victory. There were even such reports circulating in the form of handbills It is intriguing to note that a certain William Soir mentioned that "Pulaski's Legion brought with them (into Charleston) 180 greencoats or Tories and 4 Indians." (*Boston Gazette*, July 12-19, 1779). Contemporary accounts confirm that the British had a strong support of Indians and Loyalists.

Anyway, the following account was printed in almost all the American papers:

> ...The enemy began to cross Ashley Ferry in the afternoon of the 11th. Their advance party, composed of light infantry cavalry and savages, took a post half a mile from the ferry. Genl. Pulaski after reconnoitring them left a detachment to watch their movements and repaired to town in order to confer with Council. During this interval the enemy had completed their passage of the river and were advancing in three columns towards the town. Their advance guard consisted of 200 horses, 400 highlanders and Indians, their rearguard of cavalry. At the distance of 5 miles from the town, some of the Count's party were ordered to fire, principally to announce the enemy approach. The enemy made frequent halts in order to explore the ground over which they were to pass. The Count, who had ordered the infantry of his corps to form an ambuscade, directed a detachment of volunteer horse which he fell in with to second his infantry and made his dispositions for inducing the enemy to detach their cavalry from the head of their column. An accidental fire began and both our cavalry and infantry charged, but the latter were exceedingly embarrassed and encumbered in their movements by the volunteer horse owing to misunderstanding of orders. Despite these difficulties and the superiority of the enemy's numbers the ground was obstinately disputed. But at length the order for retreat became necessary and the enemy by their prudence in not advancing escaped the fire of the artillery from our works. The enemy loss was 45 soldiers and officers and ours 30 in all.

Bentalou in his *Pulaski Vindicated.* (Baltimore, 1824, p.27) gives the following assertion:

> ..the Legion departed for that long march as soon as every necessary preparation could be made and reached Charleston at the very time when the British General Prevost, having suddenly and rapidly advanced from Savannah, appeared before that city, on the 11th of May, 1779, in the confident expectation that it would surrender to him on the first summons. The unlooked-for arrival of Pulaski baffled all his hopes. Already had the Governor and Council agreed on terms of capitulation, not the most honourable, when Gen. Pulaski, accompanied

by the brave Col. Laurens, repaired to the Council Chamber to protest against that precipitate measure-declaring that, as a Continental officer, he would defend the city for the United States. Prevost was immediately informed of that determination. Pulaski saw the necessity of reviving the drooping spirits of the inhabitants. Accordingly, he sallied out with the Legion, who had just arrived. In that sortie, the Colonel of the legion was killed but Prevost abandoned his enterprise and retreated over the islands...

Judge Johnson, the worthy pupil of Charles Cotesworth Pinckney, denied the narration of events by Bentalou and replies in part:

"Would anyone believe that there is scarcely a word of truth in all this paragraph? That is, in the services attributed to Pulaski; in the claims to our gratitude which the writer is asserting." (The Author of the Sketches of the Life of Greene [W. Johnson], *Remarks Critical and Historical*, Charleston, 1825, p.29)

To which in his turn Bentalou said:

Early in the Spring of 1779, Pulaski was ordered to march his legion from their winter quarters in Jersey to Georgia, then recently invaded by the enemy. He himself took what was called the upper road, but, for the greater facility of procuring subsistence, and to take care of such of the sick and convalescent as could bear the journey, he detached by the lower road a troop of dragoons and a company of infantry, with instructions to the commander of the detachment to recruit, and obtain what supplies he could, from the state governors. At the time they reached Williamsburg, then the seat of government in Virginia, a small British fleet had entered James River, and landed some troops. Mr. Jefferson had just then succeeded Patrick Henry in the government of the state, and the commander of the detachment tendered his services to the governor on the occasion. This occurrence retarded the march of the detachment, which did not reach Charleston till the enemy had retreated. Pulaski, therefore, had not the whole legion with him on his arrival at Charleston; nor, indeed, did he bring with him all the forces he had taken with him by the upper road. For learning on the way the incursion of the enemy into South Carolina, he hastened forward with the most able of his men and horses. But had he even with his whole legion reached Charleston on the 8th, three days before the arrival of Prevost, my chronology would still have been sufficiently accurate for my purpose, which was to show his arrival time enough to be present during the siege. From the pains which the Judge has taken to prove the arrival of Pulaski three days before Prevost, one would think he had fallen into the absurdity of supposing me to have imagined, that the mere terrour of Pulaski's name and legion had caused the British Commander to raise the siege. Whether is it absurdity or disingenuousness that leads him afterwards to impute to me the assertion, that the sortie of Pulaski caused Prevost to raise the siege and decamp?

But I leave the reader to decide how far this consequence was brought about by the part subsequently taken by Pulaski, together with Laurens, in supporting Moultrie in his resolve "to fight it out," and in remonstrating with him against the capitulation proposed by the Governor and Council. It is certain that Prevost decamped after learning the determination of the commander of the garrison. Thus the firmness of Moultrie saved the town, and it is admitted that Pulaski was one of those who gave him the support of their opinion before the Governor and Council. "Gen. Count Pulaski and myself," says Moultrie, as quoted in the Remarks, "advised them not to give up the town," and the Remarks themselves inform us, that "on this occasion Moultrie was instructed by the Governor and Council, to give a negative to the demand on the terms proposed." Our author makes the Vindication say, that the terms of capitulation were agreed on when Pulaski arrived. If he will take another look at the passage, he will find it to state, that they were agreed on when Pulaski repaired to the Council Chamber. I do not know whether I was mistaken in saying that they were agreed on, when they were proposed, and the question was whether to accept them or not. It is, at most, a verbal criticism, not worth disputing about.

But nothing exasperates our Remarker so much as the passing observation I let fall, on Pulaski's desiring to raise the drooping spirits of the inhabitants of Charleston. Indeed he tells us plainly, that he will not control his feelings. I wish he would, however, because nothing is so prejudicial to the right use of the judgment, as giving loose to one's feelings. Many worthy men, with understandings quite as good as our author's, have, from this very habit, found them entirely useless all their lives. As I am no rhetorician, I am as unable, to cope with his declamation on this theme, as I am to understand how I gave occasion for it. Gordon, who had, I presume, no disrespect for the inhabitants of Charleston, and who wrote too long ago to be one of the "impudent" confederates against the author of the Sketches, has a passage which I will quote, both because it is much stronger than my own, and because it informs us by what means Pulaski succeeded in reanimating the spirits of the besieged. Pulaski, however, by discovering the greatest intrepidity, and by successful personal encounters with individuals of the British cavalry, had a considerable influence in dispelling the general panick, and in introducing military sentiments in the minds of the citizens. The people of besieged towns feel pretty much alike in like circumstances. Nothing, however, is more possible and indeed reasonable, than that the citizens of Charleston felt as our author tells us they did. As this spirit would naturally cause them to be angry and despond at the proposition of a surrender, so any circumstance which was likely to avert it, would inspire opposite sentiments. Yet this is the assertion, or rather the implication, which seems so ludicrous to our author, that he can scarcely suppress his sensations: that is, I suppose, he would laugh if he were not too angry. It may, however, be in the recollection of those who were in Charleston at that period, and who still live, how, on the arrival of Pulaski, all the young men who could procure horses, united to place themselves under his command. Such is the effect of what the Judge calls fearless rashness, in exciting popular feeling. (A Reply to Judge Johnson by Paul Bentalou, Baltimore 1826, p.28-31)

Pulaski's sortie, evidently because of the behaviour of raw volunteers, was a failure. But regardless of its military value it could have a beneficial effect on the drooping spirits of the Revolutionares. The defeat at Germantown turned out to be as good as a victory. The truth of the matter was irrelevant. The way of showing it was what counted. Besides, Pulaski had the opinion of an heroic and able general. He represented a part of the Continental forces, whereas the citizens of South Carolina were inclined to believe that while Congress used their State troops gladly,it was prepared to abandon their state. Moultrie's Memoirs are of evidential value in supporting Bentalou's version. As to Moultrie and the Council's willingness to fight and defend the city, see: Edward McGrady, *The History of South Carolina*, N.Y. 1969, p.355.

Joseph Johnson, the brother of Judge Johnson, gave the following interesting description in his *Tradition and Reminiscences of the American Revolution*, (Charleston, 1851):

On the very day that Prevost crossed the Ashley river, Count Pulaski crossed the Cooper river with a few choice troops, both cavalry and infantry. Although his reinforcement was not great, numerically, yet his arrival was highly important and encouraging to the inhabitants, at that critical moment. One of them, Mr. George Flagg, was riding up the Dorchester road, that day, and saw the vanguard of the British army crossing Ashley Ferry; he hurried back to Charleston and spread the alarm. Being introduced to Count Pulaski, an expedition against the British was immediately determined on. Mr. Flagg was requested to be the guide, and Pulaski may have said something about his being one of the aids. They encountered the British in the only road at that time leading to the city, about the place of Noisette's Garden, a little south of the forks.

The charge of Pulaski's cavalry was in character with their leader-desperately brave, but of short duration-and in the result inefficient. It was what is now called feeling the enemy; and although few were killed, it made an impression on the minds of the British, who did not dream of an encounter with Count Pulaski, or any such attack by regulars. They therefore, became more cautious in their advances, Pulaski's horses being jaded and fatigued by their long journey, were unfit for the route which ensued and a number of his men were lost in the pursuit. Among others of note, was Colonel Kowatch, the second in command, a very experienced, able officer.

The British buried him where he fell on the west side of the road, at the south-west corner of it and Hager-street, on the llth of May 1779. Colonel Kowatch was a Prussian by birth, and had distinguished himself in the army of Frederick the Great, of Prussia, from whose own hands he had received a complimentary badge of honor.

After the revolution, Mr. Flagg frequently travelled in the Northern States, and always with the title of Colonel Flagg, aid-de-camp of Count Pulaski, a traveller's title. He often told of this engagement as one in which he was present, and told it with animation; but he only sometimes told how expeditiously he leaped the ditch to get out of the skirmish, and made his escape to the city in safety. (p.218)

So Judge Johnson's brother's version is corroborative of Bentalou. Johnson noted also that James Simons probably attached himself to Pulaski on his arrival in May, became his aide, and was present with him in various expeditions and at the siege of Savannah.

On the British side, C. Stedman noticed Pulaski's arrival but omitted the whole incident. But Brigade Major F. Skelly gave it due attention:

12 May. The Dragoons commanded by Capt. Tawse and the Lt. Infantry under Majr. Gardner advanced very near the Town. Cpt. Moncrief with the Cavalry went to reconnoitre. Polaskey (a great partisan) had advanced his Legion consisting of about a hundred Foot and eighty Horse. The Foot under a Sr. Coll was posted behind a kind of breastwork thro' which was a large entrance. Polaskey with his Horse, (the best Cavalry the rebels ever had) advanced towards our Dragoons. Capt. Tawse charged them, intirely routed them, pursued them thro' the breastwork, attacked their Foot, and drove them to the woods. The Lt.-Col who commanded the foot was killed and fifteen or sixteen of his men. A

Captain and a Sub of the Cavalry were taken and several of their privates killed and taken. In all they loss'd between forty and fifty men. Our loss was three Dragoons killed and three wounded..." (*Magazine of American History*, Aug. 1891, p.153)

Captain Celeron and Lieutenant De la Close were taken prisoners by the British but released on parole.

About 24 hours were spent in negotiations, and finally the enemy withdrew without attempting to storm the town. And Moultrie noted:

The next morning not seeing any of them, Count Pulaski went out on horseback and made two or three circuits at full speed; and not discovering any of them, returned in, and made his reports and then collected the cavalry and followed; but they had crossed the Ashley River before he got there; I had given orders to him to endeavour to find out where Genl. Lincoln was, with his army.(Moultrie's, p.435)

The Boston Gazette reported:

...The Count attacked a detachment of the enemy, took several prisoners and obliged the remainder to save themselves by flight...Early in the morning of the 13th Count Pulaski went out with a small party of horse to reconnoitre, and the surprise can scarcely be conceived, which was occasioned by his sending an intelligence of the enemy having decamped and recrossed Ashley Ferry.

About that time Pulaski sent to Moultrie the following undated letter:

Sir,

I shall remain here, about the environs of Dorchester bridge. The 40 horse remaining, are not in a state to furnish me with the least necessaries to form a party of observation: all the volunteers have left me: I do not know if those I left near the ferry, and other places, have made to you any report. I repeat to you, my general, that it is very necessary to fortify the town better...at present we have the time, of course let us make use of it...I have sent all along the river a patrole...the instant I receive any information of Gen. Lincoln, I will advance with my party. I have nothing more to say but that, I am, etc... (Moultrie's, p.438)

The following fragment of Moultrie's letter proves to Lincoln the importance of those 40 horses of Pulaski's. "I cannot give you any further account of enemy's motions; all my intelligence hitherto has been from Count Pulaski, who I suppose is now with you... (May 15, 1779, p.442 ibid.)

M. Griffin, without giving a source, quotes the following letter, dated June 1, 1779, of Charles Cotesworth Pinckney to Lincoln which either proves some misunderstanding or malice on the part of the man, the peak of whose military career consisted of shooting at the passing British fleet.

> I think it exceedingly fortunate that you countermanded Count Pu-
> laski's intended attack at Wappo as from every account the enemy were
> very well posted behind entrenchment and in readiness to receive him
> (Martin Griffin, *Catholics in the American Revolution*, vol. 3, p.98)

General Lincoln reached Dorchester on May 14th after Prevost had crossed Ashley Ferry. The British general remained there for some days, then moved towards the coast and took possession of James Island which was separated from the mainland by the Stono River. That river was connected to Ashley River by Wappoo Creek. Prevost kept a post on the mainland, covering a ferry across the Stono. As said Moultrie; "The enemy being on James Island and Vappoo only about 2 miles from us (in sight from the church steeple) and having a sufficient number of boats to transport their troops at one time over to Charleston, kept us continually upon the watch..."

The British post was thought to be of much consequence and Lincoln decided to attack it. "We marched yesterday morning towards the enemy, but on their being reconnoitered by Count Pulaski, he thought them too strongly posted and of too great force for us to attack, and therefore ordered the troops to retire..." (Stono, June 1, 1779, Moultrie's, p.465).

This account is collaborated by Col. Grimkie who wrote on June 21: "A proper and well concentrated attack upon the enemy at Wappoo, while they were divided in their force, was countermanded, almost at the very moment of assault on their works: in consequence of which Genl. Paulaski had withdrawn his legionary corps from the service in disgust..." (Moultrie's, p.496)

That account which is confirmed by General Huger (ibid. p.466) is in contradiction to Charles C. Pinckney's letter. On the next day Pulaski wrote to Moultrie as follows:

Farr's Plantation, June 2d, 1779.

> On reconnoitering the enemy we have had a skirmish. Two of my offi-
> cers are wounded, and the enemy retired near a thick wood. We had
> determined to re-attack them in their lines, which were formed near
> the ferry; but on their receiving reinforcements made us change our in-

tention. Today we are informed that there are some of the enemy's galleys in the river. I cannot find a favorable opportunity to act.

I remain, &c,

C. PULASKI.

(ibid. p.467)

Judge Johnson in his "Remarks" takes this letter to mean that Pulaski decided to attack:

> Yet Pulaski mediated and attempted an attack upon him in his entrenchments (Stono Ferry), in which service cavalry as usual was called to participate. (p.34)

It is my impression that Pulaski in this letter referred to a single enemy detachment. He had a subordinate position and his forces were too weak to make the decision for a general attack on his own.

On this subject, Bentalou wrote somewhat mysteriously:

> As to the affair of Stono Ferry, if I did not know the temper of the author to Pulaski, I should doubt, as every reader must, whether the mention of it in the Remarks, were intended as a compliment or a censure. I may, therefore, leave it as it is; yet I could disclose a fact in regard to that affair, which would reflect the greatest honour on Gen. Huger.-He is no more; but if his papers are preserved, and among them could be found a letter received at the moment when he and Pulaski were on the eve of attacking this post, it would explain why they were disappointed in the execution of an enterprise conceived and determined on in perfect accord, and in which they counted confidently on success and honour;-a disappointment which almost drew tears from Gen. Huger, and which was the subject of vexation to Pulaski to the day of his death. (p.38)

On the whole Pulaski, at last in his element in spite of the failure of the Charleston sortie, was " charmed"with himself and his corps, as is evident from his letter addressed to John Jay:

JACKSONBOROUGH ROAD, 6 MILES FROM STONO FERRY,

June 4, 1779.

GENTLEMEN: General Lincoln will inform you of the detail concerning my corps. For myself I am charmed with being able to inform you in particular that the conduct of my corps in this country is as useful as it was displeasing in Pennsylvania. I am vexed at their cowardly proceeding and scorn them enough not to desire to be revenged. I will send, by order of the general, my accounts to the auditor of the army. I have lost about 40 men upon the field of battle. I have as many deserters. I have yet 180 men. There are but few who are not engaged for the war. The money, which I received for the enlistment of them is not sufficient. I have expended 12,000 pounds for the detail. You will be pleased, gentlemen, to make an advance to my treasurer and he will send the sum hither.

I am, while I wait your orders, gentlemen, your most humble, &c,
C. PULASKI.

(Endorsed:) No. 20. Letter from Count Pulaski, June 4, 1779. Read July 23. Referred to the Board of War.)(PCC.247,164,106)

General Lincoln considered an operation against the British who were weakened by Lieutenant-Colonel Prevost leaving for Savannah with the grenadiers and vessels. Moultrie was to co-operate via James Island. Pulaski's services were much wanted, and Governor J. Rutledge wrote to Moultrie on June 17, "...Pray get Paulaski with all the Horse to join Gen. Lincoln as soon as you think they can; I will send to Allstone to do so." (ibid. p.481)

Lincoln decided to attack Stono on the morning of 20th June. He had considered either that Pulaski was of such great valor that he had to send him to Moultrie or wanted him out of the way.

FROM GEN. LINCOLN.

STONO FERRY, June 19th, 1779.

Dear Sir,

You will please, immediately on the receipt of this, (unless you should see some good reason) to throw over on James-Island, all the troops which can be spared from town; shew them to the enemy on John's-Island; carry your boats up Wappoo-cut, ready to throw your men on John's-Island, in case an opportunity should offer without risking too much. If you should hear any firing in the morning at Stono-ferry and find the enemy on John's-Island moving from you, you will endeavor to tread on their heels. I have written to Count Paulaski, to aid you in your movements.

I am, &c.,
B. LINCOLN.
(Moultrie's, p.439)

Moultrie was much blamed for not co-ordinating his action with Lincoln due to his negligence in the matter of boats. But it seems from this letter that Lincoln thought that his force would be sufficient and his request for assistance was conditional "unless you should see some good reason." The lack of boats was a good reason undoubtedly. Besides, Moultrie was requested only to pursue the retreating enemy.

Lincoln attacked and was repulsed by Maitland. Pulaski's cavalry, with a small body of North Carolina horsemen under William Richardson Davie, attacked bravely but failed, and Pulaski certainly had a reason for being disgusted because he was denied action and requested to do patrol duties. On the 22nd he received the following instruction:

TO GEN. PAULASKI.
HUDSON'S, JAMES'-ISLAND, June 22d, 1779.

DEAR SIR,

> I was just now honored with your favor. I have ordered the bat-teau to the cut ready to bring over any horses. I shall have a bridge made over there, very soon; in the mean time, a dozen horse will be sufficient to assist us in patroling the island, these we can swim over the cut for the present service. Any information that may fall in your way, I make no doubt, but that you will acquaint me with.
> I am, &c.
> WM. MOULTRIE.

So hotly contested Stono was abandoned by the British on June 25th. They moved through the islands until they reached Port Royal where they established a strong post at Beaufort, under Colonel Maitland, while Prevost, with the rest of the army, went to Georgia.

When Prevost marched through South Carolina, the Negroes, who cared more for their personal liberty than for the sovereignty of the United Colonies, flocked to the Royal Army. When he retreated, a number of Negroes were left behind. If we are to believe Ramsay, the British chopped off the hands of those wretches who clung to their boats. Others perished in woods, and the bones of still others wre strewn on Otter Island.

I wonder where John Laurens would have found those three thousand Negroes who were supposed to fight for American liberty under white officers.

Lincoln established himself at Sheldon with about eight hundred Continentals, watched the enemy at Beaufort, but the heat of the sultry and sickly weather prevented any further operations for the time being.

If Pulaski joined the Masonic Order, it was probably during July or August.

While the war with the British subsided, the war with the Congres-

sional auditors continued. Captain Baldesqui was detained in Philadelphia until he could produce competent vouchers and settle the
accounts of the Legion. In despair Pulaski wrote to Congress a letter
which might be called his testament:

Gentlemen: Every information from the Northward that has
reached me since my departures from there, strengthen my opinin,
indeed-convinces me that there is some malignant Spirit constantly
casting such an inpenetrabile mist before your eyes as to render it im-
possibile for you to see and judge of my conduct with propriety and
as belongs the character of Gentlemen in your Exalted Nations. As
an enthusiastic zeal for the glorious cause with animated America as I
came over and a contempt of death first introduced me in your service so I flatered myself I should be happy enough to acquire honor
and to give satisfaction, but such has been my Lot that nothing less
than my honor which I will never forfeit retains me in a service
wich ill tractement makes me begin to abhor. Every proceding respecting my self has been so thoroughly mortyfing that nothing but
the integrity of my heart and my zeal supports me...I am accustomed
to explain myself very freely and I must do it now. Is there any one
act of mine ever since the battle of Brandywine down to the present
period the campaign of Charleston, that has not demonstrated the
most disinterested zeal for the publick cause? I believe the most...of
my enemies cannot it, then that I have so little credit among you
Gentlemen, that no one thing wherein I am concerned is done to
my satisfaction? Since the fatal instant that I undertook to Raise my
corps with I cloathed, recruited and exercised in the space of three
month time I have been and still am persecuted, I cannot express my
indignation when I...the infamous chicane by which I was compelled to appear before court Like a criminal. The Delay of Congress
to send me against the Enemy was grounded upon a pretence of mis-
behaviour of my corps to several of the inhabitants even while certificates from magistrates wherever my troops are quartered evidenced
the contrary, altho my corps behaved with firmness at Little Egg Harbor and several officers and soldiers fell or were wounded their only
reward was slander My often reteated request to have the amounts of
the corps settled while I was present, has been rejected and after a
whole years delay when several officers whose presence was necessary to prove these amounts were either killed or gone out of the
service it is pretended that they shall be settled with greatest exactness. Lieu. Col Bose ist killed, Major Montford and cap. Baillivy
have quitted the service and gone to Europe, Col. Kowats is killed
and Ltn. Seydling prisoner with the Enemy, each of those gentlemen

were intrusted with some department. You must remember that my request to settle those amounts while it could be done with care and while those gentlemen were present was exputed a thousand times, therefore if there is any irregularity in the vouchers it cannot be imputed to me or cap. Baldesqui and those who occasioned the Dealy ought to be answerable for the whole. Besides the sum which seems to extravagant to you is but a mere triffle to the States, indeed to me for tho I do not abound in Riches yet it is not impossible for myself to repay the whole expenses of my Legion. The value of paper money at present is 20 for 1 in coin, so that if I apply 30,000 livres towards it, that will produce a sum of 600,000 in paper money at Least for times the amount of the Expense that are dispended and with which I am upbraided, give me Leaves, Gentlemen to be plain with you. You are in this case rather ungenerous and there are foreigners to whom that attention has not been payd wich they had just grounds to expect from you. You can not be ignorant that I have spend considerable more that the sum in question of my own for the pleasure of advancing your cause. You must be sensible also, that I did come to America destitute of resourses to be a burden of you, that I have a letter of credit on Mr. Morris and that I was know by almost every foreigners of character. I have lately received a Letter from my family advising that they dispatsched 100,000 livres in hard money to me, should it fortunately come safe, the pleasure to me wl be truly great to repay you to the utmost farthing the whole charge of my Legion. Change you then your opinion of one foreigner who from his entrance into your servive has never the cause to be pleased, who in Europe is by Rank superior to all that are in your service, who certainly is not inferior in zeal and capacity, and who perhaps may have been considered as one who came to beg your favour, be more just, gentlemen, and know that as I cannot submit to stop before the sovereigns of Europe, to I came to hazard all for the freedom of America and desirous of passing the rest of my life in a country truly free and before setling as a citizen to fight for liberty, but perceiving that endeavour are used to disgust me against such a motive and to regard it as phantom I am inclined to believe that enthusiasm for Liberty is not the predominante virtue in America at this time. I have been informed that the board of war instead of detaining or punishing deserters from my legion have discharged them from the service, can this be called a proper conduct towards men who rob the states of the boundy and other wise? I have also been informed that one man hearing of this generosity and who had stolen a horse to desert with, apply to them was not only favoured in like manner but even presented with the horse. The officers who would have done their duty in maryland whether they were send to recruit men have been traversed by the orders of the same board, the state of maryland imposed a penalty of £100 upon any men who should inlisted in my corps. Capt. Bedkeer who was left with a detachment of light horse to collect men remaining behing sick or on furlough with horses belonging to the legion and entrusted with the sum of 5,000 dollars for the recruiting service has found protection with the same Board who have rendered him independend althro he has failed in the duty of an honest man. What does all this indicate? has is not the appearance of an invidious design of disaffected persons to urge me to omit the service in disgust without minding the justice of their procedings. Such a persons denounce to your tribulane as per-tubators of the publick welfare in the military line. It Is my disposi-tion to speak so as to be perfectly understood I honour you without baseness, flattery is noxious in private as well as public bodies, it is the vice of those base animals who endeavour to persecute and in-jure me. I was present when gen. Lincoln received an express with a letter mentioning capt. Baldesqui's detention and the order for ap-pointing another paymaster which office I believe is not very neces-sary, the few men me have left might be payd by the general paymaster of the army and there will be no further confusion of de-tails. More over it seems that the destruction of the corps is intended which will be easily performed. The campaign is at hand, perhaps I may still have occasion of sheving that I am friend of the cause with-out being happy enough to please some individuals.

Charleston, Aug. 1779

(PCC 247,164,108)

Pulaski's vexation was caused by the action of the Treasury, which reported on Monday May 17th, 1779, that:

in obedience to the order of Congress they have referred the accounts of General Count Pulaski's Legion to the auditors of account for the main army. For want of regularity in keeping these accounts and of proper vouchers agreeably to the directions of Congress and the Board of Treasury Auditor Johnston has reported to them that it is impractica-ble to settle that account as appears from his report and remarks accom-panying their report.

On which report Congress resolved:

That the commanding officer of the detachment of the army serving in South Carolina and Georgia be authorised to appoint a paymaster to the said legion and that Captain Baldesqui, the present paymaster, be detained until he shall have produced competent vouchers, and settled the accounts of the said legion. (JCC)

On July 28, 1779, Captain Joseph Baldesqui wrote to Congress that he had gone to camp to settle his accounts, but the auditors were so busy that they could not attend to him for a month. Baldesqui went for private reasons to Boston but gave the auditors all the documents received from Pulaski. He fell sick in Boston and found that the auditors had checked accounts and made report to Congress which induced it to pass a resolution which was published to his disadvantage.

Baldesqui stated that Pulaski had begun the Legion's expenses three months before he was appointed, and that Pulaski and his officers lost some vouchers as Pulaski confirmed to the auditors himself. Baldesqui had a general receipt from Pulaski giving an exact account of all sums received. Further on Baldesqui stated that Pulaski had laid out for the Legion at least 50,000 dollars of his own money. Would the regularity of public business not permit to trust Pulaski's honor, Congress should settle the accounts as they would like and Pulaski would pay. (W.T.R. Saffel, *Records of the Revolutionary War*, N.Y. 1858).

That letter was read in Congress the next day and it was resolved "That the Board of Treasury be authorized to cause the accounts of the said Legion, for the reason set forth in the said letter, to be settled in such proofs as in the discretion of the auditors or commissioners of accounts shall be judged satisfactory." (JCC)

Captain Baldesqui in defense of his integrity wrote a long memorial which was read in Congress on December 11, 1779, and referred to the Board of Treasury (247,4l,I,p.266-271) where he stated that he was enclosing certificates of auditors Johnston and Howell, showing that the accounts had been settled to his honor and satisfaction, and requesting the full exoneration.

On December 28th, 1779, the Board of Treasury reported that the auditors certified that Baldesqui had settled his accounts as paymaster of Count Pulaski's Legion to the first of March 1779, and that he had discharged his duties with strict honor and integrity.

So much for the accounts which spoiled the last months of Pulaski's life and put Baldesqui through hell on earth.

★ ★ ★

In Charleston, Pulaski had attended to (his cousin?) Ignacy Jan Zielinski, who was seriously wounded during Pulaski's attack at Charleston, and who eventually died of wounds on September 25, which is confirmed by a letter from Saville printed in *Niles Register* for October 2nd, 1847.

Another of Pulaski's friends and companions, the famous "King of Madagascar,"Maurycy Beniowski, tried to reach him about that time. Wrote Horatio Gates to His Excellency John Jay, Esq., on August 21, 1779:

> The Quartermaster at Boston sent me last week a Foreigner who came from L'Orient...That foreigner says he is one of Count Pulawszski's brothers, that he was twice taken by the English, the first time in a vessel from Hamburg, with three hundred Hussars, their arms and accoutrements, all of which were shipped in consequence of a plan sent to Europe by his brother, the General of that name in our Service and the joint expense of that General, and Pulawszki's family to the amount of £25,000 sterling...
>
> I am informed that some persons in Boston suspected this foreigner of being an imposter, but, Sir, as he demands no money on the strength of his Brother's Name: as he solicits no more than a reasonable support until he can join the Count in Carolina, and was even determined to undertake this journey on foot, could he not obtain his moderate request? I conceived the Dignity of the United States did not permit an Officer to doubt a stranger in such a Situation, and that Honor as well as Humanity, point to outdo the Necessity of risking a trifling Imposition.
>
> Having supplied him with a Continental horse and a warrant for a hundred dollars, I now send him to Congress, not doubting that I shall meet with their approbation of my conduct, respecting the relief I have afforded in their names to a stranger, who announced himself as the brother of a General in our Army... (PCC 171,252-53).

On September 4, 1779, Congress read a report from the Board of War stating that they conversed with Beniowski and they knew nothing from any testimonials he produced except that he had a letter to Pulaski who he claimed as his half-brother. It would seem that if he were an impostor he would hardly wish to go to places where he could be detected. Congress, convinced by the logic of this argument, resolved: "That Mons. le Baron Benyowski be supplied with a horse and one thousand dollars to enable him to proceed to General Pulaski, now with the southern army."

Beniowski was not a relative of Pulaski but his friend from exile in France, and an old comrade in arms. His and Baldesqui's letters confirm Pulaski's claim that he paid a good share of the Legion's expenses out of his own pocket.

★ ★ ★

Charles Hector, Count D'Estaing, after abandoning the expedition against Rhode Island, sailed from Boston on November 3rd, 1778, for the West Indies where he gained fame by capturing the island of St. Vincent without a fight, and successfully storming Grenada with its "impregnable" defenses, then beating Admiral Byron. Shortly after Savannah was lost Congress sent a fast ship in January 1779 to D'Estaing, asking him for help. Also Governor Rutledge, General Lincoln and Plombard, the French Consul in Charleston, wrote letters to the French Admiral pointing out to him advantages which could be achieved should he co-operate with Lincoln in the recovery of Georgia.

D'Estaing agreed, especially as the hurricane months in the West Indies were approaching, and he sailed out from San Domingo on August 16th. Two fast ships of the line were in advance of the fleet. At the beginning of September, D'Estaing's fleet was close to Charleston, and Viscount de Fontages was sent to inform Lincoln that the French Commander was ready to co-operate. On September 5th, General Lincoln ordered all officers and soldiers to join their regiments, and on the 8th the Continental soldiers were withdrawn from the forts and replaced by militia. According to Edward McCrady (*History of South Carolina*) the scarcity of arms and ammunition made it necessary to furnish them to the militia from the arsenals of South Carolina, and a detachment of the Georgia Continental troops under Lachlan McIntosh was asked to take charge of them and march to Augusta. There Pulaski was ordered to join McIntosh who was then required to march towards Savannah to open communications with the French.

Hugh McCall in his *History of Georgia* repeats his statement previously written in reference to the British siege of Charleston that Pulaski, to whom the command of the American cavalry had been confirmed, had had his post on the ridge fifty miles north-east of Augusta, for the convenience of obtaining forage and provisions and to be within easy march of Charleston and Augusta. (The place was probably Bull's Plantation [Doc. Am. rev. K.G.Davies, Irish University Press.)

According to the account of the *Boston Gazette* for November 15, 1779, about that time "Count Pulaski advanced with cavalry, took the enemy's picket and also surprised their captain and three privates at Ebenezer. That active and enterprising General Count Pulaski with his cavalry had so thoroughly cleared the way and broken up all the enemy's advanced posts as to afford Major-General Lincoln the opportunity of an interview with the French General at the Orphane House on the 16th. When the plan of operation was settled."

266

It was on September 11, 1779, that Pulaski with a few of his horsemen crossed Savannah River ahead of the American armies and reconnoitered the vicinity of Ebenezer, roughly twenty-three miles west of Savannah. On the evening of the 12th he sent a message to D'Estaing and informed him that General Lincoln with artillery and about 600 infantry would pass the most difficult place that night. General McIntosh was on the march. His forces consisted of about 1000 infantrymen, 8 cannon and 260 cavalry. (Archives Nationales/Marine/ B4 168, p.205)

D'Estaing, after coming ashore, sent a letter to Pulaski expressing a hope that Pulaski would be the first one to join him and complimenting him on his sublime bravery and activity which made nothing impossible for him (Archives Nationales/Marine/04 168, p.232)

On the morning of the 14th Pulaski sent a note to Lincoln, "I give myself the pleasure of sending the expedition of Count dEstaing, and I shall do my utmost to join the Count as soon as possible with my Detachment" (Am Hist. and Literary Autographs Catal. 159, p.27)

He requested infantry reinforcement, and was about seven miles from Savannah at Widow Gibbon's. (Polish Museum, Chicago) On September 16th D'Estaing sent a threatening message to General Prevost, asking him to capitulate to His Most Christian Majesty. The British General played for time and meanwhile Colonel Maitland with the garrison from Beaufort sneaked into the town. The defenses under the direction of James Montcried were strengthened tremendously. Consequently Prevost returned an answer to D'Estaing that the town would be defended to the last extremity.

A consensus of opinion among the historians is that had D'Estaing stormed Savannah immediately upon his arrival, the town would have been taken easily.

Lincoln, whose army reached Savannah River on the 12th but was delayed because of the difficulty in finding boats, joined D'Estaing on the 16th. As an assault seemed impracticable, the Allies decided on a siege.

The story of Pulaski's activities is related in the following manner by Bentalou (*A Reply*, p.32, 33). And let us note that according to that author Pulaski proceeded from Charleston, not Augusta:

> After the retreat of Prevost from Carolina into Georgia, Gen. Lincoln retired to a healthy situation in the vicinity of Beaufort, Pulaski remaining meanwhile at Charleston, both inactive certainly, but in expectation of D'Estaing, who at length, on the 1st of September, arrived on the coast of Georgia, with a large fleet, and between three and four thousand land troops. His arrival roused the whole country. D'Estaing sent the chief of his staff, the Count de Fontanges, to Charleston, to confer

with Lincoln on their ultimate combined operations; and when it was understood that D'Estaing was to land his troops at Beaulieu in Georgia on the 11th of September, in concert with Lincoln, who was to cross the river Savannah on the same day, Pulaski, who had not 'withdrawn in disgust,' left Charleston in order to join Lincoln, and they reached Zubley's Ferry on the Savannah together, on the day agreed on.

Here we found no boats, the enemy having destroyed them, and those which were expected down the river, having not yet arrived. But a single canoe having been found at length, and Lincoln being extremely anxious to pass some horse across the river, in order to reconnoitre, and follow the movements of the enemy, Pulaski determined to accomplish it, by sending over in the canoe a man at a time, with his accoutrements, and swimming the horse alongside. In this manner between twenty and thirty horse accomplished a landing on the other bank, of whom Pulaski gave me the command. Our road lay through a defile, formed by a causeway carried through a swamp, several bridges of which it was necessary to mend, in order to pass the horse over. The distance to the high grounds was, I think, about three miles, on reaching which we discovered two redoubts in front of the defile. It was lucky for us, as there was no going to the right or the left, and no retreat in the rear, that the enemy had abandoned these a short time before. I have no disposition to relate the particulars of a service rendered perilous by the smallness of our number. Wholly insulated from our army, which was separated from us by a river which it had no means of crossing, our only safety, during that night and the following day, was in wakefulness and activity. Fortunately we found all the outward posts and redoubts evacuated, and the enemy concentrated within the lines at Savannah, in sight of which I came late in the evening of the next day, my men and horses extremely fatigued. I then retreated on the road leading to the ferry I had crossed. About midnight I was challenged, and, to my great relief, it proved to be Pulaski, with the remainder of the legion and some volunteers, (for he was seldom without a number of them,) who had thus rapidly followed on my footsteps. We took the first road to the right, through the woods, and took up our quarters for the remainder of the night, in a large plantation.

Early next morning a man in a red coat was discovered riding through the woods. Dragoons were sent in pursuit of him, and he was soon taken and brought to our quarters. He proved to be an express sent by D'Estaing with a letter to Lincoln, and also one to Pulaski, in which he informed him of his landing, and said, among many other flattering things, that knowing Count Pulaski was there, he was sure he would be the first to join him. Though it then rained heavily, Pulaski instantly hastened to D'Estaing at his landing place, where they cordially embraced, and expressed mutual happiness at the meeting. On the next day D'Estaing, not wishing to wait for Lincoln, informed Pulaski of his intention to march to Savannah, and said that he counted on his legion to form his van. In pursuance of this wish, we set out immediately, and reached Savannah some time before D'Estaing, where we engaged and cut off an advanced picket of the enemy's infantry. D'Estaing, on his arrival, displayed his forces, and sent in his summons: the result is well known. On the next day Gen. Lincoln joined us with his troops, and the two commanders in chief of the combined forces, determined on a regular siege, and finally to storm the place.

The French camp, which was originally pitched south-east of the town, was quickly changed and located almost directly south of Savannah. General de Dillon commanded the right, D'Estaing the center and de Noailles the left. General Lincoln's command was posted to the southwest, the front of his line towards the east and his rear protected by a swamp. About midway between the armies, towards the north, was Pulaski's cavalry camp.

On 19th September, Pulaski with a body of cavalry attacked a British troop which landed on Egeechee River. He returned the next day with prisoners, and drove the others back to their ships.

The relations between the allies were not cordial, and the American soldiers were forbidden in the French camp. They did not look inviting to the French, with their long uncombed hair and unshaved faces. Their arms were a medley of rifles, old muskets and fowling pieces. Shoes consisted mainly of moccasins cut from hides, and their uniforms were in rags. Only Pulaski's Legion impressed the French. According to an officer of the Agenois Regiment the lancers were well equipped and excellently mounted.

But though the French were splendidly uniformed their morale was not so good, and desertions were a popular way of avoiding the misery of the service. The sailors were dying by the dozens of malnutrition and scurvy, and they lived in terror of their officers who were highly critical of D'Estaing.

D'Estaing had different opinions about his subordinates but a uniform one about the American officers. They were forgetful, full of petty jealousy and incredibly ignorant of their own country. General Lincoln suffered from somnolence, falling asleep on every occasion which, however, was forgiven him, in sharp contrast to Pulaski's alleged cat-nap at Germantown.

On the night of October 1, a lieutenant of Pulaski's Legion, Cezary August Elholm, took part in one of the most famous feats of the war of American Independence. Colonel John White, Captain George Melvin, a sergeant, three privates and Elholm proceeded to reconnoiter the position of Captain Thomas French who had been cut off from Savannah and fortified his camp on Ogechee River. This Loyalist detachment consisted largely of convalescents from Subury garrison and was not able to reach Savannah before the blockade.Colonel White directed a number of fires to be lighted in view of the camp which gave the appearance of a large force there and summoned Captain French to surrender. That ancient ruse succeeded and they capitulated. (PCC 247, 167, 197)

On October 2nd Pulaski wrote to D'Estaing:

> Yesterday an American officer commanded the picket. His accustomed laziness...caused that in opposition to my orders he did not occupy his post at the hour..."

As the result his cavalry did not come up promptly at the alarm. Pulaski was blamed for this, and lost a cavalryman. But as he wrote:

> I have studied my profession for 18 years and would blush to commit such fault that would cost a life of a man. I suffer, however, to hear several officers younger than I am amuse themselves by expressing unfavorable opinion of me..." (Archives Nationales, Marine, B4 168, p.206)

On the 4th, Savannah was heavily bombarded with considerable damage to houses and some loss of lives, mostly women, children and Negroes. Prevost requested D'Estaing to allow women and children to leave the besieged town, but this was refused with regret by D'Estaing who had to yield to the austerity of his functions, deploring at the same time the fate of those persons who would be victims of Prevost's conduct and delusions.

On the morning of the 8th, Pierre Charles L'Enfant with five men marched through a brisk fire from the British lines and attempted to set fire to the abatis, but the green wood refused to ignite in the damp air. D'Estaing had been a month on the American coast and was impatient to leave. Therefore, he decided on an attack, to which the Americans agreed, though they had the assurance of their engineers that it would take ten days to cut into the enemy's lines. It had been decided that the attack would take place on the morning of October 9, 1779, and as the story has it, the British were at once informed by their supporters about the plans.

The town of Savannah was on the southern bank of the Savannah

River. Its northern front was secured by the river and its western side was covered by a thick swamp and woody morass. The other sides were bounded by a line of works, the right and left defended by redoubts. There were batteries in the front, and impalements and traverses were thrown up in the rear. The whole extent of works was surrounded with abatis and a ditch. The Sailor's Battery was covering the wooded marshes to the west called Yamacraw, which could give the attackers concealment up to within 50 yards of the fortifications. There was a piece of flat land leading towards Spring Hill where the British had a strong redoubt. In the area between Spring Hill and Sailor's Battery there were two more redoubts and a second battery. Smaller structures and a strong line of earthworks protected the right flank of Spring Hill or Ebenezer Road redoubt. Continuing east, there was a fourth redoubt, then a fifth, and smaller works were located along the line.

As is evident from this, there was no possibility of action for the cavalry unless the infantry made a large opening. According to Lincoln's order, the infantry destined for the attack of Savannah was to be divided into two bodies. The whole was to parade to the left of the line at one o'clock, and the French were to form in three columns, two for assault and the third for reserve. The diversions on the west and east were planned under Dillon and Huger, but they both failed. The main attack was to be against Spring Hill redoubt.

Again, as in the decision to winter at Valley Forge, it was Pulaski who objected. In his memorandum to D'Estaing, he proposed three separate points of attack. One assault was to be attempted on the British right flank along Augusta Road, and another on the left wing was to be made, while the main attack should be launched near the right center of the British line. While I am not able to evaluate Pulaski's plan, I know that the disaster which met the D'Estaing-Lincoln plan could not have been worse. (B4, 168, Archives Nationale, Marine.)

Everywhere there was confusion and again an unrealistic plan of operation misfired. The French were late and the entire allied army started to march towards their lines of departure in one long column of about 4,500 at 4 o'clock in the morning. Before they were greeted by a murderous fire, they heard the weird skirl of bagpipes, which dampened the spirits of the attackers.

The French column reached the position on the right of the line of departure about dawn and D'Estaing led it forward to the attack without waiting for the others to file off to the left.

The French troops passed the abatis, crowded into the ditch and ascended the berm under heavy fire in front and on its flank. As Thomas Pinckney wrote, in spite of the efforts of the officers, the column became confused and broke away towards the woods, and the second and third French columns shared the same fate.

Colonel Laurens, with the light troops, advanced by the left of the French column, attacked the redoubt, succeeded in gaining the exterior slope and planted the South Carolina colors beside the French flag. During this flag planting, William Jasper was killed. Captain Tawse of the South Carolina Loyalists, who defeated the Legion at Charleston, fell defending the gate of the redoubt after plunging his sword into the body of his third assailant.

At the critical moment Colonel Maitland sent in the Royal American Regiment grenadiers and marines, who charged the attacking column, already melting under the deadly enfilading fire from the British ships and the batteries of the fortifications extending in the semi-circle from the river as well as under the individual fire of the British. Moultrie said the British loaded and fired without any danger to themselves since the Americans were so crowded in the ditch and upon the beam that they could hardly raise an arm, being so huddled together.

Laurens' men under the impact of the counter-attack retreated. When McIntosh arrived at the scene at the head of the second American column, it was a mass of confusion, and the wounded D'Estaing was trying to rally the French.

Now let us recapitulate the instructions for the American cavalry under Pulaski. According to Lincoln's order:

> The cavalry under the command of Count Pulaski will parade at the same time with the infantry and follow the left column of the French troops and precede the column of the American light troops. They will endeavor to penetrate the enemy's lines between the battery on the left of the Spring Hill redoubt and the next towards the river. Having effected this, they will pass to the left toward Yamacraw and secure such parties of the enemy as may be lodged in that quarter. (Charles C. Jones, *History of Georgia*, Boston 1883, p.95)

The instructions for the infantry and cavalry were probably amplified by oral orders. The British had been letting horses out of the abatis for grazing, so it would be logical to assume that if Lincoln had given Pulaski such specific instructions as to the place of attempted penetration, it had to be that spot. Also as nobody in his senses would expect the cavalry to storm the heavily constructed fortifications, Pulaski's action had to depend on the success of the assault on Spring Hill redoubt, or on infantry filling the ditch, pulling the abatais apart, or at least securing and clearing that opening through which the British let their horses out. To accomplish this mission, instead of getting into the unfortified town with its straight streets, Pulaski was supposed to attack the enemy towards the left, i.e., the Sailor's Battery which would have made more sense if Dillon had succeeded in his mission, but not otherwise. As it happened, Dillon's column got lost in a swamp and emerged in plain view of the British, who promptly opened fire on them and Dillon retreated. The cavalry under Pulaski was to precede the American column commanded by Laurens until it approached the edge of the wood and then was to wait for an opportunity for action. Pulaski, however, could not stand patiently by in view of the American retreat and, leaving the command to Colonel Horry, he tried, in place of the wounded D'Estaing, to rally the troops. While doing this, he was mortally wounded (W.B. Stevens, Joseph Johnson), leading not an absurd cavalry charge "but a desperate push at the British lines." (Robert Beatson, *Naval and Military Memoirs*, vol. IV, p.526, London, 1804).

During his life Casimir Pulaski was a controversial figure, and he remained such in death. There is no single authoritative account of his death. The scene is described in the following manner (*Pulaski Vindicated*, pp.31,32,33) by his faithful companion Paul Bentalou:

Savannah was neither a fortress nor a walled city. It was merely a town fortified with batteries, redoubts and abatis. When summoned by D'Estaing to surrender the place, Prevost requested time to deliberate, and this was inconsiderately granted. The interval was employed in introducing into the town a considerable reinforcement, and in strengthening its defences. Resistance was then resolved upon. A storm or a siege, therefore, became inevitable. The latter was preferred. After the necessary preparations, a heavy cannonade was opened upon the enemy's works, and briskly kept up for several days, but without the desired effect. D'Estaing's marine officers remonstrated against his continuing to expose so valuable a fleet to the fury of the elements at this tempestuous season, or to the possible arrival of a superior British naval force-and loudly urged his departure. An assault was consequently resolved upon. This assault was to be made on the right of the British lines. Two columns, one French and the other American, were to attack, at the same time, each a particular redoubt. In the rear of the columns the whole cavalry, American and French, was to be stationed, under the command of Count Pulaski. Should, as was confidently expected, the redoubts be carried and the way opened, that intrepid leader was, with these united troops of horse, to enter the place sword in hand, and to carry confusion and dismay among the garrison. D'Estaing led in person the French corps of attack. Wishing to avoid a circuitous advance round a swamp, and supposing the ground at the bottom to be sufficiently firm, he marched directly through it. The enemy had been informed of his plan by spies. They knew the intended point of attack, and the direction in which the approach of the assailants was to be made. Accordingly, they collected all their force where it would be required, and at the first alarm opened a tremendous and deadly fire. Pulaski, impatient to know when he was to act, determined, after securing his cavalry undecover as well as the ground would admit, to go forward himself, and called to accompany him one of the captains of his legion, who is yet living but far advanced in years.-They had proceeded only to a small distance, when they heard of the havoc produced in the swamp by the hostile batteries. D'Estaing himself was grievously wounded. Aware of the fatal effects which such a disaster was likely to produce on the spirits of French soldiers-and hoping that his presence would reanimate them, Pulaski rushed on to the scene of disorder and bloodshed. In his attempt to penetrate to the murderous spot he received a swivel shot in the upper part of his right thigh; and the officer who had accompanied him, was, while on his way back, wounded by a musket ball.-The enterprise upon Savannah was abandoned by the allied armies. The Americans and the French, having witnessed each other's zeal and courage, and acquitting each other of any intentional share in this disastrous result, separated in perfect harmony. Count D'Estaing re-embarked his troops and artillery, and Pulaski, with his wounded officer, was conveyed on board the United States brig, the Wasp, to go round to Charleston. They remained some days in the Savannah river; and during that time the most skillful surgeons in the French fleet attended on Count Pulaski. It was found impossible to establish suppuration, and gangrene was the consequence. Just as the Wasp got out of the river, Pulaski breathed his last, and the corpse immediately became so offensive that his officer was compelled, though reluctantly, to consign to a watery grave all that was now left upon earth of his beloved and honoured commander.

The Wasp entered the harbour of Charleston with her flag half hoisted. The mournful signal was repeated by all the shipping in the port-and all the forts and batteries responded to it in the manner usual on occasions of deep and universal sorrow. The Governor and Council of South Carolina, and the municipal authorities of Charleston jointly adopted resolutions to pay to the memory of General

Pulaski the most respectful and the most splendid funeral honours. A day was set apart for the celebration of the obsequies-and the Quarter-master General of the United States, at Charleston, directed to make and to defray all the preparations necessary for that melancholy solemnity. The procession was grand, magnificent, suited to the occasion. The pall was carried by three American and three French officers of the highest grade-followed by the beautiful horse which Pulaski rode when he received his mortal wound, with all the accoutrements, armour and dress which he then wore. So immensely large was the mournful procession that it was found necessary to make a circuit round the whole city to the church, where an eloquent and impressive discourse was delivered by the chaplain of the army.

According to William Bacon Stevens (*History of Georgia*, Philadelphia, p.217, 1859) Pulaski was struck by a grape shot from a bastion while rallying the troops, and was taken out of the field by his comrades. That fact is confirmed by Captain Hugh McCall who said: "Count Pulaski attempted to pass the works into the town, and received a, small cannon shot in the groin, of which he fell near the abatis...On the retreat, it was recollected by his corps that Count Pulaski had been left near the abatis: some of his men displayed great courage and personal attachment in returning through the firing, though covered by the smoke, to the place where he lay and bore him off" (*History of Georgia*, p.445-446).

Basically the same story is related by Major Thomas Pinckney: "Count Pulaski, who with the Cavalry, preceded the right Column of the Americans, and proceeded gallantly until stopped by the Abbatis, and before he could force it, received his Mortal Wound. (*The Siege of Savannah*, ed. Franklin Benjamin Hough, Albany 1866, p.166).

Further on, Pinckney claims that Pulaski said to Colonel D. Horry; "Follow my Lancers to whom I have given my order of Attack" (ibid. p.167)

David Ramsay, who was present at the siege of Savannah but whose histories are impersonal, reported that: "Count Pulaski, at the head of two hundred horsemen, was in full gallop riding into the town, between the redoubts, with an intention of charging in the rear when he received a mortal wound." (*History of Revolution*, vol. 2, p.40).

This version is duly repeated by William Gordon (p.330), and not unsurprisingly by Botta (vol. 3, p.78). But what is more surprising is that Harry Lee also wrote about the charge: "Count Pulaski, at the head of two hundred horse, threw himself upon the works to force his way into the enemy's rear. Receiving a mortal wound, this brave officer fell, and his fate arrested an effort which might have changed the issue of the day." (p. 143)

Moultrie noted:"Count Pulaski at the head of his cavalry received his mortal wound from one of the galleys." (2,p.41). The *Rivington Gazette* reported it as a grape shot, the *Connecticut Journal* a bar shot, but a French officer noted that General Pulaski received a long-bar-relled musket shot in his thigh. (*The Siege of Savannah*, ed. Charles C. Jones, p.34).

In *Traditions* (p.302) Joseph Johnson quoted James Simons who had written: "In this action (the attack on the lines of Savannah) General Pulaski (who commanded the cavalry) received his death wound. James Simons was close by his side, and was his extra aide de camp. James Simons had a feather shot out of his cap, and was one of three out of nine, who escaped with his life on this occasion."

It is also possible that Pulaski was wounded while dashing across the British fire line to the French. (Henry Archacki, *Straz*)

Accounts of the contemporary historians and witnesses are as confusing as was the battle scene. D'Estaing's version lies in between the accounts of Pulaski being wounded by a random shot and being killed while charging. D'Estaing noted, according to O'Connor's Journal and Report to M. de Sartine (Dec. 5, 1779, B4 166, B4 142, Archive Nationales, Marine), that Pulaski had "fell by his own fault as he had been at the spot where he should not had been, too soon advancing to avail himself of the passage to be open for him." Evidently, he is unaware of the fact that Pulaski rushed to his aid to rally the troops.

Moultrie stated in the appendix to his memoirs: (W. Moultrie, App. III, *Memoires*, etc., N.Y. 1802) "Several persons hearing that he had been mortally wounded at the assault on Savannah conceived the idea that in a fit of reckless fury he must have attempted to storm the place at the head of his cavalry, and what was, at first, the surmise of the ignorant, passing from mouth to mouth, became the fixed opinion of the credulous."

But to the popular mind Pulaski's death still looks like the description in the apocryphal memoirs of Major Rogowski:

> For half an hour the guns roared and blood flowed abundantly. Seeing an opening between the enemy's works Pulaski resolved with his Legion and a small detachment of Georgia cavalry to charge thru, enter the city, confuse the enemy and cheer the inhabitants with good tidings. General Lincoln approved the daring plan...Imploring the help of the Almighty, Pulaski shouted to his men, "Forward!" and we, two hundred strong, rode at full speed after him, the earth resouding under the hoofs of our chargers. For the first two moments all went well. We sped like knights into the peril. Just, however, as we passed thru the gap between the two batteries, a

cross fire, like a pouring shower, confused our ranks. I looked around. Oh, sad moment, ever to be remembered, Pulaski lies prostrate on the ground! (Compilation by Wm. H. Richardson, The Pulaski Sesqui-Centennial, Jersey City, N.J., Oct. 20, 1929, pg. 40)

In the possession of the Georgia Historical Society there are a number of letters collected by James Lynah, the grandson of Dr. James Lynah of Charleston, S.C. According to them Dr. James Lynah extracted an iron grape which mortally wounded Pulaski. He performed the operation in the field in view of the Savannah lines and was assisted by his surgeon mate's son, Edward Lynah, and a Negro called Guy who later waited on Pulaski.

There is a version that it was Dr. Elisha Poinsett who attended his deathbed (*U.S. Magazine*, I,3, Feb. 1838, p.361-69).

It is probable that Casimir Pulaski had two friends close to him at his last moments: Maurycy Beniowski and Felix Miklaszewicz. (PCC 91,78,461; 99,78, XV,616; also J. Johnson's *Traditions*, p.246).

The place where Casimir Pulaski rests remains unknown. Perhaps he was put into a watery grave, having a sailor's burial instead of a cavalryman's.

Joseph Johnson wrote in his *Traditions*...:

Another report of his interment has lately been received from my friend I.K. Tefft of Savannah. Charles Litomisky, a Polander, said that he was at the siege of Savannah, as aide de camp to General Count Pulaski, and had the consoling satisfaction of supporting this hero in the struggles of death and that he assisted in consigning his mortal remains to its kindred earth under a large tree, about the bank of the creek leading from Savannah to Charleston. I believe this statement to be correct. (p.245)

Henry Williams, making a speech during the laying of a cornerstone of the Pulaski Monument in Savannah on October II, 1853, said:

On this day seventy-four years ago Pulaski died, yet remarkable to relate surrounded as he was by friends and companions in arms, prominent as was his station, and gallant as were his deeds, no evidence exists which designate with certainty the place where his remains were deposited. Whether the sea received him, or whether he lies under some spreading oak upon St. Helena's Island in our sister State or sleeps beneath the sod of Greenwich by the banks of our own beautiful streams, an hour's pilgrimage from the spot where he fell, remains to this day a mystery.

EPILOGUE

IN THIS MONOGRAPH I have followed Casimir Pulaski's life from the moment he stepped off the brig *Massachusetts* on to the American shore in July 1777, until his death in October 1779. It was difficult, but I tried to keep my commentary to a minimum for the sake of objectivity, putting aside personal opinions as much as possible. Often I was tempted to paraphase the General's reports and letters, and write my own story. But he spoke well over 200 years ago and still does today, so I quoted him at length.

The Johnson–Bentalou polemic had to be examined in detail, researched in depth, discussed at length, and judgments expressed. The American historians and writers like Jared Sparks, Lossing, Gordon, and Haiman have generally ignored Johnson and accepted Bentalou. There is a good basis for this choice since Bentalou was at Brandywine and Germantown with the German Bn. and then served in Pulaski's Legion, from the beginning to Savannah, where he too was wounded. Therefore, Bentalou can speak from personal knowledge where Johnson publishes his purpose and motivation in attacking Pulaski—to minimize his contributions to the American Revolutionary cause. Sometimes when one has an axe to grind, and he grinds it "exceedingly fine," he may slip and grind his own fingers.

Curiously, Pulaski escaped the effects of the myth-making process so prevalent in the histories of the Revolution. By this, I mean the serious works, not the eulogic elaborations and addresses produced for the "Pulaski Patron Saint" occasions. To his contemporaries who include early American and English historians, Casimir Pulaski was a famed general, a great partisan, that intrepid and heroic Count Pulaski, perhaps unlucky at times-but then which of the American generals did not meet his Egg Harbor? Now as Pulaski's bicentennial anniversaries (as of arrival, nominations, battles and death) passed, but the continuation of attacks initiated over 150 years ago still can be expected. I take the liberty of answering some accusations even before they appear in print.

It is highly improbable that Pulaski was asleep at Germantown or drunk. He was a teetotaler. It is absurd to claim that he stole the Legion's money, for, on the contrary, there is strong evidence, referred to in this book, that the U.S. Treasury owed him money. I cannot see the point in the incredible allegation that he had pretended death on board the *Wasp* in order to escape from America. I agree with Georgian historian Joseph Vallance Bevan, who said in 1825: "In fact, none of the vulgar stories commonly repeated about himself (Pulaski) or his conduct during the siege appear to be entitled to the least degree of credit."

My task in writing this work was made especially difficult as there is no scholarly history of the American cavalry. If such a work existed, it would be difficult for its author to avoid showing the significant part played by Pulaski during the inception of the Continental cavalry, for it is a fact that Pulaski was the "Father of American Cavalry," and that he and Michael Kowacz wrote the first Continental Army regulations, thus forestalling Steuben.

Unfortunately for the memory of Pulaski, the cavalry became an extinct branch of service. Therefore, the military historians of the Revolution hardly noticed its existence for the reasons explained in this work. Thus, the closest approach to an appraisal of Pulaski, as the chief of the cavalry, was made by Charles Francis Adams and Karol Zbyszewski. (*Studies Military & Diplomatic* N.Y. 1911 & *Wczoraj na Wyrywki*, London, 1964).

Why did he come to America? Pulaski put his reasons for contemplating the voyage in the following letter to Deane:

Oct. 17, 1776

Sir: Ever since I was compelled to leave Poland I have sought opportunities for the exercise of my military acquirements. My endeavors having failed during the war between the Turks and the Russians, and having, moreover, involved me in disaster and irreparable loss, I was forced to certain measures that have delayed the expression of my ardor to contribute in my person to the success of the English provinces of America.

It is now nearly a year since I contemplated the voyage, and I was encouraged thereto by persons of the greatest distinction, to whom I confided my intentions, but being unacquainted with any one knowing the state of affairs in your country, I was obliged to remain inactive, in spite of my good intentions.

By chance I have met Mr. le Chevalier Rabier de la Baume, who perfectly understands my situation, and who knew me by reputation in Poland; and it is he who advises me as to whom I should address on this subject.

You have now, Sir, the motive that impels me to send one of my friends to speak with you, and after your conversation with him, I will come to a decision.

I beg that you will accord to this officer the same confidence that you would give to me, as I have intrusted to him whatever communication I might desire to make to you. (D.P. XIX, 323)

According to Samuel L. Knapp, it was Dr. Joseph Warren who wrote to Pulaski and "opened to him our scanty knowledge of the science and art of war and stated the necessity we should be under, soliciting aid from the great captains of Europe." And Dr. Warren was supposed to have written to Pulaski: "Our people ransack all history for stimulating examples of courage and your defense of Poland is on every tongue. Hasten, my dear Count, to our shores; here you will be hailed with enthusiasm, and a post of honor and danger will be given you as soon as Continental Cogress is appraised of your arrival." (S.L. Knapp, *Polish Chiefs*, N.Y., 1832)

While Knapp's intuition is to be much admired, the historical reliability of his work is very doubtful. There is no doubt that Warren's alleged letter reflected Pulaski's expectations. When he arrived in the United Colonies as a young general of 30, he had already achieved a European fame well deserved in a grueling, partisan war waged for years against the Russians and the Polish Royal troops, loyal to a king elected by the nobles through Russian threats, bribery, corruption, and bayonets. He was unaware that foreign volunteers, often called foreign adventurers and mercenaries, were not really welcome in America. Shortly after his arrival in America, he wrote to Washington: "That country (Poland) no longer exists for me; and here, by fighting for freedom, I wish to deserve it. Life or death for the welfare of the state is my motto and thereby I hope to earn the esteem of the citizens of this country..."

But frustrated towards the end of his life he wrote the following to D'Estaing: "...I serve in the American Army with the view of pleasing France. I left my native land expecting to find asylum in that kingdom. In passing to Turkey I obtained the recommendation of the Duke de Guiton. My prospects were flattering. Change of circumstances has not changed my heart. If your Excellency wishes proof of it, give me the opportunity, and I will profit by it. I hope to merit your approbation."

In one sense, it was unfortunate for Pulaski that the past glory of the Polish cavalry penetrated even to Northern America, and he was appointed the chief of a practically non-existent Continental cavalry. Had he been granted an infantry brigade (and he had all-round military experience) as Lafayette, De Calb, Conway or even Steuben, he might have been spared all the future frustrations. As it happened, he was appointed the commander of an incipient force over the heads of a jealous Balme and Moylan. Let me remind the reader that this post was refused by a cautious Reed and Cadwalader. Nominated, Pulaski did everything possible to shape the horsemen into an effective cavalry force.

Unfortunately, as he said in one of his letters a workman needs his tools, and those were refused him.

There were numerous reasons why Pulaski could not succeed at his task of shaping the Continental cavalry into an effective fighting force. Some were of a very concrete nature–difficulties with fodder, the high prices of horses and equipment and a dearth of recruits. But the main obstacle was the attitude towards cavalry shared by Washington and most Americans.

There was no real understanding of the tactical use and function of the cavalry in the Revolutionary Army. What cavalry the Americans had were modelled on the British Dragoons, the mounted infantry, and the British were not specialists in cavalry, for their wars were of Colonial conquest and the skillful manipulation of foreigners for the sake of the balance of power, while their forte was in Naval warefare.

During the first part of the Revolutionary War, the cavalry was hardly used on either side, though the British dragoons were feared. It is obvious to a military historian that the victory in this conflict would fall to the first side to use cavalry seriously tactically, and effectively. A hard–hitting, striking force of cavalry in Long Island, could have made a difference. (The Americans would detach men from the cavalry for messenger service, escorts, patrols, scouting, guard duty, etc. When men were detached for such service, there usually weren't enough left for tactical use as a striking force. Pulaski, as he wrote to his sister might have 50 men left from 4 regiments for tactical, offensive fighting, but he hit superior enemy forces with these dragoons on countless occasions.)

Throughout Colonial American history, cavalry was of minimal importance in its wars. No traditions of cavalry developed, while Poland was world famous for its cavalry expertise, featuring the hussars or heavy cavalry or its light cavalry, including the Lisowczyks made famous in Rembrandt's painting. Pulaski was well versed in the military cavalry traditions and became famous for his own skills and exploits as a cavalry leader. He knew the Polish battle tactics and the tactical use of cavalry including the following:

1. At Kircholm, 4,000 Polish hussars charged a larger force under Charles IX and left 9,000 Swedish dead on the field.

2. At Chocim, 65,000 Poles and Cossacks were surrounded by a Turkish force 3 times as large. Under bombardment and siege for nearly a month, the Polish cavalry rode out, charged, and routed the Turkish force.

3. At Vienna in 1683, an allied force of 68,000 (of whom about 26,000 were Poles) under the supreme command of King John Sobieski defeated over 140,000 Turks, thus saving European Christendom. The Polish hussars broke the Turkish center with their charge and captured the tents of the Grand Vizier in the ensuing rout.

Such was the glory of Polish cavalry arms which inspired Pulaski! It was in his blood! Custer, Stuart, Jubal Early, and others learned the proper use of cavalry in the Civil War.

Pulaski attempted to organize the cavalry. He and Kovatch wrote the regulations for with basic training the cavalry needed drill, discipline, and order. Pulaski tried to introduce lances and the Polish-Hungarian saddle style. He overcame every difficulty and finally sent a fully armed lancer for Washington to see. To be a cohesive and effective cavalry tactical force, he wished to be subordinate only to the Commander-in-Chief, in accordance with the contemporary European usage, and similar to Knox. His efforts were met with suspicion, jealousy, intrigue and accusations. Even worse for him was the lack of action, after Brandywine and Germantown. And let me recall to the reader that it was Pulaski who opposed the passive "death camp" at Valley Forge, advising instead a winter campaign. He was proved right. He knew from past winter campaigs in Poland that the cavalry (both horses and men) must remain active to maintain combat efficiency.

Pulaski was not only a talented cavalry leader, but in the Bar Confederation, he commanded infantry as well, withstanding the famous siege of Czestochowa. Pulaski was an excellent strategist, a splendid tactician, and he had a good grasp of the whole strategic and economic situation in the Colonies. But his versatile talents were not utilized and, what was worse, he became aware of the dislike for the cavalry permeated from the very top. In Washington, Pulaski met a horse lover, but not a cavalry leader or even a general who was cognizant and appreciative of the tremendous tactical value and advantages of that branch of the service. Calvary could strike first, soften up the enemy for a follow-up attack by the infantry, outflank the enemy, go around and hit the foe in the rear. Cavalry could go deep in the enemy rear, cut off their supplies, lead the adversary to believe he was surrounded and cause great panic, confusion, and routs. They could make victories or turn defeat into a victory. Their mobility made them priceless. It was all in vain for try as he so persistently did, he could not educate the Americans to see the value of cavalry as a tactical force. Even if he did succeed, there never was enough cavalry remaining after detaching them for various non-tactical services, as escorts, etc. And not only Pulaski but all the cavalry leaders were disparaged.

From a cavalrymen's viewpoint, the difference between Pulaski and Washington, if I can hazard a modern parallel, was akin to that between a taxi-driver and the commander of a tank division. On the American side, there were problems of forage, high cost and unavailability of good horses, costs of necessary equipment and arms, recruitment of experienced horsemen (for it took time to learn to ride), and a general unfamiliarity with cavalry tactics and the tactical use and deployment of cavalry.

There is no specific evidence but it is my impression that Pulaski was not an admirer of Washington's generalship. He did not find the respect for or understanding of cavalry which prevailed in Europe. This was a shock and came as a bitter blow for a proud cavalryman to swallow, then accept, then ignore, and finally to keep on fighting. Washington had the responsibility of the Army and the Revolutionary Cause upon his shoulders to make him wary, hesitant, and slow to cautiously decide while the other had the dash, decisiveness, impetuosity, and "perpetual motion" of a cavalry leader. They were as different as the cautious Omar Bradley and the explosive Gen. Patton.

I have not seen Pulaski's name mentioned as a member of the Washington military family. On the contrary, his name is associated often with those men who opposed Washington: Horatio Gates, H.R. Lee, Thomas Pickering, and the Adamses. Pulaski's bitter enemies were Joseph Reed, Stephen Moylan and Thomas Cotesworth Pinckney, all men close to Washington. It was Charles Lee, who had called Pulaski's Bar Confederates "banditti," but who pronounced Pulaski's cavalry principles to be the best in the world. It was Horatio Gates who recommended Pulaski's Legion, and it was H.R. Lee whom Pulaski asked for protection. Disenchanted with the cavalry command, for after detaching men for various functions, there was very little cavalry to command or to fight with and hoping to be able to command an independent strike force, Pulaski opted for an Independent Legion as a means of seeing more action and to contribute meaningful services to the American cause for freedom.

That the Continental cavalry disappeared from the stage of the Revolutionary War with Pulaski's withdrawal was irrelevant to his enemies.

Pulaski's Legion was conceived as a kind of compensation for a troublesome foreigner. Pulaski thought of the Legion as a small and independent army, and that difference in views became the source of future conflicts. The peak of Pulaski's humiliation was his arrest on the order of Reed's associate, Judge McKean.

Once in the South with his corps, Pulaski was in his element. Behind him were the jealousies and intrigues of Philadelphia, echoing only in the matter of the Legion's accounts, which darkened the last days of his life. But at present the men in the South were chivalrous, friendly and hospitable, and the horses were splendid. The volunteers flocked to his standard, and, most important, there was action at last. Immediately the matters of seniority and independence of command lost their importance for Pulaski. Before leaving for the Southern Department he had asked to be dependent only on the Commander-in-Chief in that territory, but we do not hear of him raising that question later. He gladly accepted the orders of McIntosh and Moultrie. In the actual combat zone, the need for co-operation was obvious to him; and the nuances of seniority disappeared on the battlefield. then the French arrived and they were kindred Europeans, whose language he spoke.

Perhaps all the troubles and difficulties suffered by Pulaski could have been endured with a greater patience by a man of lesser caliber or one who came to America for pecuniary reasons, and not in search of glory. Pulaski was not only sensitive, however, but proud and ambitious. Already in 1771, Dumouriez had written: "Pulaski is a quick-tempered young man, even more proud than ambitious, very attached to the Prince of Courlandia, exceptionally brave and rather sincere in his behavior." (W. Konopczynski, *Konfederacja Barska*, Bibl. Narodowa, p.113). Such character did not make his life easy in Poland nor did it in America. "Light Horse Harry" Lee says that Pulaski's name was dear to him and continues the tribute:

He was sober, diligent, and intrepid, gentlemanly in his manners, and amiable in heart. He was very reserved, and when alone, betrayed strong evidence of deep melancholy. Those who knew him intimately, spoke highly of the sublimity of his virtue, and the constancy of his friendship. Commanding his heterogeneous corps, badly equipped and worse mounted, this brave Pole encountered difficulty and sought danger. Nor have I the smallest doubt if he had been conversant in our language and better acquainted with our customs and country, but that he would have become one of our most conspicuous and useful officers. (Compilation by Wm. H. Richardson, The Pulaski Sesqui-Centennial, Jersey City, N.J., Oct. 20, 1929, pg. 41)

This opinion is expecially valuable coming from a cavalryman of fame. It is interesting to note in passing that J.J. Louvet de Couvrai also noted Pulaski's melancholy. (*Love and Patriotism*, Boston, 1789, p. 57)

There is one more of Pulaski's alleged attributes of character which I have not seen discussed by any of his biographers. Was there a streak of cruelty in his nature? Ferguson accused him of ordering prisoners killed. And the authoress of a loyalist poem, "The Times," writes: "What a devilish figure, this with devilish voice? Oh, 'tis Polaski, 'tis a foreign chief...'No quarters' is his motto...He fears not in the Field, where Heroes Bleed, He starts at nothing..." (Am. His. Rec. vol. II, p.439)

According to Rivington's *Royal Gazette*, October 28, 1778, one of the delegates, on hearing about a manifesto of the English commissioners, dared to make a speech for conciliation with Great Britain. In answer "the President sent a message to fetch the Polish Count, Pulaski, who happened to be exercising part of his legion in the courtyard below. The count flew to the chamber where the Congress sat, and with his saber in an instant severed from his body the head of this honest delegate. The head was ordered by the Congress to be fixed on the top of the liberty pole of Philadelphia, as a perpetual monument of the freedom of debate in the Continental Congress of the United States of American." (Frank Moore, *Diary of the American Revolution*, p.101)

This is obviously a fabrication, but it is characteristic that its hero became Pulaski, for he was impatient with disloyalty and lack of patriotism. Let us remember that Pulaski, angry with some men, wants them to be sent to work on the galleys. He has no hesitation about forcing Quakers to swear allegiance to Congress. Jedrzej Kitowicz in his memoirs (Pamietniki, 1845) mentions that Pulaski ordered a girl spy to be hanged. It is known that the Confederates in Poland had a ruthless attitude to known and suspected spies, and freely and severely exacted contributions and supplies. But the Bar Confederation war was a more desperate struggle than the American Revolution.

Accusations of a similar nature were made in America against Pulaski, the foreign chief in the Revolutionary War. Here, however, he had no political allies, family links or position, and also he was not a leader of a patriotic and popular cause. Nobody sang songs praising him; nobody expected his horsed swordsmen to come to the rescue. Instead, people were afraid that their fodder would be taken, that his soldiers would be quartered in their houses, and Pulaski could not distinguish between subtleties of political orientations in the population. There were, to use the revolutionary nomenclature, those well affected, those disaffected and those indifferent, and all of them complained to Congress about Pulaski and his soldiers if a chicken was stolen, a bucket of grain fed to his horses, a receipt given in an improper manner or a recquisition paid in worthless paper money.

Pulaski was hated too by the British, and he feared falling into their hands so much that against Dr. Lynah's orders he asked to be removed to the French ship, risking his life rather than a possible capture. Much of that hatred towards him could be due to the fact that Pulaski's character was shaped by war. His father Jozef was the main promotor of the Bar Insurrection in 1768, and Jozef's three sons played important roles in that struggle. Franciszek died on the battlefield (according to Kitowicz, his mistress fought at his side), while Antoni was captured by Russians, and only Casimir, a youth of 21, was left to carry on the torch of insurrection after his father was betrayed. For four long years he was a leader in the bitter civil war connected with Russian intervention on the Polish king's side and Russian occupation of Poland. His personality was shaped by the necessities and cruelties of war; he had to be both a fox and a lion, he had to lead his soldiers against an enemy superior in numbers and equipment, an enemy sometime led by Suvorov. To survive, and even triumph ocasionally, he had to be ruthless, cunning, talented and persevering.

Casimir Pulaski was of small stature but physically strong. Thus, he was described by Waldo and Kitowicz who both pointed to his unusual dexterity. Lee and Kitowicz remarked on another unusual characteristic: Pulaski was a teetotaler, however, he was a gambler. Perhaps, not so strange in a man who risked his life a thousand times.

There is no evidence of a softening feminine influence in Pulaski's life. That man who spent his life on horseback, in battles and in camps had no time for love. The only woman linked romantically with Pulaski was Franciszka Krasinska, morganatic wife of Prince Karol of Courlandia, the man whom Pulaski would gladly put on the throne of Poland. Theirs was most likely a platonic affair. Kitowicz mentions that Pulaski was restrainded towards women.

It is not strange that Polish poets and many historians saw Pulaski as a knight in shining armor.

Pulaski failed in an attempt to kidnap Stanislaus, the King of Poland, the Russian puppet, and had to flee his country. Attempting to create the Polish Legion to fight for Poland's liberty in a foreign service and on a foreign soil, he became precursor of an idea of such struggle. He did not succeed as the Turks were defeated in their war with Russia, and he found asylum in France, becoming one of the first in the long line of political emigrants leading up to the present. But an ex-ally, a "regicide," cut an embarrassing figure for the Court of Versailles. In vain, Pulaski tried to enter the Spanish or French service. He almost starved and found himself in prison for debtors, freed only by the ashamed protectors of the Bar Confederation. Thus turned by the forces of circumstances into a soldier, Pulaski sought employment in the only occupation he knew. At last the American Revolution supported by France gave him an opportunity, but somewhere at the back of his mind was a thought about trading in America. But he had nothing to be ashamed of in that.

Whatever the motives which caused him to fight for American liberty, he was the most talented and experienced general of that war. In addition to being a brilliant strategist and tactician, he was a good organizer. But he was prevented from using his gifts, and ironically it was only after his death that the cavalry played a considerable part in the war. He lived too short a time to achieve a more significant role in events. He had impressed the minds of his contemporaries with his potential, and they felt guilty for frustrating him. Both sides considered his death one of the main events of the siege of Savannah. When news of it reached the Army on November 17, 1779, parole was "Pulaski" and countresign "Poland." King Stanislaus August Poniatowski of Poland (whom Pulaski regarded as a Russian puppet said; "Pulaski has died as he lived—a hero—but an enemy of kings." (Wytrwal, *Poles in American History and Tradition*, Endurance Press, Detroit, 1969, pg. 74)

There were other tributes:

The great French philosopher, Jean Jacque Rousseau, said of Count Pulaski that he "saved his unhappy fatherland, for he redeemed the glorious name of Poland, for he restored her moral forces." (Wytrwal, supra., pg. 74)

Major F. Skelly, brigade major of the British forces at Charleston said that the Pulaski Legion was the "best cavalry the rebels ever had." (Wytrwal, ibid.)

The Marquis de La Fayette wrote: "He was one of the first members of the Confederation of Poland, the most distinguished officer and the most dangerous enemy of the tyrants of his country." (The Executive Documents of the Senate of the United States for the Second Session of the Forty-Ninth Congress, Washington Govt. Printing Office, 1887, vol. 2: Nos. 11-125, pg. 9)

Congress voted a monument to him but never constructed one. It was not until 1855 that the grateful people of Savannah and Georgia erected a splendid edifice to his memory. Monuments aplenty have since been erected, towns and counties named after him, presidential and gubernatorial proclamations issued year after year, Pulaski parades annually held in his memory—but for all of this he remains relatively an unknown general of the Revolutionary War.

NOTES

1) "Franklin has engaged Pulaski, one of the King of Poland's assassins and five or six French officers to go to America on board a vessel that will sail to Nanty..."
(Lord Stormont to Lord Weymouth, Paris, June 4, 1777)
(B.F. Stevens, *Facsimiles of Manuscripts in European Archives Relating to America*, London, 1891, vol. 16, 1545)

2) Pulaski landed at Marblehead on July 23, 1777, arriving on board the three-masted privateer brig. *Massachusetts*, under Captain John Fisk (Gardner W. Allen, *Naval History of the American Revolution*, N.Y. 1913, (reprint 1962), vol. l, p.236)

"Pulaski is to embark at Nantes aboard Massachusetts armed vessel. Capt. Fink..." Stormont to Weymouth, 19 June 1777, B.F. Stevens, Facsimiles, vol. 16, 1552.

In the collections of the Georgia Historical Society in Savannah there is correspondence from James Lynah, the grandson of the surgeon of the same name who removed the deadly bullet from Pulaski's wound. Lynah made an interesting research in connection with Pulaski and among his letters are two from Rev Dr. W.L. Johnson of Jamaica (Jan. 12, 1854 and Feb. 28, 1854), who stated that his neighbor from Trenton, N.J., Dr Nicholas Belleville (Capt. Le Brun de Bellecour, Maryland Hist Mag. XIII, 3, p.224) " came to this country with his friend Pulaski. They landed at Salem."

Pulaski supposedly met Belleville in Paris and went to America via London and Liverpool.

3) William Heath, *Memoirs of the American War*, reprint, Books For Libraries, N.Y. 1970, p.134

Wladyslaw Wayda misquotes in the originals of Pulaski correspondence enclosed in his *Pulaski w Ameryce*, Warszawa 1930. Not a "noble Pole" but "Polish nobleman." Also the correct date of Heath's entry for that day is July 26, not June 26.

4) Executive Document, No. 120, 49th Congress, 2nd Session, Senate "Message from the President of the U.S.A.," March 3, 1887. p.7. This document is also referred to as an Executive Document.

5) The whole fantastic project could originate not only under the influence of Maurycy Beniowski but also under the influence of the tales of Michal Dzierzanowski, another famous adventurer of those times. There is also a slight possibility that "Madagascar" was a code name for Kamtchatka, or that the Colonies thought about making peace with England and attacking their erstwhile ally.

6) Executive Doc. p.7. Some other foreign officers hit on this idea too, (De Bois, Breligneu. Vide: Papers of Continental Congress, Microcopy 247).

7) For instance the position and property of Stanislaw Poniatowski, the father of the king of the same name, was about equal to the position of Pulaski's father Jozef. King Poniatowski's brother became prince by a special decree of the Sejm (Diet).

8) When Congress was not eager to honor Dekalb's contract assuring him of a rank of major-general, he wrote on August 1, 1777, to Congress: "What is deemed generosity in the Marquis de Lafayette would be downright madness in me, who am not one of the first-rate fortunes. If I was in his circumstances I should perhaps have acted like him..."

Further on he stated: "It will look very odd, and I think very diverting to the French Ministry, and to all the military men, to see me under the command of the Marquis de Lafayette."

He ended his epistle with a hint of a civil suit for damages. He also asked, in case his request was refused, for return of expenses for travel to America and back to France. Dekalb's letter was passed to the Committee on Foreign Applications. His request was rejected but Congress voted $4,000 for Dekalb and his company. (*Journal of Continental Congress*, vol. 8, p.637).

9) "...ought not this weak or roguish man to be recalled?" Lovell to Whipple, July 29, 1777 (E.C. Burnett, *Letters of Members of the Continental Congress*, Washington, 1921, vol. 2, p.431. This work is referred to further on as LMCC).

A motion to recall Deane was put on August 5 and on November 21, 1777; Congress resolved to recall him. In spite of his role in establishing Roderique Hortalez et Cie, which supplied the revolution in America, and getting the support of France, Deane fell heavily with the leading faction in Congress. Among other reasons, he was condemned for sending to America without authority numerous French officers.

10) "...The trouble which your Excellency receives from Foreigners commissioned by Congress has made the Committee appointed to examine their pretensions averse to offering any resolution for places

above the rank of subalterns." James Lovell to Washington, May 26, 1777 (LMCC, vol. 2, p. 375, also Lovell to Franklin, ibid., p.398.)

11) "...We are yet in Philadelphia, that mass of cowardice and Toryism. Yesterday we buried Monsieur Du Coudray, a French officer of artillery who was lately made an Inspector-General of artillery and military manufactures with the rank of Major-General. He was drowned in the Schuylkill in a strange manner. He rode into the ferry boat and rode out at the other end into the river, and was drowned. His horse took fright. He was reputed the most learned and promising officer in France. This dispensation will save us much altercation... John Adams, Works, 2, p. 437.

> The Du Coudray treaty is not yet determined upon, but I think there will be few advocates for confirming it. The 4 engineers who were the only persons absolutely sent for, are arrived; and though modest men, upon a very modest treaty, yet positively refuse to be under the command of Du C - y who has duped Deane to make him Commander-in-Chief of all the artillery and engineering through the States..."
> L.M.C.C. 2, p. 403.

12) Said John Adams: "I have been distressed to see some members of this house disposed to idolise an image which their own hands have moulded. I speak here of the superstitious veneration that is sometime paid to Genl Washington. Although I honor him for his good qualities, yet in this house I feel myself his Superior. In private life I shall always acknowledge that he is mine." (L.M.C.C. vol. 2, p. 253)

13) "Whether, if Duke Ferdinand had commanded at Germanstown, after having gained by the valour of his troops, and the negligence of his enemy, a partial victory, he would have contrived by a single stroke of the Bathos, to have corrupted this partial victory into a defeat? In one of the numerous publications which have lately infested Philadelphia, it was brought as a crime against Mr. Deane that he had directly or indirectly made some overtures to Prince Ferdinand of Brunswick to accept the command of the American Army who must, of course, have superseded General Washington. The crime appeared to all the foreign officers who are acquainted with the prince's reputation as a soldier, in so very ridiculous a light they never think or speak of it without being thrown into violent laughter." Charles Lee, July 6, 1779, p.156, *The Life and Memoirs of Major-General Lee*, N.Y. 1813. Also see: J.B. Perckins, *France in American Revolution*, reprint 1870.

14) Louis XV was married to Maria Leszczynska, the daughter of Stanislaw Leszczynski (1677-1766), king of Poland 1706 and 1733.

15) The documents of the Bar Confederation are lost or not easily available for a historian abroad so the figures are only an approximation. A French adviser to the Bar Confederacy reported on April 30, 1771: "...(Pulaski's) army consists of more or less 600 hussars, 300 dragoons of lejb-regiment, 100 infantry, and nearly 3000 Polish cavalry divided into 77 regular squadrons, and 10 or 12 irregulars. He has, too, quite good Tartars and 50 Bosniques and 40 Cossacks."

But further on the French general states that all of them dispersed and actually Pulaski had at his disposal about 1200 men. (Wladyslaw Konopczynski, *Konfederacja Barska*, Wybor tekstow, Krakow, 1928, p.114).

16) Gen. Brigadier Prudhomme de Borre was accused of cowardice and resigned. From Trenton on September 18, 1777, he wrote: "...It is not my fault that American troops run away ..." (Microcopy 247, Roll 91, Item 78, p.257).

17) This description confirms Stedman (C. Stedman, *The History of the..American War*, London, 1794, p.292), and Bentalous's assertion in *Reply*, p.19: "...enough light baggage remained to form a column of waggons."

18) *Journals of the Continental Congress*, Gaillard Hunt, editor, Washington, 1904, vol. 8, p.745 (15 Sept. 1777).

It must be realized that Congress at that time was quite a small body. In the period when Pulaski was appointed generally about 25 men were taking part in deliberations, and the influence of James Lovell was enormous

19) Sullivan was blamed in Congress for the Brandywine defeat, and recalled until the inquiry into his handling of the Staten Island expedition was finished. Washington protested, pointing to the scarcity of generals and the probability of the next major engagement. Sullivan was acquitted.

20) Alexander Hamilton was no admirer of foreigners: "...They (Congress) have disgusted the army by repeated instances of the most whimsical favoritism in their promotions, and by an absurd prodigality of ranks to foreigners and to the meanest staff of the army. They have not been able to summon resolution enough to withstand the impudent importunity and vain boasting of foreign pretenders but have manifested such duplicity and inconstancy in their proceedings as will warrant the charge of suffering themselves to be bullied by every petty adventurer who comes armed with ostentatious pretensions of military merit and experience. Would you believe it, Sir, it has become almost proverbial in the mouth of French officers and other foreigners that they have nothing more to do to obtain whatever they please than to

assume high tone and assert their own merit with confidence and perservance..."(Alexander Hamilton to George Clinton, 13 February, 1788, quoted in Jared Spark's *The Writings of George Washington*, Boston, 1834, vol. 5, p.508.)

21) It is interesting to note that Pasquale de Paoli was a national Corsican leader who fought against the Genoan and French oppression. The French, who were so eager to help the cause of American liberty, were less concerned about the case of Corsican liberty and Paoli found asylum in Britain.

Nobody, it seems, cared much about Polish liberty, though Turkey reluctantly got involved in a war with Russia for that cause.

A dispatch brought into Philadelphia by Col. Alexander Hamilton was that the British were about to cross the Schuylkill and caused panic among the statesmen who escaped by a ludicrously involved route up the river and then southwest, making the better part of a circle to Lancaster. There they had a session on 27th September, but Congress moved behind the river to Yorktown.

> ...the movement was made not by a Vote but by Universal Consent, for
> every Member consulted his own particular Safet... Thomas Burke,
> Sep.20, 1777 (L.M.C.C. p.499, vol. 2).

22) In the 1st Regiment of Continental Dragoons (Blands 1st Va Cavalry) the Lieutenant-Colonel was Benjamin Temple and the Major was John Jameson; in the 2nd Dragoons (Elisha Sheldon's Conn. Cav.), the Colonel was Samuel Bladger, the Major Benjamin Talmadge; in the 3rd Regiment of Dragoons (Baylor's 3rd Va), the Lieutenant-Colonel was Benjamin Bird and Alexander Clough was the Major; in the 4th Dragoons (Moylan's 4 Pa. Cav.) Anthony White was Lieutenant-Colonel and the Major was William A. Washington.

23) Anburey gives such a description of Colonel Bland's troops in Virginia, that I quote it for all it's worth: " the colonel has with him here, for the purpose of express and attendance, the most curious figures you ever saw; some like Prince Prettyman, with one boot, some hoseless, with their feet peeping out of their shoes, others with breeches which put decency to the blush; some in short jackets, some in long coats, but all have fine dragoon caps and long swords slung round them, some with holsters, some without but gadamercy pistols, for they have not a brace and a half among them, but they are tolerably well mounted and that is the only thing you can advance in their favor. The Colonel is so fond of his Dragoons that he reviews and manoeuvres them every morning..." (Thomas Anburey, *Travels through the Interior Parts of America*, London, MDCCLXXXIX, p.320).

A Quaker girl, Sally Wister, who left a charming journal, had a houseful of Light Horse officers. Uniformly they made a good impression on her and thus she describes Captain Cadwallader Jones of the Third Regiment: "..tall, elegant and handsome,-white faced, with blue regimentals, and a mighty airish cap and white crest; his behaviour is refin'd-a Virginian." (*Sally Wister's Journal*, Albert Cook Myers, editor, Philadelphia, 1902.)

24) Members of Philadelphia City Troop, according to William B. Reed, were: John Dunlap, James Hunter, Thomas Peters, William Pollard, and James and Samuel Caldwell. The full list of names is in Wilkinson's *Memoirs*. The troop was commanded by Captain Morris and was discharged, with Washington's thanks, on 23 January, 1777. It was on duty at Brandywine and Germantown. If Pulaski in reality led combined troops of Morris and Lewis at Brandywine he had perhaps about 50 men. With such a number as he wrote to Rulhiere he attacked a thousand infantry. Was it at Brandywine?

25) In fact Washington's army was naked as witness numerous contemporary accounts which used that word repetitiously. About that time Stephen Moylan wrote to Robert Morris, requesting shoes and blankets for his men

26) Lt.-Col Thomas Seymour was appointed colonel in 1776 and commanded all the Connecticut Horse at New York. Elisha Sheldon who accompanied Washington on his retreat through Jersey was Major under Thomas Seymour. There were two other Seymours under Sheldon; Horace and Thomas. All of them, it seems, were related, coming from Hartford (*Record of Service of Connecticut Men*, Hartford, 1889).

Elisha retired to Vermont.

The following letter printed in Peter Force's, Fifth Series, vol. I, p.514, should be of interest to any student of the American cavalry:

COLONEL SEYMOUR TO GOVERNOUR TRUMBULL.

Hartford, July 22, 1776.

HONOURED SIR:-As the troops of Lighthorse returned yesterday from New York, I thought it my duty to give your Honour the earliest account of our conduct and proceedings, with every attending circumstance I before mentioned the immediate forwarding of your Honour's orders to the Majors of the several regiments named therein, as soon as they came to my hand. The companies made so great despatch in their march, that most of them came on (though well-spirited) without the precaution of a blanket, or even a change of clothing. They had conceived the idea, from the suddenness and urgency of the orders, that they were immediately to be called to action, and soon to return, which made them too incautious. I must, however, in justice, say, that a better body of substantial yeomen never appeared on such an occasion. They were admired and applauded for their spirit and zeal.

We no sooner arrived at King's Bridge, on Monday morning, than the General's letter met us, copy of which I now enclose. This at once seemed to check and mortify. We had no idea of sending back our horses, especially as the men had left their farms and crops in the most critical situation, and must return as soon as possible. I ordered them, however, to halt at the bridge, and, with Majors Starr and Sheldon, waited upon General Washington. He soon told us that forage could not be had upon the Island, (the drought being extreme that way), and that he would by no means be justified to pay for it, if it could be found. This again flung us into some perplexity, for we thought at least if there was so great need of the men, from the danger of a sudden attack, as the General often expressed it, that the Continent ought to undergo the burden of detaining us. There was, however, no reasoning upon the subject. We then proposed finding pastures for our horses, at and this side of the bridge, and depend upon the Colony, and so tarry a short time, rather than be turned directly back, which might throw a discouragement upon the honest intentions and wishes of men forward to serve their country on any emergency. To this the General graciously consented; and after much difficulty to obtain pastures for a small space, we marched into the city, through dust and sweat. Our numbers were soon trebled, and the sound of it rung through the enemy's camp. The same day our horses were sent out, and the men were put into houses, with nothing but the clothes on their backs, for lodging. As soon as a return of our men could be made, a number were ordered upon guard. This was something unexpected, but cheerfully submitted to. Soon after, a further order came for mounting guard, and for eight of our men to go to King's Bridge upon fatigue, there to remain one week. The first of these requisitions was complied with, but the last declined, as unreasonable for men under our circumstances. Colonel Silliman, as well as others, advis against submitting to fatigue; that it was counter to the laws of the Colony, and what your Honour had no idea of subjecting us to. Major Hart, with me of course, (by direction of General Wadsworth) waited upon General Washington, and stated the case, mentioned the exemptions of our law, &c, at same time suggested that the men would freely furnish guards of every kind, and man the lines, as they had done, if they might only be ex-

cused from working parties, for which they were in no measure prepared. We were answered, that no distinction could be made between our men and the rest, and if they would not submit to these
terms, they might be dismissed. This reply, after we had come so far,
left everything at home in the most suffering condition, had made
such despatch, and placed out our horses at so much risk and expense, and had done every other duty in the time of the alarm, and
also at other times (except that of the pick-axe, the shovel, and the
wheelbarrow,) was indeed very humiliating. We could not account
for such treatment, unless it was from the quarter of such who always viewed the existence of a body of Lighthorse with a jaundiced
eye. It was the opinion of several General Officers that we ought to
be excused; that it might be done consistently, and that we deserved
thanks and applause instead of the reverse. And, in short, if so large
and respectable a body of men, scattered through the Colony, are to
be blamed, under particular circumstances, for not complying with
every formal round of duty in camp, from which they knew themselves excused, it must rather create disaffection than otherwise. We
are, however, willing, if we have done amiss, to stand amenable at
your Honour's bar.

We left the city on Thursday noon last, when the most, if not all
of our inlisted levies had arrived. About seven thousand of the Fly-
ing-Camp had also reached the Jersey shore. These at least must
treble our number to that of the enemy. Lord Howe also arrived the
Friday before, without fleet or army (save a ship or two). Under
these circumstances, no prospect of any sudden attack, our horses
not to be kept any longer, the pressing circumstances of our affairs at
home, and the general opinion that we could not be needed soon,
(even General Putnam said we were not wanted,) together with the
sudden and unexpected reply from the General, all induced us to return.

I have troubled your Honour too long with a relation of facts, but
thought it necessary, that no mistake might arise from differing accounts. I ought to mention one circumstance further: that is, that
just before I left New York, after the men were all gone, Generals
Spencer and Heath called upon me, and said there was a misunderstanding in the matter, and that they had just come from the General, and he meant to excuse us from fatigue. The matter was now
over, the men gone and irrecoverable. And besides, the General had
otherwise expressed it the evening before, when Major Hart, with
me, waited upon him for the purpose.

I can't help remarking to your Honour, that it may be with truth said, General Washington is a gentleman of extreme care and caution; that his requisitions for men are fully equal to the necessity of the case; and that if more attention was had to the Northern Department it would be as well.

It is much to be lamented that our numbers of volunteers are so slow and deficient. Am persuaded that detachments must, after all, take place, as our only remedy.

I should have stopped here, but am this moment informed by Captain Hooker that Mr. Webb, General Washington's Aid-de-Camp, has written your Honour something dishonourable to the Lighthorse. Whatever it may be I know not, but this I do know, that it is a general observation, both in camp and country, if the butterflies and the coxcombs were away from the Army, we should not be put to so much difficulty in obtaining men of common sense to engage in the defence of their country.

Your Honour will excuse my freedom and prolixity in this, as it proceeds from no other motive than a sacred regard for the community of which I have the favour to be a member.

I am, with every sentiment of esteem and regard, your Honour's most obedient humble servant,

THOMAS SEYMOUR.

27) Francois Louis Teissedere de Fleury (born 1749). A professional soldier. Left for America with Coudray. Joined the American Army as a volunteer. Was commissioned as captain of engineers on 22 May, 1777. For his gallant behavior at Brandywine received from Congress a horse. He withstood the siege of Fort Mifflin. Was wounded on 15 November. Promoted to Lt.-Colonel, worked on a project of attacking the British shipping on Delaware with rocket-propelled boats. Joined Lafayette on Canada expedition. Voted one of only eight Congressional medals. Discharged in January 1782.

28) Wayne took revenge for Paoli: "Our people remembering the action of the night of the 20 of December, near the Warren, pushed on with their bayonets, and took ample revenge for that night's work. Our officers exerted themselves to save the poor wretches who were crying for mercy, but to little purpose. The rage and fury of the soldiers were not to be restrained for some time, at least not until a great number of the enemy fell by their bayonets." (Dawson, *Battles of the U.S.A.*, Documents, p.326).

General Wayne commanded the advance, and fully expected to be revenged for the surprise we had given him. When the first shots were fired at our pickets, so much had we all Wayne's affair in remembrance that the battalion was out under arms in a minute ..." (*Diary of Lieutenant Sir Martin Hunter* as quoted in Commager, Morris, *Spirit of 76*, p.625).

29) It was a large stone residence which belonged to a loyalist judge Benjamin Chew. Perhaps it was his pale face Graydon saw peering through a window at Washington's parade through Philadelphia, and perhaps Judge Chew derived some satisfaction from the role his house played. Eventually Chew was deported.

30) "What, to call this a fort and lose the happy moment?' exclaimed Reed as quoted in Fisher's *Struggle for Independence*, vol. 2 p.39. According to Thomas C. Amory, *Memoirs of General*, Sullivan, PMH, vol. 2, p.201, and on what basis I do not know, Pulaski was with Sullivan, Knox and Washington.

31) James Wilkinson, *Memoirs of My Own Times*, Philadelphia 1816, vol. l, p.363. Spark's *Writings of Washington*, vol. 5, p.364, Fred Cook, *What Manner of Men*, N.Y. 1959, Alfred C. Lambdin, Battle of Germantown, PMH, vol. l, p.368.

32) Johnson writes in his *Sketches* that it was Moylan with three regiments of horse who guarded the flanks of the retreating army. But Pulaski's cavalry was blamed for the disorder. On the other hand Pulaski was supposed to be on picket duty, but it was Allen McLane who attacked Mount Airy. Anyway, according to Bentalou at Germanstown there were only three regiments of horse and if Johnson is right it would mean that Moylan was leading cavalry, not Pulaski, a rather intriguing point.

33) In the case of the artillerymen, Washington, to avoid the problem of seniority, thought about creating a separate corps of artillery, and also about pre-dating American officers' commissions to give them seniority over their French competitors. In those matters Washington was facing an open revolt of his generals.

34) Washington to Conway, December 30, 1777. "Sir, I am favored with your letter of yesterday, in which you propose in order to lose no time to begin with the instruction of troops. You will observe by resolution of Congress relative to your appointment that a Board of War is to furnish a Set of Instructions, according to which the Troops are to be Maneuvred. As you have made no mention of having received them, I suppose they are not come to you. When they do, I shall issue any Order which may be judged necessary to have them carried into immediate execution...Your appointment of Inspector-General to the Army, I believe, has not given the least uneasiness to any officer in it...you may judge what must be the sensation of those Brigadiers who by your promotion are superseded. I am told they are determined to remonstrate against it..." (W.W. 10, p.226).

35) Dekalb had the following opinion about the choice of place: "On the 19th instant, the army reached this wooded wilderness, certainly one of the poorest districts of Pennsylvania, the soil thin, uncultivated and almost uninhabited, without forage and without provisions! Here we are to go on to winter quarters, ice. to lie in shanties, generals and privates, to enable the army, it is said, to recover from its privations, to recruit, to re-equip, and to prepare for the opening for the coming campaign while protecting the country against hostile inroads...The idea of wintering in this desert can only have been put into the head of the commanding general by an interested speculator or a disaffected man..." (Commager & Morris, *The Spirit of 76*, p.646).

> ...Among the many reasons offered against a winter Campaign... one of the most prevalent was a general discontent... Committee of Congress to Washington (L.M.C.C. vol. 2, p.585).

36) George Washington to Brigadier-General Preudhomme de Bore on August 19, 1777: "...I thought it might be more agreeable to you to have one of your own Countrymen in your family, and that it would be means of giving a handsome employment to some one of those French Gentlemen of merit, who are commissioned in our Army without being attached to any particular Service..." (W.W.9 p. 96).

37) For a pathetic description of that action see *Trenton Gazette*, March 11, 1778. The author could have been Livingston.

BIBLIOGRAPHICAL NOTE

The detailed bibliographical information is given immediately in the relevant text in the belief that such a method of direct reference is preferable to time-consuming and tiresome consultation at the end of the book or chapter. For the same reason most of the "footnotes" were incorporated in the body of this work. Only books and articles bearing directly on the subject matter are quoted. Anyone interested in works on the American Revolution will find bibliographies in Mayo Boatner's *Encyclopedia of the American Revolution*, N.Y. 1966, and in H.S. Commager's and S.E. Morton's *The Spirit of 1776* or in any other authoritative modern work on that period.

I should like to recommend two works of a general nature: D.S. Freeman's *George Washington*, N.Y. 1948-57, and Alexander A. Lawrence's *Storm over Savannah*, Athens, 1951.

The bulk of the documents relating to the American services of Casimir Pulaski is deposited in the National Archives, Washington, D.C., in Papers of Continental Congress, in the War Department Collection of Revolutionary War Records, and also in the Library of Congress, Washington Papers, the Manuscript Division. Photostats of portions of the French Archives Nationales, Marine, connected with the Revolutionary War are in the Library of Congress. Most of these documents are available on request on photostats or microfilms. Recently a computerized catalog of the Papers of the Continental Congress has been made available. Whenever possible, I tried to depend on the original documents. Many of them are printed for the first time in this work.

Of the printed sources *Writings of Washington* is of great importance. I mainly used John C. Fitzpatrick's edition, *Washington, 1931-41*, which I abbreviated to "W.W." A number of Pulaski's related documents are printed in the *Journals of Continental Congress*, Gallard Hunt, editor, Washington, 1904-37, referred to in my work as "J.C.C.," and in *Letters of Members of Continental Congress*, edited by Edmund Cody Burnett, Washington, 1921-36, and referred to as "L.M.C.C." Some of Pulaski's letters were printed in Jared Sparks's *Letters to Washington*,

Boston, 1853. *Message from the President of the USA*, 49th Congress, 2nd session, Senate Executive Document, No. 120, March 1887-"Ex. Doc." is also an interesting publication, containing a number of Pulaski's documents.

Correspondance du General Casimir Pulaski avec Claude de Rulhiere, Institute Historique et Litteraire Polonaise, Paris, 1948 offers a fascinating collection of documents, but little known to Pulaski's biographers. Some of them are translated in R.D. Jamros "Pulaski," 1979, Savannah, Georgia. Neither this work, nor *Janina Hoskins' Selective List of Reading Materials in English on Pulaski*, was available during my research.

Martin Griffith, in *General Count Casimir Pulaski, Father of the American Cavalry*, vol. 3 of *Catholics and the American Revolution*, Pa 1911, published a number of Pulaski's documents, as did Dr. W. Wayda in *Pulaski w Ameryce*, Warszawa, 1930. Professor Wladyslaw Konopczynski's biography *Kazimierz Pulaski*, Krakow, 1931, remains the most authoritative work on the Polish part of Pulaski's life.

Contemporary journals, memoirs and other works were also consulted and, as mentioned previously, the exact bibliographic information is given in the text.

BIOGRAPHICAL NOTE

Casimir Pulaski was born on 4 March 1747, on the family estates in Winiary. His father Joseph, a lawyer by profession, was one of the Polish potentates and actively engaged in politics. Casimir (or in Polish, Kazimierz) received his education in the fashionable academy run by the Teatyni Fathers.

In 1762, while in the service of Prince Charles in Courland, then a Polish suzerainty, he received a rudimentary education in the military arts during a brief encounter with the Russians at Mitau.

After that Casimir returned to his family estates to enjoy the peaceful life of a young squire until 1768, when he helped his father Joseph and brothers Francis and Antoni to organize an anti-Russian and anti-royal insurrection called the Bar Confederacy. At that time Poland, though formally free and huge in territory, was practically a Russian satellite, and King Stanislaus Poniatowski, an ex-lover of Catherine II, was her puppet. The Bar Confederacy was the first one in the long line of Polish insurrections against Russia.

Immediately, Casimir Pulaski was recognized as an outstanding military commander in that partisan war. But eventually, after many successful battles and skirmishes and defending fortresses, he had to leave the Podolia region where the insurrection started for Malopolska from where he renewed his military activities. Also in that year he was elected Marshall of Lomza Province which gave him an official position. Meanwhile his father died a Turkish prisoner, his brother Francis was killed in a battle and Antoni was taken prisoner by the Russians.

Casimir had proved himself to be an outstanding leader, a superior strategist and tactitian. His personal courage and endurance was proverbial and legendary. In 1771 after he overwhelmingly defeated, at the siege of Czestochowa, a Russian army supported by the Prussian artillery, his name became famous all over Europe.

But the war was in an impasse. The Russians and supporting Loyalist troops could not extinguish the ever-rising flames of the insurrection while the partisans could not win large battles with the regular troops nor take over towns and cities.

In 1772 the political leadership of the Confederation decided to kidnap the king and force him to abdicate. In an attempt Stanislaus Poniatowski was actually kidnapped, but he succeeded in escaping.

Casimir Pulaski was blamed for organizing the action. The tide of public opinion turned against the Confederacy, and in spite of the Turkish-Russian war, and much delayed French financial and some military help, the insurrection expired.

Casimir Pulaski went into exile. He tried to organize a Polish Legion to serve on the Turkish side in their struggle with Russia but that war soon expired too.

Casimir Pulaski found himself in an especially difficult situation as his estates in Poland were confiscated and he had no money nor credit abroad. In addition he was sentenced in absentia to death for the crime of regicide which did not help his position at the royal courts; and in spite of his military achievements and fame he could nowhere receive an army commission.

But Pulaski gained at least a sort of political asylum in France from where after surviving an extremely embarrassing financial distress, he proceeded on his career in America in 1777.

COMMENTARY
By Michal I. Zawadzki, Ph.D.

A DOCUMENTARY MONOGRAPH on Kazimierz Pulaski in America has been overdue for a long time. Without such a work, creator and the first general of the American Cavalry would continue to be dutifully worshiped among Polish Americans but patronized by many American historians.

Szymanski uses more source materials than any other author who wrote on Pulaski's life and military career in America. But his work is much more than a collection of edited documents. It shows the man, his character and his role on the background of a realistically presented American Revolution.

Especially worthy of notice is that the author stresses the tension between Gen. Washington and Pulaski, a point completely overlooked by the previous Pulaski biographers. He explains Pulaski's dilemma not only by lack of cavalrymen and horses, insufficient supplies and weapons, inflation and sagging revolutionary enthusiasm, but also by Washington's misapprehension of the function of cavalry as an independent branch of the armed forces and its tactical and strategic objectives.

Another significant suggestion offered by the author is Pulaski's association with men critical of the Commander in Chief's military leadership, such as John Adams, Charles Lee and Horatio Gates, and others.

In his comprehensive work Szymanski discusses at length various unknown or little knownn facts, for instance, permission given to Pulaski to recruit the British prisoners of war and its strange withdrawal; the question of his alleged membership in Free Masonry; Legion's finances and Pulaski's personal expenditures toward its equipment (here the author reconstructs for us the Legion's uniforms and its martial array which included lances and tomahawks!).

He solves the various puzzles intriguing Pulaski's biographers such as his reason for the overstay in Boston, the much discussed nationality of Capt. Joseph Baldesqui or the real first name of Capt. Zielinski, and gives the most probable version of Pulaski's death.

After reading this monograph one puts away the book with a strong feeling of knowing the man and documented conviction that Kazimierz Pulaski was an outstanding general, excellent organizer and innovator, whose merits were only partially appreciated during his lifetime, and are unfairly not recognized today.

—Michal I. Zawadzki, Ph.D.

COMMENTARY
By Dr. Edward C. Rozanski

KAZIMIERZ PULASKI, the famed Soldier of Liberty whose military innovations and deeds earned him the hero title and veneration in two nations – Poland and the United States – is often portrayed in usually short and shallow historical essays as an enigmatic man and a victim of several misfortunes.

In this respect he shares the lot with another "foreigner" of the American Revolution, Tadeusz Kosciuszko, whose military genius as a strategist and fortification expert is only now being recognized in several studies published in conjunction with the Bicentennial of the American Revolution.

In the supposedly authoritative *Dictionary of American Biography*, we find such nonsensical, unsupported with facts and unsubstantiated whedling about Pulaski by some uninformed or ill intentioned egghead:

> His American career was tragic for it was a chronicle of disaster and embittered dissapointment. He was fortunate in his last days, for his gallant death served to ennoble even his mistakes in the eyes of posterity."

This is written about a man whose bold actions saved Washington's Army from dire consequences at Brandywine; who reorganized and disciplined cavalry regiments in the Continental Army and issued the first professional Cavalry Regulations in the United States; who organized and largely financed an Independent Corps of Light Cavalry and Infantry, which became known as the Pulaski Legion.

Certainly, Pulaski met with many dissapointments during his service in the American Revolution: perhaps the biggest and most aggravating was the fact that the American Command was wont to assign its cavalry units to supportive action only. To Pulaski, reared in centuries-old traditions of the Polish hussars, schooled in the typically Polish strategy of rapid field movement evolved from encounters with

Tartars and Turkish forces, this unintentional slighting of cavalry was almost intolerable.

The independent Corps of Light Cavalry and Infantry was to fill the void Pulaski felt in the make-up of the Continental Army.

Personal heroism of Pulaski is praised in the *American Military Biography*, wherein we read about his action at Savannah: Pulaski "made a bold effort at the head of two hundred horses to force his way through enemy's work...but while advancing at the head of his men, exposed to the tremendous fire, the intrepid Pulaski received a mortal wound." A laudable comment but characteristically of doubtful historical accuracy.

The last scholarly, but limited in its scope, research on Pulaski in America was published in the Polish language by Dr. W. Wayda to honor the sesquicentennial anniversary of Pulaski's death. Prior to this, in 1905 the works of Prof. Wladyslaw Kozlowski was published. The exact bibliographical material and data is being provided by the author, and may I say that Kazimierz Pulaski deserves more exposure in the scholarly circles.

In contrast, his career in Poland is well documented especially through the research of Prof. Wladyslaw Konopczynski-but perhaps, it would not be out of place to follow Pulaski's achievements in Poland since Szymanski's work deals only with his American service.

Born in the Mazowia region of Poland, in 1747 the youthful Pulaski became the chief leader of guerrilla war led by the Confederation of Bar (1768-1772) against the Russian aggression. His exploits, especially the defense of Czestochowa, proclaimed his fame throughout Europe. His action was very effective in the most adverse situations against overhelming odds. He was a master of partisan encounter.

To forestall the downfall of the country, the Patriots decided to kidnap King Stanislaus August Poniatowski who was dominated by the Russians. Pulaski took part in the undertakings which having failed forced him to escape from Poland. The Confederation of Bar fell apart. Pulaski proceeded to Turkey where he endeavored to organize a Polish Legion to continue in the struggle for Polish freedom. Russia defeated Turkey, and Pulaski was once again on the move, this time to friendly France. There he met the American agents serving Congress, namely Deane and Franklin, and with their letters of recommendations and the "secret blessing" of the French Court, Pulaski left for America to arrive here on June 23, 1777.

Szymanski's monograph, deeply researched, documented with never published facts, and primary sources from many archives, spells out the best work in recent years.

Szymanski's style is unique, giving all the facts and reserving his comments for the epilogue. Through the author's pen, Kazimierz Pulaski emerges as one of the dominant military figures of the American Revolution. At the same time the book entwines the history and the beginnings of the American Cavalry.

The author had many accomplishments in his literary career in Poland. In 1959 he decided to leave Poland and continue where freedom prevails. His talents are outstanding in both English and the Polish language. He is an honor graduate in Polish Language and Literature at London University, and Ph.D. History graduate of Polish University in Exile, London as well as Master of Political Science C.S.U.L.B. As editor he served the Polish Press in Australia, England and the United States.

This monograph is a milestone in our histography.

—Dr. Edward C. Rozanski

Index

POLISH HERITAGE COOKERY

Robert & Maria Strybel

Features:
- Over 2,200 authentic recipes
- Entire *chapters* on dumplings, pototao dishes, sausage-making, babkas and more!
- American weights and measures
- Modern shortcuts and substitutes for health-conscious dining
- Each recipe indexed in English and Polish

Acclaim from the press:
"*Polish Heritage Cookery* is well-organized, informative, interlaced with historical background on Polish foods and eating habits, with easy to follow recipes readily prepared in American kitchens, and, above all, it's fun to read."
                              —Polish American Cultural Network
"A culinary classic in the making, this comprehensive collection of over 2,200 recipes is by Polonia's most famous chef."
                              —Zgoda
"This cookbook is the most extensive and vaied one ever published in English."
                              —Polish Heritage Quarterly

$29.95

*   *   *

To order your copy(s) send a check or money order in the amount of $29.95 for each cookbook, plus $4.00 shipping & handling for the first book, $.50 for each additional, to:

HIPPOCRENE BOOKS, 171 Madison Avenue, New York, NY 10016

Polish Literature and Folklore from Hippocrene

THE DOLL
Boleslaw Prus

Prus's legendary portrait of Polish society in the 19th century celebrates its twentieth year in English translation."A fine novel, clearly in the tradition of Dickens, Balzac, Zola, and Peréz Galdós. *The Doll* would undoubtedly be a classic in America if it had been translated 50 years ago....The lively, idiomatic translation is a real achievement." —*Library Journal*
Anniversary Paperback Edition
   700 pages   *$16.95p*   *ISBN 0-7818-0158-3*

PHARAOH
Boleslaw Prus; translated by Christopher Kasparek

First published in 1896, and now recently translated, *Pharaoh* is considered one of the great novels of Polish literature, and a timeless and universal story of the struggle for power.
   691 pages   *$25.00c*   *ISBN 0-87052-152-7*

THE DARK DOMAIN
Stefan Grabinski; newly translated by Miroslaw Lipinski

These explorations of the extreme in human behavior, where the macabre and the bizarre combine to send a chill down the reader's spine, are by a master of Polish fantastic fiction.
   192 pages   *$10.95p*   *ISBN 0-7818-0211-3*

TALES FROM THE SARAGOSSA MANUSCRIPT, or, Ten Days in the Life of Alphonse Van Worden
Jan Potocki

The celebrated classic of fantastic literature in the tradition of *The Arabian Nights*. "A Gothic novel, quite an extraordinary piece of writing." —Czeslaw Milosz
   192 pages   *$8.95p*   *ISBN 0-87052-936-6*

THE GLASS MOUNTAIN: Twenty-Six Ancient Polish Folktales and Fables
Uretold by W.S. Kuniczak; illustrated by Pat Bargielski

"It is an heirloom book to pass on to children and grandchildren...A timeless book, with delightful illustrations, it will make a handsome addition to any library and will be a most treasured gift." —Polish American Cultural Network. 8 illustrations.
   160 pages   *$14.95c*   *ISBN 0-7818-0087-0*

OLD POLISH LEGENDS
retold by F.C.Anstruther; wood engravings by J. Sekalski

Now in its second printing, this fine collection of eleven fairy tales, with an introduction by Zygmunt Nowakowski, was first published in Scotland in World War II, when the long night of the German occupation was at its darkest. 11 woodcut engravings.
   66 pages   *$10.00c*   *ISBN 0-7818-0180-X*

THE TRILOGY,
by Henryk Sienkiewicz

Available from Hippocrene Books

"Kuniczak's modern translation is brilliant, timely and necessary...If you are going to read only one literary work in your life about Poland, read the Sienkiewicz Triology."
—*Christian Science Monitor*

THE TRILOGY tells a tale of war and adventure, recounting the violent fall of the Polish-Lithuanian Commonwealth in the 17th century after 200 years as the leading power in Europe. The first book, WITH FIRE AND SWORD, is set during the Cossack rebellions and bloody Tartar wars which cost Poland its hold on its eastern lands. THE DELUGE plays out against the Swedish invasion of 1655 and the dynastic wars in which Poland lost its Baltic territories. FIRE IN THE STEPPE concludes the Triology with the Polish-Turkish wars, hastening the rise of the Russian Empire.

"The Sienkiewicz Triology...stands with that handful of novels which not only depict but also help to determine the soul and character of the nation they describe."
—James Michener, from the Introduction to *With Fire and Sword*

WITH FIRE AND SWORD

"Most highly recommended." —*Library Journal*, starred review

"In this robust, modernized translation by Polish-born American novelist Kuniczak, we feel the Poles' resilient spirit of freedom and their national pride as the same spirit sweeping Eastern Europe today." —*Publishers Weekly*

"A suspenseful tale of bloody insurrection, heroism and romance in the best Dumas tradition...Kuniczak succeeds in producing a novel that is considerably more vivid, gripping and contemporary." —*Milwaukee Journal*

    1130 pages   *$24.95*   *ISBN 0-87052-974-*

THE DELUGE

"Old fashioned fiction of the highest order." —*New York Times Book Review*

"The convincing translation by Polish-born American novelist Kuniczak adds luster to a robust populist epic...Around the constants of love and war, Polish novelist Sienkiewicz weaves a fugue of betrayal, redemption, faith and passion." —*Publishers Weekly*

"The Deluge is historical fiction at its best...This massive epic of love, war and adventure comes to life in English in an innovative modern rendering...The Deluge is literature in the grand manner." —*The Chicago Tribune.*

    1,762 pages   *$45.00 (2 vol. set)*   *ISBN-87052-004-0*

FIRE IN THE STEPPE

"Fast-moving action...often mingles with genuine tragedy as well as with lighthearted humor, all those hallmarks of a perfect, realistic novel." —*World Literature Today*

"Like Volodyovski himself, this work champions romance through his enduring love for Basia, the impish soldier/princess. Then together these lovers command the martial stage, standing against the Turks' surging might and the Tartar Horde, standing firm on the rock of Kamyenetz in defense of Poland, church, and God. Great literature stands on such enduring themes and in this inspiring work, Sienkiewicz taps the essence of not only a nation but all people." —Starred review, *Library Journal*

    750 pages   *$24.95*   *ISBN 0-7818-0025-0*